THE DAUGHTERS OF THE DARKNESS

BY
LUKE PHILLIPS

Print Book ISBN: 978-0-9562987-4-4
e-book ISBN: 978-0-9562987-3-7

For my mum, for whom Africa was merely the back garden, hippos, crocs and all, and always inspired my imagination.

Acknowledgements

The book you are about to read would not have reached you without the considerable help of a great number of people.

First, I must thank those who contributed to the book itself. That includes Richard and Dani of Valle Walkley, who have provided the stunning and sensational cover art. It also includes a whole suite of beta-readers, Liz, Ian, Rosie and Abigail, whose feedback helped make the story, characters and scenes within, that little more polished and presentable.

Thank you also to the Field Museum of Chicago, who answered my questions on one of their prized exhibits, and to the museums of Natural History of both London and Paris, who helped in my search for the Barbary lion.

I also need to thank those who support me and keep me going long enough to write whole novels. Rosie Marr, you have been a constant source of encouragement, timely time-outs and help. And to my family, thank you too for another few years of patience and practical support.

And lastly, thank you to you, the reader. Thank you for choosing this book. I hope you enjoy it. If you do, please consider leaving a review on Amazon or Goodreads, it really makes all the difference.

Modern Day Man-Eating

As you pick up this book and begin to weave your way through the story, you may find the theme of active man-eaters a little surprising and out of place in a modern age. However, the truth is that predators have never stopped doing what they have always been capable of, when the opportunity and right circumstances present themselves.

The statistics show that man is still very much on the menu. In sub-Saharan Africa, approximately 3,000 people are taken every year by crocodiles. 1,500 Tibetans are killed by bears. 600 Indians are preyed on by leopards whilst another 85 are taken by tigers. The king of beasts naturally tallies the most kills, with lions taking 700 people on average annually.

Some of them become revered and infamous. The Tsavo Man-eaters, who feature in the legacy of the fictional lions in this book, were very real, as is the tigress in Nepal known as the claw. A lion given the name of Osama killed more than 50 people in Tanzania between 2002 and 2004. He was less than four years old, and suspected to be part of a local pride that deliberately targeted humans. The story you are about to read is not as far-fetched as you think.

Another Osama, this one a crocodile, ate its way through 83 villagers in the waters of Lake Victoria before being captured in 2005. After sixty years of snatching victims from the banks, capsizing boats, and even boarding the wooden vessels to find his prey, he now lives out his days as breeding stock for Uganda Crocs Ltd, makers of fine leather handbags.

Human-predator conflict isn't restricted to the more far flung places of the world either. Hans Kruuk, a carnivore zoologist for the University of Aberdeen, concluded that wolf predation on humans is still a factor of life for Eastern Europeans, after a lengthy study of their death records.

In the U.S too, although rare, predator related death is a possibility. Mountain lions take an average of one person every four years. Bears (polar, brown and black species combined) take to man meat about twice a year. Wolves barely register, with one human fatality every five years in the last twenty. Only a total of three fatal coyote attacks have ever been recorded.

The risk is minimal, and I do mean minimal. You are eleven times more likely to win your state lottery than fall victim to an American predator taken to a palate of people. Death by dog is fifteen times more likely, and death by cow or horse, 32 more times likely.

But there is one killer that just can't even begin to be compared to - us. Americans kill over 3,000 mountain lions every year. In the last two decades, over 100,000 black bears have been killed in the eastern United States alone. About 1,750 wolves are culled or simply hunted across North America annually.

The story you are about to read is fiction. The facts are very different. I hope you enjoy the book and find a new respect for our predators in equal measure.

PROLOGUE

TSAVO, KENYA – SEVEN YEARS AGO

Amanda Walker woke with a start, sitting up in her sleeping bag and instinctively reaching for the old Marine Corps fighting knife she kept under her pillow. For a few seconds, she sat completely still, trying to work out what had woken her. Her first thought was that a snake had decided to curl up in or near the sleeping bag. It wouldn't be the first time. When she couldn't detect any movement, she relaxed a little and began to listen.

The door of the canvas tent was still tied shut. There was a soft breeze and she could hear the song of crickets carried on it. Then she heard something else. Soft murmurs, coming from outside. She looked over at her husband, Thomas. Even in his sleep he looked exhausted. She turned up the collar of his shirt to cover the insect bites on his neck. He had fallen asleep in his clothes almost as soon as he had returned from the day's tracking. His fitful slumber and the sheen of sweat on his skin told her he was fighting another bout of Rift Valley fever. She smiled to herself and affectionately ran her fingers through his hair. She would let him sleep, but she couldn't ignore the sounds. They had heard the man-eaters calling close to the camp during the day.

Just like her husband, she had gone to bed in her clothes, and she tucked the knife into the back of her shorts as she pulled the mosquito net up and made her way to the door-flap of the tent. She undid the top tie whilst yawning silently and peered out. The camp's outbuildings were across the way, but no lights were on in the windows. Nothing seemed to be stirring. Then she heard the murmur again. Standing on the veranda of one of the buildings was a little boy. His skin was incredibly dark, showing up the blue and mauve tones of the night sky above. He was completely naked and held his hand over his mouth as he sobbed, staring into the darkness in wide-eyed terror.

As Amanda undid the rest of the flap ties, the boy noticed her immediately. As she watched him streak out of the camp, she immediately realised he wasn't one of the children who lived with the crew and staff. He moved with absolute silence, his feet hardly touching the ground as he ran. The moon was full and bathed the scorched ground in an eerie light. Amanda couldn't help the pang of panic she felt and took a few steps in the direction the boy was headed, intent on following. She hesitated. Thomas would be angry if he knew she had left the tent during the night. All the better reason to let him sleep, she decided.

She began to follow the little boy. The red dust stuck to her bare feet and the ground was still warm from the baking heat of the day. She crossed the road that led into the camp and paused for a moment as she looked out over the long grass. Thomas really would be angry at the thought of her going any further without a gun or an escort. But she could see the path the boy had taken and now she was growing concerned. She had already imagined the possibility the boy was from a local village, where maybe the man-eaters had attacked. What if he came for help? Amanda thought. She pushed on into the long grass.

She moved carefully and quietly, moving the brush aside and listening intently with every step. She could barely see over the top, so instead she crouched and followed the path the boy had made, peering ahead.

"Kito," she whispered softly, "kito?"

The Swahili word was often used affectionately by mothers to children. The literal translation meant 'precious one'. Amanda had considered the boy was so young that he may never have met a white person, and her appearance could have startled him. If he heard her speaking softly and in Swahili, he might stop running.

The moon was directly above her, making her long blonde hair look silver in the strange light. Somehow it made her feel alone and exposed, and she shivered with the cold she suddenly felt. Instinct overrode her, and the hairs on the back of her neck stood on end as she reached the abrupt end of the trail. The boy had seemingly disappeared into thin air. The tall grass ahead of her swayed silently in the wind, moving back and forth as if caught in the breath of some invisible giant beast. She crouched, spinning on her heels to face the direction she had come from. She began to tremble as she closed her eyes and listened, as the crickets stopped singing one by one until there was silence.

For a moment, she couldn't bring herself to open her eyes. She gritted her teeth and blinked, peering out into the grass around her. At first, she didn't see anything. Then a pair of amber eyes flashed in the darkness, then another. More eyes, like burning coals in the shadows, appeared over to her left. Even in her fear, she was amazed at the pride's ability to work together in silence and in the dark. She could feel them closing in on her. She estimated them to be no more than twenty yards away, and they were obviously hunting. She was in no doubt what, or rather who, the prey was.

She decided she had only one chance. The camp was three hundred yards ahead of her, beyond the long grass and across the road. She leapt upwards, her bare feet tearing into the ground violently as she sprinted through the grass. The greenery around her seemed to ripple with tawny-coloured flashes of fur. The lions began to call to each other quietly, emitting little coughs and grunts that came from both sides. She knew they were verging in on her, attracted by her flight and the noise she made as she ran. Her muscles burned as she willed herself faster.

She could now see the road and she felt a momentary swell of relief. She was going to make it. She knew the lions would at least hesitate before they broke cover, giving her the few seconds she needed to make it into the camp. She decided she was at least close enough to start screaming and raise the alarm. She opened her mouth just as the silhouette passed in front of her. She found herself suddenly stunned and winded as she was dragged to the ground. A large, pale coloured paw pushed her face into the dust, stifling the scream that waited to burst from her lungs. It had been the perfect ambush. The big female had always been behind her, waiting for the rest of the pride to drive Amanda into her waiting jaws. She went for the knife, but knew she would never reach her attacker face down in the dirt as she was.

The hot, wet breath of the animal lashed her skin as she tried to struggle free. Then came the torturous moment she felt the pressure of its teeth upon her neck just before they punctured the skin. Tears welled as she thought of Thomas and what he would discover come the morning. She convulsed as agonising pain momentarily rippled through her body. She kicked out a few times in her violent death throes as she asphyxiated, then her body went limp as her windpipe was crushed and the nerves at the top of the spinal cord were severed. As the big female began to feed on the kill, the other members of the pride drew close, waiting their turn to feast.

CHAPTER ONE

CANNICH, SCOTLAND, PRESENT DAY

Thomas Walker leaned back into the deep green leather of the desk chair, letting out an audible sigh. Even from his study, he could hear the television in the living room down the corridor. Meg, the chocolate and grey merle coloured Border collie, trotted up to the open doorway. She tilted her head and made a questioning huffing noise, clearly confused that she could hear Thomas's voice from down the hall and yet saw him there, right in front of her. He couldn't help smiling though. Catherine, his fiancée, was watching an old episode of Hunter Hunted. The year before, they had discovered a remarkable feline predator in the Highlands of Scotland, and tracking and eventually killing it had brought them considerable fame. For Thomas, it was his second dose, taking his fifteen minutes up to a full half hour. Hunter Hunted had been his first, a popular TV series centring on his adventures and that of his wife, Amanda, as they hunted man-eaters across the world. Amanda's death in Kenya, seven years ago, had signalled the end of the programme. But now, with his name and actions back in the limelight, an ambitious reporter had seen an opportunity.

Kelly Keelson had become a figure as strongly associated with the story of Scotland's spate of big cat attacks as he was. Her reports had helped clear his name after it had been dragged through the mud by a politician named David Fairbanks. He and Thomas had clashed before, when he had openly criticised the show and the circumstances of Amanda's death, whilst on holiday in South Africa. They clashed again after, as Fairbanks rose through the government ranks to become the Minister for the Environment. The bad blood with Fairbanks had dried up when he was killed by the great cat, but not before he had tried to kill Catherine. It wasn't something Thomas liked to dwell on, but Keelson had fed the eager public stories new and old, as well as re-runs of Hunter Hunted via her own, newly formed production company. But she hadn't stopped there. Thomas was thumbing through her proposal for a new series. He picked up the phone and dialled Keelson's number. She answered almost immediately.

"So, what do you think Walker?" Keelson asked with glee. "I'm already being swamped with offers after just putting out a few feelers. There's a tigress in Nepal called 'the claw' that has killed eleven. Mumbai in India has an especially nasty leopard problem, which would be interesting given the city surroundings. Or for something completely different, how about a croc in Burundi? You've never done a crocodile before, and this one's been called Osama. He's meant to be 24 feet long and..."

"Take a breath Keelson," laughed Thomas, rolling his eyes. "There's a reason I've never done a crocodile before, I'm not that bloody stupid. You're also forgetting I've already said no, several times."

"You're just playing hard to get. Come on Walker, you can't tell me those new royalty cheques are hurting. There's much more where that came from," Keelson added coolly.

"I'm not exactly hard up. And you should realise I got out of the business a long time ago for a good reason. You can only cheat death so many times, and I think he's beginning to take it personally."

"So that's it, back to putting flea collars on foxes and such like?" Keelson retorted, trying to bait him.

"Yes, exactly that. I'm a conservationist, and I like to think things have moved on from blowing holes in animals we have a problem with," Thomas replied curtly.

"Tell that to Suru, who lost his mother, father and two children to 'The Claw'. Or the families of the 300 people Osama chewed on. You know it's not that simple, you're a realist," Keelson challenged, changing tack.

"I am a realist. And I know I can't take all my memories, baggage and a new fiancée into that kind of danger again. I'm damaged goods, whether you like it or not," Thomas admitted.

There was a pause, and Thomas knew Keelson wasn't going to push him anymore, at least not today.

"Okay, but I'm not giving up. I actually think this would be good for you. Not many people get second chances. Just think about it."

"I wouldn't expect anything less from you Kelly," smiled Thomas.

He couldn't help feeling a little fond of her as he put the phone down. She never pushed past the point he could take it. They had found a mutual respect for each other over her handling of the cat story, and the numerous phone calls and emails since. He stood up and stretched. It had been a relatively quiet Sunday afternoon up until that point. He walked round the large oak desk and passed through the door into the hall. Meg barked and wagged her tail with excitement, darting between his legs as she scampered ahead of him. Her missing hind leg made her gait lop-sided, but didn't seem to slow her down. The victim of a mountain lion attack in the

States, she was another reminder of the risks posed by what Keelson was suggesting.

He put his head round the door of the living room. Catherine was curled up on the sofa. Just seeing her soothed his weariness a little. She embodied cosiness with her short, flame-coloured hair, a thick jumper wrapped around her, and the massive blue-grey hulk of Arturo, the Italian cane corso mastiff they had adopted, draped over the sofa with his head on her lap.

Catherine's eyes were glued to the screen. His gaze followed hers, and he saw his younger self on the television. His dark hair now had a little more grey in it, and his bright blue eyes didn't shine with quite so much arrogance, at least he hoped. He recognised the episode as one of the early ones. The subject of this particular show was Vladimir, a Kamchatka brown bear that had terrorised a Russian mining town in the Olyutorsky district, killing five and mauling many more. Thomas had eventually shot Vladimir after cornering the bear in a platinum mine. Like many of the rural areas of the Russian Federation, the resources of the wildlife department were limited, and mainly centred on hunting permits. Dealing with killer bears had proven beyond their remit. They also feared and revered the bear, giving it something of a mythical status, as was often the case with many of the man-eaters he faced during the course of the show. An animal had only to survive an attempt to kill it, or prove more cunning and confident than its counterparts to be elevated to legendary status by the local people. Not that Vladimir hadn't been impressive in the flesh though. Kamchatka bears, the biggest sub-species of brown bear in Europe, were almost as large as their Kodiak cousins in Alaska. They also featured oversized, broad heads, giving them a rather formidable appearance. Vladimir had measured over nine feet in length and weighed 1,437lbs. The bear's 17-inch-long skull sat on a shelf in his study.

"How's your girlfriend?" Catherine teased, not looking up.

"Stubborn and determined," Thomas sighed.

"No wonder the two of you get along," Catherine smiled cheekily, this time looking round to meet the playful, mock look of annoyance he was fixing her with.

He leaned over the back of the sofa and bent down, kissing her softly on the lips.

"I'm going to get some air, want to come?" Thomas asked.

"I wanted to go for a run later. I'll pass if that's okay, unless you want company?" Catherine offered.

"Meg will suffice. Although now I'm thinking of you getting back and hitting the shower," he quipped, raising an eyebrow.

Catherine fingered the open top of his shirt and pulled him closer, returning the kiss.

"Best not be too long then, hey," she whispered.

Thomas held her gaze for a moment. He glanced at Arturo, who looked up at him with amber coloured eyes, his head still resting on Catherine's lap.

"Yeah, I wouldn't move if I was lying there either," Thomas laughed. "Come on Meg. Let's leave these two to it."

Meg barked, wagging her tail with obvious enthusiasm. Thomas walked back through to the hall. He pulled on his leather walking boots whilst sitting on the stairs and stood up, looking out of the windows on either side of the front door to check the weather. It was a fresh, early September afternoon and the sun was shining brightly. He could see the wind moving the tops of the Scots pine trees along the track, and he pulled a black fleece gilet from the rack, putting it on unzipped over his shirt. He opened the door and stepped out.

Meg rushed past him, heading for the path that would take them to the secluded south-western shore of Loch Mullardoch.

"Good choice," agreed Thomas, taking after her.

He looked up at the imposing peak of Sgurr na Lapaich before it disappeared from sight amongst the trees. There was no snow at this time of year, and its rust and moss-dappled summit stood tall in the centre of the other Munros of Glen Cannich. He followed Meg into the shade and seclusion of Mullardoch forest. A calming breeze touched his skin and he let out a long breath, enjoying the taste of the fresh heather and spruce-tinted air. Meg stopped a little way ahead and turned back to look at him.

"Go on, I'm coming," he reassured her. She trotted off again with a bark.

Thomas looked around at the familiar scenery. The forest floor was carpeted in long, lush clumps of cocksfoot and dogstail grass, dotted with the tall stems and purple bells of foxglove. As he walked further in, he caught the scent of honeysuckle, masked slightly by the thick ozone smell of the rich lichens that clung to the rocks and fallen timber all around him. He rolled his shoulders and cracked his neck as he let go of all the anxiety and bluster he'd felt build up during the conversation with Keelson.

He looked up sharply as he heard a group of siskin making their way through the boughs above, their trilling and wheeze-like chatter making them hard to miss. Their bright yellow and black colouring stood out against the dark branches and tree tops. One paused momentarily on a high sprig to look down at him, chirring cautiously to the others. They moved off, flitting from tree to tree until they disappeared altogether in a noisy babble.

He soon came to the mountain stream that led down to the loch. It didn't take too long to reach the stony shore from there, the path through having been flattened by the many excursions over the last few weeks. He found the rocky seat he'd used on each occasion, cushioned as it was by moss and lichen, with pinkish heads of butterwort flowers poking up from the crevices around it. He sat with his eyes closed for a few moments, enjoying the touch of sun on his skin and the warmth it brought. Meg scampered over the rocks, splashing into the cold water lapping the shore. Thomas watched as she chased the brown trout parr through the shallows, each fish no longer than a few inches at this early stage of their life. They were right to stick to the shallows, as their cannibalistic brethren in the deeper waters of the loch would happily eat them. Meg wasn't having much luck, but he wondered if he might. He got up and carefully started walking along the loch.

He stepped silently onto a granite slab that stretched out over the water from the shore. He got down onto his knees, and then his belly, dipping his hands into the clear cold water as he started to feel beneath the rock's lip. It had been eroded away by the water into a perfect lie for a trout. Thomas held his breath so he was less likely to flinch when his fingers found the wet flesh of the fish. He smiled when they did, and he began to stroke its belly, using his left hand to coax the trout into a trance whilst his right one moved towards its head. As soon as he was sure he had it, he grabbed the head and cupped the body of the trout, bringing it up and out of the water with a flick of his wrist. The fish sailed over him and he expected to hear the smack of its body against rock, but instead he heard the light snap of teeth. He turned to find Meg behind him, the trout between her jaws and her tail wagging.

"You old sneak," chuckled Thomas.

Meg stripped the trout expertly, holding the tail in her front paws and ripping the flesh free from each flank. She finished her meal in a few bites, leaving the head, tail and a few tatters on the rock. Thomas picked it up and threw it into the loch, knowing there was still plenty to interest the local otters, but he was surprised by a high pitched, yelp-like call from the trees. He glanced up to see the glaring yellow eyes of a white-tailed eagle in a large pine some fifty yards away. He recognised it as a sub-adult, still growing into its dark chocolate, second winter plumage. Only its nape and beak hinted at the paler colouring it would take on as an adult. No wonder he hadn't seen it nestled against the bark of the tree. He smiled, glad to see the bird back in Scotland. The reintroduction programme had started in 1975 on the Hebridean island of Rum, and they had slowly begun to colonise the west coast during the late eighties. The east coast reintroduction on the other hand had only started in 2007, and he was fairly certain this was an east coast juvenile that had started heading west in search of a new territory. As he called Meg to him and headed back towards the pines, he caught sight of the eagle as it launched from the tree and drifted down effortlessly towards the remainder of the trout still floating on the water's surface. An outstretched talon of ebony reached out lazily and plucked it from the loch, a gentle, singular beat of its wings being all the eagle needed to glide to shore and out of sight. Thomas knew it would be eating quickly and in the open, where it could spot danger easily.

As he made his way back through the trees, Thomas considered what an exciting time it was to be a conservationist in Scotland. Eco-tourism was on the rise, and species long since lost to the land were being returned to it with the help of people like him and Catherine. The white-tailed eagle was just one example of a successful reintroduction, after having become geographically extinct in the country in 1918. Its arrival hadn't been without controversy, with farmers worried about their livestock and even concerns about public safety being voiced. But, as the bird he had just seen had proven, the eagles were as much scavengers as they were predators. No doubt lambs were taken by the 'flying barn doors' as they were known locally, but usually as carrion. The Scottish weather was still a far bigger killer of vulnerable animals than the eagles were. The scaremongering vexed him. It led to the illegal shooting and poisoning of the birds. But it was more than that. Somewhere in time, people had lost the awe and reverence they had for the majestic birds. On Orkney, 5,000-year-old early Bronze Age tombs had been discovered, where the worthiest were laid to rest after they had been left for the eagles to feast upon. Later, in the 16th and 17th centuries, Scottish families considered it good luck to have eagles nest nearby. People now were much more skittish and less awestruck. And he knew the public faced a greater challenge to come.

After the discovery of the creature he had killed, other big cats had been tracked down throughout Britain. Although they were recognised species such as mountain lions and leopards, it had quickly come apparent they were relatively few in number. Plans were now being discussed as to how those that remained should be dealt with. Capturing or killing the animals was proving as difficult as it had been before their presence had been officially recognised. So, another scenario was being considered, the reintroduction of a cat that had once been native to the UK. The lynx. It was hoped that although smaller than the pumas and leopards, if introduced and supported in sufficient number, they would put further pressure on the small populations of surviving cats by reducing prey such as deer. Thomas had his doubts. He knew only too well that desperate cats wouldn't just give up. They'd fight to the death, or turn to other food sources, ones the lynx would be unable to compete with them for. But he also knew he would love nothing more than to be able to walk through the forest and catch a glimpse of the rust coloured, spotted hide of a lynx. Only time would tell if he would one day be able to do so.

It didn't take long for the granite and whitewashed walls of the house, named Sàsadh, to come back into view. The trees began to thin and he found himself on the track that led to the house, a few yards further down from where he had first entered the forest. Meg trotted ahead of him, past the converted stables that now acted as a garage, and up to the front door. Thomas whistled, and she looked back towards him.

"You know better than that, muddy paws," he said, nodding his head towards the back.

Meg huffed a grumble, but scampered back over to him as they both walked round to the boot room. He swung the door open and she dutifully stepped through onto the tiled floor. Thomas took off his own boots and grabbed a towel from the rack. He knelt beside Meg and carefully cleaned her paws of mud before letting her scamper down the corridor. He placed the fleece gilet back on the rack as he passed, and headed back to the study. Meg was there before him, sprawled in front of the desk. He made himself equally comfortable in the leather desk chair and clicked on the keyboard to bring the Apple laptop to life. He went to his inbox, thinking he should let the local RSPB officer know about his sighting of the eagle, but was surprised instead to see a new message waiting for him. It was from a friend he had not seen in seven years. They weren't regularly in touch. Jelani had been part of the tracking team on Hunter Hunted. There was no subject to the message, just the date and time. Kenya was two hours ahead, so it had been sent in the late afternoon. Thomas began to read it, his curiosity giving way to horror almost immediately.

Thomas, my friend

I know you were fond of my brother, Jabari. I am writing because I thought you would want to know that yesterday evening, he was taken by lions. The lions. The lions that took Amanda. The pride now numbers at twenty-two and they are growing bolder. My staff fear a local crime lord and self-proclaimed witch doctor named Kanu Sultan, who they believe sent the 'critters of the bush' after myself and Jabari for running a business that caters to Europeans and Americans. Most of my staff have fled, leaving me with few to run a camp and lead safaris. I do not believe I will last long – something that is undoubtedly in the hands of Kanu.

I have sent word to O'Connell for help, but do not know if or when he will arrive. I know you have painful memories of Tsavo, and I do not ask for your help lightly. But in my heart, I feel it is the right thing to do for both of us. We both now have unfinished business with the Simba Giza.

Your friend, Jelani.

Thomas's brow wrinkled as he read through the email again. Simba Giza. The Daughters of the Darkness. It was the name the local population had given the pride, and it was an apt one. The reason he and Amanda had gone to Tsavo in the first place was because of the legendary man-eaters that had brought terror to the region in 1898. Colonel John Henry Patterson had spent nine months trying to hunt them down as they picked off his labourers from the camps of the Uganda railway. Although not proven and often disputed, Patterson put the number of people killed at 135. Thomas had no problem believing it. A recent study he'd written for Scientific American had found that man-eating was still an issue in eastern Africa. Over the last twenty-five years, in Tanzania alone, over 1,200 people had been taken by lions. About a hundred people a year still found themselves on the menu for the king of beasts across Africa, and those were just the ones known about and reported. But the Tsavo lions, known as The Ghost and The Darkness thanks to a Hollywood film, were still the continent's most famous killers.

Thomas slumped forward onto his desk, his head in his hands. It had been seven years since he had scattered Amanda's ashes in sight of Mount Kilimanjaro, in the shade of a flat-topped acacia tree. The wind had taken her from him, disappearing into the red, dust-veiled river gorge. He wondered if he would be able to stand there again as he reached for the phone, hitting redial.

"I'm surprised to hear from you again today Walker," Keelson admitted on answering. "Please tell me you're considering my offer?"

"I'm not interested in a new series. But what if I were to let you come along on a one-off?" Thomas asked.

"I'm listening," Keelson replied.

"You're aware from when you interviewed me that I never went after the lions that killed Amanda. I've just had word that they are still enjoying themselves immensely, at the expense of a friend of mine. I think it's time for me to break up the party permanently. Would you be interested?"

"Are you kidding? This is better than anything I'd suggested," Keelson said, "We'll have networks frothing at the mouth for this."

"I'm not interested in the money," snapped Thomas, "but it would be useful to have the political weight of a network behind us, and your connections might help ease a few closed doors open."

"I'll start making enquiries, but I know we'll get it," Keelson assured him.

"Good. I have a number of conditions. You'll need to get special permits, arrange transportation, and hire people. I'll send you a list, but check with me if you're unsure of anything. This isn't going to be straight-forward, but I'll put you in touch with the right people where I can," Thomas said, and put the phone down.

He sighed, what he had just said and done not quite registering. It became suddenly clear as he noticed the shadow in the doorway. Catherine's turquoise-green eyes were wide in shock, and burned with fury.

"Going somewhere?" she snapped.

"It's not that simple," he challenged back. "I have to go. I owe it to my friend, myself even."

"And the first person you wanted to discuss it with was Keelson? You didn't think it was something we should have talked about first?"

"It's not like that," Thomas protested. "I had to get Keelson on board to get the ball rolling. I was angry." Thomas said, flushed.

"So am I. Tom," Catherine said, glaring. "I'm going on my run. That's an example of me telling you what I'm going to do before I do it. You may want to start trying."

A few moments later, Thomas heard the slam of the front door. He sat at the desk dumbfounded, his eyes glancing at the picture of Amanda that sat in a frame on the shelf. Slowly his gaze moved downwards, coming to rest on the museum replica of a lion skull below it and the pristine, four-inch-long teeth on either side of the upper jaw. He shuddered. The ghosts and darkness of Africa were all too real for him.

CHAPTER TWO

Kanu Sultan stepped out into the courtyard of his compound. The sun was all but gone and he let the warmth of the last few rays linger on his skin as night crept slowly from the east. He had chosen his new home well – a dense marshland nestled between the three national parks of Tsavo East, Tsavo West and Chyulu Hills. Several other smaller wildlife conservancies were on his doorstep, but like the one he now occupied, they had been abandoned following his arrival in the territory. It was a hunter's paradise, benefiting from the movement of animals between the parks and being close to water, offering a place for them to slake their thirst. Thirteen miles from the nearest road, the remote location gave him privacy and security, but was still central enough for him to have a wide influence over much of the area. Roughly equal distance from his native Mombasa to the east and the more tourist-friendly Nairobi to the west, much of southern Kenya was within his reach, as was the border with Tanzania.

Kanu walked past one of his men, a former Kenyan Army paratrooper who remained statuesque at his post as he went by. Kanu hand-picked most of his men from either the paratroopers or the Presidential Escort Regiment, Kenya's best. He also made up their number with some local Maasai, and he paid all of them well. Although relatively small, the force was elite enough to make his reputation formidable and kept his activities safe from government interference. Out here, he was the authority. And it was that authority he was about to exercise now.

At the far-left corner of the courtyard, he turned, making his way down a flight of stone steps that led to a makeshift prison block. Weeks before, it had held expensive wines and brandies for the paying guests of the game lodge that now served as his personal quarters. He walked down the dimly lit corridor to the end cell, the only one occupied. He stared in, the flash of his white teeth against his dark face alerting the dishevelled man on the other side of the iron bars to his presence.

"I respect a man who takes risks in business," said Kanu. "It's why I asked you, with respect, to go elsewhere. Unfortunately, like most Afrikaans, your greed and disrespect have brought an end to your good fortune."

"Stepped on your toes did I, kaffa?" the man leered, easing himself up onto his feet from the floor, using the wall to support his weight.

Kanu stiffened slightly at the insult, glancing down the corridor as he heard the hurried footsteps of one of his men. His eyes told the young Maasai to stop where he was, only momentarily glancing at the sack the warrior held out in front of him, its heavily twisted top held firmly between both hands.

"Racism is born of fear Mr. Van Zyl, and fear is natural when facing death. Did you know the kingdom of Kaffa was once a state of what is now Ethiopia? Its first capital was named Bonga, as was the district around it. It was one of the prime trade routes for slaves, which is why both Kaffa and the term Bonga Bonga land came to be used by the whites in such a derogatory way. It was where the slaves came from."

"Getting back at the whites is it then?" Van Zyl sneered. "Bit late don't you think?"

"Hardly. You are a dealer of drugs. Instead of plying your

trade to wealthy visitors in Nairobi as I suggested, you targeted the poor and vulnerable on the streets of Mombasa. The same streets where I grew up and watched men like you destroy whole families and neighbourhoods. You did not do as I asked Mr. Van Zyl, and that situation demands nothing short of my full attention," Kanu replied.

"You're a fucking hypocrite Kanu. You're a dealer too. Admit it, this is about shutting out the competition."

Kanu stepped closer to the bars, his eyes fixed on his captive.

"I don't mind you selling drugs Mr. Van Zyl," he said in barely a whisper. "But I do mind who to. And you are wrong, I am not a dealer like you: I am a trafficker. I organise, sell and allow safe passage of product, be it arms or narcotics, through the territory. What I don't allow is for those items to be used against my people. There are plenty of opportunities outside of Kenya, and even a few within its borders. You were urged to explore them. Now you must face the consequences of not doing so."

Kanu carefully stepped back, taking a large iron key from his pocket. Van Zyl watched him as he slowly placed it in the lock of the door and turned it. As a heavy sounding clunk signalled the release of the door, Van Zyl shot forwards and pulled it open as he attempted to dart between the two men in his way. Kanu was ready for him, pouncing forward and punching him in the chest with both fists, his forearms straight as spears. Van Zyl was knocked head over heels backwards. He crumpled onto the floor by the back wall.

Before Van Zyl could get up, Kanu quickly took the sack from the Maasai. In one flowing movement, he took the corner in one hand and pinched the top open in the other, as he upended it and flung it forward. Van Zyl screamed as an enraged snake leapt towards him, its open mouth and two-inch-long fangs all he saw before he instinctively raised his arms to shield his face. He was surprised at the heavy impact he felt as the snake hit him. He panicked and threw the snake aside, but not before its teeth sank into the biceps of his right arm. The snake hit the floor with a thud and immediately made for the darkness underneath the cot bed. Once there, it coiled and lay with its eyes fixed on Van Zyl. It made no noise, but its forked tongue tasted the air every few seconds.

"My apologies for the theatrics Mr. Van Zyl," Kanu said. "The gaboon viper has to be somewhat provoked into delivering an envenomed bite. They're actually quite docile. But I find them hard to resist, being the largest of their kind. The fellow who just bit you weighs 20lbs."

Van Zyl spat. His mouth tasted dry and his tongue felt heavy and swollen.

"Not exactly common in this part of Kenya, people might get suspicious don't you think?" he said, beginning to feel slightly faint.

Kanu smiled. "Oh, we're not quite finished yet Mr. Van Zyl. When you're found, I doubt they'll think to check for a snake bite. I just needed to slow you down."

Kanu nodded to the Maasai, who had been joined by another of his men. They both stepped into the cell and picked up Van Zyl, dragging him out and back along the hall towards the stairs. Kanu slipped into the empty room behind them and picked up the snake with ease by the tail. It sought out the open sack as soon as he offered it, and he knotted the top as he walked out. At the top of the stairs, he handed the Maasai the sack.

Van Zyl was thrown across the flatbed of a large green Toyota Land Cruiser truck. Kanu climbed into the open back with him. He looked the man over as the truck pulled off. It passed quickly through a large archway made up of the black volcanic stone of the region and ploughed forward into the African night.

Kanu smiled down at the pale, sweat-strewn face that looked back up at him from the bed of the truck, the eyes bulging and bloodshot.

"I would have allowed you a slightly more luxurious last ride, Mr. Van Zyl. I personally would have preferred the air conditioning. But your body is no longer in control, and I couldn't have you shitting and pissing yourself over my leather seats," Kanu explained.

He brushed aside the dying man's shirt. The welted, swollen purple flesh of his shoulder and neck were already beginning to blister. The man could no longer talk from his enlarged tongue. Soon his eyelids would also be too heavy to keep open. Kanu knew the man's pulse would be racing and slowing with complete irregularity. If simply left, his death could still take up to an hour. He looked up and began to peer into the darkness.

After driving for nearly thirty minutes, Kanu finally thumped on the cabin roof of the old Land Cruiser, giving the signal to stop. The driver pulled over into the long tussock grass.

"My pets are close, Mr. Van Zyl; you will not suffer much longer," Kanu laughed, towering over him.

Van Zyl barely felt the rough grasp of the two men who picked him out of the flatbed and threw him to the ground. The impact of the dry, rock strewn earth on his blistered and swollen flesh sent a wave of pain through his body. He continued to writhe and struggle as he heard the truck pull away, but he no longer had the strength to stand. The sound of the engine dulled, faded and then disappeared altogether.

He lay stricken. His arms and chest felt as though they were on fire, and his skin felt tight, as if it were too small for him. With great effort, he opened his bruised and tumid eyelids, and gazed at his hand. His arm had ballooned. Its purple and yellow colouring was punctured by cracks that streamed with thin, cherry-red blood. He knew he would not stop bleeding now. He closed his eyes, knowing he would not be able to open them again. He gagged and choked on the froth filling his throat, turning his head to the side to try and vent it. His strength left him and he waited for death. Just as his thoughts threatened to fade, a sound piercing the night stabbed him with a momentary surge of adrenalin and renewed panic.

The diabolical laughter crept closer on swift, padded feet. It made the animal sound nervous, but it was a sign of pure confidence. Van Zyl convulsed involuntarily as the hyena sniffed at his head. The animal let out a yip of excitement, leaning in closer to lick the man's forehead and scalp.

Another sound penetrated the night. A low, deep rumble of warning. The hyena gave a scream of fright, only pausing to snap off one of Van Zyl's ears as it loped away. Blind and half deaf, his body shutting down in shock as his flesh was putrefied by the snake venom, Van Zyl still had time to sense the presence of the large, heavy animal as it came closer. The press of its paw on his chest was the last thing he felt as he slipped into unconsciousness. Moments later, a pair of five and a half inch fangs smashed through his temples.

~

She dragged the body further into the grass, seeking the cover of scrub and thorn. Deep in a thicket, she lifted her head and let out a thunderous roar, calling in the rest of the pride. She listened to them slink closer as she began to feast on the body.

~

A breath of wind carried the whisper of the roar to Kanu's ears as the truck rolled through the night back towards the compound. He smiled.

CHAPTER THREE

Catherine ran hard and fast. Her trail running shoes bit into the dirt as she tore along the Scottish mountain path. Arturo loped along behind. At first, he had bayed loudly and joyfully as they went, but now the big dog just concentrated on keeping up. Catherine knew she wasn't putting too much pressure on him. He was doing exactly what his breed was meant to do, coursing game over long and rugged terrain. She shuddered slightly at the thought of being game, and the memory of being trapped against the dark walls of the mine shaft flashed through her thoughts, the green eyes of the cat peering up at her out of the gloom. She gasped, stumbling a few steps before coming to a stop. She stood bent over, her hands resting on her knees as she caught her breath. Arturo stopped beside her, panting happily. He barked, as if querying which way to go next. Catherine stood up and looked about.

The renovated deer farm Thomas had made into their home and named Sàsadh, meaning a place of comfort, was behind her, as were Loch Mullardoch and the forest. She had the choice of two paths. One led south east to the research centre where they worked, the other south west, towards the lofty pyramid shaped peak of Carn Eige. She took the upward path, away from home and work. She had fought her fears over the last eighteen months. She had started climbing much to Thomas's dismay, her frantic scrabbling in the mineshaft a private source of shame. She had vowed it would never happen again. She had also been pleasantly surprised when Thomas had flown her out to Prague for her birthday. First, he had booked them into one of the Reindl Atelier suites of the Le Palais Art Hotel, which had thrilled her. Her art had been an important outlet for her as she had recovered from the impact of their experience. Thomas seemed to genuinely appreciate her artwork, and several of her colourful and abstract pieces now adorned the walls of Sàsadh. But in between the sumptuous luxury, and visiting the Antonín Dvořák museum and the Leica Gallery, they had also visited a former communist compound. There, the ex-soldiers had trained her to use a variety of weapons, from small handguns to semi-automatic rifles and a shotgun. She had even fired a Desert Eagle pistol. For the rest of the day, Thomas had suggested she become his bodyguard. But the message behind the fun was clear: he was completely behind her desire to learn how to protect herself.

The trip to Prague had been necessary for the handgun training, because they were illegal in the UK. But on their return, he had helped her acquire her shotgun and firearms certificate. She wasn't as good a shot as Thomas, and had no real interest in shooting, but she appreciated the sentiment. To combat the more human elements of her fear, she had started intensive Muay Thai lessons at a gym in Inverness. The feeling of being defenceless haunted her. But these practicalities weren't how she chose to deal with her fear and trauma. She expressed it in her paintings and out here on the mountain, and by throwing herself into her work. She had been campaigning hard for the lynx reintroduction programme, as well as passionately speaking against the possible repeal of the 2007 hunting act. But today it was the mountain that offered her solace and therapy. She needed the space.

She ran on and upwards, the landscape becoming sparser

as she left the tree line behind her. As she glanced to her right, over the tops of the spruce and pine trees, she caught the glimmer of afternoon sun reflecting off the far away surface of the loch. She focused on the path again, watching her footing as she jogged along the path. The blur of dark hide streaking across the trail from the left sent her into a panic, and she lurched aside. As her heart pounded in her chest, she had the sense to drop to her knees and throw her arms around Arturo. The big black dog tried to surge forwards momentarily, but stopped as soon as he felt Catherine's embrace and her unspoken command. She watched as the stag bolted down the mountainside, its hide discoloured by the boggy peat it had been rolling in. She let her nerves recover before starting off again, this time at a gentle walk. She wasn't far now from where she wanted to be.

She sat on a rocky outcrop behind a thick entanglement of gorse. She watched as a male whitethroat sat perched on a thorny stalk amongst the bright yellow flowers, repeating its scratchy, rapidly uttered warble as it claimed its territory. The song was hardly delicate, but the bird was handsome with its rust-brown back and grey-capped head. Further down, Arturo ran from rock to rock, chasing the voles that hid there. She looked up to the ridgeline and was just able to spot the two saplings that marked the entrance to the cave where the giant hybrid cat had cornered her, before Thomas had followed them in and faced it down. And now she felt trapped again, but this time by him. His absolute stubbornness meant they were going to do whatever he had agreed to with Keelson.

She sat with her back to the mountain, feeling warm and content in the sun and cocooned between the rock and the gorse. She ran her fingers through the fine powdery soil around her, and was surprised to find a silver and brass coloured bullet casing. She picked it up and examined it. The spent 9mm ammunition had come from the gun David Fairbanks had fired at her. Although he had failed to kill her with it, the sound of gunfire had brought the cat out from its lair. She remembered the sprint from her hiding place, and the sounds of the cat tearing into Fairbanks's flesh behind her as she made for the darkness of the cave. The cracking of the bones and ripping of sinew hadn't frightened her. The pleasure she had felt from hearing it had. She put the casing into the pocket of her hoodie and let out a deep sigh.

She hugged her knees as she looked down the valley, back towards the loch. She squinted as some large bird lifted off from the trees by the shore, mobbed as it went by a pair of hooded crows. It had to be an eagle, and as it drifted closer she saw it was. It followed the thermal of air up and over her head, on towards the peak above. The deeply fingered wing feathers let her know it was a white-tail. She knew Thomas would be excited to know one was in the area and smiled. She couldn't decide if his stubbornness was something she loved or hated. Most of the time, it was just something light hearted she teased him about. But this was different. She was hurt and angry he hadn't thought to discuss it with her first. He didn't think about the consequences, what it might mean for their work or the preparations they would need to make in order to go travelling. It wouldn't have even occurred to him that somebody would need to look after the dogs. He had made the decision on a whim and instinct as always.

She looked about and realised that this was where her own instinct had told her to come. Where she had seen, and faced death. It had guided her here. She was invisibly tied to the place, just as Thomas was to Africa. She wondered what Thomas would think if he knew this was where she came to think. She had never confided in him about it. She smiled acceptingly. There was a comfort in knowing they were both occasionally ruled by their emotions. He blamed her red hair, which made her wonder what his excuse was. Arturo barked, turning his head in her direction and looking up at her.

"Time to go home," she said.

As she stood up, her phone beeped in her back pocket. She knew it was Thomas. She opened the message and read the simple text. Marry me here, it said. Below the text were stunning vistas of African landscapes, sunsets and wildlife. She couldn't help the little flutter of excitement she felt as she scrolled through the images. Let's talk when I get back she replied. You're still in trouble, just not quite so much. There was a glow of warmth in her chest as she remembered the elaborate proposal in Rome the year before.

She jogged slowly and easily back along the trail, Arturo loping by her side comfortably. Great swells of relief washed over her as she covered the three miles back to Sàsadh. Africa was somewhere she had always dreamt of going. She caught her breath on the drive before heading to the boot room entrance. As soon as they got through the back door, Arturo slumped down onto his blanket next to a dozing Meg. He growled softly and affectionately as Catherine cleaned his paws. The mindless activity helped clear her head and she felt calm again.

She made her way out to the hall, where she came to a halt. The staircase was strewn with scarlet and pink dried rose petals. She followed them up, giggling slightly at the extravagant gesture. Thomas seemed to have no ability to gauge his romantic offerings, making them all or nothing, with a preference for the all. She stepped along the hall to the bathroom, following the path of petals as she went. She swung the door open and beamed.

More petals laced the clay coloured tiles. At the centre of the room, the grey and pink hued stone bath was filled, and as she stepped closer she caught the fragrance of the jasmine, ylang-ylang and clary sage scented foam. Sitting beside the bath was an ice bucket containing a bottle of rose Veuve Clicquot. A crystal glass champagne flute sat on the rim of the bath with a singular, sliced strawberry delicately perched over its outer edge. He had turned the lights low and pulled the blind to the only window, making the red-walled room feel even warmer. Several lit candles sat on the floor to add to the cosiness. She tested the water with her fingers, as she walked past the bath to the dressing table and large framed mirror sitting against the far wall. She slipped off her running gear and left it in a messy pile underneath the table, grinning that it would slightly ruffle Thomas's desire for neatness when he saw it. Then she paused, running the forefinger and thumb of her right hand over the band of white gold on her ring finger, its channel set with brilliant round diamonds surrounding the six-pronged centrepiece, a 2.3 carat stone. She had hit Thomas hard enough to leave a bruise on his chest after looking it up on the Tiffany website to see how much it had cost. She eased the ring off and left it on the top of the table.

As she turned, she met Thomas's gaze from the open doorway.

"I'm sorry," he said, "but in my defence, if you haven't learnt that I don't always think things through by now, it's probably too late."

"It's okay," she smirked. "I mean, it's not, but we'll talk about it later. I would just have preferred if I had been the first person you spoke to about it rather than Keelson."

"Who?" Thomas quipped, staring at her soft naked skin.

"That," she purred, "was the right thing to say."

She stepped over to him, taking his hands in hers and placing them on her waist. They pulled her tight to him. They kissed softly and slowly as she began to strip away his clothes until they were both naked, tentatively touching each other with a nervous eagerness. She led him over to the bath and they stepped in together. She sat down in the warm, milky water with her back to him. She felt his legs sidle past her and he began to bathe her, his hands cupping the silky liquid and letting it fall over her neck and shoulders. A stream cascaded between her breasts, and suddenly his hands were there too, rubbing and stroking to her delight. She leaned back, nestling her lips into his neck to nuzzle softly. She arched her back, lifting herself and squeezing his legs back between her own. They made love slowly and tenderly at first, but giving way to their passion as it broached. They giggled together as each impassioned lunge sent a wave of water over the top of the bath. They held each other for some time afterwards before she stood up, looking down at him coyly.

"I'm still going to need that shower," she whispered.

Thomas watched her go and moments later heard the shower begin to run in the adjoining room. He leaned over the top of the tub and grabbed a towel from the rail. His first instinct was to follow her in, but he held back, knowing they had a serious conversation ahead of them. He tied the towel round his waist and walked out of the bathroom and across the hall to the bedroom. He passed through into the oak lined walk-in wardrobe and started taking the heavy, leather luggage down from a back shelf. As soon as the preparations were made, they were heading to Africa.

CHAPTER FOUR

MKUU, TANZANIA/KENYA BORDER

The battered and dented white Mitsubishi Shogun bumped along the dry, dust encrusted track. Robert Botha looked across to his client, an Italian named Leonetti whose wallet outweighed his shooting skills by some margin. They had been out since dawn after hearing the lions during the night. And the Italian wanted a lion, badly. Robert watched the man as he nervously gripped the Famars .416 Rigby Africa Express rifle, his knuckles white with the pressure.

"Ease up old boy, we'll find them before you have to leave. The plane will be landing at the lodge at 4pm, and trust me, it won't leave without you after what you've paid," Botha reassured him.

The man smiled, and seemed to relax a little as he let out a breath and wiped the sweat from his brow.

Botha stood up from the raised bench seat that sat squarely against the cab of the Shogun and looked out over the top. He scanned the road ahead and immediately banged hard on the roof of the truck. His driver, Enzi, brought the vehicle to a juddering halt as Botha jumped over the side. He knelt by the track, examining the large fresh pugmarks. The lions had used the road because it was the easiest route through the scrub, but it made him wonder where they were going. He was worried they were heading for the river and the Kenyan border, where they would not be able to follow. But further up at a bend in the road, the prints led off into the acacia-potted wilderness.

Botha walked back to the truck.

"Looks like we're on foot from here my friend," he said.

The Italian climbed down from the seat and over the side of the truck. Abasi, Botha's tracker and gun bearer, climbed out of the passenger side of the Shogun. He carried the two long wooden sticks that would make up a gun rest and slung Botha's Weatherby rifle over his shoulder. Botha and Leonetti followed him past the bend in the road and into the surrounding scrub. The tall, dark-skinned Maasai scanned the landscape ahead. He walked forty yards before stopping again, his gaze set on a thick tangle of scrub in the shade of a thorn-studded acacia tree.

"What is it Abasi?" Botha whispered as he joined him.

"There is a kill. See the tai?" Abasi asked.

Botha looked to the horizon. The dark silhouettes of griffon and white-backed vultures, or tai in Swahili, were easy to spot against the azure sky. They rode the thermals in a slow arc, their outstretched wings carrying them with ease over the savannah.

"They have not landed," Abasi stated simply.

Botha nodded. The lions were still feeding, or at least guarding the kill. He turned and beckoned Leonetti to them.

"We'll stay downwind and head towards that clump of trees. We think the lions are laid up there. Go slow and go quiet, okay?"

The Italian nodded, his shirt already drenched in perspiration. Botha nodded to Abasi, signalling they were clear to move off. The men skirted the scrub together, and clung to the thin pieces of cover between them and the yellow-flowered candle bush where they planned to try for a bead on the lions. When they reached it, they knelt and took a draw of water from the canteen Botha carried. The going had been hard, hot and slow, but they were now within shooting distance of the acacias and the shade they offered.

Abasi seemed to squint as he searched out the dark recesses beneath the trees. Finally, he relaxed and rammed the two sticks into the ground, their crossed ends forming a natural rest for the client's rifle. Leonetti was brought up, and he placed his gun between the two pieces of wood whilst Botha pointed out where he should be looking. Botha used a pair of old Zeiss binoculars as Leonetti searched through his scope. He found the animal easily. The scrawny looking young male seemed to be alone. But it was a prize worth taking. The pale colour of the hide looked slightly out of place against the tawny scrub, and hinted the animal was something unusual. Over the last decade, east Africa had seen more and more so-called white lions in their populations. The reason for their strange appearance was unknown, but it would make for quite the trophy.

"You've got a whitey," Botha whispered. "Not every day you get a chance at one of those. He's sitting up nicely, all you have to do is squeeze the..."

The explosion of sound rolled around the arid dustbowl surrounding them as a lick of flame erupted from the end of the rifle. Botha watched with annoyance as a giant pock mark was etched into the trunk of the acacia, a few inches from the lion's head. The animal jumped up immediately, melting into the undergrowth seamlessly as it dashed behind the tree. You can lead a horse to water Botha thought bitterly, looking to the sweat sodden Italian for an explanation.

"I went for the other one," Leonetti stammered, "I only saw a shadow, but it was there. It made the other one look-a-like pussy cat."

Botha sighed. It wasn't the first time a client had shot at shadows. The heat and sun played tricks on the eyes as well as the mind out here. He had wanted the man to get his lion, but he knew they were out of time.

"Well let's go see what old Simba was snacking on hey," Botha offered.

The three men walked slowly over to the tree, careful to watch in case the lion decided to make a return. With ten feet still to go before they reached the acacia's welcome shade, Abasi stopped suddenly, throwing his arm out to the side to hold back the others. Through a thick swarm of jade-bodied blowfly, the torn remains of a man lay scattered in a heap amongst the crimson stained grass. There wasn't much left. The abdomen had been opened, the spilled guts devoured and fought over. The trampled and flattened brush showed several lions had fed here. The sheered, neatly gnawed rib cage had been broken through so the prized morsels within of heart, liver and lungs could be extracted. The legs had been severed below the knee, ripped off as individual prizes to be consumed away from the slathering mob. Botha spotted a crunched, nearly fleshless foot laying a little way off from the body. The skin and meat from the man's cheeks had been licked away by the sandpaper tongues of the cats. Only a few flaps of skin and tattered strings of flesh still clung to the broken and battered body.

As Botha took a step closer, an ear-splitting roar rose up from the scrub where the young male had disappeared. Abasi's eyes grew wide as the sound echoed away into nothing. Botha could read the uneasiness on the man's face.

"I think we're in danger of overstaying our welcome,"

Botha said. "We'll call this in when we get back to camp. Besides, we've lost them now. They're headed to the Kenyan side of the river, and there's no sport shooting there I'm afraid."

Without a word, the three men worked their way back to the truck, each offering nervous glances behind every few steps.

A few hours later, Botha watched both his client and a small metal container containing the remains of the man they had found board the Vulcanair P68C TC plane at the camp's private runway. He waved them off as the twin engines pulled the plane into the sky, but the day's events vexed him. Although the client had enjoyed a fine safari of nearly thirty days, he suspected he would not see Leonetti again. Not getting his lion meant the Italian might venture further south for his next hunt. Namibia and South Africa offered more certainty these days. The camp at Mkuu was spectacular in location, right on the border of Tanzania and Kenya, in the shade of Mount Kilimanjaro itself. But the hilly outcrops, thickly packed wooded gorges and fierce desert scrub made sport shooting difficult. That was exactly what he had intended when he had set the place up, a safari experience that harked back to the golden era of hunting. A place where the danger was real and the animals were wild. But shooting had changed. Game farms offered a sure thing for the fraction of the price, with the story behind the kill left to the client's imagination once back home. He sighed, pondering if he should consider moving south too.

~

She waited in the grass, hunched and coiled. She had watched as the strange upright animals had left the kill, only to return and remove it. She had nearly charged, but instinct held her to the warm earth under her belly. As the light had begun to dim, the wind had changed and now the pungent scent was carried straight to her. It was immediately recognisable, a sweet, honey-like odour combined with a taint of leather or hide. The aroma was never alone, often wrapped in other scents, some bitter, some more delicate. But she had become accustomed to it and now recognised it as prey.

She was wary of the dark sticks the animals carried. She had learnt to no longer answer their thunderous noise with a roar. Although it brought the prey to her, she had seen others killed in their proximity. She now only ever roared when she was sure of the prey's position and a successful strike. Patience was something she had learnt as she sat above the entrances to warthog burrows, often for hours before the animal emerged. And no such vigil was necessary for this animal. They seemed careless.

The change in the wind brought confidence and she finally stirred with a flick of her tail. The tall savannah grass consumed her, the light dappling her silhouette and outline until it was just a glimmer. She knew these things by instinct, this being her favoured time of day to hunt. As she padded through the scrub, her ears pricked up and faced forward. She made little, rumbling grunts as she went. The other members of the pride flanked her but never out stepped or overtook her. They followed the scent laden trail from the cover either side of the dry red track that cut through the landscape. She knew this area was free from lions, as she had killed a large male and taken over a family group here. The surviving members had joined the pride amicably after that. But she still showed caution this side of the river. There was less prey here, and she couldn't tolerate the disturbance and taking of a kill.

Night was beginning to descend, but the scent trail remained thick and pungent. The pride stepped out of the grass together, entering a scrub-strewn gap in the cover. She stopped, her ears pricked at the distant sound of fire and the animals up ahead. She held her head high as she took in the smell of smoke laced with the teasing taints of hot fat and blistered meat. As she headed straight across the sparse ground, the others flanked and spread out on either side. They reached a maze of rocks and flat-topped acacia on the other side of the break and sunk to their bellies, inching forward as their amber eyes sought out the emergence of prey from the inky blackness. They made no sound now. Each tawny coloured cat made minute adjustments to their approach, pushing their noses into the wind until they could see the prey ahead of them. Some stood, straining forward as their heavy padded feet and unsheathed claws anchored them to the ground. Others hugged the earth, every muscle tight and wound for the rush to come. They waited.

~

Botha sat back in his canvas chair and watched the men begin to pack away for the night. They secured the food stores inside coolers and metal containers then loaded them onto the back of the shogun for added protection. He grabbed another bottle of Castle Draught beer from an ice box being carried past him, giving the man carrying it a nod as he did so. The lager was South African, like him. He had allowed the men to celebrate the end of the safari as usual, despite his misgivings of how the last hunt had gone. His crew behaved themselves, accepting the cold beers gratefully and not over indulging, something he took a dim view of. He pressed the condensation laced glass bottle to his forehead and closed his eyes for a moment as he enjoyed the cool comfort it brought.

When he opened them again, he settled his gaze on the dying fire. A log crackled and fizzed, its scorched bark popping in the dry air. He rolled and cracked his neck and looked up, above and through the wisped tops of the flames. There in the darkness he saw two golden embers of light. It took a few moments for his tired gaze to realise it wasn't part of the fire he was looking at, but its reflection in the mirrored irises of a cat. As he stared, he thought he could begin to make out the white guard hairs of the chin. At first, his fatigued mind told him it was a caracal, a small golden coloured cat that often hunted birds and mammals in the grass beside the camp. As the shadow took form, suddenly and silently rushing forward, he realised to his horror that it was a lioness.

He sprang from the chair as the great tawny beast leapt from the other side of the fire, its hubcap sized paws reaching out for him through the harmless and dying licks of flame. Botha only had time to half scream a warning, his words cut off as 350lbs of hard packed muscle hit him like a locomotive. He was thrown back nearly six feet onto his back. As his head struck the stony ground and the wind was knocked from his lungs, the momentum of the lioness brought her head and body smashing into his. Her open jaws found flesh and her top set of four inch fangs sank into his shoulder and the back of his neck, whilst the bottom set broke through its side and his right cheek bone. The crushing force splintered his jaw and ruptured his vertebrae, but he was still alive when the lioness split him open from belly to groin with a rake of her rear claws. As the lioness lifted him from the ground, she bit down harder, strangling the remaining life from him in a few seconds.

Roars erupted all around the camp. The men panicked, running in every direction as they sought an escape. None materialised. Rippling, bounding shadows spilled into the camp, swamping the fleeing men. One man ran for the truck, only to be brought to the ground and dragged off into the darkness, his screams coming to a sudden, cut-off end moments later. Another ran for Botha's tent, hoping to find the South African's rifle there. He did, and he died reaching for it as a lioness entered the tent and pinned him against the canvas, her growls drowning out his fearful sobs as she straddled him. A moment later he was rendered silent with a crushing bite to the chest that penetrated his heart and lungs.

Abasi sprinted away into the darkness, along a track that he knew would lead to the main village of Mkuu some three miles away. He didn't look back as the sounds of roaring and screams melted away into the night. He had always been swift and was running flat out. Guiltily, he hoped the lions would be content with his co-workers. He made it nearly two hundred yards before he found out he was wrong. As the moon broke free of a cloud and began to paint the savannah below from its still low position in the sky, a pale, grey coloured blur burst out of the undergrowth and barrelled into him. His tall, six-foot frame crashed and tumbled some way through the patchy and dry Bermuda grass. As he lay dazed and stunned, he thought of the white hunters he had helped purge the land of game. He knew they were rich beyond his understanding whilst he had remained poor. And now the land was poorer too. Was this the price to be paid for such disrespect and squander? The head man of his village had always preached that the Earth had a memory. It was what they believed. Perhaps she held a grudge too.

He was aware of a shadow passing over him. He cried out in pain as his feet were pinched between the jaws of the great cat. As he was dragged into thicker cover, his arms and legs were torn by the acacia thorns on all sides. He tried to reach up and claw at the animal's ash-coloured flanks, only to be ripped back down by the barbed branches. He gasped as they came to a stop deep in the thicket. There was no light here and he scrabbled with his fingertips for a way out. A deep, angry rumble penetrated the darkness and reverberated around the ragged walls of his prison. Abasi felt the hot breath of the animal on his face before a dry, rasping tongue raked across his cheek. A flick of a claw opened up his throat, and he gurgled and spat out his last breaths as the animal lay down by his feet and began to lick and clean them of flesh.

CHAPTER FIVE

It had been a painful and slow-turning three weeks for Thomas whilst Kelly made all the necessary arrangements, but he was pleasantly surprised by what she'd been able to pull off in that time. The seventeen-hour flight had been interrupted by a stop in Turkey, to take on supplies they weren't legally or otherwise able to procure in the UK, but it had been without incident. The Alenia C-27J Trojan cargo plane Keelson had somehow acquired on loan from the U.S.A.F was certainly more comfortable than some of the more antique aircraft he'd been in, but it was still a bare basics military transport. Catherine had tried to sleep a little, but the constant reverberation and juddering of the plane was something she wasn't used to. Keelson had kept herself busy checking and re-checking everything on board and didn't seem tired even now.

"I admit I'm impressed Kelly," Thomas said as she sat down on the troop bench opposite him. "This must have cost you a pretty penny or two."

"The yanks had the plane in storage at RAF Lakenheath. We gave them the opportunity for some much needed flying time in Middle East-like conditions. We're practically just paying mileage, more than worth it to get the assistance of bona fide flyboys I'd say," Keelson grinned. "Besides, the vehicles and most of the small arsenal you insisted on bringing were all on you. The rest is just crew and production."

Thomas glanced over at the two-man team piling equipment cases to one side at the back of the plane. One in particular, he was very pleased to have with them. He hadn't known that Danny Reeves's son was also a wildlife cameraman, but Kelly had. Her eulogy and tribute to Danny's ultimately ill-fated efforts to track down the marauding cat in the Highlands had clearly had an influence on bringing him into the production. Somehow, it felt right to have a Reeves behind the camera, just as Danny had been when they had made the Hunter Hunted series. Although only in his early twenties, Mason looked a lot like his dad. His thick black hair had a slight curl to it, and his five 'o' clock shadow was pretty much permanent Thomas guessed. He was slighter than his father had been, but still well built. Thomas had insisted everyone, including Mason, had experience filming wildlife, and predators especially. He caught his eye, and the cameraman walked over to join them.

"I haven't had a chance to thank you properly for dropping everything Mason," Thomas said.

"It was a no-brainer. Dad would have loved this. I think he wanted it actually. I'm sure he'll be watching over us," Mason replied, with the flash of a kind and genuine smile.

"I certainly hope somebody is," Catherine butted in, stifling a yawn as she stretched her arms above her head.

"Better get ready and buckled in," Keelson stated, "we're coming into Jomo to meet representatives of the Kenyan government and wildlife authority, before we fly on to the camp at Galana where we'll be based."

As he did up his belt, the desert-camouflage painted wingtip of the plane Thomas could see through the port side window, began to dip as they circled around and prepared to land at Nairobi's Jomo Kenyatta International Airport. A few moments later, there was a screech of rubber on tarmac and a thud as the plane touched down.

The two pilots stayed behind to check over the plane and

take on more fuel and supplies whilst Thomas, Catherine, Kelly and Mason gingerly made their way down the back ramp of the plane. The other member of the production crew joined them, an Indian sound engineer named Karni Bachchan, who was also a gifted editor and digital specialist. Thomas had been shown his impressive credentials by Keelson and both he and Mason had a number of warzone and wildlife encounters between them, with BBC and National Geographic documentaries to their names.

At the bottom of the ramp, a Kenyan official waited for them with three armed guards. Thomas guessed he was in his late forties from the hints of grey in his short cropped black hair and his somewhat portly appearance. He beamed a wide smile at Thomas and took his outstretched hand in both of his.

"Welcome back to Kenya Mr. Walker," the man said, his enthusiasm instantly warming him to Thomas. "I hope you had a pleasant flight. My name is Hali Diallo and I am a secretary in the Ministry of the Interior. I am to escort you to your meeting."

"Thanks for the warm welcome Hali. This is my fiancée Catherine Tyler," Thomas replied.

Hali took Catherine's hand and shook it as vigorously as he had Thomas's, which made her laugh.

"Is this your first time to our beautiful country Ms. Tyler?" Hali enquired.

"Yes," Catherine replied, "but I've always wanted to come here. I studied zoology at university and the wildlife at home isn't quite as exciting, well at least until recently," she smiled.

"Yes, I have heard of your adventures of course," Hali laughed loudly. "If you and your crew will follow me, we have some refreshments ready for you."

They didn't have to walk far. Hali directed them to a new looking open hangar on the other side of the runway. Thomas noticed it was on a small, seemingly private offshoot of the main strip, above which he could see several commercial airliners on approach. More armed guards, all Kenyan Army, were lined around the entrance of the hangar. Hali strolled past them as if they weren't there, heading towards the back, where Thomas could see a partition wall consisting of large windows and solid, lightly coloured panels made up an office space. Through the glass he could see a number of officials seated around one end of a long rectangular table.

"Are we expecting trouble?" Thomas whispered to Kelly just before they passed through the door of the office.

"Nope. But that doesn't mean there won't be any," she replied quickly, but with a confident smile.

"Please help yourselves to refreshments before we begin," Hali beckoned towards a table covered in fresh sliced mango, watermelon and pineapple.

Thomas could smell the rich Kenyan roast coffee and made straight for the pot of percolating black liquid, pouring himself a cup whilst Hali made the introductions.

"My colleagues Mr. Bah, Ministry of Defence, Mr. Kone, Ministry of Foreign Affairs and Dr. Yeboah of the Ministry of Environment."

Each man nodded as Hali said their names. Thomas and the others took their seats. The office was air-conditioned, but the heat and being back on the ground were already having an effect. He felt groggy and tired, but he smiled as he watched Catherine take a huge bite out of a large, triangular piece of pink fleshed watermelon. She wiped the juice from her chin, a glimmer of a giggle in her eye as she caught his smile. Bah was the first to speak. He had the look of a military man, with a crew cut of short black hair and a slight build stuffed into a caramel coloured suit. He studied Thomas with sharp brown eyes.

"Mr. Walker, we want you to know that you have the full support of the Kenyan government, but that said, our support is very limited. The majority of our forces are deployed protecting villages on the east coast. The threat of terrorism is very real for us, as I'm sure you're aware of the attacks we have sustained over the recent months. Our main focus is in countering Al-Shabaab's road blocks and protection rackets operating in the area, new ones of which seem to appear every day. We are also bedded down in the north of Nairobi, where some districts are now controlled by their forces."

"I completely understand," Thomas replied, "we are very grateful to have your blessing to be here at all. I'm very saddened by the attacks on your wonderful city and country, but I thought we'd be out of harm's way in Tsavo?"

"Perhaps not," interjected Hali. "We are aware of a local crime lord operating along the Tanzanian border not far from Tsavo. We suspect he runs guns and drugs for Al-Shabaab, amongst others. When the lions attacked a camp a few weeks back, just over the border in Tanzania, he declared they were under his control and that he was taking back the land from the corrupt whites who have destroyed it. He calls himself Kanu Sultan."

"That's clever," Thomas smirked. "A self-declared wildcat king."

"You know your Swahili Mr. Walker," acknowledged Dr. Yeboah.

Thomas turned to him. The man was tall and thin, with

short grey hair and a neat beard and moustache. He wore a dark pinstriped suit with a grey jumper underneath. He had kind eyes, which met Thomas's gaze through a pair of gold rimmed rectangular glasses. He had a quiet air of intelligence about him.

"But you should be aware that Kenya has changed, in many ways for the worse in your absence," he continued. "We have lost something like fifty percent of our wildlife, in part at least to a prolific bush meat trade. Outside of the national parks, where you'll be, the predators are finding it hard to find prey. Reports of aggression and man eating are also on the increase as they clash with farmers and villagers."

"And we are concerned that should the situation be misreported in the press, or worse, things went badly for you, it would affect our already now fragile tourism industry most severely," added Hali.

"I can assure you we're not here to cause trouble," Kelly said. "In fact, I'd like to think we're here to help. We're very grateful for your hospitality and support. As you know, we'll be working with an established safari company in Tsavo, and I'm sure that can only end up being very positive for tourism. I don't want to seem indelicate either, but the historical significance of man-eaters being in Tsavo, and Thomas's involvement should also prove positive for you. It will give the news cycle new feed other than terrorism to chew on, if you'll pardon the pun."

"You didn't want to seem indelicate?!" Catherine snapped, glaring at Keelson, who blushed and sat back a little.

"She's right," Thomas said quietly, his tiredness showing.

"We agree, generally," Bah continued. "But we wanted you to know what to expect, and to unfortunately basically tell you

you're on your own."

"We're here to hunt the man-eaters," Thomas declared, "we'll stay out of the limelight until the job is well and truly done. Kelly will liaise with you every step of the way with whatever progress we make."

"Thank you Mr. Walker," said Hali. "It's not that we don't appreciate you being here, it's just a very difficult time for the government, and we are naturally cautious of the risks involved. More so of course for you in the literal sense, but we will be held accountable if you fail."

"I understand," Thomas said.

There was an uneasy silence for a few moments, and Kelly took it as a sign the meeting was over.

"Thank you gentlemen, we have another flight and some arrangements to make before we can get set up in Tsavo, but we appreciate all your support and assistance," she declared, getting up from the table.

The others stood and they exchanged handshakes. Hali nodded to Kone, the one from the Ministry of Foreign Affairs, who passed him a manila file. He headed over to Thomas and handed it over. Inside, he found two hunting permits, one for the lions and the other allowing him to take two buffalo, five impala and unlimited bush pig, as well as game birds like francolin and sand grouse to supply the camp with meat if needed. There was also a declaration of special judiciary from the Kenyan Wildlife Service, giving Thomas authority over National Park rangers and staff in case it was ever questioned. Thomas knew that such permissions were very rare and the government were doing all they could to support them.

"Thank you," Thomas said. "Kelly has all of the details and will keep in touch with you and your office directly. I presume we can leave it to you to keep your colleagues informed?"

"Of course, I am sorry we cannot do more, but I think you probably have greater resources than we do at the moment," Hali admitted.

As they left the hangar, Kelly, Mason and Kali peeled off to the side. The camera equipment had been unloaded from the plane and they gathered around it, deep in conversation. Thomas and Catherine waited for Kelly to join them.

"We're going to drive to Tsavo from here and get some stock footage along the way. We've hired a truck and the boys are just off to get it. We'll see you there," she explained.

"That's a good 150 miles, rather you than me," Thomas laughed.

He waved at the two men and Keelson as he and Catherine walked back up the loading ramp of the plane. With a pneumatic whir, it began to close behind them and he heard the twin turboprops splutter into life. With the paperwork in his hand and just the short flight to the camp ahead of them, he suddenly felt a little dizzy. For the past three weeks, it hadn't really felt like it was happening, especially with Keelson handling most of the arrangements. He looked over the assorted gun cases and the customised Land Rover that made up most of the cargo. They brought him little comfort. Once again, he was on the trail of man-eaters. But this time, it wasn't a lone animal in the Highlands or an isolated case in some distant jungle. This time, he was going back to Tsavo and facing a whole pride with a legacy, one that included his dead wife.

CHAPTER SIX

There was a jolt as the big plane turned and began to drop towards the short, dust-red landing strip gouged into the savannah. Catherine leant forward, tensing and clutching at her stomach as they dropped again. Thomas placed his hand gently on her back to comfort her. It didn't help. The plane landed heavily, sending a ripple of jolts and bangs along the fuselage. Catherine snapped off her buckle and jumped from her seat, dashing towards the small toilet behind the cockpit. The slam of the door and the roar of the turboprops almost drowned out the sound of her retching, but not quite. Thomas stared at the closed door between them uneasily.

I might have to make alternative arrangements for the return trip he thought.

As the engines coughed and began to splutter as the plane powered down, Thomas unbuckled himself from the troop bench and looked out of the window. Africa glared back, the bright afternoon sun burning at his retinas. He could see an old battered open top Land Rover sitting a little way off, and a group of four men standing around it. He turned round as Catherine reappeared, looking a little pale. He grabbed a bottle of water from his pack. She took it from him and supped at it in large gulps.

"Rough flight, but we're here now," he cooed, stroking her hair as she leant against him for a moment.

"I'm just so tired," she spluttered. "Sorry."

"Nothing to apologise about, don't worry. We've all done it," he assured her. "But make sure you have enough to drink, it's going to be important you keep hydrated whilst we're here."

She stood up slowly, using his arm for support.

"I am glad we're here," she whispered, giving him a hug.

"Come on," he said, "there's somebody I want you to meet."

They walked down the ramp at the back of the aircraft hand in hand. They turned away from the plane and out of the strong glare of the sun, heading towards the shade of a huge, thick trunked baobab tree, under which the Land Rover was parked. As they drew near, the man behind the wheel of the vehicle jumped out and raced towards them. The native Kenyan wore a khaki coloured safari shirt and shorts, and was almost as tall as Thomas, but with a barrel chest and thick arms. Thomas dropped Catherine's hand just in time as the man drove into him with a powerful embrace that knocked the breath from him.

"Thomas my old friend," the man declared. "I thank you for coming. It is so good to see you after so long."

"I had to come. I'm sorry about Jabari," Thomas replied, gripping the man by the shoulders. "Jelani Jang, may I introduce you to Catherine Tyler. It's her first time here, and I expect her to get your full safari experience."

"Welcome Catherine," beamed Jelani. He leant in close to her. "As you are currently my only client, it shouldn't be difficult," he whispered.

"I'll leave you two to get acquainted," suggested Thomas, "I need to help get the gear unloaded."

He turned back towards the plane. Jelani's men had already started taking some of the smaller packs from the cargo hold, and were beginning to collect them into piles on the ground. He walked up the ramp and called two of them over.

"Your rides for the trip to camp gentlemen," he explained, throwing them a set of keys each as he did so. "Pack them up as best you can, but we'll let the cars do most of the grunt work."

The men grinned and climbed onto the two Can-Am Outlander ATVs. They turned the engines over and then pointed the black and orange painted 4x4s down the ramp, putting on a turn of speed as they hit the dust and pulling up by the piles of gear. Thomas turned to the customised Land Rover Defender Pickup. When it had first been built for him for the Hunter Hunted series, it had been the same dull green as most safari vehicles. Now it had been completely overhauled by a company called Twisted Automotive. The new tobacco brown coloured paintwork glimmered even in the dark hold of the plane, completely in contrast to the black custom bull bar, snorkel, cargo rack, winch and light rig. It sat purposely on its 18-inch, five spoke alloy wheels – also painted black and clad in heavy duty all-terrain tyres.

He opened the driver's door and climbed in. Inside, the car had been further transformed. The sport seats were clad in deep mahogany and chestnut leather, and housed inbuilt fans for cooling. A polished maple wooden steering wheel with three aluminium spokes had replaced the factory issue, and all of the electronics, from the climate system to the folding canvas roof that covered the front cabin, had been fully upgraded with modern parts. The suspension and brakes were race-tuned, as was the reinforced floor and chassis. It was the same car, yet felt completely different. He turned the key in the ignition, smiling as it growled into life first time. Modern reliability was also something new. He rolled the car down the ramp, turning to the left and rumbling past the men packing up the ATVs. He gently pressed the accelerator, releasing a tiny whine from the pent-up supercharger before he trundled to a stop in front of Jelani and Catherine.

"Mine's bigger than yours," he said with a smug laugh.

He climbed out and handed the keys to Catherine.

"She looks a little bit different from when I last saw her," Jelani said, surprised.

"Ten years is a long time, especially when you've spent seven of them in storage," Thomas said. "She needed some TLC, but there was only one car I was ever going to bring here. Cath, may I present to you the Big Cat."

"Wow, another Land Rover. At least it's a different colour from the one we have at home," Catherine answered, seemingly unimpressed.

"Seeing as you're going to be driving her back to camp, why don't you take her to the end of the runway and back to get a feel of her?" Thomas suggested, still smiling.

Catherine climbed up into the open cabin of the Big Cat. She shook her head and rolled her eyes as Thomas and Jelani watched her in silence. She turned the key and focused her gaze towards the end of the runway some 600 yards away. Without hesitating, she floored the accelerator and the tyres bit into the dry ground, tearing her away from the two watching men in an instant. She swung the car out to the side, clearing Jelani's parked Land Rover by a few inches and drifting out onto the strip, her quick and seamless gear changes answered by a happy roar from the engine and the rising chirr of the supercharger. She raced down the runway, a ragged cut in the scrub that ended in a thick mire of acacia trees and thorn bushes. They loomed closer as she thundered towards them, but she held her nerve, determined to show Thomas up. She lifted off the accelerator and let the car slow a little before yanking the wheel hard to the right and pulling the handbrake. The Big Cat seemed to pirouette on the spot, its sliding bulk sending a spray of fine rust coloured dust up into the air as she straightened up for the return run, gunning the engine again as she did so. As she built her speed up, she aimed squarely at Thomas and Jelani, who were leaning up against the other Land Rover in the distance. At the last moment, she floored the brake, locking up the wheels into a juddering halt that sent Thomas and Jelani diving for cover. She casually climbed out of the cab as the dust settled, leaning up against the car. She looked extremely smug as Thomas picked himself up and dusted off his hands.

"The Big Cat, so called because of the supercharged Jaguar engine. I have been watching the show remember," she smirked.

"My friend, I like her," Jelaini laughed, slapping Thomas heartily on the back.

"So do I, most of the time," Thomas replied.

"Go and get your other toy, I know you want to," suggested Catherine.

"Well, if you insist," Thomas said with a mock shrug.

He disappeared up the ramp again, pulling the cover off the last bit of kit left on the plane. He threw his leg over the coffee coloured fuel tank and took a seat on the tan, weathered, single-seat leather saddle. The coiled suspension rods bowed with the pressure. With a heavy kick, the four-stroke twin engine started, and he revved it a few times with a flick of his wrist to warm it up. It was a Triumph Bonneville; one his father had built and modified into a scrambler when he'd retired. The chunky, knurled Continental tyres were perfect for the unforgiving tracks and off-road demands of the Tsavo savannah, as were the raised exhaust, reinforced frame and skid plate. He gave the throttle a little flurry as he left the ramp, spinning the bike round before heading back over to Catherine and Jelani.

His dad had always ridden bikes, but Thomas had never really trusted himself on them. That hadn't stopped him getting his license and owning the odd one or two, but he rarely took them out, and it had been a little while since he'd been on one. But the bike felt steady and comfortable, and he felt confident enough within the limits of the four-stroke.

"Just remember, if you come off that thing and it doesn't kill you, I will," Catherine warned.

"Yes, Ma'am," Thomas replied.

Jelani, Catherine and Thomas helped the men finish packing up the cars. The two Land Rovers took the bulk of the equipment, with the ATVs taking the smaller packs. Thomas slung the canvas rucksack that he had carried throughout the flight onto his back. It contained the documents Hali had given him, a few bottles of water and his personal identification, as well as a little bit of money.

"It's just over ten miles to camp," Jelani explained. "It will take us about half an hour to get there."

"Let's get the show on the road," Thomas grinned.

He climbed back onto the bike as the cars and ATVs started off, catching Catherine's wry smile as she glanced back at him. She seemed to be feeling better, and he was glad she was enjoying herself. He gave a quick wave to the pilots, who he knew were heading back to the Ramstein Air Force base in Germany. Neither he nor they knew when they would be back, only that it would be when the job was done. The thought cooled his excitement as he kick-started the bike and tore off after the little convoy.

The landscape was an entanglement of parched, red rocky outcrops, densely wooded thickets, jagged river gorges and clear open savannah punctured and potted by dark volcanic escarpments. The air was hot and dry, and the dust it carried sucked the moisture from Thomas's throat and mouth. He felt alive and excited for the first time in the long twenty-four hours they had been travelling, the sensory overload seeping into him all at once. He opened up the throttle of the bike, quickly catching up with the ATVs and passing them to coast alongside Catherine in the Big Cat. She caught his eye through the open window and with an upward nod, directed his gaze to the scrub alongside the track to their right. A Rothschild's giraffe and her calf were moving away from them, the orange and chocolate colour of their patterned hides blending perfectly into the Tsavo landscape.

Thomas kept the bike alongside Catherine, enamoured by the look of wonder on her face. Her brilliant turquoise eyes sparkled with excitement as flurries of grassland pipits and golden palm weavers burst from the scrub to feast on the insects the vehicles flushed from the track. She slowed down to watch a white browed coucal flap off from its perch on a thorn bush, smiling happily as the crimson-eyed cuckoo babbled its objections at being disturbed. He sighed with relief, glad that she was happy to be in Africa.

The convoy bumped and trundled along the track, eventually leaving it altogether as Jelani led them along the crest of a ridgeline that ran alongside a wide river. Thomas could see that the trail culminated in a large flat kopje, a table-like rock grouping sticking up out of the landscape. Just on the other side of the rock formation he could make out the sand coloured canvas and fabric of the tents and structures. As they drew closer, he could see they had been reinforced with wooden sides and doors, adding to their luxury and security. Each had permanent floors built of thick, planed slabs of acacia.

"Looks a little more luxurious than what we had back in the day," Thomas exclaimed, pulling up next to Jelani's open topped Land Rover.

"Welcome to Anga ya Amani. The name means peace and sky. It was abandoned about a year ago," explained Jelani. "It's a beautiful location, but hard to get to, and it's harder to convince the tourists to stray from the National Parks in the current climate. On the bright side, it was a bargain," he smiled.

Thomas smiled back understandingly. Jelani couldn't resist a good deal, and was a formidable negotiator. Watching him at work in a market, going stall to stall and refusing to take anything but the best produce at the best price was something he remembered fondly. He could only imagine Jelani would have been just as tenacious in the acquisition of the camp.

Jelani directed Catherine to park next to a tent in the centre of three.

"This one's yours," he declared to them both.

The tent was fronted by a large deck that housed a woven rattan sofa to one side, and a matching dining table and chairs to the other. It had a large, enclosed porch, entered through a pair of wide, glass-panelled, wooden framed doors. A pair of canvas flaps then opened into the main chamber of the tent, a smooth acacia trunk at its centre acting as the totem and support for the structure. Thomas was glad to see the thin gauze of mosquito nets covering the openings at the top and along the sides.

"I'll give you the tour," suggested Jelani, as Catherine climbed out of the Big Cat and stretched, giving Thomas a mischievous and happy smile as she joined them.

Thomas took her hand as they followed Jelani. He noticed the other two tents were similarly appointed.

"These three tents are for you, your Miss Keelson, and O'Connell should he actually turn up," Jelani explained.

"Who's O'Connell?" Catherine asked.

"The Irish bum who's good with a gun," chimed Jelani and Thomas together, laughing.

"He's a hunter and tracker. A good one," Thomas added, still chuckling. "He has trained some of the best capture and conservation teams all over the world. I asked him to join us when the government hired us to look at tracking down cats in the UK, but he told me it would be a conflict of interests. I don't think he approved. He used to help us out from time to time, especially in Tanzania."

"He's coming from Tanzania?" Catherine asked, surprised.

"He's a good friend," Jelani admitted. "That said, Tanzania is only about eighty miles south of here. You have come a great deal further."

A little way back from the grouping of three tents, Jelani showed them the two separate bath huts. They were relatively simple, with woven screen walls and open panels between the A-frame of the roof. Each contained a toilet, bath, basin, and a shower tiled and lined with polished slabs of the black volcanic rock the camp sat upon.

"Our water comes from a volcanic spring, so we have a

plentiful supply," Jelani continued. "The tanks are refreshed automatically overnight and are just behind the huts."

"It's a lovely setup," Thomas remarked. "One of the nicest camps I've ever operated out of that's for sure."

"Thank you," Jelani replied with quiet pride. "The kitchen and food stores are also behind here; it just means there is still some space between them and the accommodation if anything other than us gets hungry."

They walked back through to the three main tents, which opened out onto the top of the kopje. Some weathered wooden chairs sat at its centre, around a large stone encircled fire pit where one of Jelani's men stacked logs for burning. The kopje was raised high above the river below, giving them beautiful views through the gorge on both sides. The braying call of a hippo echoed in the distance and Catherine's eyes lit up at the noise.

"We have both hippo and crocodile in the river, so I don't recommend swimming, but we have the high ground here and most of the wildlife skirts round us on their way to drink at the pool a little way down. You can just see it from the top here, and very easily through a scope or binoculars," Jelani explained.

Thomas and Catherine followed him as he led the way along a path to another grouping of tents. These were a little smaller and seemed more functional.

"This is where your crew and mine will be based. My tent is also here." Jelani said. "I've also set up a firing range on the other side there so you can test your weapons before heading out."

"That's thoughtful, thanks," Thomas acknowledged. Testing weapons after a flight was a good habit to get into, allowing a hunter to make changes to scopes and sights as required before heading out into the field. He was impressed Jelani had remembered such a detail.

Thomas walked back through the camp, surveying it as he went. When they reached the kopje again, he called over two of Jelani's men to them. He sent them over to a pile of cases, where they extracted a collapsed frame of metal and carbon fibre. They quickly unfolded it and started assembling the loose parts. When they had finished, Catherine and Jelani could see it made up an open framed gun rack, with a top shelf attached for hand guns.

"I had this custom made," Thomas explained. "I know the setting is beautiful and we're all rather in awe at the moment, but we need to remember we're here for a reason and this is man-eater country. I want a couple of guns on the rack at all times and within easy reach, just in case."

"Thanks, think I just came back to Earth with a thud," Catherine sighed. "Do you mind if I go and start to unpack, I'm not going to last much longer."

"Mansa," cried Jelani, calling the man who had been stacking the firewood earlier over to him. "Mansa, please help Ms. Tyler with her bags, and then draw her a bath."

The thin but muscular man had short cropped greying hair and dark bronze coloured skin. His eyes were grey too, but shone kindly at Catherine.

"Mansa is in charge of looking after our guests at Anga ya Amani, and our splendid cook. He will make sure you have everything you need," Jelani said.

"Thank you, a bath would be lovely," Catherine said with relief. She followed Mansa away towards the tents.

Thomas and Jelani busied themselves setting up the rest of

the camp exactly as they wanted it. The vehicles were re-parked at the head of the trail after they had been unpacked, ready and pointing back out into the savannah. Thomas set up a string of motion detectors and lights along the corridor between the main tents and the crew camp, connecting them to power leads that snaked back to the main generator. The men helped erect a gazebo and lined it with bench tables to act as an equipment tent. They then carried a larger folding table to its front. Thomas checked and opened each case, directing the men who carried them to the equipment tent or the gun rack depending on contents.

He walked over to the equipment tent and opened a small case on the floor. It contained a set of Thermoteknix Ticam 750 thermal imaging binoculars. Made with military grade software and boasting lenses capable of pinpointing a man over a mile away, he put them down on the table, ready for use come twilight.

Thomas smiled, listening to the laughter of the men as they worked. The clatter of pots from the kitchen and other sounds of a camp being set to work floated up into the hot afternoon air. He felt relaxed, as if he had come home. It was a curious sensation. He knew he was here for a purpose, and that this was where Amanda had died. He felt conflicted, his whole being warmed and welcomed by the African sun whilst cold memories tugged at his conscience, challenging his happiness. His smile faded.

He looked up and watched a little family flock of speckled mousebirds pick their way through the top branches of a nearby tree. Their excited, repeated chirps were a sound he knew well, being a relatively common bird of Kenya. He watched them fly off, darting over Catherine's head as she emerged from the tent. She was wearing a pair of white linen shorts and a lightweight, navy blouse. Tufts of her red hair peaked out from underneath the white straw Panama hat she wore, complementing its copper coloured trim and bow. She looked beautiful, as if she had been on safari every day of her life. He walked over to her, his smile returning.

"Wow, you look good," whispered Thomas as he embraced her.

"Why thank you kind sir," she cooed, slipping her hand around his waist as they began to walk together.

"Fancy some range shooting to get used to the feel of a gun again?" he suggested.

"Yes, if it gets it out of the way. I know you want to play with your toys," she laughed, "Mansa said dinner would be a while."

"That reminds me, I should probably do a little scouting for game later, if we're going to keep the camp in meat."

"Can't we just go to the supermarket?" she half-joked.

He could see she wasn't completely at ease with shooting game, even if it was for food. He had come to terms with it, but it still wasn't necessarily something he enjoyed.

"I know it's not ideal circumstances, but it's just not practical in the long term. The meat will also need to hang for a little while too, so it's best to get it out of the way," he explained softly.

"I'm not a hypocrite or anything," she winced, "I'm sure I'll tuck in and find it delicious. I'm just not used to it."

"I know," he said, shrugging. "Neither am I. But look at it this way, we're very restricted to what we can shoot, only very numerous and pest species like the pigs. And we'll keep it to a minimum, okay?"

"I trust you," she said, "but you know me, I had to say something."

"It's true, you do talk a lot," Thomas said with a mischievous smile.

She nudged him playfully in the ribs.

"Like all your best jokes, that's one of mine," she laughed.

They stopped by the gun rack, now adorned with weaponry. Thomas's Holland & Holland .465 rifle sat at the far right, a Leica scope already attached to it. Next to that was a William Evans St James over-and-under 20 bore shotgun, which he intended to shoot game birds with. Its neighbour was a more powerful 12 bore side-by-side game gun by Purdey. The rack was well designed, with an ammo shelf sitting at the back, where boxes of cartridges sat behind each gun accordingly.

"Believe it or not, this isn't everything we have, but I want our shotguns and rifles to hand if we need them," he explained.

"It's a little unnerving if what Hali said about the lions attacking that camp is true," she said, "and when you say ours?"

"These two are for you," he replied, gesturing to the other end of the rack.

There were two guns purposely placed at the far left, a shotgun and a rifle. Thomas watched her pick up the shotgun, a Beretta Diamond Pigeon 20 bore.

"Is it wrong that I find that quite sexy," he said as she opened the barrels and posed with it hung over her arm.

"Getting on my bad side could definitely be more dangerous for you here," she laughed.

"When isn't it?" he replied.

She put it back down on the rack and picked up the rifle.

"That's the one you'll need when you mean business," Thomas explained. "It's a Marlin guide gun, and it fires 45-70 rounds. It should put down anything you fire it at, but it's light and short too."

"What are you trying to say," she quipped, raising an eyebrow.

"That you can handle it, and that's all," Thomas replied, holding up his hands. "It's a powerful gun, but it's lever action, so you'll need to practice."

"I even like the colour," she smiled, admiring the silver Leupold scout scope that matched the stainless-steel finish and the black and grey stock.

"I also want you to get familiar with the handguns, just in case we have a close call. That one on top is for you. It's not necessarily legal for you to have one here, but I'd rather you had it," he said quietly.

Catherine instinctively slung the strap of the rifle over her shoulder, which made him happy. She picked up the revolver, a Smith & Wesson 686 Deluxe with a three-inch barrel. It was finished in stainless steel and had textured wood grips. He reached behind the rack and pulled out a small, red leather clip holster and handed it to her. She fitted it to her shorts and placed the gun into it, where it became partially covered by her blouse.

"Let's fire a couple of shots off down at the range. It would be a shame not to after Jelani has set everything up," he said.

Thomas pulled another holster from the rack, already containing his own revolver, a Colt Anaconda with a six-inch barrel. It looked similar to Catherine's, except his was an older and much larger gun.

"Ideally, I don't want guns on the rack that we haven't shot, and we never take a gun into the field that hasn't been fired, okay," Thomas explained.

"Why's that?" she asked.

"It doesn't make sense to trust your life to an untested gun," he shrugged. "Colonel Patterson found that out for himself when he was hunting man-eaters here over a hundred years ago. He borrowed a doctor friend's more powerful rifle, only for it to misfire on him when one of the lions ambled up. He was very nearly lunch."

They picked up their guns and ammo and walked down the path that led to the working side of the camp, where Jelani had set up the firing range in a small avenue between the scrub opposite the tents. Some empty oil barrels with sandbags on top of them marked where they were to fire from, and a table with a soft leather top and fleeced blankets hung over its side provided a place to put the guns. It was only a short walk, but the weight of the weapons made it a hard one, and they were both glad to reach the table.

Thomas looked over the range. Jelani had been thorough, setting up steel targets along the banked curves at various distances. There were numerous animal shaped ones, with Cape buffalo, coyote, boar and bird plates dotted around at various distances. Double-tap duelling trees and gongs were lined up in banks extending down the range. A little closer there were even some zombie shaped targets, as well as traditional card and paper bullseye ones. Thomas put the boxes of ammunition onto the table, then each of the guns, pointing them down range.

"Why don't we try that lever-action out first?" Thomas suggested.

He picked up the gun and grabbed a handful of bullets from the box. He showed her how to feed the six rounds of ammunition into the rifle before shouldering it. He chambered a round with a pull of the lever and snapped it back up quickly. With his eye on a nearby zombie target he pulled the trigger. Catherine flinched at the sound, which almost drowned out the resounding ping as the big bore bullet smashed into the target, just left of centre.

"Your turn," he said, carefully handing it over.

"How much did you want to be John Wayne when you were little?" Catherine sighed.

"It was Clint Eastwood actually," Thomas replied.

He was glad to see she knew what she was doing. She showed no hesitancy or fear as she checked her footing and shouldered the rifle. Something troubled him though, something that had been gnawing away at him for some time. Catherine had changed over the last year. Her softness could disappear at a moment's notice, her demeanour becoming cold and hardened. He was used to her fire and temper, but not the feeling of being kept at a distance. When she was feeling vulnerable, she closed up and became aggressive. He could see it in her eyes now, a steely determination, and a faraway look that burned with something akin to hatred. She struggled for a moment with the lever action before it broke open, but she snapped it back up confidently enough. She took a breath and held it as she pulled the trigger. A puff of dirt erupted just to the left of the zombie target. Thomas saw the pent-up frustration flush over her face and vanish just as quickly as he stepped forward. There was no struggle or hesitation this time as she reloaded, the gun still at her shoulder. It was Thomas's turn to flinch, close as he was as the second shot cracked. A metallic ping rang out as it hit the far left of the zombie silhouette.

"It shot left for me too," Thomas said quietly. "Let me adjust the scope for you."

She handed the rifle to Thomas. The coldness had gone.

"I thought this might be fun, but if you're not in the mood..."

"It's not that," she sighed. "I just always wanted to come to Africa, to go on safari. Bringing guns was never part of the dream."

Thomas nodded, understanding. He looked down for a moment, screwing off the caps for the elevation and windage adjustment on the top and side of the scope. He glanced at the grey indent where Catherine's shot had hit the target, before turning the windage dial a few clicks. He handed the rifle back to her.

"I'll make you a deal," he offered. "Hit that target in the centre and tomorrow, you get a full day of safari with Jelani and I as your personal guides. No man-eaters and no guns."

Her eyes lit up mischievously, making him smile. She shouldered the rifle again. A second later she fired, the satisfying sound of an echoing, bell-like ring signalling she had hit the target well. He almost didn't need to glance to see she had hit dead on centre. Boosted by the hit, she chambered and fired the three remaining shots at some of the other targets, each marked by a successful ping of impact.

"See, you just needed the motivation," he said kindly.

"And your adjustment of the scope," she smiled. "Thank you. You're right, that was kind of fun."

They each took turns to shoot, making adjustments to the rifles where necessary. Having fired both his rifle and shotguns satisfactorily, Thomas pulled out the Colt revolver. He loaded it with the silver cased 44. Magnum bullets from the box and cocked the hammer. He took careful aim at a coyote shaped target on the 75-yard bank. Pulling the trigger, he didn't hesitate or wait for the ping, moving onto the gong targets to its right. He grinned proudly as he knocked the empty casings from the cylinder onto the table. The coyote target had fallen over completely, whilst the weighty gongs were left swinging from the impacts of the heavy rounds.

"Show off," smirked Catherine. "Bet you can't do it twice in a row."

"What do I get?" he asked, raising an eyebrow.

"Respect and less of a hard time," she shrugged.

Thomas chambered another six rounds quickly. He took aim at another coyote target to the left of the gongs and fired. He shifted his aim, minding his footing and the wind as the gongs swung back and forth from the previous impacts. As the cylinder of the revolver clicked round for the final bullet, he took in a breath and held it. His trigger finger squeezed just as he felt Catherine's hot breath on his neck, then her wet tongue as she gave a quick playful lick of his nape. He flinched and shot high, his miss being marked by an explosion of the spongy bark of a baobab tree behind the gongs.

"You're as good as licked if you get distracted," Catherine giggled. "You worried the hell out of that tree though."

"Cheat," Thomas scoffed.

"Come on Rambo," she laughed, "I'm starving. And as you missed, that ringing sound can only be the dinner bell."

They walked hand in hand back up the path to the main camp. Other than the colt which he holstered, and Catherine's Smith & Wesson, they left the guns on the table. Thomas nodded to two of Jelani's men nearby, who took up the guns and followed them. Catherine had been right, and they found Jelani and Mansa waiting for them at the top. Out on the kopje a dining table and chairs had been brought out, set up a little way back from the fire pit and its own wooden armchairs. They would be treated to a beautiful sunset view of the gorge as the day ended. Mansa gave them a little bow as they approached and directed them to their seats. Jelani joined them.

"The range is fantastic," Thomas acknowledged.

"I gathered from the noise you were enjoying yourselves," Jelani beamed.

"I've promised Cath a day of safari tomorrow if you're up for coming with us?" Thomas asked.

"Of course," he nodded. "O'Connell will be here too by then and can be my assistant."

"Let me know how that works out for you," Thomas laughed.

The first course was a fragrant salad of mango and avocado served with a chilli dressing. Catherine devoured the food, listening in silence as Thomas and Jelani talked about the camp, and the men who had stayed loyal whilst others had left in fear of the lions and Kanu Sultan. Mansa brought out the main course, roasted guinea fowl, with fried slices of sweet potato and a caramelised onion and red berry gravy. She had hardly eaten on the plane, but she was now ravenous and reminded of her hunger by the wafting aromas coming from the kitchen. As the dessert arrived, a soft orange and lime sorbet, she was startled to hear a lone and curious sounding howl float up from quite nearby.

"A hyena," explained Jelani.

"I know," said Catherine, her mouth still partially full, "I was just surprised to hear it so close."

"It can smell dinner," he smiled. "They sometimes come into the camp after dark to look for scraps – but the men wash everything down and lock supplies away in metal boxes. We also have a watch throughout the night and keep the fire lit, which keeps them at bay."

"That reminds me," said Thomas, "ask the guys to take the straps off the rifles in the rack will you. Old leather and cloth is almost as good as that guinea fowl to a hyena."

"Believe me, it isn't," Jelani smiled.

Mansa and another man cleared away the remnants of the dinner. Catherine slumped up against Thomas, nuzzling her head into his shoulder. She wrapped her arm round his, comfortable and satiated for the first time in 36 hours.

"I would offer you a sundowner," Jelani said, "but I think perhaps an early night is calling for you. My men will help your Miss Keelson when she arrives."

"I'm going to have a look around first, maybe bag a few birds to replace your diminishing stocks," Thomas replied. "The food was truly excellent."

"I'm definitely heading to bed. I'm bushed," sighed Catherine happily.

They excused themselves and walked back to the tent, arms around each other's waist, their backs warmed by the glow of the sunset.

"Don't be too long," Catherine murmured.

He kissed her on the forehead as she slipped through the doors and shut them behind her. He turned around and walked over to the gun rack, picking up the Evans 20 bore shotgun and filling the pockets of his lightweight shooting vest with shells. He wasn't planning to go far, just a little way beyond the firing range into the scrub. He was fairly certain that if he edged towards the river gorge, from there he would find some guinea fowl foraging in the cool of the evening, or even some sandgrouse going to roost in the thorns if he was lucky. He shouldered the shotgun and stepped off the path, into the scrub that ran alongside the shooting range.

~

She stirred, having been awake for some time, but hesitant to move from her spot deep in the thicket until the heat of the day had dissipated. Her thick, smooth coated tail thrashed the ground with pent up energy, as if her muscles and sinews had been storing the solar rays she had soaked up during her rest. She stood, stretching her front paws out in front of her as she arched her back. She rubbed her chin and both sides of her forehead against the dry, dusty ground, marking it with scent from the glands beneath those sensitive areas of skin. She scraped the dry earth with her back legs, raking and disturbing the soil so as to distribute the pungent marking further. Satisfied, and with a deep purr emanating from her throat, she trotted forward through the scrub.

She had been curious at the sounds she had heard during the day, edging closer before the sun had risen high in the early morning. Although she had raised her head at the explosive sounds that had come later, it was much quieter now and she headed in the direction they had come from. As she entered into a heavier cluster of trees, the rich, honey-like scent she was now familiar with hit her nose and stopped her in her tracks. She dropped to the ground instinctively. She lay with her ears pricked and swivelled towards where both smell and sound came from. She rose into a crouch, ready to spring if necessary, but her curiosity tempted her forward. At the foot of a sausage tree she paused. She could make out the white structures ahead and sensed the movement of animals beyond them.

New scents were brought to her on the breeze. Metallic and chemical taints that she did not recognise and made her lips roll back, baring her fangs at the unwelcome taste. There was too much noise and open country here. She flanked left, following the land downhill. In her peripheral vision, she could see more white structures further down, before a gully that opened up between the trees. She avoided this, skirting round and away into the shadows. Then she caught the movement in the distance, heading across her path. She hunkered down immediately, craning her head forward with her eyes and ears fixed directly ahead.

~

Once clear of the shooting range, Thomas swung right, heading towards the bank that ran along the gorge. He began to stoop as he went, breaking his upright silhouette and making it harder for him to be spotted. Although stalking birds, he still made occasional changes to his path, staying downwind as much as possible. He was all too aware that the cool shadow of the scrub would be an ideal place to lie up for predators and prey alike.

He stopped in a dense ring of thorn bushes. He heard a piercing cry, like a child's squeaky rubber toy. He smiled, recognising it as the call of a crested francolin. It was a species he had thought he might encounter, as they had an inherent trust of man and often foraged for food near bush camps. He crouched for a while, letting his eyes get used to the sepia tones of the little patch of woodland. He spotted the plump brown and cream coloured birds scratching around the roots of a sausage tree about thirty yards away, their dappled tones the perfect camouflage. His eyes darted to the forked trunk of an acacia tree to his right and he slowly edged towards it. Very carefully, he brought the gun up and rested it within the fork. Only the tip of his head was visible from the other side as he broke the barrels and plied them with the pair of yellow, shot-filled cartridges. As quietly as possible he snapped them shut and shouldered the gun.

Looking down the sights, Thomas could see he had an opportunity to take all three. Two of the birds were standing close together, almost butting heads as they pecked at the ground beneath them. The other bird was standing a little further off, still making the brazen call he had heard. If he was fast with the trigger, he could take the two together with one barrel, and the loner with the other. The foraging pair wouldn't be a problem, but the strutting cock bird was already on alert and would fly up at the report of the first shot. He would have to pick him off mid-air, but he was up for the challenge. Thomas took a sharp intake of breath and held it. He waited for the two birds scrabbling at the dry earth to line up, as the neck and head of one disappeared behind the other. He squeezed the trigger, and a fraction of a second later saw the birds drop onto their backs, their feet still twitching as he swung the gun upward and fired again. Caught in its ascent, the third bird folded its wings, its head falling forwards in death as it bowled over in the air and began to drop to the ground. It disappeared out of sight on the other side of a thick clump of wait-a-bit thorns. Thomas sighed as he stood up and walked over to pick up the brace, before venturing towards the barbed brush that possibly held the other.

~

She looped in a wide arc around the man she was following. He moved cautiously and carefully, putting her on alert. She recognised his approach and demeanour as that of a predator. She became curious, interested in what the man could be hunting. She again hunkered down, watching. Her eyes were fixed on his position, but she lost him in the distance as he too lowered into the brush. She waited, not daring to move or give her position away. The man had altered his course several times, forcing her to stay upwind. This made her hesitant, but she slowly relaxed as curiosity took the place of her desire to hunt. As a thunderous crack ran out through the woodland, she flinched with the surprise, the sound muffling her answering snarl. Her tail swished with purpose, its soft, barbed tip brushing the scar on her left flank with each flick. It had been left there by a noise maker just like the one this man carried.

Spurred into action, she was already up and padding away silently when the second shot rang out. Freezing again, but ready to pounce, she caught the movement above her. Instinct anchored her to the ground as she resisted the urge to spring, instead letting the dead bird crash to the floor a few feet from her. Swiftly she dashed forward, scooping the francolin into her jaws as she passed. She did not look back, quickly putting distance between her and the noise maker as she weaved through the thorny maze of scrub, confident she would not be followed.

~

Thomas paused on the other side of the wait-a-bit thorns. Where he had expected to find the bird, lay only a few belly feathers. Where the rest of it had gone was only too clear. The pug mark was almost as wide as it was long, some six inches either way, not quite as long as his outstretched hand, but considerably wider. He had almost mistaken it for a leopard print at first, but it was far too large. The pads were broadly spread, typical of a male, but narrow and teardrop in shape like a female. It could only be a large lioness he concluded. Suddenly distracted from his thoughts by the shiver sent down his spine as he realised how close the cat had been, he stood up and slowly began to back towards camp, his gun trained on the bush as he went.

CHAPTER SEVEN

Thomas stared at the sky through the mosquito-mesh tent top. The night was filled with sound. Cicada beetles and crickets chirped from the grass, only stopping when stumbled upon by the equally vocal sharp-nosed grass frogs and square-marked toads that hunted them along the camp edges. The creaking call of a marsh owl floated up from the river gorge. He tried to sleep, something Catherine was having no trouble doing. She was sprawled out over the bed with one hand tucked beneath a pillow, the other behind her back and the sheets wrapped around the bottom half of her naked body. Thomas smiled as every now and again her contented snores added to the night chorus. He closed his eyes, drifting away as best he could. Soon he slept, albeit fitfully, as his slumber was penetrated by the screams of startled prey, the devilish chuckles of hyena and the bickering of hippo down in the gorge. Finally, deep sleep came and he fretted no more.

He woke some hours later, startled and sitting bolt upright in the bed. Catherine stirred beside him, dozily coming round. He leapt up, grabbing a pair of shorts from the chair and pulling them on as he dashed for the tent door. Pulling it open, he stepped outside. Everything seemed quiet, but he spun on his heels as he heard rushed footsteps coming along the path. In the dim glow of the moonlight, he could just make out Jelani's outline as he came closer. Thomas took a few quick strides from the tent, walking out onto the kopje. Then he heard it. It was very distant, but it was unmistakably the sound of a car horn. He also thought he could make out what sounded like shouts and metallic bangs at the edge of his hearing.

"Sounds like trouble," stated Jelani as he joined them.

Suddenly, a red explosive streak rocketed into the night sky to the north, beyond the trees. The signal flare spluttered before bathing them with a pinkish glow as it fizzled on its way back down to the ground.

"Looks like it too," sighed Thomas.

He turned and quickly ran back to the tent. He dressed and hurried out again, surprised to find himself closely followed by Catherine. She had managed to pull on some clothes, but was still in a daze from their rude awakening.

"What's going on?" she stammered.

"A signal flare just went up. Looks like someone needs help, and it's most likely to be the crew," he explained.

"Do you think it's the lions?" she asked.

"I'm hoping it's more like engine trouble, but we won't know until we get there," he said. "I would suggest you stay here, but that's not going to happen, is it?"

"Not now I'm awake it's not," she stated flatly.

"Okay Annie," he sighed, "let's go get our guns."

Thomas threw the keys of the Big Cat to Jelani. He scurried away towards where they had parked the vehicles earlier. At the gun rack, Thomas picked up the Holland & Holland .465 rifle and slipped on the shoulder holster for the big Colt revolver. As Catherine went to pick up her rifle, Thomas passed her the Purdey 12 bore instead.

"You're riding shotgun," he said, also passing her a box of shells.

Jelani roared into the compound behind the wheel of the Big Cat, pulling up beside them.

"Are you carrying?" Thomas asked.

"I wasn't going to walk up that path on my own," shrugged Jelani, lifting his own shotgun from the front passenger seat.

Thomas walked to the back with Catherine, dropping the pick up's tail gate. He climbed up and turned around to help Catherine clamber into the truck bed beside him. They stood together, holding onto the light rig over the top of the cabin. He looked at her, amused to see she was smiling as Jelani turned the car around fast, gunning the engine and out onto the trail.

"I can't help it, it's exciting," she laughed, making Thomas laugh too.

Jelani swung the car off the trail into the long grass. Thomas guessed he was cutting across to another road, where the crew or whoever fired the flare must be approaching from. The car bucked as it hit small rocks and holes in its path, forcing Thomas and Catherine to hold on tightly as the Big Cat forced its way through the grassland. Thomas caught a glimpse of a dik dik in the spotlights, a tiny species of antelope that disappeared quickly back into the inky blackness around them. Suddenly, the car turned with a jolt and he saw they were back on a trail, one that led north west and into the trees and scrub. Jelani gunned the throttle and the supercharger kicked in a moment later, the big tyres biting into the trail with renewed purpose.

Thomas looked to the East, back towards the camp. The darkness behind was changing hue, turning indigo and violet with the coming dawn. It had been a short night it seemed, and he still felt tired. He turned back to the trail ahead. He could hear the honking car horn much more clearly now, and raised voices. But above them he heard something else, a sound that made him reach for the rifle and clip a five-cartridge magazine into it. The reverberating bellow sounded again, and Thomas raised the gun, pointing it over the top of the cabin roof and up the trail. His eyes began to search for movement on either side of the track.

As they thundered round a bend, they all saw the headlights of the car up ahead. As they drew closer, the powerful lamps of the Big Cat's spotting rig bathed the haggard crew and Kelly Keelson in penetrating light. They were all perched on top of the luggage rack of the battered Land Cruiser's roof. Thomas couldn't help letting out a chuckle. As he gazed over the vehicle, he saw the cause of their predicament. The front driver's side tire had been torn from the rim, ripped almost in two. A series of gashes and dents along the doors and panels on the same side of the car revealed the full extent of the assault.

"Where is it?" Thomas cried out to Keelson.

"Back in the brush, behind the car," she yelled back. "It's big."

"They're never small," Thomas replied, but under his breath.

"What?" Catherine asked.

With a belching roar, the thickly knotted elephant grass to their right exploded in a blur of movement. A glancing blow was delivered to the rear end of the crippled Land Cruiser as the enormous animal turned and ran alongside the vehicle. Thomas marvelled at its size. Startled by the glare of the Big Cat's spotlights, the bull hippopotamus trundled to a stop. Its broad muzzle and over developed jowl quivered as testosterone pumped through its veins. It half opened its mouth, a sign of uncertainty. This new intruder had caught it off guard. Thomas watched closely. If it opened its mouth fully towards them, it would be a sign of submission. Keelson was right though, it was big. Standing over five and a half feet at the shoulder and weighing what Thomas estimated to be 4,000 lbs, it was old too. He knew that male hippos never stopped growing, only reaching that kind of size after a long and successful life of dominating their patch of river. It was unusual for a male to be so territorial on land and at night, but perhaps his size gave him confidence. As if sensing Thomas's line of thought, the big bull shot forward like a juggernaut, its head down and tilted towards the car. Thomas lifted his rifle and fired a shot into the air, which had the desired effect of deflecting its charge back into the long grass.

"A fine way to be welcomed," mused Kelly as she began to climb down from the roof.

Before Thomas could warn her, the hippo appeared out of the gloom like a freight train emerging from a tunnel, thundering head on towards the Land Cruiser. Thomas raised his rifle again, but didn't have time to put a bead on the bull before it smashed into the vehicle's side. He watched in despair as Keelson lost her grip and was thrown several feet into the elephant grass. As she scrabbled to her feet, the hippo dashed left again with a shake of its head. As it passed, it hooked the bull bars of the crippled Toyota with its lower right tusk and ripped them away from the car with ease. Thomas heard it grating along the ground as the hippo plunged back into the grass.

"Behind us," Catherine yelled as it appeared again, crossing the track before entering the thick scrub on the other side.

"It's coming for you Kelly," Thomas warned, raising his

rifle.

He tried to follow the path of the bull, closing his eyes for a moment to allow his hearing to tune in to its grunts and the smashing of the brush as it bulldozed through. He raised the gun, only to pause as another sound distracted him. It was the scream of a high revving car engine making its way down the track at speed. As Thomas opened his eyes, he saw it had caught the attention of the bull as well. It swerved away from Keelson and into the path of the oncoming vehicle, its bright lights now visible through the swathes of elephant grass it was ploughing through. The driver was clearly coming straight for them, possibly after hearing the shot he'd fired, Thomas considered.

The bull was in full charge, and opened its mouth in a giant four-foot gape that revealed the pair of two-foot long, tusk-like canines in its lower jaw, as well as the enlarged, knife sized incisors above and below. The car kept coming though, altering its course to meet the hippo head on. Just at the last moment, the driver hit the brakes, slowing down but still sliding towards the bull over the long grass with the momentum. The hippo bellowed before it smashed into the front of the car, its teeth locking over the top and bottom of the impressive bull bars at the front of the vehicle. Now bathed in the dazzling light from the other car's array, Thomas only saw a silhouette as it popped up over the roof line of the jeep, but he caught the glint of the heavy rifle the stranger carried. The hunter stood over the hippo, separated by only a few feet of twisting and grinding metal as the bull thrashed and bucked in a test of strength. A moment later, a flash and a roar erupted from the end of the barrel and the bull slumped to the floor. There was a sudden silence.

"And may the good Lord take a liking to you too," said a voice with an Irish accent out of the dark.

CHAPTER EIGHT

In the early light of the dawn, Thomas inspected the damage to the Warthog, Jericho's own customised Jeep Wrangler JK8 pick-up. It had come through its encounter with the bull hippo remarkably unscathed, with only a few scratches to its black powder-coated bull bars, their unique design and size lending the car its nickname. The gun-metal grey paintwork made the flashes of red from the exposed shock absorbers and the interior stand out. The car sat high, lifted on huge black wheels encased in heavy duty all-terrain tyres, just as on the Big Cat. He let out a satisfied sigh as he turned his head, listening to the raucous bellows of the hippos down in the river gorge.

Jelani's men had been quick to make their way out to where the bull had been killed, butchering and cleaning it there in the field before bringing the good meat back to camp. The size of the old bull meant that at least for the time being, there would be no shortage of meat for them all. It relieved some of the pressure and conflict he felt about having to fill the larder. He walked out onto the kopje and sat down in one of the wooden chairs. He stretched out his feet, resting his tired and aching muscles.

At the sound of clinking glass and footsteps crossing the kopje towards him, he opened them again. Jericho O'Connell regarded him with a mischievous glance as he fell into the chair next to him, passing over a bottle of Kenyan Tusker lager. The bottle was cold, still covered in a crisp sweat of condensation. Jericho had already taken the tops off and Thomas took a long swig.

"Jelani tells me that old bull had been a pain in the neck for some time," Jericho grinned, "it sounds like the younger males are pleased to find him gone."

"Indeed, probably can't believe their luck with all the ladies suddenly at their disposal," Thomas mused.

"Ah, it'll do the herd good to have some new young blood take over. Those old bulls too often turn into calf killers don't you know."

"Aye," Thomas smirked, mimicking Jericho's accent and opening one eye again.

He knew Jericho was right. Older hippo bulls only became more aggressive and less tolerant as they aged. They patrolled the swamps, rivers and grasslands on a constant short fuse. Their territorial instinct and urge to control and mate with their captive bands of females often lead to the slaughter of calves, even their own, just to bring a female back into heat. It didn't always work out so well for the male though. The bulls had strict rules of engagement that they adhered to, always attacking head on in a show of brute strength and size. The females had no need to do this, and Thomas had observed them on several occasions attacking from the side, successfully driving off males and saving their infant in the process. Alas however, he had also seen calves killed in the jaws of determined bulls too. Hippo society was one of Africa's most brutal.

"You'll be glad to know that I'm your official game guide, so I'll be filling in the paperwork for the big fella, and anything your good self actually gets round to shooting," Jericho smirked back.

"It is good to see you Jericho," Thomas said, sitting up and slapping the man's knee.

Jericho hadn't seemed to have aged much over the last seven years. His blonde hair fell in thick strands around the side of his face and his blue eyes shone with charm and mischief. His skin was a little weather worn, but still managed to be caramel coloured despite the relenting attention of the sun. Thomas couldn't recall ever seeing him without a strap of thick stubble covering the lower part of his face, and today was no exception. As he stood up, Thomas saw a flash of Jericho's toned midriff beneath his shooting vest. Jericho was very well built, pretty much the same height as Thomas but much more muscular.

"Have some decency to put some clothes on will you, you'll show me up," Thomas sighed, also standing up.

"That's gonna happen whether I'm dressed or not," Jericho smirked.

Thomas and Jericho walked over to the dining table and chairs sitting on the outcrop. There was a cool breeze, and they supped at the beers in tired silence. After a little while, they heard Catherine and Kelly making their way over to them, chatting as they walked.

"Jericho O'Connell, meet Catherine Tyler my fiancée and Kelly Keelson, our producer," Thomas said, introducing them.

"Some boys have all the luck, don't they?" Jericho smiled as he reached out his hand.

"Mainly bad in his case," laughed Catherine. "Thanks for the timely arrival last night if this one has forgotten to say," she continued, ruffling Thomas's hair fondly as she stood behind him.

"No need. I was actually following the car because I thought they might be poachers. I've had some trouble with a rather well organised crew recently, and I didn't recognise the car. I kept my distance until I heard the shot, but didn't know quite what you'd stumbled into until I caught up. I only realised it was you when I heard Jelani laughing, probably at the sight of Thomas in his pyjamas no doubt."

"Still, thank you," Kelly offered quietly.

"Good morning," beamed Mansa as he arrived at the table, carrying a large tray piled high with plates of scrambled eggs, sausages, bacon and sweet smelling 'chapo' flatbreads. There was also a large cafetiere of coffee, adding to the rich aromas surrounding the breakfast table.

"Mansa, could you arrange for my two to be fed, they'll soon get up once they smell breakfast," Jericho asked.

"Certainly," Mansa answered with a courteous bow, "although Saka has already helped with some of our surplus."

"You brought them?" Thomas exclaimed with some excitement.

Jericho grinned, then put his thumb and index finger of his right hand into his mouth and gave a loud, sharp whistle. There was an instant reply of a booming bark as a large, tan, short-furred dog appeared in the open doorway of Jericho's tent. It had a muscular and regal appearance, with dark coloured ears and a black muzzle and nose. It sauntered over, wagging its thick, stout tail as it came. Catherine recognised it as a mastiff type, but wasn't sure what breed the impressive dog was. The dog trotted straight past Jericho and up to Catherine, placing its great head in her hands.

"Well he likes you," laughed Jericho, "this is Rhodes. He's a Boerboel, a South African mastiff."

"He's lovely," beamed Catherine, making a fuss of the big dog.

"And here comes the other one," Jericho smiled.

Thomas saw her saunter out from behind the kitchen, gulping down a scrap of meat as she did. She froze as she saw the table of people ahead of her, bobbing her head in uncertainty. Then her amber coloured eyes locked on his. She gave a quick yelp then let out a babbling yikker as she lurched towards him.

"Is that what I think it is?" Catherine gasped.

"If you think it's a scrawny looking thief and a pain in me ass, then yes," Jericho sighed.

"You have an African hunting dog as a pet?" Catherine asked.

"You can blame yer man for that," Jericho sniggered.

The lithe, thin canine covered the ground quickly, her long legs making short work of the distance. She barged past Jericho and rammed her head into Thomas's chest with a powerful butt. She continued to squeal and yammer as she rubbed the sides of her head along his welcoming arms and shoulders. Her movements and behaviour seemed more cat-like to Catherine.

"You can stroke her, she's fine with it," Thomas said quietly to Catherine.

Catherine reached out, running her fingers through the coarse, scraggy fur. The hide was covered in inkblot shaped blotches of white, yellow, black and brown. Catherine reached up and began to scratch the dog behind its huge, bat-like ears. The animal instantly sat down and leaned into her, enjoying the sensation so much that one of its hind legs began to hammer against the ground.

"She's remarkable," said Catherine.

"Her name is Saka," Thomas replied. "It means hunter in Swahili."

"She's also one of the rarest mammals in Africa," Catherine exclaimed.

"True," admitted Thomas, "but it's not what you think. Her mother abandoned the den after a rock python entered it and ate Saka's siblings. She was only three weeks old, but she scrambled out, presumably over the snake whilst it had its mouth full. But it was too late. I found her by the side of the road, fending off a honey badger. I did track back to the den, but the snake was still curled up inside, digesting her brothers and sisters, and the pack was long gone."

"Oh," Catherine said apologetically.

"She's also donated three litters of pups to captive breeding programs here in Kenya," Jericho added, "so she's played her part. East and West Tsavo are one the last few places you can find them in the wild in East Africa. She's also pretty handy to have about the camp. She still hates snakes, and will catch and kill any she can."

"Quite the little fighter hey," Catherine cooed as Saka tilted her head back towards her, now rubbing her head on her lap as she had done to Thomas.

The dogs bumped heads casually and walked side by side out onto the kopje. They lay down a few yards from the table, seemingly enjoying the touch of the early morning sun. As Thomas and the others helped themselves to the lavish breakfast, the dogs were thrown the odd sausage or sliver of bacon. There was certainly enough for all.

"Jelani is going to stay here and sort out the camp as well as taking care of reporting the hippo, so I'll take you out today," Jericho explained. "He can look after these two whilst we take a day of safari."

"I think the guys and I are going to acclimatise today and

take stock of the equipment, get set up, that kind of thing," Keelson added. "Mason did manage to get some great footage of the hippo attack though, so he's pretty pleased."

"He's his father's son all right" Thomas laughed.

Suddenly, Saka sat up, her large black ears pricked and pointed down the gorge. She stood slowly, leaning into the wind. After a while, she turned and looked at Thomas. He stood up and walked over to her, stroking her back with the tips of his fingers as he stood beside her. He cupped his hands behind his ears and listened in the direction Saka was staring. He turned back to the others, all watching him from the table.

"Elephants," he grinned. "Time to get out on that safari I'd say."

CHAPTER NINE

Thomas emerged from the tent, dressed in sand coloured lightweight trousers and a matching shooting vest. Underneath was a light blue linen shirt, which he'd rolled the sleeves of up to the elbows.

"My, don't you look quite the Bwana," Jericho called over from the gun rack.

Thomas walked over to join him. He was at least glad the Irishman had found a shirt, and was sporting a pair of safari trousers. As Thomas approached, he noticed he was filling an ammunition belt with the torpedo shaped bullets for his own weapon, a Merkel 500 Nitro Express rifle.

"That thing's a howitzer," grinned Thomas. "We're just meant to be enjoying the wildlife today, remember."

"Well like my old scout leader used to say, be prepared," Jericho smirked. "Plus, I know you. You can't help but go looking for trouble."

"Don't normally need to," shrugged Thomas, "it usually has a pretty good bead on where I'm at already."

"Well, if it wasn't for bad luck my old Bwana," Jericho smiled, as Catherine joined them.

"Why do you and Jelani keep calling him Bwana?" Catherine asked.

"It's a rather old fashioned, but respectful word meaning boss in Swahili," Thomas explained.

"And they don't have a word for fugly," Jericho said with a wink.

Catherine laughed. Thomas was glad that even just a few

hours of sleep seemed to have lightened the mood, and he knew Jericho was helping with that. She looked much less tired today, and the sparkle in her eyes had been refreshed. The slight curl in her red hair made it hang down in tufts on the side of her face, peeking out from the rim of her hat. She brushed a few stray strands form her neck, smiling at Thomas.

"Mansa is preparing a picnic lunch for us," Jericho explained. "I've put plenty of water into the car, but fill up a canteen anyway."

Mansa appeared from the kitchen, carrying a picnic hamper and a large canvas bag. He passed them, heading in the direction of the cars.

"I presumed you didn't mind taking yours, seeing as mine's only got the two seats," smiled Jericho.

"God, that means I have to let you drive," groaned Thomas.

Thomas helped Jericho load the Big Cat with a few supplies. He put both their guns into the rack on the back of the custom light rig. He checked over the first aid kit, and put the lunch into an air tight and refrigerated container underneath the rear bench. Finally, he made sure the jerry can on the back of the truck bed was attached and full, just in case. He walked back round to find Catherine sitting in the front passenger seat. She smiled smugly, as she finished fitting a small zoom lens to her Fujifilm camera.

"I have a present for you," he said softly, taking out a leather pouch from behind his back, passing it to her.

She took it from him and opened it up. She took out the cocoa coloured binoculars and looked at him quizzically.

"I thought you might find these a bit handier than the big 12x50 pair you have. They're made by Swarovski and treated for the light conditions of the Serengeti. They also weigh a lot less, being 8x30s. They'll be great for spotting before you take a snap," he explained.

"Thank you," she beamed, leaning out of the window to kiss him on the cheek.

"Ready to hit the trail?" Jericho asked, climbing into the driver's seat.

"Absolutely," replied Catherine, as Thomas took his seat behind her.

Jericho glanced back at him with a sly smile then turned back and started the car. They rolled out of the camp, with waves to Jelani and the men as they turned onto the dirt road that had led them to the camp the day before. As Jericho slid the rest of the windows down, Thomas reached through from the back to the centre console, and flicked the switch that turned on the cooling fans built into the seats. He slumped back into his own with a satisfied grin as Jericho rolled his eyes.

As they bumped along the track, they found their first subjects. An ostrich family were foraging through the rough edges of the road, making the most of the natural border to the grassland on either side. Jericho slowed, keeping his eye on the impressive black and white male as it stepped towards them, putting itself between the car and the female and her chicks. It turned its head to the side and opened its beak threateningly, ruffling its wings from side to side as it did so. As they got a little closer, Catherine realised just how many chicks the pair had, with at least thirty of the brown headed balls of fluff following the female off into the grass on the left-hand side of the road.

"It's a crèche," Jericho explained, seeing her surprise.

"These two must be a dominant pair, and they look after and raise the majority of the offspring. There will be a few more females and sub-adults around somewhere though."

Catherine nodded as the car pulled off again. The male, standing at over eight feet high, watched them warily as they passed. It followed behind them in a sudden charge, catching up with them in a few lengthy strides. Catherine couldn't help but notice the impressive spur at the end of the largest toe on each foot. She didn't find it difficult to believe the legendary power of an ostrich kick, said to be capable of killing a human or lion that got too close, maybe even disembowelling them. But the male's charge became half-hearted and it soon peeled off back into the grass after a few seconds. Just as Jericho had said, as they rounded a corner, they caught sight of another mottled brown female and a larger juvenile joining them. Catherine took a quick glance at the snaps she'd taken on the camera's screen. She shot Thomas a huge smile when she looked up.

Their next encounter was also avian in nature. The grey-backed secretary bird stalked the grassland to their right, seemingly oblivious to their presence. Its red eye patch and yellow hooked beak gave it a menacing and purposeful appearance, but with its black tipped wings and tail, Catherine found it beautiful. As it strutted close to them, it suddenly darted forward, flapping its wings and thrashing at the ground with powerful strikes of its long yellow legs. It dashed forward again, using its wings to flush out whatever it was striking at. Just as quickly, the bird stopped, ducking its head out of sight, only to reappear again with what Thomas recognised as a brown house snake in its beak. It proceeded to swallow the reptile whole, taking it down in a series of large gulps. The bird then cocked its head and continued its patrol of the straw-coloured grass as if nothing had happened.

Further along the trail, Jericho swung the car onto a lower road that took them to the river. He confidently swung the car into the shallows, creating a wash that surged from the front and sides of the vehicle. Jolts were sent through the chassis as the Big Cat bucked over unseen rocks and gouges along the riverbed. With the water lapping at the tops of the wheels, Thomas was glad the snorkel exhaust was still functioning after all these years. Jericho looked round at him with a grin as they pulled out onto the track on the other side of the crossing.

There were fewer trees and belts of woodland this side of the river, with more open grassland and rust coloured rocky outcrops. The landscape was still dotted with flat-topped acacias and the occasional bulbous trunked baobab tree though. The sun was climbing high now, and the heat of the day was seeping into the cabin of the car. They trundled forward, following the river again from the other bank, climbing a little as they followed the ridge.

They pulled up and watched a troop of olive baboons cross the road, their passage guarded by a large male, who yawned at the car, displaying his two-inch long canines and gums by throwing back his head. He let out a loud grunt that built into a howl as he sat up on his haunches, asserting his dominance in a threat display. When the rest of the band had crossed, the male rolled into a standing position and sauntered after them, with an occasional glance over his shoulder as they passed.

A little further on, Jericho brought the car to a halt as they crested the ridgeline. He pointed down to the opposite bank of the river, where hundreds of small holes had been bored into the crumbling earth. Emerging from them were beautiful pink and green coloured birds with long, curved black beaks.

"Carmine bee-eaters," Jericho explained. "They breed at the hottest time of the year, when the river is low and there is less risk of flooding."

They sat and watched the birds sunning themselves on the bank, spreading their wings out wide on the ground.

"Because they live in such large colonies they are prone to parasites, so they literally burn the bugs off their backs," Jericho continued.

Suddenly, in a huge swirl of commotion, the colourful birds rose into the air, bolting across the water towards them. Thomas glanced instinctively up river and caught sight of a huge shape plummeting through the air towards them. The great chestnut bodied bird shot past them in a powerful glide, revealing its gleaming white head, breast and tail. The African fish eagle reached out with a yellow talon and plucked a bee-eater from the air with ease, a single beat of its wings taking it to the top of a thorny acacia where it picked its meal clean before tearing into the meat. Their sheen dulled by death, the pink, teal and yellow coloured feathers floated down from the tree in a morbid, rainbow cascade.

Catherine's camera whirred and snapped as she took picture after picture, never rushing a shot and carefully repositioning each time. Happy, she glanced back to Thomas with a beaming smile, her eyes electrified with excitement.

"That was amazing," she laughed, throwing her hands up joyfully. She reached behind her and took Thomas's hand, squeezing it lovingly.

"It's all down to the guide," Thomas smiled.

"To be sure," nodded Jericho with a wink.

Catherine reviewed some of the shots of the eagle's attack,

occasionally lifting the camera up to show Thomas her work with some pride. He shone with his own pride. Her natural skill with a camera was something he had been enamoured with since they had been together, and many of her best shots now sat framed along the walls of his study. Even at the office at the Highland Wildlife Research Centre, Thomas had encouraged her to put pictures up. He thought it was the perfect place for them, and many guests and visitors had admired her skill, just as he was doing so now.

They continued along the trail, with Catherine taking pictures as they went, trying to capture the strange, red coloured landscape and its scrubby countryside, peppered with thickets and termite mounds surrounded by slabs of dark volcanic rock. It seemed eerie to Catherine, never really opening up into open grassland, making it feel claustrophobic and impenetrable.

They stopped for their lunch on a small kopje that overlooked the river gorge. Thomas pointed out a pair of klipspringers that studied them cautiously from its furthest outreaches. The small, strong and stocky looking antelopes were buff in colour, with washed out chins and muzzles. Their flanks were grey, giving way to white underbellies. Catherine couldn't help but laugh as they flicked their zebra-striped ears towards them every now and then, giving them a distinctly odd appearance.

Jericho lay out a large woollen blanket on a flat piece of rock and unpacked the picnic. Thomas and Catherine joined him. She watched as Jericho reached over the side of the truck-bed and pulled his gun off the rack, resting it up against the door of the Big Cat, close to where he sat.

"I guess you can never really get away from the fact that

there are animals willing to kill you out here," Catherine said, almost to herself.

"It's not especially open here," replied Jericho, "you never know what might wander out of the bush. Man-eaters are just one thing we have to worry about. But an elephant, buffalo, rhino or hippo will happily make a mess of you too, given the opportunity and motivation."

Catherine loaded a plate with a tomato and sweet corn salad. As she put it down to grab a piece of the cold, roasted francolin meat Thomas offered her, she noticed one of the klipspringers take a few bold steps towards them. She looked back round to Thomas, who smiled at her.

"They're either not very used to people, or far too used to them," he observed.

Catherine held out the plate, curious to see if it would approach closer. It did, taking a few more tentative steps. It continued edging closer until it could swipe a mouthful of leaves off the plate, skipping nimbly back to the other straight after. Satisfied, the two small antelopes disappeared from sight over the other side of the outcrop.

"Jelani tells me this was a favourite picnic rock of Colonel Patterson, the hunter of the original Tsavo man-eaters himself," remarked Jericho, "which is quite likely given that the place is hardly riddled with pristine spots."

"I know he was partial to a swim in the river, and this wouldn't be a bad place to do it," Thomas added.

"The guy was an idiot," Jericho replied, rolling his eyes. "The only thing that got him through the whole debacle was the luck of the Irish. Swimming in a crocodile infested river is just more proof."

"I don't think you're being especially fair to him," Thomas

said. "He was an experienced tiger hunter, but I know what you mean."

"Aye, but he tried to hunt lions like they were tigers. Sitting up in trees, or worse, on a damn machan. How many times did he position himself over an old kill, expecting the boys to come back, only to hear his men being ripped to pieces elsewhere in the camp? And how many pot-shots did he take at them? By the time he was through, he could have just used a magnet to draw them into camp with the amount of shrapnel he'd riddled their hides with."

"He definitely made mistakes," Thomas sighed.

"He repeated his several times. That's not bravery, that's thick-headedness," scolded Jericho.

"Can't imagine where he'd get it from," Thomas grinned.

"You're just lucky this Irishman has more sense," Jericho shrugged.

"You hide it well," Thomas replied.

"I find the specimens themselves interesting," Catherine interjected. "Both were over nine feet long, considered very large, and were virtually maneless. And they were very pale in colour too. And if even just some of their reported behaviour was true then they were definitely out of the ordinary."

"Well you don't kill 140 people by being ordinary," Jericho laughed.

"That's a highly dubious number given recent research," Catherine snapped back. "Studies of certain isotopic signatures in their bone collagen and hair keratin suggested that the first lion Patterson shot ate around 24 people, whilst the second scoffed a mere ten. Even the railway company records state only 28 losses."

"Patterson's numbers may well have been exaggerated, but

the studies you mention don't account for the practice runs that all man-eaters make, or the number of people they kill and don't eat," argued Thomas.

"They were also killing people for over nine months. Those isotope readings were taken on specimens over a hundred years old in very poor condition, with no accurate way of measuring assimilative breakdown of the elements. It also presumes that the lions ate each person whole. What if they just took the good bits? Many man-eaters do you know," added Jericho.

"We know," replied Thomas and Catherine together.

Thomas leaned over and stroked the top of Catherine's hand with his thumb as he took her hand in his. His heart thumped loud in his chest as his head was flooded with images of the Highland cat's rampage.

"Anyway, this was meant to be a day without man-eaters," Thomas stated. "Let's get back to our day of safari."

They packed away the picnic and climbed back into the car. Jericho continued to follow the track west along the riverbank. As they rounded a sweeping bend, they were greeted with the noise they had been searching for. Loud rumblings and excited trumpets resonated from just up ahead of them. Jericho changed down a gear and turned off the track, ploughing through the river again at another crossing point. The water came up to the wheel tops this time, but they were soon climbing the opposite bank. Jericho turned the car west again. As they cleared a thick patch of scrub, he brought the car to a halt and pointed up river.

Ahead of them the river widened, and a sandbank at its middle split a deep pool off from the main current and flow, although it was still open at both ends. A group of about twelve elephants were using the pool as their personal spa. Catherine was surprised by their dark red colouring that matched the landscape. Some were lying on their sides, lazily lifting their trunks above the water. Others kneeled, semi-submerged and clearly enjoying the coolness of the mud and water. The group was made up of females, and the matriarch stood at the water's edge, close to a slightly smaller cow who was nursing a calf. The water lapped up past the calf's tummy, and it seemed unsure if it should panic or delight in this. With a gentle and encouraging nudge from its mother, the calf took a lunge into the water and began splashing wildly. Catherine laughed as it made a mock charge through the water towards the matriarch, who cuffed the youngster gently with a touch of her trunk behind its outspread ears.

Catherine took out her camera again and attached the largest of her zoom lenses. She leaned out of the window, taking the time to wait for the right moment and shot. As she focused on an elephant lying on its side, she noticed it suddenly rise, seemingly agitated. The animal was the closest one to the car. It stood at about eight feet at the shoulder and must have weighed every bit of 6,000lbs Catherine guessed. The elephant spread its ears wide and rocked on its feet whilst emitting a deep, menacing rumble. Catherine followed its gaze into the water on the other side of the sandbank and let out a tiny gasp as she saw what lurked there.

It lay in the water, not visibly moving its body or limbs, but still edging towards the sandbank. Its long, pointed snout slipped through the water, gliding along the surface with deliberate slowness. Catherine caught the glint of the green iris housed within its bony, scale enforced socket. The crocodile wasn't huge, but at nearly twelve feet it was still over twice as long as she was. She shuddered at the thought of lying beside it in comparison. As Catherine took her eye away from the camera, she looked to find Thomas and Jericho also transfixed by the scene before them.

With a fearsome and loud trumpet call, the elephant swung around and charged through the water towards the opposite bank, her large bulk pushing the young calf aside and separating it from its mother. The other elephants followed in a panic, stampeding up the steep bank. Catherine held her breath as she watched the calf regain its feet quickly and begin to follow the others. Its mother called out in anguish as her back legs slipped and she stumbled. She crashed to the earth, sending a huge section of the bank tumbling into the river, in a mudslide that momentarily consumed her calf and pushed it back into the water.

The crocodile flew up the sandbank, but suddenly paused there. That's when Catherine noticed the other one. It had just silently appeared in the mouth of the pool down river from them, surfacing like a submarine at the sound of the thrashing calf in the water. This crocodile was enormous, at least another six feet longer than its smaller companion. Its broad body and thick snout, as well as its huge size, suggested this was a mature and very old male. As Catherine looked at the smaller one perched on the sandbank, she wondered if it was maybe a female, and perhaps its mate. She began to dig her fingernails into the leather headrest she was gripping as she watched the huge crocodile slowly begin to beat its tail and slip towards the flailing calf.

"Oh to hell with that," declared Jericho, suddenly starting the engine. "That's the only calf in the herd this year."

"Go for it, the old girl can take it," nodded Thomas.

Without waiting for further encouragement, Jericho gunned the car down the bank. Catherine gripped the headrest harder as they plunged bonnet first into the water, sending an impressive bow wave ahead of them. The roar of the engine and the displacement of the water was enough to send the smaller crocodile sliding off to the side, back into the water. But as Jericho turned the Big Cat and sent it flying over the sandbank, the big male didn't budge. As the water level rose to the tops of the wheel arches, Jericho stopped and began to back off a little, reversing onto the surer footing of the sandbank behind.

The mother elephant and the rest of her herd made screaming trumpeting calls as they ran back and forth along the edge of what was now a four-foot cliff between them and the calf. The sound was deafening. The baby instinctively reached up for them with its trunk, looking for reassurance and help as it stood in knee deep water at the pool's edge. Catherine watched as the elephants knelt and groped at the calf with their trunks in desperation. Once or twice, it tried to clamber up the bank by rearing onto its hind legs. Each attempt sent a small mudslide back down into the water in its wake. Catherine suddenly got hopeful, realising that the thick clay was beginning to pile up and soften the steep angle of the bank. Then she looked back to the big croc. It had snuck even closer, now just a body-length away. The calf wasn't going to make it.

Catherine glanced at the water lapping against the side of the door. She wasn't thinking, acting only on instinct as she shot up from her seat and reached for the open roof above. Thomas watched in horror as Catherine slipped past him, hoisting herself skyward before he could grab her. She threw her legs over the roof and slipped down the windscreen and over the bonnet of the car, splashing noisily into the water. She surged forwards through the coffee coloured froth, only looking at the calf and trying to stop her panicked thoughts settling on the encroaching crocodile.

Thomas and Jericho moved like lightning. By the time Thomas was standing next to the Irishman, Jericho had reached behind to the rack and was passing him his gun. Thomas leapt up, throwing himself forward to firmly plant his feet on the bonnet. He saw Jericho train his nitro express double rifle at the crocodile's head, allowing him to focus on Catherine. He turned back towards her with a shudder as he heard a sound like rolling thunder, followed by the crack of a nearby acacia as it fell to the ground.

The bull elephant was immense. It brushed the tree aside as if it were kindling and stepped out onto the bank. Thomas guessed he stood nearly fourteen feet at the shoulder and that his red, pot-marked hide encompassed a mass of 14,000lbs. His eight and a half feet long ivory tusks must have weighed more than a 100lbs each alone. They curved skywards in a smooth arc, but the bull pointed them down towards Catherine and the calf. He spread his ears out in a display of unmitigated aggression and lifted his forehead high as he let out a murderous, rage-filled bellow. Thomas brought up his rifle. He hadn't missed the dark stains on the bull's face that indicated he was in musth, which explained his close presence to the herd. At such a short distance, he knew he would have to angle the shot steeply from beneath the centre of the bull's forehead. If he went for what most people would consider between the eyes, even his large calibre bullet was unlikely to penetrate the 9 or even 10″ thick skull and its kinked sinews and muscle padding. He aimed at the third fold on the bull's trunk, where he knew the bullet was most likely to pass through the sinus cavity and into the brain. He took a breath and placed his finger on the trigger.

Catherine edged closer to the calf, talking quietly and kindly to it as she approached. The calf raised its trunk and turned towards her. As it did so, it noticed the crocodile again. It didn't hesitate to decide that Catherine was the better option, and quickly stepped behind her. It began to clamber at the bank with renewed panic. Catherine reached out, touching the baby on its back as she sidled up to it. She felt it tense and rear backwards, but she knew its focus was now on the crocodile, which had begun to edge forward again. Catherine pressed her back up against the calf's behind and anchored her feet into the thick mud beneath the swirling water. She began to push with all her might, her eyes fixed on Thomas's. Then, in her peripheral vision, the hulking form of the crocodile began to emerge.

The raking actions of the calf had begun to form a channel up the bank. As Catherine pushed from behind, the baby suddenly found footing again and hauled itself a little way up. Catherine had to pull with all her strength to release her feet from the clamping embrace of the river mud, but as she did, she felt the calf move upwards again. She squeezed and wriggled against its doused hide, trying to help it ascend one more step and to safety. Then suddenly she felt herself falling, the wall of elephant at her back suddenly absent. She closed her eyes as she saw the crocodile lunge.

It seemed to happen in slow motion for Thomas. The crocodile rose from the water, its mouth open and ready to take Catherine between its sixty conical shaped teeth. Its seven-foot-long tail propelled it through the water at unthinkable speed. Thomas's mind was flooded with images of the death roll he was about to witness and he imagined Catherine's face slipping beneath the water, where the croc would keep her until she drowned, perhaps lodging her corpse in the roots of a tree until the meat was bloated and tender. But not before it popped one of her limbs for a more immediate snack. He swung his rifle back towards the croc only to see the water in front of it explode in a fountain, followed by another to its side.

His ears were ringing, and he knew Jericho had fired. He had decided to try and scare the croc rather than kill it, placing a shot practically on top of its nose. But it was only then that he realised where the second explosion had come from. It had been the elephants. A boulder the size of a bowling ball had smashed into the crocodile's side moments after, hurled down the riverbank by the calf's mother. Seconds later, a large thorn encrusted limb of the felled acacia dropped from the sky onto the croc's stunned head. With a thrash of its tail the croc spun and surged out of the pool, disappearing as soon as it reached the deep channel of the main river.

Catherine sat trembling against the muddy bank for a few moments before she remembered the bull elephant. She jumped to her feet and spun around, still shaking violently from fear and now the cold, thoroughly drenched as she was. The bull took a step forward, a reverberating groan emanating from deep within its throat. It folded its ears back and reached out its trunk. Catherine froze as the tender tip gently touched the top of her head, brushing aside a wisp of her hair as it did so. The bull tenderly explored her nape with the two opposing lips of its trunk. The bull took a big sniff, and the warm air against her skin tickled, making her shiver. Then, as she watched the calf scamper away by the side of its mother, the great elephant took a step back. For a moment, the three people and the elephant locked eyes, before it turned away and followed the group of females at a distance. Just as Catherine's legs gave way to the shock, she found herself caught by Thomas, who lifted her up and carried her back to the car as Jericho backed it up further onto the sandbank.

"Well my old friend, it looks like you have some competition," smiled Jericho. "I think old Sefu took a liking to Catherine there."

"Sefu?" Catherine stammered.

"It means sword. He's probably one of the last great elephants in Kenya, and as you just found out, the Tsavo river herd benefit from his protection. As now do you I'd rightly say," Jericho winked.

CHAPTER TEN

Thomas stared into the fire, set within a ring of stones on top of the kopje. Dinner had passed with little comment between him and Catherine and now she had wandered back to the tent. He had gone from feeling shocked, to angry, to perplexed by her actions at the river with the elephants. He knew she had scared herself a little too. Her face had been ashen for most of the journey back to camp and he had seen her hands trembling. He was alarmed at the recklessness of her actions.

"A good laugh and a long sleep cure all manner of things you know," Jericho offered as he took a seat next to him, passing him a cold bottle of lager and taking a swig from his own.

"I just have no idea of how to even bring up what we witnessed today," said Thomas, shaking his head.

"Carefully I'd say. In my experience, telling a woman she's done something you're displeased with has the same effect as baptising a cat," Jericho replied.

"I have to admit, part of me is absolutely glowing with pride," Thomas said, sitting back.

"Then maybe that's the part to listen to," Jericho offered.

They both supped at their beer quietly, watching the fire.

~

Catherine sat on the bed in the tent. She hugged her knees, resting her head on them as she closed her eyes. She was determined not to cry, but her whole body shook with the effort of damming the flow of tears. She didn't quite know herself why she had felt so compelled. She was a wildlife biologist and knew better than most that nature was red in tooth and claw. But there was something about how the elephant calf had seemed helpless and panicked. The seeming arrogance and surety the crocodile displayed as it crept closer. She had first considered that it was perhaps just some natural maternal instinct that had kicked in, but she knew that wasn't it, or at least not the whole picture. The scenario had just seemed horribly familiar. The feeling of being trapped against her will had welled up within her. More than anything right now, she wanted to be able to retreat to the top of Carn Eige with her thoughts. Back where she'd found the bullet casing. Where she had watched David Fairbanks die as he in turn tried to kill her.

She was startled by the sound of soft footsteps coming along the side of the tent. She lifted her head, tense and alert as she followed the sound towards the door. She was surprised to see a tall, native boy step inside. He was thin and lanky, with tightly cropped black curls of hair. His skin was especially dark and he met her gaze with deep, chestnut coloured eyes. He wore only a pair of faded orange jeans, with old green trainers on his feet. His chest and top were bare. He looked at her questioningly.

"Bwana?" the boy uttered.

Catherine's brow furrowed, but she pointed out towards the kopje. As the boy turned and left, she jumped up from the bed to follow him.

~

Thomas turned as he heard several raised voices. Jelani and Mansa were striding towards a young boy approaching from the direction of the tents. Catherine was quick to get between them and the lad, who seemed frightened and skittish at their sudden appearance. Thomas jumped up to intervene, with Jericho close behind.

Jelani and Mansa were both talking at the boy, their Swahili too fast for Thomas to follow, although it was clear they were demanding to know who he was and what he was doing at the camp.

"Leave him alone and back off," warned Catherine, stepping towards the two men.

They immediately fell silent, surprised.

"I speak English," stammered the boy. "I need the Bwana."

"What do you need him for?" Thomas asked, stepping in beside Catherine. He glanced down the track, where more men appeared, heading towards them, and followed by Kelly, Mason and Karni.

"Chui," the lad gasped.

Thomas tensed slightly. Chui was the Swahili word for leopard. He felt a sinking feeling in his gut as he remembered Dr. Yeboah's warning about the increase in aggression and man-eating as Kenya's predators found their usual sources of prey diminishing.

"This past year three children have been taken. Tonight, a young girl," the boy explained, panting slightly as he did. It was clear he had been running to bring them the news. "You are nearest Bwana, others not come."

"They won't come because they know Kanu Sultan controls that territory," Jelani interjected.

Thomas noticed the boy visibly stiffen at the mention of the crime lord.

"Shit," Jericho chuckled, "a man-eating leopard, in this bush, at night, in the back yard of an arms dealer. I guess that's one way to go."

118

"I don't know what you're laughing at, you're coming with me," Thomas replied.

"Just remember you're the one with the paperwork to shoot the mean stuff. I can't do that for you," Jericho reminded him.

"You will come?" the boy asked, wide eyed.

"Yes, we will come," Thomas nodded. "Where?"

"My village, to the west," the boy replied.

Thomas brushed past Jelani and Mansa and walked over to the equipment tent and gun rack. He pulled a large, elongated and weathered looking holdall out from underneath a shelf. He unzipped it and started taking the contents out and placing them onto the table. Catherine joined him.

"This is my leopard kit," Thomas explained. "Hunting leopards in thick brush is especially hazardous to one's health, so it pays to be prepared."

First out of the bag was a brown leather jacket. The soft looking brown hide was creased and pot-marked all over. It looked as old and weathered as the bag it had come out of. Thomas turned the collar out, showing her the strip of aluminium sewn into it.

"Leopards like to attack from behind, with a bite to the neck or the base of the skull. And if they do get behind you, you absolutely will not hear them coming," he said.

Catherine wasn't convinced the upturned collar would be much defence against a leopard's fangs, even if laced with metal.

"Kevlar has been woven into the lining and innards, it's basically armour," he added, as if reading her thoughts.

He took out a small tin and checked its contents, revealing them to be four morphine syrettes. He also took out a couple of buckle tourniquets, a bottle of hydrogen peroxide solution and bandages, placing them all on top of each other. He put them into a small backpack he retrieved from the bottom of the holdall and passed it to her with a shrug.

"Is all this necessary?" Catherine asked. "You seem more rattled by a single leopard than the idea of taking on an entire pride of lions."

"I am. I don't like leopards," Thomas replied.

"And with good reason," chimed Jericho as he joined them. "They don't call the leopard the flying chainsaw for nothing. You see, a leopard will hit you with teeth, front claws and back all at the same time. Thomas and I once ran a camp here in Kenya next to…shall we say a slightly less reputable operation. One of their guests was ill-mannered enough to put a small bullet into a big leopard, which is never a great combination. Their pro went after it, as is expected by man and beast given the circumstances. Ten minutes later he reappeared, resembling a meatloaf wrapped in a safari shirt. They got most of the major holes in him plugged whilst they whistled up a rescue plane."

"When it arrived," Thomas continued, "another hunter got off and took over the safari. He was a well-known professional, and his first order of business was to settle the score. Only the leopard took issue with this, and sent him back to camp with some lovely new scars to be, and in time to catch the plane back with Bwana number one."

"So, plane number two and hunter number three arrive later that day," Jericho said, taking over the story again. "He dropped his kit at the tent and headed for the bush. The cat nailed him from behind, carving enough meat off him for a decent BBQ, and was so pissed off by then that he decided to savage two other crew members for good measure before anyone could get a shot off."

"That's five-nil to the leopard," shrugged Thomas. "Then Jericho and I were called in."

"So, in we go," Jericho laughed, shaking his head, "and you can imagine we were erring on the side of caution by this point. I'm tracking, Tommy is on point. Bang, out of nowhere comes Spots, rising up into the air like Mother Mary herself. Your man here gets a shot off but that doesn't stop the old flying fur coat either. Next thing, I'm prizing a dead leopard off the great white hunter, and he's got a broken thumb and two busted ribs as a thank you."

"Was that actually meant to reassure me?" Catherine said, a little shocked at Jericho's flippancy.

"No, but this might," Thomas replied, placing a strange looking gun on the table.

Catherine glanced at it. It looked like a shotgun, but had three barrels, one on top of the bottom two. They were shorter in length than usual, as was the stock.

"It's a Chiappa," Thomas explained. "It's a Turkish gun, made for the American home defence market. But I thought it would make an ideal leopard gun. I can shoot it from the hip, and it's short enough to manoeuvre in heavy scrub. A leopard isn't going to give me the time to raise my rifle to my shoulder. But with three barrels, I can empty two slugs and a backup of buckshot into him before I'm out of options."

"And we're burning moonlight," added Jericho, grabbing his own bag. As they passed by the gun rack, he also picked up his shotgun, as Thomas slipped on the holster containing the Colt Anaconda.

Thomas, Jericho, Catherine and the boy climbed into the

Big Cat, just as Keelson, Mason and Karni drove up the track from the staff camp in the hired Toyota pick-up.

"What's your name?" Thomas asked, turning round from the driver's seat to the boy.

"Musa," he replied sullenly.

"Where's your village Musa?" Thomas asked.

"Not far, twenty minutes running," Musa replied, his eyes wide as he took in the cabin of the car.

Musa directed them back along the track they had taken the night before. They passed the deep patch of scrub where the hippo had attacked, and then rumbled into a thicket of interlocked acacias. The Big Cat pulled and ploughed through the ruts and bumps of the track with ease. They eventually left the thicket behind them, pulling out into a stretch of open savannah.

Catherine took the Thermoteknix thermal imaging binoculars from the bag Thomas had hastily put together. She brought them up to her eyes, switching them on as she began to scan the darkness beyond the car. Her world suddenly became illuminated in washes of grey, white and black. Off in the distance, she could just make out a lone elephant, tearing strips from a baobab tree. Closer, a warthog dashed off into the grass as they passed by. She slowly panned forwards, catching the bright, hot-white flares of lights in the distance.

Thomas brought the Big Cat to a halt on the outskirts of the village. Men were walking the streets with flaming torches. There seemed to be a great deal of activity, and people were soon flanking all sides of the cars. Musa jumped out almost as soon as they stopped, with Thomas, Jericho and Catherine following.

An elderly man came forward and the crowd parted for

him as he approached. His eyes glistened with tears and he began to speak. His dialect seemed to be a mixture of Swahili and a more primitive bushman language, interspersed with clicks and whistles that Thomas was not familiar with. Musa quickly began to translate.

"The girl was taken at the other end of the village," he said. "This is Whistle, her father and the head man of the village."

Thomas and Jericho bowed their heads as a sign of respect.

"She went to wash the dinner pot after supper, but the leopard was waiting and took her as soon as she opened the door. They know it was a leopard, as they heard nothing."

"Take me there," Thomas demanded.

They walked through the small collection of huts that made up the village. Catherine noticed that most had wooden-framed, woven doors and thatched roofs. Some had mere blankets thrown over the entrances. She doubted any of the simple dwellings afforded much protection from a determined leopard.

The party came to a stop outside the last hut. A woman appeared in the open doorway, still wailing and clutching at her remaining children; another girl, and a boy much younger than Musa. He was no older than five, Catherine guessed.

Thomas's eyes however, were drawn to the large, undisturbed pugmark left in the dust at the hut's entrance. Guessing by its size, roughly five inches square, Thomas thought it was most likely a front paw print. And he knew by the position of the cat's equivalent of the big toe that it was the left paw. Just to the side of the hut, he found where the little girl had been ambushed. The ground had been thrashed in the swipe, with only a large globule of dried blood giving away what had happened. Thomas took a few steps into the darkness, picking up the leopard's trail with ease. The pugmarks were easy to follow and there was no hint of a drag. The leopard was carrying his meal.

"He's a big fella," remarked Jericho, reading the same signs as Thomas.

"Healthy too," Thomas added. "No indication of a limp or other wounds that might hinder him."

Thomas and Jericho walked slowly back to the car. Thomas took out the three-barrelled shotgun and broke open the breach. He popped two rifled slugs into the bottom barrels, adding a final shell containing 12-gauge buckshot into the top one. He then took out the Colt Anaconda and opened the cylinder, filling the six empty chambers with silver cased, brass topped 44. Magnum bullets. Finally, he put on the jacket and flipped the collar up. He gave a quick shrug as Jericho shot him a sarcastic smile.

"Well, you've gotten your armour on. Now you just need to slay the monster," Jericho said with a smirk.

He stepped aside and Thomas caught a glimpse of Keelson and Mason filming them.

"Was that little quip for the benefit of the camera?" Thomas asked dryly.

"Nah, it was for the benefit of the woman behind it," Jericho grinned.

Thomas walked back up through the village. The head man and his wife watched them pass, mumbling a blessing as they went by. Catherine touched the tips of Thomas's fingers with her own. He glanced at her, catching her quiet and frightened gaze.

"They're superstitious," Thomas whispered. "They think the leopard is a demon, or something supernatural, especially as it has killed here before. That's why they won't try to kill it themselves."

"But can't we wait until daylight?" Catherine pleaded. "I'm worried you're being pushed into going after it in the dark just for the cameras."

"It's extremely unlikely, but what if the little girl is still alive?" Thomas replied.

He caught Jericho's knowing look. He didn't think she was.

"Can't Jericho go with you?" Catherine asked desperately.

"He's not licensed to kill a protected animal like a leopard. Only I can do that," Thomas replied. "But don't think that'll stop him if I get into trouble. He won't be far behind," he added as reassuringly as he could.

They came to a stop at the edge of a trail that led away into the scrub. Another pool of thickened blood marked it. It almost looked black in the moonlight. Jericho knelt beside it, illuminating it further with his torch. He looked up at Thomas, his expression serious and foreboding. Thomas knew it too. The girl was dead. The heavy splash of blood came from an artery, opened as the leopard had adjusted its bite for better purchase through the thick vegetation.

"Looks like this is where you leave us," Jericho commented. "Hopefully only temporarily though," he added.

Thomas caught Catherine's rigid, pale expression as she glowered at Jericho with disgust.

"I'm not going to take any chances," he explained softly to her, recapturing her gaze and attention. "I'm just scouting things out. It could be long gone."

Jericho fixed him with another knowing look.

"Keep quiet and listen out for my first shot. Then you can follow me in," Thomas nodded to Jericho.

The Irishman nodded back, somewhat solemnly.

Thomas looked at Catherine, and just as he had her convinced they were in the middle of a silent exchange of deepest meant love, he smiled and winked. He laughed as he saw some colour return to her cheeks, and she shook her head, smiling back and rolling her eyes. He turned and stepped into the brush.

Within a few steps, he was wrapped in the embrace of night. He went a little way further, waiting until he was sure he was out of sight of the others before sinking down onto one knee. He stayed there for some time, keeping his gaze downward to avoid the glare of the moon. Slowly, his vision became used to the darkness. The inky black changed hue to navy and indigo and he stood up, beginning to creep forward.

The leopard's trail was easy to follow. The animal had been blatant, using a game trail that ran behind the village and away from it to the west. He couldn't see the pugmarks here, but a path of flattened grass stretching across the meadow in front of him shone like a slick of oil as it glistened in the moonlight. Thomas waded in after the cat, the grass coming up to his waist. His senses became even more heightened and he crept forward cautiously, pausing every few moments to listen to his surroundings.

The silence told him what he already knew. The leopard was still close by. As he edged across the meadow, he began to see the border of a small thicket emerge out of the darkness. Instinct told him that this was where the leopard was. He paused again, checking the wind was still in his favour. He began to creep forward, ever hoping some animal or bird would spot the leopard for him and give him an idea of its position. It came just at the edge of the first thick clump of trees.

The squeal of the baboon floated up into the night air. Thomas froze as he realised the sound didn't come from the thicket, but behind him. There was the softest grunt of displeasure, followed by another shrill squeal of the baboon that was cut off mid-cry. Thomas turned. A ghostly form shimmered along the trail behind him so silent and fast, his eyes didn't register it at first. His instinct kicked in just in time and he threw himself onto his back, raising the shortened shotgun as he did so. There was a blur above him and Thomas squeezed the trigger. Not hesitating, he rolled and spun, coming up onto one knee as he raised the gun to his hip, firing again as the leopard disappeared into the thicket.

Thomas sat there for a moment, panting for breath and close to swearing at himself. The leopard had stuck around to see if anybody had followed him, possibly having learnt this from a previous man-eating attempt. He remembered reading about Jim Corbett and the legendary leopard of Panar. That man-eater had learnt to do the same thing, having realised that an obliging hunter would regularly sit up in a tree and wait for him above a previous kill. Corbett himself had nearly been killed doing just this. It was only the alarm of the straying baboon that had saved Thomas, alerting him to the leopard's approach.

Thomas began to edge forward again, quickly finding a shiny, greasy looking blood trail. He knew that meant he had hit the leopard in the gut. He now had no choice but to follow it into the thicket. The leopard would lie up and exact its revenge on any human being it could find if he didn't. At the same time, the animal would be in considerable pain and couldn't be left to suffer. He felt the splash of blood and gore on his shins from the wet grass as he pushed through.

The blood trail was thick, and at first Thomas began to hope that he would find the leopard dead just up ahead. But as he parted some brush, he realised that would not be the case. The half-devoured remains of the head man's daughter lay face down in the mud, in a mangled crumple. The leopard had killed her with a single bite to the back of the head, the two large dark voids still visible at the base of her skull. Her vertebrae would have been crushed instantly, and as he had discovered, she soon bled out from the mirrored lacerations to her throat. Her killer had eaten on the run, taking bites from her calves and buttocks. Beside the body was a fresh pool of blood, only a few minutes old, still sticky and wet. Behind her, a flattened trail through the bushes showed him where the leopard had gone.

He waited, hearing the shouts of the others as they approached.

"Careful, it's not dead, just injured," he called out.

Jericho appeared behind him moments later, panting hard from the brisk run across the meadow. His eyes fell to the corpse of the little girl, and he immediately turned.

"I'll be right behind you once I've dealt with this, but you better get after it," Jericho whispered.

Thomas crawled forward on his hands and knees, jumping up as soon as he was able. The blood trail was still fresh and easy to see in the moonlight. He kept the gun at his hip, swinging it slowly from side to side. The night was absolutely silent, probably due to the sounds of his own shots. But it could also easily be because of the presence of the leopard. Now though, there was absolutely no way of telling. The leopard would not give up its position again. Unlike a lion, which would give a sporting roar as it charged towards you, a leopard was always stone cold silent in its delivery of death. Just as it had tried before, it would launch at him from behind, or come from the front, ready to eviscerate with powerful scrabbling kicks from its hind legs, as it buried its fangs into his head for good measure.

With his gaze still fixed to the trail, Thomas froze as he passed under a flat-topped acacia tree. The splatter of blood hit his shoulder and he picked up its lingering taint as he realised what was about to happen. The leopard had doubled back again. It had relied on him following its own gore trail past the tree, where it now waited for him. A second drip hit his shoulder, shaking him from his dread. He spun on his heels, lifting the gun and letting off the final blast of shot. As he did so, he was engulfed in a blur of amber. His world went black.

Moments later, he came round to the sound of Jericho's belly laughs and raucous applause. A few feet from him sat the dead leopard. As Thomas rolled over, suddenly aware of a shooting pain to the side of his head, he saw that both rifled slugs had hit their target. One bloody wound showed where the gut shot had done its damage. The second had hit a little way back from the shoulder, possibly smashing bones and organs in its path. He realised that if the second slug hadn't hit its mark, he probably wouldn't be sitting there. The leopard had indeed waited for him in the tree, but had succumbed to its wounds and blood loss before it could reap its revenge.

"You took a beating from being hit by 150lbs of falling pussy cat," Jericho chortled, "and a fang gave you a glancing blow to the head on the way down, but you're okay."

"I don't feel it," Thomas exclaimed.

Catherine joined them, kneeling beside him with the open medi-pack from the leopard bag. Thomas winced as she pressed a peroxide-laced cotton wad against the cut on his head.

"You'll have some lovely bruises," she remarked, still examining him.

Thomas watched as Jericho led the head-man over to the dead leopard. Wiping fresh tears from his eyes, the old man gave the animal a kick as he drew a knife and cut off one of its ears. This was the tradition of the tribe, to trade blood for blood, flesh for flesh. Thomas felt his stomach turn a little. The conflict he felt was always the same. The leopard was guilty of one thing; being a leopard. The male animal before him was beautiful, in its prime. Jericho had closed its eyes and shut its mouth to cover the lolling tongue, so now it looked like it was sleeping peacefully. It didn't deserve mutilation and humiliation in death for simply being true to its nature. But he knew that couldn't justify the taking of the headman's daughter. He took a sharp intake of breath as the image of her torn remains flooded into his head again. He knew killing the leopard was warranted, but that didn't make it easy or ease his conscience.

Thomas sighed as Jericho and Catherine lifted him onto his feet, and he hobbled with their support back along the trail towards the village. Soon, the villagers were singing victoriously as they made their way through the brush, and Thomas couldn't help but feel that some good had come of it. They felt safe and protected, something that had been missing from their lives for some time.

~

Musa shivered as he sat in the back of Kanu Sultan's car. He couldn't help compare it to the one the white man had driven, although it seemed even more luxurious and larger. The cold crisp air of the interior seemed strange to him.

Kanu Sultan stood close by, watching the procession through the village with a handheld night-vision camera. He smiled at Musa as he climbed back into the car and put it down.

"It looks like Mr. Walker passed his first test Musa my friend," Kanu grinned. "I expect you to look after him now you have been reacquainted. Africa is such a dangerous place, and it would be unfortunate for him to leave here unharmed."

CHAPTER ELEVEN

She watched the glow in the sky to the east gradually brighten, as she lay in the cool shade of the thicket. Although she felt the scampering of the agama lizard on her hind quarters, as it boldly foraged for flies, she stayed completely still. Only when it jumped up onto her flank did she flick it away with a swipe of her tail. She yawned and stood up, shaking her head groggily as she did so. She stretched, dipping her hips and arching her back with her front legs taut and rooted to the ground. She marked the dry, dusty earth liberally with urine before moving off. As she did, she caught the male's scent from close by. He had been following her for some time now.

She had known the male since he'd been a cub. She had a bond with him like the rest of the pride, but his attentions made her skittish. She emitted a low, rumbling growl to let him know not to come any closer for the time being. Her head turned sharply as she heard him pad off through the scrub to her left. A far more aggressive, barking growl lingered in her throat this time. She walked slowly, her tail swishing back and forth and occasionally bumping along the ground. She was aware of his presence almost instantly. The rich, intoxicating perfume of her urine and scent marking was too much for him to resist. She was in heat, and the male knew it.

She had watched him the previous day, as he had approached the new cubs. His playful cuffs and bites had nearly cost one its life. There was a new vigour to his actions that made her feel unsettled. Although she had birthed offspring herself, they never survived more than a few days.

But she felt a protective bond nevertheless towards the cubs of the other females. They mated with lone males they encountered or those that came in to try and take over the pride. None lasted long. She found it difficult to tolerate their presence, as if they were alien to her; and she was never able to submit to their rule. Her size and strength gave her an advantage over them as it was, and more than anything, it was her maternal instinct that made her drive off the males. In the past, their adolescent curiosity and rough housing had resulted in death, for both them and the cubs.

Young males were usually evicted from the pride at the first signs of their transgression into adulthood. She had tolerated this male for a little longer. He hunted well and had succumbed to her leadership, at least until now. She paused as she crossed a trail, looking back over her shoulder. She couldn't see him but knew he was close. She hunkered down onto her haunches and waited for his approach.

~

Thomas helped himself to the pile of sticky brown sausages in the serving dish Mansa brought to the table. He added them to his already brimming plate of scrambled eggs, slices of deep fried sweet potato and crispy bacon.

"I guess that's one way to get your strength back," Jericho commented as he joined him. "I've spoken to Nairobi on the radio. Apparently, that leopard has been on some ranger's to do list for the past year. You're in their good graces."

"I should bloody well hope so," Thomas growled, shovelling another mouthful. He felt a little sour that both the leopard and the villagers had, in effect, been let down by the authorities.

"When you've finished your meal sire, we have some

company," Jericho nodded towards the trail at the camp entrance.

A crowd of villagers were gathered there, some carrying baskets of vegetables and fruit, while others had game birds hung from broad poles balanced on their shoulders. One was pulling a goat along on a short rope. Thomas stood up as he finished his mouthful and began to walk over. He knew that it would be considered a great insult to refuse the gifts, and Mansa would be more than happy with the additions to the stores. This morning there had been a feast in the village to celebrate the passing of the headman's daughter, something akin to a wedding breakfast. These gifts to the killer of the leopard were part of the festivities. The villagers saw it as the lifting of a curse and the exorcising of a demon.

Thomas looked over the crowd but failed to spot Musa, the boy who had come to them for help. The funeral for the headman's daughter had taken place almost as soon as they had returned to the village, her remains burnt on a hastily constructed pyre. Thomas was sure the boy had not been there either. As he shook hands and embraced the men and boys who collectively greeted him, he was distracted by Musa's continued absence.

~

The young adolescent male padded up to her from behind. He paused a few feet from her, rolling back his lips and exposing his fangs in a half-snarl as he took in her scent. She growled a warning, but did not move or change position. Her muscles were hard and coiled in readiness though. He straddled her, quickly taking her neck in his jaws to limit her movement. She allowed him to do so, still rumbling her warnings with low, penetrating growls. A jolt of pain rippled down her back as he began to mate with her. She tried to shake off the clamp of his jaws, but stopped when he increased the pressure on her neck. She tried to turn and bat the male away with her paw, but could not reach. As the pain became unbearable, she bellowed an incredible roar and threw the male off with a shake of her shoulders. She spun at him, striking a dizzying blow with her paw that left the male stunned and bloody. He didn't wait around to attempt a second mating, and instead dashed off into the brush. She knew where he was headed and quickly followed.

~

Thomas caught the sound of the roar even above the chanting and chatter of the crowd. He turned quickly towards Jericho. From his blank expression, Thomas could tell he hadn't heard it. He tried to tune out the background noise, but it was no good. The roar had dissipated and reduced to nothing. He also knew that the sound could travel at least a few miles, perhaps even up to five. And it had only been at the edge of his hearing. It still put the lions close by.

He turned back to the crowd, homing in on a bare-chested man Jelani was talking to. From the brace of francolin he carried, and the homemade slingshot casually stuffed into his shorts, Thomas presumed he was a hunter. He made his way over to them.

"This is Badru," announced Jelani as he introduced the man. "He tells me that the village has been cursed by Kanu Sultan's demons and you are the only one to vanquish them so far. Even the wildlife service feared to come, but not you."

"Have you seen Kanu Sultan?" Thomas asked.

"Yes, many times," Badru answered in passable English. "He brings offerings to the families of the dead. He says they have died in battle, that if we help him he will give us more farmland. Land stolen by the government."

"Do you mean the National Parks?" Thomas queried.

"Some," acknowledged Badru.

"The chui was only one demon," Thomas stated, changing tactic. "I am after the many."

"You hunt the Daughters of the Darkness?" Badru asked hesitantly.

"I do," Thomas nodded.

"They cannot be killed," Badru shrugged "they are controlled by Kanu himself."

Thomas knew that this wasn't the time to argue. Badru would not be convinced until Thomas killed at least one of the animals. He also knew from Jelani's email and his now wide-eyed expression that he too believed there was something supernatural about the pride.

"Having killed one demon, why would I not be able to kill more?" Thomas challenged.

"The chui was a test Bwana, Kanu wanted to see if you would stand up to him," Badru sighed, as if bored with Thomas's inability to understand the situation.

"Will you perhaps help me to find them at least?" Thomas asked.

Badru paused, his eyes flicking from Jelani and then back to Thomas. His gaze eventually settled on his feet.

"I will help you, because you tried to help Sanura," he remarked. "I will show you where they were last night."

"Thank you Badru," Thomas nodded appreciatively. Sanura was the name of the little girl the leopard had killed. As he looked at the sorrowful expression on the hunter's face, Thomas wondered if the hunter was in some way related. It was quite likely in a small village. "We won't tell anyone that you helped us Badru," Thomas reassured him. "I am curious though, the boy who came to us for help last night, Musa, where is he?"

Badru looked at Thomas curiously then let out a loud dismissive laugh.

"Musa is not of the village, he belongs to Kanu," he explained with a smirk. "If he was the one to warn you of the chui, do you not now see that Kanu controls what he calls the critters of the bush?"

Thomas was a little shocked. He hadn't contemplated that Musa had not come from the village. The fact that the boy had said so meant he had deliberately lied, and Kanu had indeed sent a spy into his camp. Jelani's worried expression showed he was thinking the same.

"I think we'd best thank our guests and get on the trail Jelani," Thomas suggested.

Jelani nodded and began to usher the gift-brandishing villagers towards the kitchen and stores.

~

The adolescent male tore into the clearing, his rage fuelled by the deep, painful slashes to his snout. The heat and humidity made them sting and ooze. He let out a menacing snarl as he barrelled towards the three closest lionesses, but he changed direction as they stood up together in readiness to intercept him. Ahead, he spotted a lone lioness carefully herding her three cubs into the long grass. Instinct took over as he thundered towards them, his mind set on death and mating again. The lioness roared back savagely at his approach, but hesitated, lacking the strength to fight him off without help. She braced for the spring and positioned herself between the charging male and the cubs.

The blow came without warning. The male was knocked tumbling and scrabbling into the dust. Before he could regain his feet, she attacked again. She pinned the male down with the natural weight of her front paws, extending the scythe-like claws into his flesh and drowning out his roars with her own. She slashed away at his flank with rakes of her hind feet and the extended, hooked talons on each toe. As she subdued the male with her weight, the thin ridge of greyish black hair along her spine rippled with pent up energy. She opened her mouth wide as she buried her fangs into his throat, picking him up off the floor and dragging him away. She spun, using the momentum to throw the male several feet and onto his back. Before he had time to recover, she sprang onto his back and sank her teeth through the top of his skull.

She paced back and forth, watching the male for any sign of life, growling and snarling with each pass. Eventually satisfied, she looked around at the lionesses surrounding her. Most were on their feet, looking back at her. As one of the cubs bounded up and stood between her legs, she lowered her head to lick it and purred a greeting. She issued a few grunts as she walked off, the others falling in behind her in silent procession.

~

Thomas walked along the trail with Jelani and Badru up ahead of him. He knew Jelani would be trying to glean as much information from the hunter as possible, something he might not be as able to do as a foreigner. They hadn't walked far out of camp before Badru had directed them onto a game trail that led south-east. They soon found the pugmarks of several lions lacing the red dust. The pride was moving slowly, their close-together and splayed tracks belying the casual pace as they walked along.

A little further on, Badru came to a stop and waited for Thomas to reach them.

"They rested in the thicket there," he pointed up the trail.

"Thank you for your help Badru," Thomas replied.

Badru turned and nodded silently before loping back off in the opposite direction. Thomas could tell from his expression that he thought their investigation was a pointless one. As he noticed Jelani's nervous glance, Thomas stepped forward and took the lead. As a precaution, he slipped his rifle from his shoulder and clipped a five-cartridge magazine into the receiver underneath. He chambered a round with a quick snap of the bolt, noticing Jelani had brought up his shotgun too. They cautiously made their way into the thicket.

Thomas was relieved to hear the chatter of weaver birds and the buzz of insects as they made their way through. The pugmarks were harder to follow here, and it was soon clear the lions had split up and taken several different routes through the maze of thorns and thickly entwined branches.

"Stay close," Thomas indicated, as he and Jelani skirted round the broad trunk of an acacia in opposite directions.

"Don't worry," Jelani replied nervously, but with a smile.

Thomas read the ground like a map, stooping as low as he dared as he followed the change in pace and direction of the lions. He was confident he was on the trail of a group of three females, indicated by their relative small size and rounded toes.

"They have cubs," Jelani called out from somewhere to his right.

Thomas wondered how old they were. If they had already

become accustomed to human flesh, then they were as much a danger as their parents.

"How old?" Thomas yelled back.

"Not yet weaned," Jelani replied.

Thomas sighed with relief, pleased that there might still be hope to turn the behaviour of the pride back towards natural prey. He knew that would still mean culling the ones teaching man-eating to the others. And for that to happen, he would have to assess and identify them at close quarters. The handing down of the man-eating trait to other generations, as well as the sheer numbers of the pride, meant relocation was pointless. But he was still determined only the killers would be killed. The rest of the pride could be rehabilitated and protected, of that he was certain. He was just as determined to show that there was nothing supernatural about their behaviour.

He caught sight of Jelani again as he rounded the acacia and stepped into a small clearing. He noticed the tracks clumped together as he glanced back down at the ground. The tracks Jelani was following brought him round towards Thomas again, where they rendezvoused. It was clear the animals had regrouped and come to a halt in the small clearing. They looked around, wondering what might have caught their attention. All of the pugmarks seemed to face east, and as Thomas looked into the distance in that direction, he noticed the clearing was overlooked by a small hill with a single baobab tree, silhouetted against the sun at its crescent shaped top. Thomas wondered if something up there had caught their attention, as there seemed little else to look at in the bleak surroundings.

Silently they continued along the trail until Thomas picked

up the spoor of a male. Judging by the size of the pugmarks, he suspected it was a young, adolescent animal. As Jelani went to take another step, Thomas slapped a hand on his chest to hold him back, making him look up. The cloudless blue sky was strung with the black outlines of gathering vultures, as they circled closer in a slow and cautious descent. Thomas and Jelani stepped forward together, their guns trained on the narrow path ahead.

When they stepped out into another clearing, the warranting of the vultures became immediately apparent. The torn and broken body of a young male lion was strewn across a bloody stretch of gore soaked earth. Thomas felt a great swell of pity as he noticed the short and barely formed mane of the animal and the pale colour of its pelt, almost white rather than the typical golden tawny hue. It had been suggested that the lack of a mane and the unusual colouration were genetic adaptations that helped the Tsavo lions cope with the more arid conditions they lived in, but no one was sure. Thomas examined the wounds on the lion's skull, impressed at the suggested size and skill of the killer.

He paused over the imprinted pugmarks left in the dust in front of the male's body. He recognised them as belonging to the same animal that had stolen the francolin he had shot a few days earlier. He noticed the same narrow, elongated toe pads and overtly large size that had surprised him before. He looked up at Jelani, as if for an explanation.

"In Tsavo there is no king, only a queen," Jelani offered.

Thomas nodded silently.

"All that's missing is the stone table," Thomas replied with a half-felt smile, as he looked over the male's broken body again. "Fancy a walk to the top of that hill to see what got their attention back there?"

"The trail is cold here," Jelani replied. "They have moved into the rocks anyway."

Leaving the body of the dead lion for the vultures, they headed back along the trail to the clearing where they could see the hill. They scrambled up through the scrub until they reached its top, building up a sweat as they did so. There, under the shade of the baobab, they found nothing out of the ordinary except a glorious view of the surrounding hillside. Then Thomas knelt and peered closer at the sticky dust covering the ground. He spread both of his hands out over the two enormous sets of tracks. Two large lions, definitely males this time, had stood side by side and looked down - perhaps at the gathered pride below.

"This is the eastern border of the pride's territory," explained Jelani. "I've never known them to venture beyond here. Perhaps this explains why, and that dead male down there."

"No," Thomas said. "I'm pretty sure your queen got him. But maybe she was making room for someone else."

He stood up, gazing out across the vista.

"Either way," he added, wiping the sweat from his brow and taking off his hat, "there are some new kids on the block, and we don't know if they're friend or foe."

CHAPTER TWELVE

The following morning, Catherine found Thomas sitting alone at the dining table on the kopje, staring at a map of the area. As she walked up behind him, sliding her arms over his shoulders and down onto his chest, she caught the smell of the rich, hot coffee in the enamel cup beside him. He reached up with his right hand to stroke her forearm, but didn't look up.

"I'm surprised to find you out here without Jericho and a beer in your hand," she whispered, planting a kiss on his cheek as she twisted onto his lap. She glanced down at the map too.

Thomas smiled, sitting back a little to accommodate her, as his left hand scooped around her waist to support her.

"No Jericho today," Thomas informed her. "He's been called away to a village in the north, where there's been a report of some elephant poachers. Apparently, they're the same ones he missed in Tanzania, or at least he thinks so."

"You guys are doing an awful lot of work on the wildlife service's behalf don't you think?" Catherine exclaimed.

"You heard them back in Nairobi, they've more than got their hands full at the moment," Thomas replied.

"They're using you, and hiding behind all this superstitious nonsense to do so. And I think you know it too," she scolded, nudging him in the ribs.

"Look, I've got to ask, is that's what's got you so worked up?" Thomas probed, softly. "It's just you seem to be distant one day, on fire the next, and clingy the day after that, if you don't mind me saying so."

"I do mind you saying so," she glowered at him. "But it might have something to do with not really feeling very involved with what you're doing. I'm a wildlife biologist, but I feel like I'm just tagging along. Give me something to do. Maybe I won't be so clingy," she snapped.

"Okay, wrong word maybe," Thomas replied, squeezing her waist affectionately. "I'm just worried that you're not quite yourself. And that's bad for me, as I'm sort of in love with you if you haven't noticed."

"You do hide it well sometimes," she mocked, but she rested her head on his for a moment and wrapped her arms around his shoulders. "So, are you going to tell me why you're staring at a map like it's a magic-eye puzzle?"

"Jelani said something yesterday about the border of the pride's territory. He said they don't venture east past this hill here, where we found tracks of two males." He pointed to a set of contours on the map. "But that's not true; they have appeared almost a mile further east on several occasions, often when they've been pursued. One of the reasons the local villagers think they are demons is because they will suddenly appear on the other side of the river, with nobody knowing how. I'm looking for a logical explanation, but I can't see where they can cross. The gorge is very deep there."

Catherine leaned forward and studied the area Thomas had pointed to. She could see green crosses marked in biro where the lions had been reported, and red ones cataloguing their recent attacks. It was clear the pride avoided the hill and the high ground to the north and east. But just as Thomas described, sightings and attacks were marked again just over a mile down river.

"What kind of rock makes up the gorge?" Catherine asked,

not looking up.

"I think it's mainly volcanic, scoria basalt if my geology isn't too rusty," Thomas replied.

"But also granite too right, this lovely red dust coating everything must come from somewhere?"

"There'll be sandstone in there as well I'm guessing, but I think I see where you're going with this," he said, leaning forward.

They both gazed over the map. Catherine followed the course of the river with her finger, past the hill, where it wound north and east then doubled back to the south again. She paused at a point where the river seemed to widen, not far from where a new grouping of green and red crosses emerged. There was no bend in the river to explain the widening of the channel. She'd learnt to read maps like this as she had progressed with her climbing, looking for clues in the topography that would reveal possible routes and hidden dangers. She looked at Thomas, her eyes flickering with excitement. He caught a hint of smugness too, and he smiled back.

"There's a cave system there, probably a series of lava tubes. They're not crossing the river; they're going over or under it." Catherine stated.

"You think they've taken up spelunking as well as man-munching?" Thomas exclaimed.

"Yes, I do as it happens, and less of the sarcasm. I know I'm right," she mocked confidently.

"Well at least you now know how I feel most of the time," Thomas laughed.

"See how easy things are when I'm involved," she taunted. "Why don't we go and check it out?"

Thomas paused, torn for a moment. He was happy she was acting more like herself, and he did want her to be more involved. He knew they worked best as a team, and that perhaps Jericho being around had overshadowed that. But he also didn't want her exposed to the danger of encountering the pride so directly. Her smile was infectious though, and he knew he'd be in real danger if he even suggested something along the lines of the survival scenario sexism he was considering. He also wasn't a very good climber, and he knew he might need her help navigating through any cave system they happened to discover.

"We'll take the ATVs," he said, giving in and trying to hide the accompanying reluctant sigh. "There are some narrow trails, and the Big Cat won't be able to get up into the rocks, but they might."

They made their way back to the tent hand in hand, where they changed and packed their gear into backpacks. Thomas watched as Catherine threw in a chalk bag and a couple of head torches, as well as the binoculars Thomas had given her. They both grabbed baseball caps and sunglasses before they stepped back outside.

Thomas walked over to the gun rack, putting on the shoulder holster for the Colt Anaconda and tucking it out of sight beneath his safari vest. He filled one of the outer pockets with ammo. He knew Catherine already had the Smith & Wesson tucked away in her pack, keeping it with her just as he had asked her to. He passed her the Marlin rifle before picking up his own and shared out some rounds for each.

They stopped off to see Mansa in the kitchen tent, as they strolled back past. He provided them with two large canteens of water, a large sealed plastic bag of biltong jerky, and another with some dried sliced pineapple and mango. Thomas and Catherine packed them away and then headed over to the ATVs. He showed Catherine how to clip her rifle into the mount on the front of the all-terrain vehicle, a Can-Am Outlander XT-P, as she secured her pack to the rear rack. He then did the same to his own ATV, the exact same model as Catherine's and sporting matching black and orange paintwork.

Thomas threw his leg over the broad saddle and made himself comfortable. He gave Catherine a grin as he turned the key and twisted the throttle in one fluid motion. The 1,000cc engine roared to life instantly, and he let it rip as he tore away down the track, momentarily pulling the front wheels up into a wheelie as he gunned it. Moments later, he heard Catherine's ATV approaching from behind on his left. He turned to look, catching a glimpse of her, shaking her head disapprovingly.

Catherine followed Thomas as he turned south-east, along the same game trail he had traversed the morning before. It was only a little after ten, but already the air was thick with heat and a bead of sweat ran down her forehead, forming into a droplet as it perched on the bridge of her glasses. The ATV bucked slightly as it hit a dip, and the jolt sent the bead cascading down the lens on the right side. She shook her head slightly to clear her vision. As the trail opened up ahead, she hit the accelerator again to catch up with Thomas. He pumped his hand up and down to slow her down as she drew alongside. They trundled to a stop, the ATV engines idling quietly as Thomas pointed into the bushes.

She couldn't quite see it, but she could certainly smell it. Thomas shut down the engine of his ATV as he climbed off, and Catherine followed suit. He led her into the scrub and pulled the Colt Anaconda from its holster as he approached the carcass of the young male. He opened the cylinder and began to feed the 44 magnum shells from his pocket into the empty chambers. He and Catherine weren't the only ones interested in the carcass. A lone hyena removed its bloody snout from a tear along the lion's stomach and looked at them, indifferent to their presence. Thomas pointed the revolver into the air and fired a single shot. The reddish-brown back of the hyena rippled as it snarled, before the animal scampered into the thickly knotted scrub of the thorny acacias surrounding them. Thomas nodded to Catherine to go ahead.

After twenty-four hours in the sun, and having attracted the attention of vultures, jackals, hyenas and even smaller opportunists like honey badgers and mongoose, the split hide, splintered bones and pink sinewy flesh they'd left barely resembled a lion. Catherine knelt close to the carcass, holding her nose to protect against the putrid stench it emanated. Little flurries of black and green jewel-backed flies lifted off the taut, torn skin, invading its interior with a loud and droning buzz that never seemed to stop.

Thomas pointed out the dried blood around the fleshy wounds to the neck and skull. He could see from her wide-eyed expression that she too was surprised by the suggested size of the weaponry that inflicted the damage.

"Are you sure it wasn't one of the big males you were talking about?" Catherine asked. "I've never heard of a lone female killing a male. They just don't have the size or strength."

"I'm sure the pugmarks were that of a female," Thomas nodded. "Jelani called her a queen yesterday, and I know when we encountered them seven years ago, the pride was thought to be mainly made up of lionesses, if not entirely."

"Was she leading the pride then too?" Catherine asked.

Thomas nodded solemnly and looked away.

"Do you think she was the one that killed Amanda?"

"I imagine they all played their part, but I figure she took the lion's share of the blame, if you'll forgive the pun," Thomas replied, choking out a dry, violent laugh. "Sorry, I still don't like talking about it," he admitted, "and I know we don't talk about it enough."

"It's okay," she reassured him. "I'm just worried you carry it around with you. You're probably the strongest man I know, but even you can't bear that kind of weight indefinitely."

He smiled weakly. "Guess that's why we're here," he replied.

"Then let's get to it," Catherine replied positively.

They carefully made their way back through the brush to the ATVs and continued on their way, following the trail as it skirted around the hill that marked the border of the pride's territory. Thomas glanced up to the lone baobab, half expecting to see the silhouette of one of the males keeping vigil from their outpost. But he and Catherine were alone for now it seemed. The lions had moved on.

Thomas remembered tracking mountain lions whilst in Wyoming in the United States. In particular, he recalled a large tom he'd nicknamed Silver, after Long John Silver from Treasure Island, due to an injury that made the cat drag his left hind paw slightly. It made Silver somewhat easier to track than some of the other mountain lions in the same area. Like all predators that maintained a territory, Silver moved around so as not to exhaust the prey in any one area, and to show he was patrolling regularly. The cat had travelled in a rough figure of eight, covering his entire territory once every seven days or so. He wondered if the lions did something similar, and if so, if their wanderings could be predicted or even intercepted. He decided to make a mental note to try and pick up the trail on the other side of the maze of rocks, even over a day old as they were. They still might lead somewhere.

Lost in his thoughts, Catherine had crept ahead of him a little. He smiled as he sat up in the saddle and twisted the throttle. As he began to accelerate, the rumble of the exhaust was answered by something in the brush off to the left. Thomas twisted his head in the same direction to try and pinpoint from what, and where, the noise was coming from. The strained bellow that rose up out of the thorns confirmed it. He caught a glimpse of tough black hide as it shuffled off. The Cape buffalo made grumbling, ranting snorts as it left. Thomas let out a sigh of relief as he passed, glad that one of Africa's most disagreeable residents hadn't taken an interest in them. Then he realised the buffalo had trundled to a stop.

Watching him as he passed, Thomas caught the eye of the buffalo as it expelled a sticky, mucus-drenched breath from its nostrils. It lifted its head, exposing the fused boss of its horns, their curved and deadly tips over a yard apart. Time seemed to stand still, but then the buffalo lurched to the right, crashing through the undergrowth with the momentum of a wrecking ball. Thomas could see the buffalo was on an intercept course with Catherine's ATV, cutting through the thorny acacias and scrub at a steep angle straight towards her. He gunned the throttle, tearing along the track, whilst relying on the buffalo's focus on Catherine to make up some of the distance in safety.

As the black mass of muscle burst into the open, Catherine caught sight of it too. She hadn't heard it over the sound of her engine. Instinctively she hit the gas, speeding up. The buffalo kept coming, close enough now for her to feel the thunderous strike of its hooves as they smashed into the trail alongside her. The animal's stink hit her nostrils just before the beast itself veered towards her in a broadside charge. Catherine hurled herself from the saddle of the ATV, crashing into the underbrush in a cloud of thick red dust. Moments later, the buffalo collided with the black and orange frame of the 4x4, throwing it up into the air before sending it cart-wheeling into the scrub beside her. The engine screamed for a moment as the throttle caught, before spluttering into lifeless silence as the upended wheels kicked and spun in the air.

Thomas juddered to a halt and snapped his rifle up from the front of his ATV. He could see the shiny black back of the buffalo as it began to pace at the side of the trail, its poor eyesight struggling to find its target in the spray of dust. Thomas jumped off the ATV and took a few quick paces to his left to get a better line on the buffalo. As he stepped out onto the trail, the buffalo raised its head again, catching his scent and proclaiming its disgust with an angry snort. Thomas fed a three-and-a-half-inch long brass round into the chamber of the rifle, and took careful aim through the scope. The buffalo was a big bull, nearly eleven feet long and easily 2,000lbs. He lined up the crosshairs about a third of the way up the chest, directly between the front legs. As the bull snorted again and took a step forward, Thomas squeezed the trigger and felt the slam of the rifle against his shoulder, as the 480-grain projectile rocketed towards its target at 2,375 feet per second. There was a wet slap as bullet met flesh, and Thomas lowered the rifle knowing that his shot had smashed into the buffalo with the same power as a racing truck, wrecking the top of the heart where all the major blood vessels connected, before blowing out its lungs for good measure. Only, that's not what happened.

Thomas watched, absolutely stunned as the buffalo stared him down. He saw the fixed gaze of the bull turn from defiant challenge, to deathly, blood curdling rage. As a stream of claret coloured blood and gore spilled from the hole in its chest, the bull stumbled forward into a charge, coming at Thomas like a jet-black missile. The ground seemed to shake as the enraged bovine thundered closer and Thomas raised his rifle again, feeding in a second round. Aiming slightly from the side, Thomas made a snap decision and lined up the sights behind the lowered head of the bull. As it bore down on him, he let off the second shot. It smacked into the buffalo's spine, splintering and severing the bone and nerve column it found there. Thomas rolled out of the way as the bull slumped to the floor, rolling precariously onto its back with its carried momentum. He watched in disbelief as the tumbling corpse smashed into the front of his ATV, crushing the radiator and front suspension as if they were paper, before it flopped to the side in a lifeless slump. He let out a deep sigh before turning around to see what had become of Catherine.

She stood at the side of the trail, dusting herself off. As he ran to her, he could see she had some nasty gashes to her legs and arms, and a shiny red welt on the side of her head. She managed a weak smile as she replaced her dust encrusted cap and pulled at a few stray tufts of her red hair.

"Well I can't say you're as good as new, but are you okay?" Thomas asked, concerned.

"I'll live, I think," she shrugged.

"I'd say he definitely lost his sense of humour about

something, wouldn't you?" Thomas said, looking back at the bull.

"What happened?" Catherine asked. "Did you miss?"

"No," Thomas replied, a little defensive. "Hit him square in the thumper. I've heard stories of Cape buffalo having enough adrenalin and oxygen to cover a hundred yards or so after a heart shot, but that's certainly the first time I've ever experienced it. It certainly adds weight to the saying that there's more lead in the buffalo than the mines around here."

"Do you just attract dangerous animals?" she laughed, wincing slightly. She lifted her T-shirt to reveal a cluster of emerging blue and purple bruises along her side.

"You tell me – you're the one marrying me remember?" he joked softly, kissing her gently on the cheek. "Let's head back and get you seen to. Especially as it looks like we're walking."

"No, let's keep going. It shouldn't be far now, and it's just cuts and bruises. I've had worse," Catherine protested.

"Only if you're sure," Thomas agreed. He could already see her mind was made up.

Thomas retrieved Catherine's rifle from the wrecked ATV and checked it over. It seemed fine, and he slung it over his shoulder along with his own. As he looked back at the dead buffalo, he took out a magazine cartridge from one of his pockets and filled it with five bullets to reload just in case.

They walked along the narrowing trail, Thomas leading the way with regular glances back to check on Catherine. She smiled reassuringly the first few times, but began to wave his attentions away with a shake of the head, and muttering under her breath as it became a little overbearing. In the end, he gave in, and focused on the path ahead. He noticed they had gained a little height as they had trekked along, and he could now see and hear the river a little off to their right and below. As it curved away to the south, they found themselves confronted with a wall of dark volcanic rock, peppered with vesicles.

"That's a good sign," commented Catherine, catching her breath.

"What, that the trail's come to an end?" Thomas asked.

"Nice try handsome," she mocked. "I mean that the rock's porous. Water can find its way through. And you know we're climbing up to check it out, so don't play dumb. I appreciate you're looking out for me, but knock it off."

"Yes Ma'am," Thomas replied reluctantly.

She thumped him in the ribs with her elbow as she passed. The scramble up to the top wasn't difficult. From there, Catherine could see it expanded to the north, waves of lava frozen in time and turned to stone, only revealed after millions of years of erosion to create a rippling and uneven surface. Just as she had suspected, fissures and cracks riddled the rock, some going quite deep. She began to hop from one plate of stone to another, exploring the gullies in between and where they led. A little way across she stopped, and waved Thomas over.

They peered into a dark passage some six feet square and leading down. They both bagged their sunglasses as Catherine knelt and took out the head torches, passing one to Thomas. He hesitated at the entrance. A warm breeze came from within, bringing with it a scent. It was a dense, musk-like odour. It reminded him of dry hay bales that had begun to rot at their bottom with damp. It was the unmistakable calling card of a lion. He placed a restraining hand on Catherine's shoulder and edged past her, slipping her rifle from his shoulder and passing it over as he did so. As he stepped into the shadows, he flicked on the head torch and brought his own rifle up. They stood looking into the mouth of a cave. The only path led down into the darkness.

~

She moved quickly through the scrub. The sweet scent of blood on the breeze enticed her out from the kopje where she had been basking. A guttural huff from her left, beyond a bank of candle bush and whistling acacias, told her the others had caught it to. She loped purposefully through the maze of outcrops and brush, stopping abruptly a few feet from the open trail. She hunkered down into the dust, her ears pivoting in search of sound that would indicate a threat. She froze as a pale, parchment coloured hide stepped out of the scrub a few feet away. She wouldn't normally tolerate a subordinate approaching a kill before her, but this time she was curious. If there was a threat, it would soon reveal itself.

The young lioness stalked the carcass of the buffalo, approaching downwind and crawling on her belly, with her head held just above the ground. She crept forwards, shuffling in quick, silent flurries towards the dead bull. She rushed in from a few feet away, clamping her jaws around the bull's mouth and nostrils as she anchored her claws into its neck for purchase. The bull did not move. Satisfied, the young lioness stood up to her full height, relaxing her stance and flicking her tail casually as she looked back into the grass-thatched scrub.

The big female emerged from the thickly entwined maze of branches behind the bull. She walked past it, holding her head high to catch the smell brought to her on the breeze. It was sweet and honey like, and she purred contentedly as she found a spot to the side of the trail laced with the scent. Her whiskers flexed, involuntarily reaching out towards the magnetic field created by the metallic thing that ticked and hissed at her in the heat. She ignored it. She had seen things like them before in human settlements. She rubbed the scent glands below her eyes and on the side of her head through the dust that still held the honey-like aroma. Then she detected it. Thinly veiled beneath the sweet scent, was a thicker, more acidic odour. She flicked out her tongue, tasting the stronger copper and iron elements within. Blood. Human blood. She grunted a warning to the others, who stood shoulder to shoulder with the young second-in-command around the carcass of the buffalo. Silently, they dispersed back into the brush as they took up their positions for the hunt.

~

Thomas crept along the passage, the only light coming from the head torches he and Catherine wore. Their long shadows reached up onto the stone walls surrounding them, distorted and elongated by the throw of the beams.

"Remember the last time we were in a cave?" Catherine whispered.

"At least this one's warm," Thomas shrugged.

This cave was vastly different to the home of the creature they had discovered in the Highlands of Scotland. There, the air had been thick with moisture, and pools of mineral laden water coated the walls and dripped from the ceiling. This cave was warm and dry, and well ventilated.

"There must be other openings, the breeze is fresh," Catherine commented.

"Still no sign of your river though," Thomas replied.

"Plenty of evidence of something else though," she said pointedly, directing her torch towards the ground.

The prints in the dust were so numerous it was hard to

distinguish them at first, but as Thomas knelt, instinctively stretching out his fingers to gauge their size, he knew they were the pugmarks of numerous lions. There were enough of them going back and forth to suggest that Catherine's theory about the cave system being some kind of underground lion highway was probably right. As he stood up to get going again, he flinched and turned around sharply. He squinted back into the blackness as he listened intently. A knot in the pit of his stomach told him something wasn't right. He raised his rifle, aiming it back up the passage.

~

She watched as the others scaled the rocks in total silence. They made easy jumps up onto the black basalt slabs. They instinctively split up, spreading out over the barren surface and disappearing into the cracks, squirming and wriggling through the narrow openings to drop down into the maze of corridors beneath. As they stepped into the darkness, the pupils of their eyes reacted to the light by rapidly expanding, drinking in eight times the available luminosity of a human eye. A membrane behind the lens concentrated the weak light onto the back of the retina, helping paint the dark interior of the cave complex in bluish-green tones that illuminated their path. They began to pick their way through the passageways, following the warm breeze that brought them the scent of their prey.

As she took a few steps forward, a subordinate brushed her flank lightly, in an attempt to get past. She recognised it as one of the younger lionesses, and that it was excitement that fuelled her urge to drive ahead rather than a desire to dominate. Nevertheless, a barge of her shoulder and a warning snarl put the adolescent in its place. She paused, bristling with pent up energy as she listened to the echo reverberate into the darkness ahead.

~

Thomas took a few steps back, swinging the barrel of his rifle slowly back and forth as he went. The snarl had confirmed what he'd feared, that they were no longer alone in the cave. But the sound had triggered other echoes, muffled growls and scrabbling that trickled through the rock towards them. There must be other openings along the passage, he thought as his mind raced.

"Let's get moving," Catherine suggested, pulling at his arm. "Do you think it's the lions?"

"I don't think it's mice, put it that way," nodded Thomas. "I don't think we're very welcome."

"I think we're lunch if we don't move," Catherine replied. "It's too enclosed here to greet them appropriately."

Thomas followed Catherine, who now also trained her rifle ahead of her. They moved quickly, ducking low overhangs and glancing back frequently. The lions were undoubtedly getting closer, but so was something else. Catherine paused for a moment.

"Do you hear that? It's water," she exclaimed.

"And hopefully that way out you predicted," Thomas nodded.

They continued on, feeling their way along the walls as they followed the sound of bubbling, rushing water. Then Catherine came to a halt, in front of a round opening that formed a tunnel about four feet high and three feet across. Now, above the sound of the running water, was the dull echo of a roar. But it didn't come from the lions behind them. Instead, the sound reverberated along the tunnel from the chamber beyond. Catherine ducked and began to creep along the passageway. Thomas did the same, bumping his head slightly as he found the ceiling a little lower than he'd expected. He followed Catherine along the claustrophobic tunnel until they emerged onto a red-grained sandstone ledge. As they peered over the lip, it became clear where the sound of the roar emanated from. A rich turquoise waterfall dropped from an almost perfectly spherical opening in the rock beside them, crashing into a foaming pool some forty feet below. From there, they could see the winding channel that led away to the south-east.

Catherine walked right up to the lip and leaned over. She glanced back at Thomas with a mischievous smile. But he didn't have time to return it. He spun on his heels, ripping back the bolt of his rifle to feed a cartridge into the chamber. As he knelt, the beam of his head torch revealed a shadow creeping towards them through the passage, and the dull reflection of two amber discs at its centre. Thomas didn't hesitate to fire, aiming at a spot he imagined to be about two inches above the centre of the lion's eyes. The shadow slumped to the floor instantly, only to be engulfed by a second silhouette behind it. This time there was no eye shine to guide his shot, but he aimed high and let off a second round. The report of the rifle was answered with a savage roar, and Thomas saw the second lion jump backwards, crashing and scrabbling against the ceiling and the sides of the tunnel. He worked the bolt quickly and followed up with a third blast, this time aiming lower at what he hoped was the chest cavity. Evidently his shot was on target, as he watched the animal flop onto its back, on top of the first lion, and caught in the spine twisting death throes and limb spasms only a heart shot could produce. With the entrance to the tunnel momentarily plugged with the bodies of the two lions, he turned back to Catherine.

She was eyeing another ledge on the other side of the waterfall, about ten feet away from them. It appeared to lead to a path that headed down, along the wall of the cavern.

"The way I see it, we have two choices," she observed. "First, we take a running jump onto that ledge, then make our way down and try to find a way out at ground level. The only problem with that is if the lion's follow us, they're as capable as we are of reaching that path."

"What's the second option?" Thomas asked, already suspecting he knew the answer.

"We take the express route. We jump into the pool, and follow the river. That's our way out," she replied in a matter of fact tone.

"Of this life?" Thomas exclaimed.

She eyed him calmly, with her hands on her hips, as he too peered over the edge.

"How do we know the pool is deep enough?" Thomas asked.

"We don't," she shrugged, "but would you rather the alternative?"

Thomas glanced back towards the tunnel. He could hear scuffling and clawing echoing along the chamber. Something was trying to scrabble its way past the dead lions. He looked up into the numerous cracks and fissures surrounding them. He could imagine a lion emerging from any one of them just as easily.

"Okay, we'll jump. But we'll have to stow the rifles here and come back for them. They won't take kindly to a dip. The revolvers will be okay though," he sighed, giving in.

He searched around quickly for a crevice that was large enough to hold the guns, and he slipped them inside on top of each other. As he turned, he saw the look of horror on Catherine's face. His eyes immediately shot to the entrance of the tunnel. A pale, straw coloured head emerged out of the darkness. A pair of amber eyes met his, but he was already running across the ledge towards Catherine. As the lioness dragged herself clear of the tunnel, Thomas followed Catherine's lead as they leapt together from the ledge.

Time seemed to stand still as they fell feet first towards the violently foaming water. Thomas could hear nothing as he watched the surface of the water rush up to greet him. As they hit the pool, the world erupted into sound once more as the waterfall engulfed them. The icy sting of the water's touch froze his muscles. They both went deep, bubble trails escaping from their clothing as they sank momentarily into the centre of the pool. Then he felt a slight tug that lifted his body and pulled him along. There was a mild current, and it was carrying him. His head broke the surface and he took a large gulp of air. He spotted Catherine's white T-shirt ahead of him. She too was letting the current do the hard work for her, practically surfing as she used her arms to position herself dynamically in the water. Thomas wasn't quite so graceful, floating along on his back and holding his head out of the water so he could keep track of Catherine. He craned his head back towards the ledge, meeting the stony gaze of the lioness as she watched them disappear from sight.

As the current swept them round a slight bend, they were greeted by a wall of rock ahead. The tributary they were in seemingly flowed straight into it. Thomas saw Catherine begin to swim urgently to the side, where she clung to a lip of rock. He followed and soon joined her.

"Are you okay?" Catherine asked him.

"Well we're not dead yet and I'm enjoying the swim," he grinned.

Catherine nodded and began feeling her way along the edge until she reached the rock face, where the water disappeared. She braced herself against it, and the current, as she explored below the waterline with her fingertips. Then she made her way back to Thomas.

"Okay, it looks like the water flows beneath the rock here," she explained. "I'm just guessing from what I saw on the map, but I don't think it goes far, and there may be places where the chamber opens up and we'll be able to breathe."

Thomas looked around. There were no tangible hand holds to climb the sheer walls of basalt around them, polished smooth by the passage of the tributary over countless millennia.

"Unfortunately, I don't think we have much choice at this point," Thomas replied.

They stared into each other's eyes as they took a series of deep breaths. As a thunderous roar echoed throughout the chamber, they both ducked underneath the water and the wall of rock above them. Thomas felt the difference in pressure immediately as the current swept them into a dark tunnel. His natural buoyancy dragged him up to the surface, where he bumped his head against the stone ceiling. Tumbling through the water, he lost his bearings, unsure of which way was up. He calmed himself as he shut his eyes and felt his body being pulled along again by the current. Only the current had fingers, and was dragging him to the surface. Moments later, he took a long gasp of air as he found himself looking up into a sun filled sky, and Catherine stroking his hair and supporting him from beneath. He let the tips of his shoes pop up out of the water as he stretched back and winked at her.

"I think I'm done drowning for the day," he smiled.

"That's a nasty bash you took back there, your head's bleeding," she cooed, wiping away a crimson-matted clump of hair from his forehead. "Looks like we're swimming for a while, but the good news is that it's not too deep and there's hardly any undertow."

Thomas lifted his head as they drifted along slowly. The banks of the river were steep cliffs of slippery mud, backed by the solid walls of a canyon. Catherine was right, they wouldn't be leaving the river just yet.

The mild current swept them through a bend, and up ahead Thomas could see where the tributary joined the main river. He smiled at her.

"Hard being right all the time, is it?" Thomas mused.

"No, it comes quite naturally," Catherine smirked.

He noticed that she hadn't yet released her grip on him, and was keeping their movements to a minimum. Her gaze patrolled the banks of the river, presumably for an opening where they might be able to scramble ashore he thought. But he also knew she was as aware as he was that African rivers were not the safest of places to take a dip. She was instinctively trying not to draw any attention to their passage.

As he looked about him, Thomas began to recognise parts of the landscape. A large tower of red sandstone marked a bend in the river he knew wasn't too far from a crossing that led to the camp. As they passed it, he fumbled beneath the surface of the water for the Colt in its holster, under his safari vest. He took it out and held it high in the air. One of the things he appreciated about the classic revolver design was its reliability. He hadn't wanted to take the rifles into the water because he knew the wooden stocks were likely to expand and become misshapen. But the Colt and the Smith & Wesson he'd given Catherine were not only able to survive a dunking, they could even fire underwater and still be lethal to several feet. He figured they were close enough for the shots to be heard from camp. He fired off a round as they skirted the bend, listening to the echo as it ricocheted down the canyon and dissipated into nothing. He then fired again and waited for silence before squeezing off a third shot. He knew the first shot would have gotten the attention of anyone back at camp, whereas the second and third would hopefully let them know roughly where they were, and direct their attention towards the river gorge.

He felt Catherine's grip around his chest suddenly tighten, and he instinctively looked to the shoreline sixty feet behind them. The three Nile crocodiles squatted motionless on the bank, their jaws open as they basked in the afternoon sun. Their olive green and sulphurous yellow armoured hides shone brightly, peppered by black spots along their flanks and bellies. Thomas admired their beauty almost as much as their ability as apex predators. Second only in size to their salt water cousins, Thomas guessed each of the reptiles to be between twelve and thirteen feet long, about average size for a male.

Small gangs of male crocodiles weren't uncommon, especially on the borders of territories of larger males, like the one they had encountered a few days before with the elephants. Nile crocodiles were one of the most social species of their kind. Food resources and basking spots were often shared like this, but always to a strict hierarchy determined by size. Larger and older males often staked claims on quiet pools or stretches of river abundant with prey or females, but that didn't stop them joining their smaller brethren when presented with an opportunity, such as when migrating herds forded the rivers. Nile crocodiles were more than happy to share the bounty, as long as the largest of them got their share first. They had even been known to hunt cooperatively.

As if to confirm the subject of his thoughts, the largest of the three crocodiles turned its head in their direction. It raised itself up slightly, taking a wobbly step forwards. It paused, awkwardly balancing on three legs as it contemplated Thomas and Catherine, as they ebbed further away in the embrace of the river. Like lightening, the torpedo shaped reptile shot forward, slipping down a smoothly worn slide into the water that the crocodiles had clearly used many times. The clumsiness and apparent lethargy of the reptile on land was replaced by a lithe and streamlined agility in the water. It streaked towards them with powerful and purposeful beats of its tail. About thirty feet from them, it submerged submarine-like and disappeared from the surface.

"Quick," yelled Thomas, "dive under."

"What?" Catherine yelled back.

"Crocodiles don't like to attack underwater, dive, now," Thomas commanded.

Catherine took a deep breath and then dove beneath the surface, and he watched the glimmer of her white T-shirt fade as she sank. He quickly followed suit, as the two other crocodiles slipped into the river. The water was relatively clear, with visibility good to about fifteen to twenty feet. Thomas let himself sink naturally, and he hung suspended about a foot from the sandy bottom of the river, right next to Catherine. The first crocodile emerged out of the greenish fog ahead of them. It slowed, splaying its feet wide to anchor itself in the water. It seemed unsure of the behaviour of the potential prey. Thomas watched as Catherine began to lower herself further in the water, holding herself off the bottom with her forearms. He noticed as she gripped a clump of river grass and fought to stop herself rising in the current. The crocodile turned away, disappearing back into the pea soup behind. Catherine turned to Thomas and pointed up to the surface.

Their heads broke the water together, and both swivelled to see if they could see the crocodiles. The three animals were now logging, lying stationary in the water as they observed them. Thomas and Catherine let themselves drift along the river a little way, but the crocodiles followed, carried along with them by the river. Thomas was the first to notice they were edging closer. The reptiles guided themselves towards their prey with tiny undulations of the tips of their tails, homing in as they regarded Thomas and Catherine with unblinking celadon eyes. Thomas signalled to Catherine as they ducked under again.

Thomas knew that crocodiles could not focus very clearly underwater. Their eyes were protected by deployable nictitating membranes that acted like natural goggles. But although the thick lens of the nictitates did allow some vision submerged, it was considerably restricted compared to their excellent eyesight above water. Most species preferred to ambush prey from close by, lying in wait at the edge of a pool as animals came to drink. But rules always had exceptions, and he knew Niles were highly capable fish hunters, which meant they could hunt underwater if they wanted to. It was Thomas and Catherine's rough shape and size that made the crocodiles both hesitant and interested in them at the same time. It was more than possible they thought he and Catherine were strange and unusual crocodiles.

Thomas dove under again, fighting his impulse to swim away as hard as he could. The energetic splashing that would entail would definitely bring the crocodiles in. Catherine joined him, sticking close, but unable to hold her breath for quite as long this time. It was as Catherine moved up again to the surface that he saw the smears of blood that stained her clothing, at the same time reminding him of his own scratches and scrapes. The crocodiles were not going to give up their interest in them. He knew the olfactory lobes of the Niles were especially large, giving them not only an exceptional sense of smell but also the processing power to separate a scent from a conglomerate of source and track it down, such as with blood in the water. Fairly impressive for a brain the size of a golf ball Thomas thought.

Another thought crept into his mind as they surfaced again. Whether the crocodiles thought they were of the same species or not, the blood was a problem. Blood told other animals around you that you were weak, perhaps even vulnerable. And crocodiles were cannibals. Smaller, lone animals often wound up the meals of larger, more dominant ones. As he glanced back, he could see the crocodiles were growing bolder, closing the distance between them. Crocodiles were excellent problem solvers. They watched and learnt the behaviour of their prey. A crocodile might lie in wait at a village waterhole for several weeks, watching the women wade in to collect the water. Once they had the schedule down, so went the victim. The three crocodiles were clearly now anticipating Thomas and Catherine's regular trips to the surface and using the opportunity to slip within striking distance.

Just as he began to panic, he heard shouts from downstream. He turned to see Jericho, Jelani and several men standing at the edge of a river crossing. Jericho's Jeep stood in about a foot of water as he leaned up against it.

"Crocs," Thomas shouted, pointing upriver to the approaching reptiles.

Jericho's jovial smile was replaced by a look of stricken sternness. He reached through the open window of the car and pulled out a black, pistol gripped shotgun. It looked like something out of a science fiction movie. As Jericho began to wade towards them, Thomas dove and pushed Catherine ahead of him, towards the protection of the others, and spinning around as he sensed the movement of water behind him. The crocodile shot toward him like a torpedo, but his sudden movement surprised it and it broke off the charge. It lurched to its right, after the trail of bubbles left in Catherine's wake. He got a good look at the thirty or so teeth on the left-hand side of the croc's mouth, set in its fixed characteristic smile. It almost seemed smug as it gazed at him from the corner of its eye, sweeping past him in a lazy and confident glide. Thomas pulled the big Colt revolver free from the holster, and used both hands to aim it squarely at the side of the reptile's head, less than two feet from him. There was an explosion of bubbles from the barrel, followed by a sudden jerk and thrashing from the crocodile. The twelve-foot reptile rolled in the water, spewing gore and blood from its eye socket as it thrashed wildly. Its movements stopped as it began to sink, and convulsions gripped its limbs.

Thomas almost dropped his gun as he found himself grabbed from behind. He first thought one of the other crocodiles had flanked him, but he realised he'd already had far too long to think about it as he was dragged from the water by Jelani and one of his men. He was about to let out a sigh of relief, when the elongated, triangular green head of the second crocodile burst from the water, jaws agape, and filled with gleaming white teeth as it rocketed towards him. He found himself stunned and disorientated, as the top of its head exploded in a crimson spray of foam and flesh. His ears were left ringing as the dead reptile slumped into the mud in front of him. Jericho stepped up on his left, not hesitating to send another charge into the wrecked skull of the croc, obliterating it like a sledgehammer hitting a watermelon.

"Christ Jericho, you don't do subtle do you," Thomas exclaimed, as the Irishman dragged him to his feet.

"This is the DP-12 double-barrelled pump action shotgun," Jericho grinned. "It's machined from a single piece of aircraft grade aluminium. I like to keep it handy for close encounters with poachers, but I made an exception for my new luggage here."

Thomas watched the third croc appear a little way upriver, heading back alone to its slip with fast, methodical beats of its tail. He glanced over at Catherine, who he noticed was trembling. He leaned up against the tailgate of the Jeep with her as they were brought a blanket.

"It's just the cold," Catherine whispered meekly.

She was almost as white as her drenched T-shirt. All her hardness and survival instincts had evaporated within the embrace of their safe surroundings.

"And the adrenaline," Thomas added. "I'm pretty sure I'd have died a couple of times today if it wasn't for you keeping a cool head."

"It looks like you nearly did anyway," Jericho exclaimed, nodding at Thomas's bloodstained forehead and Catherine's various scrapes. "What the hell happened to the two of you?"

"Oh you know," Thomas shrugged with a flippant grin. "Buffalo, man-eating lions, waterfalls, crocodiles. The usual."

"In that case you look grand," Jericho replied with a wink.

CHAPTER THIRTEEN

The camp became a hive of activity over the next few hours. Jelani organised trailers for the Big Cat and the Warthog, as well as the film crew's Toyota, in order to retrieve the stricken ATVs, the lions, and the added windfall of the buffalo Thomas had shot. Each vehicle was filled with men from the camp, as both protection in case the lions returned and through excited curiosity. Kelly, Mason and Karni filmed and recorded Thomas as he led Jericho, Jelani and a few of the men into the cave system to retrieve the rifles. They found the two dead lionesses at the entrance of the tunnel that led to the waterfall, shoved aside but unmolested by the rest of the pride. The men chattered nervously as they stretchered the corpses back out into the sunlight, where they were immediately joined by the others. Whoops and cheers went up followed by happy shouts and claps. Jericho gave Thomas a congratulatory slap on the back whilst he tried to ignore the camera.

"Maybe next time take a radio," Kelly suggested, sidling up to Thomas amongst the throngs of men. "Or even better, your film crew."

"It was just meant to be a reconnaissance trip, but obviously, things didn't quite go to plan," Thomas replied defensively, "but you're right. I didn't think things through. I still wouldn't have brought you though," he smirked.

"Two's company huh," Kelly replied. "Just how is Catherine coping with all this and you being the centre of attention again?"

"Wow Kelly, you can take the girl out of the tabloids but

171

not the tabloids out of the girl, is that it?" Thomas accused her. "I thought we'd moved on from that?"

"I meant it genuinely and off the record," replied Keelson, clearly a little hurt and taken back by his remark. "I know I'm struggling to keep my head straight with everything that has happened so far, and I'm your producer. I've been on the front line numerous times before. Catherine hasn't."

"Sorry, I know you're right," Thomas said with a sigh. "But I did get hit in the head today in my defence, and it's been a long one. You can film us going over our plans and take as many shots of the dead lions as you want. The villagers are bound to visit the camp to see them too. They won't believe we've killed two of them."

"You've killed two of them you mean," Kelly corrected with a smile as she turned and walked away.

As he'd predicted, news of the two dead lionesses spread quickly. By the time they rolled back into camp, a large crowd had gathered. Villagers from miles around had trekked to see the bodies of the two man-eaters. As Jelani and his men laid their corpses gently onto the ground, Thomas felt a slight pang of remorse. He didn't take a life lightly, any life, and if it wasn't for the bloody entry wounds of his bullets, he could have been forgiven for thinking the two females were sleeping peacefully. *Maybe they are in a way* he thought.

Jelani had to keep the crowd back, as many of those who had come were relatives of victims of the pride. They were looking to take souvenirs from the bodies, as was their tradition. For others, they believed that great magic was contained in the teeth and claws of the two demons that lay before them, and wearing them in the form of a necklace or charm would give them great power. Keelson, Mason and

Karni were kept busy with taking stock footage as the crowds came and went. Then, tired and irritable, as well as a little disgusted by the lack of respect and feeling dismissive of the superstitious clamouring, Thomas took out the Colt from the holster and fired a deafening shot into the air. Silence fell upon the camp as all eyes, frozen and wide in shock, turned towards him.

"Show's over," Thomas grunted.

Catherine emerged from the tent at the sound of the gunshot, and he suddenly realised it was the first time he had seen her since they'd returned from the cave. She had clearly washed and changed. She wore a sea green V-neck T-shirt that matched her eyes and made them glisten in the light of the early evening sun. As she shimmied over to him, he felt his boiling blood cool and his heartbeat drop a little. She pressed against him, running the back of her index finger down the bare skin between his collar bone and the top of his chest.

"You're exhausted, and you smell. Go do something about it," she whispered.

Thomas let out a deep sigh.

"Sorry folks, I promise I won't shoot any of you," he called out. A few of the gathered villagers laughed, albeit nervously.

Jericho walked over to him and casually took the gun and holster from him.

"Just to be sure," he winked assuredly.

Thomas shuffled off to the nearest bath hut, stripping off as soon as he was inside. He noticed the fresh towels Mansa had left in a pile on the table the other side of the woven screen. He switched the water on and stepped in without waiting for it to heat up. The shower was bracing, but not uncomfortable after sitting stored in tanks all day. It refreshed his senses, and he felt his knotted muscles begin to soften and untie as the water grew warmer. He let the beads hammer against his skin for a while, before he reached for the bottle of Trumper's shower gel from his wash bag. He cleaned himself carefully, paying extra attention to his cuts and bruises.

His shower over, he tip-toed carefully back to the tent wrapped in one of the towels, thankful that the crowd had dissipated and the camp was relatively quiet and clear again. As he entered, he found Catherine waiting for him, sitting on the bed with an open first aid kit.

"Lie down on the bed," she commanded softly with a purr.

"Absolutely," he grinned, letting the towel slip.

"Cold, was it?" Catherine remarked, raising one eyebrow.

He laughed as she deftly flipped him over onto his front. She climbed onto the bed, pinning his legs between hers as she did so. She dragged the first aid kit over to her and began to clean the cuts with rubbing alcohol. When she was happy they had been disinfected, she got up off the bed. Thomas sat up as she dressed the wound on the side of his head properly. She fussed over him in silence until she was satisfied.

"All done," she smiled. "I've already done mine."

"Oh, I was quite looking forward to returning the favour," Thomas exclaimed with a grin.

"Yep, you're fine," Catherine laughed with a shake of her head. "Needed to be done though. There are things in the water here other than crocodiles, and just as dangerous in some cases."

"I know," Thomas nodded.

"Come on, dinner's nearly ready and Jericho wants to swap war stories so he can look good in front of Kelly."

"Heaven help her," Thomas replied.

He grabbed a clean shirt and a pair of cargo shorts. He dressed quickly and slipped on some sandals before walking out to join the others. He was pleased to see Kelly and Mason had joined them too.

"Where's Karni?" Thomas enquired.

"Still finishing the editing and sound tweaks from today's footage," Kelly explained.

The group had dragged their chairs from the table to sit around the fire pit. A pile of logs cracked and fizzed as a warm breeze fed the flames. As Thomas found a place to sit, Mansa appeared, carrying a tray of pink cocktails.

"Ladies and gentlemen, you have a choice of watermelon margaritas or a non-alcoholic pomegranate Mojito. Enjoy your sundowners," Mansa informed them politely, offering the tray round with a little bow.

Thomas took a margarita, taking a refreshing sip and savouring the taste of the salt-encrusted lip of the glass and the splash of lime that held it there. He noticed Catherine take the non-alcoholic option. She sat quietly, sipping on the red coloured straw deep in thought. His own were interrupted by Jericho's enthusiastic chinking of his glass.

"Cheers my old Bwana, two down, lots more to go," he grinned.

"Down the hatch my friend," Thomas replied. "I'm surprised you didn't bring some of that awful Irish stuff you call whiskey."

"I did," Jericho laughed with a cocky tilt of the head. "We'll get to that after dinner."

After Mansa served hors d'oeuvres of snapper crudo with chilli and sesame seeds, the conversation soon turned back to the man-eaters. Kelly seemed keen to get the original story of the Tsavo lions on camera, and Jericho obliged her willingly. Thomas watched Catherine quietly as the Irishman began to regale the group with the tale of Colonel John Henry Patterson, and the war he waged on the two male lions known as the Tsavo man-eaters.

"It was in March 1898 that good old John Henry rocked up in Tsavo to build a bridge as part of the great Uganda railroad," Jericho began. "He should have maybe taken note that the name means slaughter in the language of the Akamba people, as shortly after he arrived, so did a pair of man-eating lions. When the first lot of coolies went missing, being the obedient imperialist he was, he simply put it down to the natives misbehaving. But three weeks in, one of his jemadar, a Sikh, was plucked from his tent one night and dragged off."

"What's a jemadar?" Keelson asked.

Thomas noticed Mason had casually set up the camera on a tripod the other side of them, purposefully capturing the group through the flickering flames they were gathered around. He leaned back out of shot and let Jericho continue with his story.

"Well, John Henry was a British Army Officer, originally stationed in India. And many of his workers were Indians. A jemadar was a rank within the British Indian Army. They assisted British Commanders and were often in charge of troops. J. H used them in the same way to keep order in the work camps," Jericho explained. "But as the good colonel tracked the paw prints of the lion and the drag marks of the unfortunate Sikh's legs, he discovered the first of many strange behaviours the man-eaters adopted. This lion stopped several times with his still live victim to lick off the skin and drink the blood."

"That's hard to believe," Catherine interjected, sitting forward.

"To be fair, it's what Patterson states in his account," Thomas remarked in Jericho's defence. "And he later found at least two bodies that had missing skin, with the flesh left dry as if it had been sucked."

"Anyway," Jericho continued. "When they found the unfortunate first victim, his body had been torn to pieces, literally ripped apart. That's when they discovered a second lion was involved. At this point, our hero took up his favourite unsuccessful method of hunting man-eaters; sitting in a tree with a goat tied beneath it. He realised shortly after midnight, as a terrifying scream pierced the night and abruptly stopped, that our two boys had no interest in goats."

Jericho finished his drink and wiped his mouth with his sleeve, before carrying on with the story.

"Now, the lions weren't exactly hardened killers yet. Their next appearance was a slightly comical one. They burst into the tent of a Greek trader, grabbed his mattress and ripped it out from under him, carrying it off into the night without harming a hair on his head. One of them also tripped over the ropes of Patterson's own tent. It all sound's amusing to us, but the workers in the camp had another explanation. They believed the lions to be possessed by the spirits of two angry chieftains who had not yet grown used to their new bodies. The natives named them The Ghost and The Darkness."

"Not according to the Field Museum of Chicago they didn't," Catherine retorted. "That was all down to Hollywood."

"Well it sounds better than specimen number I don't recall and specimen number I don't give a damn," Jericho grinned.

"You also have to remember that the natives were dismissed by Patterson as primitive and superstitious. He would not have taken the names they gave the lions very seriously," Jelani offered. "I believe the names were those given. It is common for the people to christen animals like them as such."

Catherine sat back, slightly annoyed. Thomas couldn't help smiling as he watched her simmer as Jericho started his story once more.

"But as with all killers, practice makes perfect. Patterson's problems really started when the main body of workers moved to the other side of the river, leaving him with a single encampment of just a few hundred men. It was like he'd opened up a supermarket for the man-eaters, a virtual one stop all-you-can-eat buffet. The men built huge thorn barricades, kept fires burning and set up noise makers in the trees. Nothing deterred the lions and it was then that they carried out one of their most famous attacks. When the main camp upped sticks, they left behind their old hospital, and they hit it, no doubt drawn to the smell of blood and decay within. They carried off one man and left two severely mauled in their wake. Ever practical, Patterson has a new, clean hospital constructed. Still clinging to the hope the lions will get nostalgic, he then lay in wait at the abandoned site hoping they might revisit. Alas, they did hit the hospital again, but it was the fresh new one over a mile away. Patterson's only company that night were the mortifying screams and cries of the hospital staff and patients."

Jericho paused for a moment, savouring the silence of his audience, who were now completely gripped by the story. He gave a quick wink to Thomas, who eyed him with a shrewd and knowing smile.

"So, up goes hospital number three. They certainly needed it by all accounts. That's when Patterson decided to get creative. He arranges for a covered goods wagon to be placed on a siding, close to the second abandoned site. He also convinces the good Doctor, who by now probably wants to be anywhere but the hospital, to join him for an armed vigil from said wagon. They add the temptation of some cattle for bait and after dinner, walk over a mile in the dark to set up shop and get comfy. That there and then darlin', is why I'm happy to claim Patterson would have proved positive on the idiocy spectrum," Jericho nodded in Catherine's direction. He continued.

"Unfortunately for Patterson and the Doctor, his workers weren't so foolhardy, and completely ignored his orders to block the entrance to what was to be their protection, a fence of thorns known as a boma. They weren't going out after dark it seemed. And as Patterson peers from the open top half of the goods wagon, wondering why the lions have not visited the hospital again, he thinks he sees something crawling through the darkness towards them. Only as the lion springs is it revealed, and only the double rapport of their rifles saves them, surprising the lion and causing it to swerve away back into the night. But that did enough to give the lions pause for thought, and Tsavo became a relatively peaceful area again for a while."

"Apart from the little matter when his men tried to kill him," Jelani added with a deep and infectious laugh.

"Can't blame them for trying, it wasn't like they were getting hazard pay," Jericho shrugged.

"You mean there's hazard pay?" Jelani exclaimed with

179

another burst of laughter.

"No," said Thomas and Jericho together, shaking their heads in stern mockery.

"Anyway," Jericho continued, sitting forward, "having gotten nothing more than a good look at the man-eaters, the colonel gets serious and puts together a trap made from railway sleepers, tram rails, telegraph wire and heavy chain; basically, the raw materials he had at his disposal to build a railroad. The trap was split into two compartments, one for human bait, and the other intended for the brothers grim. Each section was separated by iron rails set three inches apart, keeping the bait safe. Patterson did offer himself up as the potential meal for several nights, but the only things interested in dining on him were mosquitoes, and he was forced to eventually seek rest. He didn't know at the time, but the lions had taken to hitting some camps ten miles away, and didn't return to Tsavo for a few months. But when they did, they did so in style. Every night, Patterson would lie in wait for them, listening to their murderous roars reach ever closer, only to grow suddenly silent. Then, inevitably, the night would be pierced by screams. The mangled, haunting cries of his workers, each night from a different place. He called it their reign of terror."

Jericho let out a deep sigh as he paused and looked into the fire for a moment.

"Many hunters, as well as Naval and Army officers, ventured up from Mombasa to assist him, but all left empty handed. As for the workers, they were now absolutely convinced the lions were the devil incarnate, and pleaded with John Henry to give up trying to shoot them, seeing it as pointless like. The lions also changed their tactics. Whereas

180

before they had been happy with a single victim between them, they now insisted on one apiece at each strike. Eventually and inevitably, the workers deserted the camp, with only Patterson's personal staff and those of the station at Tsavo remaining. The good colonel's nightly vigils recommenced, but the closest he got was on two occasions being within earshot of the lions as they dined. But a few nights later, with hired guns now manning his trap, one of the lions entered. Unfortunately, its reputation well and truly preceded it, and the men in the trap were so terrified that their barrage of shots did nothing, except hit the chain link that held the door in place, thus allowing Simba to escape."

"Nice to know we're not the only ones who have trouble with man-eaters," Catherine whispered to Thomas.

He gave a tired shrug of acceptance in reply.

"After that, things do get a little spooky," Jericho continued. "A few mornings after the fiasco with the trap, J.H is greeted by one of his men sprinting down the road, nervously looking behind him as he approaches. He tells the colonel that the lions sprang on a group of men just a short distance away, but missed and took one of their pack-donkeys instead. Having been left a heavy rifle by one of his comrades, he snatches it up and dashes off in the direction the man came from. He discovers the lions a little way off in the brush, but the snap of a rotten branch underfoot gives him away and they retreat into a thicket. Close to going mad at this point, John Henry gathers his men with oil drums, tin cans, and anything that can make noise so they can beat the brutes out of the thicket. He skirts the brush and waits as the beaters approach. Suddenly, out into the open steps a huge, maneless lion. Distracted by the noisemakers, the lion fails to notice him until he is about fifteen yards away and Patterson raises his rifle. Absolutely astonished, the lion throws itself back on its haunches with a savage growl. Cocky and confident, Patterson covers the beast's brain and pulls the trigger. But nothing happens. All he hears is the cold, dull snap of a misfire."

"This is the bit I find almost unforgiveable," Thomas remarked to the others, leaning forward.

"And why I think the good colonel was more of a gifted idiot than a skilled hunter," Jericho added. "So astonished and horrified by the misfire, he lowers his rifle to reload, completely forgetting he has a second barrel ready to go. The lion is so disturbed by the approaching din that he springs into the thicket instead of at John Henry, which gives the great hunter just enough time to remember why it's called a double rifle. He gets off a shot, and it is answered by an angry roar that can only mean the lion has been hit. Patterson jumps onto the trail after him, but loses him in a rocky maze."

"Sounds a little too familiar after today," Catherine sighed.

"Anyway, perhaps a little maddened by the continued luck of the lions compared to the Irish, J.H decides to stake out the abandoned and only partially eaten carcass of the donkey," Jericho added. "And to do so, he constructs a machan, a plank of wood supported by four poles stuck into the ground and inclined towards each other at the top. Come sundown, he climbs up and settles in for the night, a mere twelve feet from the ground, which is well within a lion's reach if it was really motivated I might add. Hours into his lonely vigil, just as he his fighting off sleep, he hears the approach of something large through the bush. Tense with nervous energy and still as a statue, he listens as it comes closer. When it lets out a deep sigh of hunger, he knows for sure it is a lion. It takes a few more steps then stops in its tracks. Silence ensues, only for the night to be penetrated by an angry and menacing growl. Patterson realises his presence has been detected. But instead of making off back into the brush, the lion begins to stalk him instead. For the next two hours, John Henry listens to the man-eater circle the machan, gradually edging closer as it does."

A smouldering log at the bottom of the fire pit, almost reduced to just glowing embers, finally cracked with a fountain of sparks, as the pile on top broke its burnt-through fibres. It distracted Jericho, who seemed lost in thought as he stared into the flames for a moment before continuing.

"The good colonel did know enough about man-eaters not to move though. He lay as still as a statue, all the while expecting the sudden rush of the lion as it either brought the platform down to the ground, or reached for him in a leap. As he feels a jolt on the back of his head, he almost screams, thinking death has found him. But as the moments pass, he realises that his lack of movement has allowed an owl to mistake his outline for a perch. But his involuntary flinch is enough to produce a sinister snarl from close by. As John Henry turns in the direction it comes from, he can just about make out the lion's ghostly form against the white underbrush of the acacias. He brings up his rifle and pulls the trigger without a second's hesitation. An almighty roar shakes the platform and J. H listens as the lion tumbles and tears its way through the undergrowth, growling and gnashing as it goes. He fires shot after shot, as each snarl reveals the position of the man-eater in the brush, until he hears it collapse. A series of deep groans rumble out of the darkness, followed by a single sigh, then silence. As his men approach excitedly, the colonel decides that retreat is the better part of valour, not wishing to endanger them in case the lion is not dead. But in the morning, he finds that he has indeed killed the first of the man-eaters. Crouched and frozen in death, ready for the spring, J. H discovers at least two of his shots found their intended target. The male lion, known as the Ghost, was almost maneless, very pale in colour, and very large at nearly nine feet and nine inches in length."

"What happened to the other man-eater?" Kelly asked.

"Oh, he made his presence felt soon enough," Jericho sighed. "After a bungled attack on a local inspector's bungalow which resulted in the taking of a goat, Patterson re-adopted his tried and tested method of sitting up close to the kill sight. This time though, he set three new goats as bait, tied to a 250lb iron rail. After a sleepless night for J. H, the man-eater appeared just before dawn and nabbed one of the goats, pulling the other two and the iron rail to their doom with it. Patterson let a few shots off, but it was too dark to follow up."

"He did manage to hit one of the goats as I recall though," Thomas laughed.

"Too true," Jericho replied with a wink. "Anyway, even Patterson was able to find the trail of three dead goats tied to an iron rail being dragged through the brush, and followed it up the next morning. A very unhappy lion charged him and his hunting party, but disappeared back into the scrub. Absolutely certain the lion will return, he has a very strong scaffold built in a tree close to where the man-eater has abandoned the goats. He sets up, with both a twin barrelled smooth bore and a magazine rifle, and accompanied by his gun bearer he settles in for another night's vigil. Amazingly, the lion does indeed present itself, and J. H commemorates its appearance by sending slugs from both barrels into its shoulder as it passes below him. Again though, Patterson waits for the comparative safety of dawn to take to the trail. Almost unbelievably, it disappears back into the maze of rocks. For ten days, they neither see nor hear anything of the lion, and presume it has died of its wounds somewhere in the bush."

"He's not big on following up wounded animals, is he?" Catherine said scornfully.

"Like I said, I'm no real fan of the man," Jericho replied, throwing up his hands in agreement.

He paused as Rhodes, the big tan boerboel, padded up to his side and laid his head contentedly on his knee. Not expecting her to be far away, Thomas looked round to catch Saka stealthily stalking him from behind. On being discovered, she let out a whining yawn and trotted past, slumping to the floor at his feet and stretching out in front of the fire.

"One evening," Jericho continued, "the good colonel hears the terrified shouts of his men calling for him, saying a lion is trying to reach them. Having learnt from their mistakes, they hadn't declared the lion dead yet, rather just missing in action, and were still sleeping high in trees surrounded by a thorn boma. Patterson doesn't fancy leaving the safety of his own enclosure either, and takes a few pot shots into the darkness. This seems to at least have the desired effect, as the men are not disturbed again that night. But come the dawn, the lion's huge and obvious pugmarks can be seen circling the tree several times, and then rather sinisterly, traipsing through each and every empty tent in the camp. Without missing a beat, J. H has another platform built high in the tree, hoping the lion will come back. Again, he takes up his post with his gun bearer, and settles in for the night. After about an hour of uncomfortable dozing, he blinks awake, certain that something isn't right. And although his man is attentively on guard, Patterson peers into their murky surroundings. He catches a tiny flicker of movement, and drawn to it, he begins to watch in disbelief as the man-eater sinks into cover, carefully stalking them to within twenty yards. He snatches up the magazine rifle and sends home a round into the lion's chest. The man-eater melts back into the darkness, but not before Patterson sends another three shots in his direction."

"Had he killed it this time?" Keelson asked.

"Well, again John Henry waits for dawn to break before he decides to check," Jericho replied. "But the plentiful splashes of blood give him some confidence. Accompanied by a tracker, J. H has the common sense to use the luxury of strength in numbers to check ahead, and about a quarter of a mile in, he finds it's a good thing too. The party are met by an angry snarl, and Patterson sees the man-eater rise up, ready for a charge. Patterson lets off three shots, which seem to only piss the thing off further, but he reaches behind, confidently expecting to be passed the second rifle by his gun bearer. Unfortunately, both servant and said firearm are disappearing up the nearest tree, and Patterson has no choice but to join them in a hurry. John Henry swings up into its branches just as the lion reaches the foot of the tree. But as it limps back to the thicket, the gun bearer remembers what he is there for and passes J. H the gun. The single round he sends in the lion's direction floors it immediately, and J. H scrambles down, finally sure he has finished him off. But as we know from any good horror movie, the monster always comes back one more time, and on his approach, up jumped the lion and charged again. This time, the close-fired shots to the man-eater's chest and head did the job, and the second Tsavo man-eater died five yards from Patterson's feet. Known as the Darkness, he too was maneless, measured nine feet six inches in length, and stood near enough four feet at the shoulder. Both big boys, as I'm sure our experts will agree," Jericho nodded to Thomas and Catherine.

Thomas sat back and gave a sarcastic smile in reply. Catherine seemed too deep in thought to respond.

"And now their legacy lives on it seems?" Keelson asked. "That's why you call them The Daughters of the Darkness I presume?"

"I am interested in the appearance of these lions, I have to admit," Catherine answered out of the blue. "The ones we saw back in the cave were also unusually pale. We are presuming they are females, but maybe the males are maneless, as the Ghost and the Darkness were. It's not that uncommon a trait for lions that live in more arid conditions, where the weight and heat of a mane would be a hindrance. It's also a two-way street. Lionesses in the Okavango Delta of Botswana are known to grow manes, giving their prides added protection through the perception of having more males."

"I'm pretty sure the tracks I found were of lionesses," Thomas interjected. "The only prints of males I've found so far were from the one unfortunate to encounter the so-called queen's wrath, and the two big guys who were hanging around on the hill."

"I've already spoken to the Field Museum in Chicago," said Kelly. "They would be very interested in adding to the existing Tsavo lions exhibit if we provide the opportunity."

"We should maybe be a little more concerned about doing what's best for this pride as a whole," Catherine argued, "before we make any deals to sell off all of their hides. Lions are a vulnerable species, and populations have decreased by 42% over the last twenty years. We need to take some responsibility for our actions."

"It's not like we can teach them to not eat people anymore," Jericho scoffed.

"Don't be so sure," Catherine replied, shaking her head. "Lions are the only social cat species in the world. They hunt, kill and feed together, and follow a strict hierarchy. If you take out the leader, the pride could be forced to move and make changes to their choice of prey."

"You've got yourself a regular Joy Adamson there," Jericho sighed, nodding at Thomas. "Being friendly towards lions didn't do her any good in the end you know?"

"What do you mean by that?" Catherine asked.

Thomas could see she was beginning to get agitated, but he wasn't sure he agreed with her completely either. He quietly watched as Jericho took up the argument again.

"Everyone seems to forget that when Joy Adamson's death was first reported, it was said to be a lion that had killed her. The original report detailed that she was taking a stroll in the bush outside her tent, and came across a lion chasing a buffalo. The lion turned and killed her. She was found by a park employee, lying face down with heavy wounds on her hands, arms and head. No question of any human foul play."

"You're going to have to let the Adamson conspiracy go at some point," Thomas laughed.

"Come on, you can't tell me that it was a little suspicious?" Jericho exclaimed. "Can you imagine the damage to the Elsa Wild Animal Appeal, or the Born Free Foundation as it is now, if it had been left that their founder had been killed by the very animal they held up in such adoration? It's even on their mascot for Christ's sake. Those hefty donations may have taken a hit don't you think, if they hadn't conveniently found some farmer to take the fall? Mysteriously forgetting the buffalo and the team of trackers who were following up the lion I might add."

"It's true," Jelani agreed. "It's very easy to cover something like that up here. Corruption is everywhere, and it has only gotten worse."

"I agree it's suspicious," Thomas replied, "but what I don't understand is that you must have been all of five years old when it happened, what do you care?"

"I care because the one thing we need to stop doing in conservation is joining in with the propaganda," Jericho replied, frustrated. "It was the 1980s when corporations started getting involved. Things are dire enough without us inventing new species or re-labelling them just to declare them extinct. We move entire villages onto barren desert to set up national parks, then wonder why we have no community support. It's like some damn marketing company took over the whole movement at some point and none of us noticed. Remember Cecil the lion, killed in Botswana by that asshole dentist who lured him out of a national park? There are two so called charities working there right now, gleaning donations from the public in Cecil's name, whilst at the same time being funded by pro-trophy hunting organisations and lobbyists."

"I completely agree with you that local communities should be at the heart of conservation," Catherine declared. "We need to look after people as well as the wildlife. But you heard what the authorities said back in Nairobi, the ecosystem is out of sync. Game animals have been killed or driven off,

189

and the predators can't find their usual prey. That's why we have a leopard and lions taking to man-eating in the same district. We have to take responsibility for what we have done to the environment, and have a duty to try and repair it, not just take out isolated animals. I could even argue that's exactly what has contributed to the problem. Every time one, or a group are killed, others will move in to the territory, as is the natural order. But they find themselves in the same predicament and turn to the easy pickings of livestock and humans when they can't find food. We need to be educating and working with local projects, providing an income for the people through wildlife and habitat management."

"Which is what we are trying to do here," Jericho said, gesturing to the camp behind them. "Jelani was born in this district, as was his brother. He employs the local tribesmen and villagers. He protects the land as much as he can. But that didn't stop his brother getting killed. I agree with everything you've said, but they are long term goals, and in a way, idealistic. In the short term, in the here and now, we aren't just up against an out of kilter environment; we're up against poachers, and a local crime lord. At the end of the day, yes, lions do need to be protected. But so do people."

"It's even more complicated than that I believe my friends," Jelani sighed. "I have heard stories of Kanu Sultan disposing of his enemies through his critters of the bush. I think that is what happened to Jabari. I think the lions have become used to being fed their human victims."

"That's horrible Jelani, I'm so sorry," Catherine stammered.

"I think we need to remember that everyone here has experienced the reality of living in the presence of a man-eater," Thomas said softly. "And that also our understanding of them has increased considerably since Patterson's day. But that doesn't change the danger they represent. At the moment, the only thing I know for certain, is that we need to know more about these lions and how they operate if we are to have any hope in stopping them effectively."

As the fire crackled and spat sparks into the warm, dry air, they were called away from its glow by Mansa. The dinner table set at the centre of the kopje was adorned with plates of sticky brown steaks, crisp fried yams, and a broad bean and sweetcorn salad. Catherine hesitated for a second as Mansa explained the steaks had come from the hippo Jericho had shot, but she took one with Thomas's encouragement. The steak was thick and broad, with slithers of yellow fat marbling the surface. Her mouth began to grow moist as the scent of charred meat wafted up from the plate. She cut a small piece from the corner and scooped it into her mouth. The meat began to melt against her tongue instantly, and she savoured the smoky yet subtle taste before it disappeared. Thomas smiled at her as she began to chisel a larger piece off the slab. By the time she looked over to meet his gaze, her eyes were lit with joy and hunger. He leant over and kissed her on the cheek.

"To us, predators one and all," Thomas called out, raising the glass of perfectly poured red wine Mansa had just handed him.

As glasses clinked together and the atmosphere seemed to relax with the application of alcohol, Thomas took a sip of the Anwilka 2005 vintage within the glass. The earthy tones to the complex hint of blackberry, liquorice and espresso were the perfect accompaniment to the lingering taste of the seared meat, and an expensive one. He noticed Catherine cover her glass as Mansa plied the others with the wine. The thin African disappeared back towards the kitchen tent. He appeared about a minute later, striding back towards the table carrying a tall glass filled with a dark pink drink. He set it down next to Catherine's plate.

"A strawberry and blood orange smoothie made with coconut milk for the lady perhaps?" Mansa said with a kind smile in his wispy crackle of a voice.

"Perfect, thank you Mansa," Catherine replied.

She met Thomas's questioning look and gave him a reassuring squeeze of the hand under the table.

"My head's not right for alcohol, especially red wine. I feel a bit fuzzy and tired still, and my stomach is a little flighty after our adventures today," she explained.

"I'm going the other way," laughed Thomas. "I'm going to try and drink the jitters into defeat."

"We can compare notes in the morning, but I don't fancy your chances," Catherine replied, resting her head on his shoulder for a moment.

"Nor do I if the Irishman has anything to do with it," Thomas whispered into her ear, kissing the top of her head softly.

The light was fading fast, and the chatter and noise around the table began to grow quieter with the subduing satisfaction of a good meal. The stars were just beginning to appear in the evening sky when Thomas noticed Saka rise to her feet. The sleek, blotch patterned hunting dog took a few steps past them, her large bat like ears unfolding and pricking up. He turned in his seat when Rhodes let out a short bark of warning and also rose, alerted by noise and movement from behind. Karni and several of Jelani's men were coming up the track from the staff camp. And they seemed in a hurry.

"It looks like we have company," Karni said to them as he joined them.

Thomas, Catherine and the others rose from their seats at once and began to follow the group back down the path. Thomas scooped up his pair of Leica binoculars as they passed the equipment table. He knew the 12x50 lenses were particularly suitable for the evening light, but he also grabbed the Thermoteknix thermal imager just in case, and passed it to Jelani. He noticed Jericho grab his nitro express rifle from the stand as they went by too. He nodded his approval over the crowd of nervous and chattering workers.

They walked straight through the staff camp and made their way onto a slight knoll. The scrub around them was relatively sparse, with only the odd tree and patchy thorn bushes peppering the broad plain stretching out in front of them. They faced west, and into the last remnants of a blood red sunset. It seemed quite eerie to see the already rust coloured earth bathed in the clotted streams of light that ran from the horizon like an open wound. Thomas felt the warmth against his skin, and so was unsure why a chill clung to him and made him shiver.

"They're still there," Karni said, "beneath that baobab tree, about 500 yards out."

Thomas followed Karni's pointing finger out to the squat, dense silhouette of the tree. He caught a glint of something reflecting the light and raised his binoculars in curiosity. In the shadow of the colossal boughs of the baobab, he could see three dark coloured vehicles. He recognised them as Range Rover Sports. Then he noticed the movement in front of the one closest to them. He refocused the binoculars as he adjusted the magnification to its highest setting.

Squatting in front of the car was a tall, well built, and dark skinned African man. He had closely cropped black curled hair and a military style moustache. Thomas thought he could make out a stubbly salt and pepper beard too. The man was dressed in a dark khaki short-sleeved shirt with shoulder straps, and he also wore tight, smart trousers of the same colour. It gave him the air of a military officer. Thomas noticed he had thick and powerful arms as he watched the stranger spread them out over the ground. As the man dropped his head towards his feet, another man approached him from behind the vehicle. Thomas took a sharp intake of breath as he saw what he carried. In one hand, he held a sharp, long bladed knife. In the other, a live trussed chicken dangled by its feet. Without looking up, the squatting man took both from the other, who quickly retreated. With a deft and lightning quick strike, the man cut off the chicken's head. A spray of arterial blood streaked from the bird's open neck as its wings fluttered with nervous impulse. The man began to pirouette, still squatting, and spraying the blood liberally over the ground. After making a complete turn, his head suddenly snapped up. The eyes were wide and intently focused on Thomas and the rest of the group. Thomas could make out the blood splatter on the man's skin. The sinister grin the man seemed to fix him with made him feel incredibly uncomfortable. He watched as the man took a small glass jar he hadn't noticed sitting on the bonnet of the Range Rover, and poured its contents onto the ground, over the still twitching body of the chicken.

"I presume that's Kanu Sultan," Thomas asked, passing Jelani the binoculars.

Jelani took them and raised them to his eyes. Thomas

noticed his posture instantly become taut and anxious.

"That is him," Jelani replied solemnly.

"What was he doing?" Catherine asked.

"It is a voodoo ritual," Jelani said, an audible shake in his voice. "He is a bokor, a man of black magic."

"I'm guessing that wasn't exactly a blessing we just witnessed then?" Jericho asked.

"No," Jelani replied, shaking his head. "It is a blood sacrifice, an invoking. He is calling forth the Petro-Loa – powerful, shape-shifting demons. We will be visited by them as lions tonight."

Jelani's men instantly began crying out and backing away, their heightened and fearful talk no doubt audible to Kanu Sultan and his men.

"Knock off the shite Jelani," Jericho snapped angrily, "control your men."

Jelani barked an order at the others as they retreated. They stopped in their tracks and hung their heads a little shamefully. Jelani continued to speak to them in Swahili, too fast for Thomas to keep track of the conversation. He did pick up that Jelani was reminding them that two of the lions were already dead by his hand.

Jelani fumbled in his pocket and brought out a necklace adorned with what Thomas recognised as the claws from a lion.

"Please put this on, it will reassure the men that we are protected. The claws are from one of the lions you shot."

Thomas took the necklace a little reluctantly.

"If it means they stay and don't make damned fools of us then I'll put it on," Thomas sighed. "But just to be clear, I don't condone this souvenir taking from the ones we shoot. Above all else, we were planning to do some research, and that means leaving the bodies intact, okay?"

"Yes boss," Jelani stammered.

Thomas could see he was clearly upset and worried by Kanu Sultan's appearance and the strange ritual they had witnessed.

"That will certainly make for interesting footage," Mason said with a grimace as they watched the procession of Range Rovers drive off and disappear.

He took the camera down from his shoulder and turned with the others, as they began to make their way back up the track towards the staff camp.

"How much danger do you think he really represents?" Mason asked Thomas as they walked.

"Hard to say," Thomas shrugged. "Can they award that feature photography Pulitzer you're after posthumously?"

"Very reassuring," Mason smirked.

Darkness was beginning to descend quickly with the disappearance of the sun over the horizon. The last of its rays were engulfed in shadow, then finally consumed by the night. A pale moon hung low in the sky, and began to bathe the trees and path ahead of them in a soft, yellow light.

Thomas listened as the nocturnal animals of the bush began to stir. The piercing whistle of a Verreaux's eagle owl, the largest of its kind in Africa, floated up from the woods to their left. Carried on the wind, he could hear the belching bellows of the hippos on the river, as they prepared to leave the water and forage along the banks and into the grassland. A jackal barked and yipped from somewhere behind them, and was immediately answered by the hysterical yikker of a group of spotted hyenas. As they reached the staff camp, they were greeted by the more familiar chirping of cicadas and crickets. The men busied themselves with lighting lamps and Thomas called Jelani over.

"It won't hurt to get some fires going and to make sure all of the tents are secured," Thomas suggested. "I don't believe in the superstitious stuff, but that doesn't mean Kanu doesn't have something planned. That was quite a statement we saw out there."

"I agree my friend, it will be done," Jelani nodded.

Thomas watched as Jericho reached up into a tree at the side of the trail, seemingly absent minded. There was a sudden scream as Kelly jumped backwards, followed by a roar of laughter from the men.

"I thought you might want to give him a little kiss and see if he turned into a prince," Jericho offered with a smirk, picking up the yellow tree frog he had just placed on her shoulder.

"Asshole," Keelson laughed, shaking her head.

Thomas couldn't help smiling. Even the frog looked a little perplexed, its lemon coloured toes gripping to Jericho's fingers as he placed it back onto its branch.

"I just needed to break the ice with the crowd darlin'" Jericho whispered, "they were taking things a little too seriously," he winked.

Keelson gave him a friendly thump in the ribs in return.

Jericho's stunt seemed to have the desired effect. The atmosphere lightened and the men relaxed as they went about their work. They left them to it as they walked back along the trail to the main camp. A few of Jelani's men followed, carrying large branches with them. When they got to the kopje, they began to arrange the dry wood into a pyramid.

New logs were added to the fire pit as well. Soon both were bellowing flames high into the night sky.

Keelson, Mason and Karni stood talking together, looking around at the others. Thomas noticed Mason had set up his camera on the tripod again. Jelani was deep in discussion with Mansa, occasionally breaking off to direct his men to some new errand. Thomas walked casually over to Jericho, who was waiting for him at the gun rack.

"Do you get the feeling we haven't seen the main show yet?" Jericho asked him, quietly eyeing the others.

"Pretty much," Thomas sighed.

He noticed Jericho was checking his nitro express rifle. He picked up his own from the rack, and slid the bolt back as he fitted a magazine cartridge. He turned as he felt Catherine walking up from behind. He handed her the Marlin rifle from the rack. She took a box of ammunition and began to feed the 45-70 Govt. rounds into the loading port. Jericho passed Thomas the holstered Anaconda he had taken off him earlier. They returned to their chairs around the kopje in silence, resting the rifles on the wooden frames and at arm's reach. Thomas slung the strap for the Thermoteknix thermal imager over the back of his chair. As they sat down, Jericho nodded to Mansa.

The hospitable African disappeared into the kitchen tent, reappearing moments later with a silver tray. On it were three crystal tumblers and a bottle of whiskey. As he set it down in front of them, Thomas nodded his approval to Jericho. The squat, cognac shaped bottle of 1987 Vintage Teeling Gold Reserve Whiskey was an example of Ireland's best. Jericho plucked the large champagne coloured stopper from the bottle, poured the three glasses, and handed them out.

"To the long wait," Jericho toasted them as their glasses clinked together.

Thomas took a sip, enjoying the instant warmth the amber liquid gave him. It was smoother than the peaty whisky he favoured, possibly due to being finished in white burgundy barrels that also gave it a fruitier flavour. He could see Catherine liked it, as she sat back in her chair and took a large sip. She savoured it and called Keelson over to them.

"One sip's enough for me," Catherine smiled contentedly, "but I'm sure Kelly would like the rest."

She offered the glass to the reporter, who gladly took it with a nod of the head. She too took a big swig. Her shoulders dropped as she instantly relaxed and took in the honey coloured liquor. She was about to say something, when a long, drawn moan drifted up from the scrub behind the camp. It was the hunting call of a lion.

Instantly, everyone went on alert. Other calls joined the first, seemingly from all sides of the camp. Thomas, Catherine and Jericho jumped to their feet, snatching up their rifles.

"Don't you hate being right all the time?" Thomas cussed to Jericho under his breath.

"This might be the first time I don't celebrate it," the Irishman nodded.

Jelani rushed out of the kitchen tent, clutching his own shotgun. He rushed off down the trail towards the staff camp. Every minute or so, another roar floated up into the night, each time sounding a little closer than before.

"They're hunting us like they hunt baboons," Catherine exclaimed in realisation as she half brought up her rifle.

Thomas looked at her quizzically, readying his gun in the same manner.

"They've surrounded us, and now they're trying to induce a panic," she explained. "Baboons usually sleep on cliff faces or high in trees. One group of lions will start roaring and tearing through the bush nearby, hoping to drive or push the baboons towards a second group lying in wait."

Thomas and Jericho instinctively turned in the only direction from which they were yet to hear any roars; the main road that led into camp and straight ahead of them. There was no noise now. Even the crickets and cicadas had stopped their song at the approach of the lions. Thomas reached for the thermal imager and flicked it on as he peered through the viewfinder.

The landscape was suddenly painted in ashen tones of grey, black and white. The high-tech gadget automatically focused as he swung past Jericho, his hot face glowing white and his features etched in grey. Thomas made sure he didn't look at the fire, to avoid the lens flaring as he pointed it into the darkness and towards the road that led into camp. The magnification was so good that he could see insects rising from the grass. He scanned back and forth, probing the tall scrub.

It was a flick of a tail that caught his eye first. It glowed just slightly hotter than the surrounding wisps of grass. As he trained his gaze downwards, he saw them. Three lionesses hunkered down onto the ground about a hundred and fifty yards away. Through the monotone viewer they looked like statues, the detail of their faces lost and their eye sockets seeming empty and soulless.

"They're right in front of us," Thomas whispered. "Three in the long grass on the right-hand side of the track, no more than two hundred yards away. When they come, we'll have about seven seconds at the most to drop them, be ready."

Another burst of unsettling grunts and coughs rose up from the tree line behind the camp. Thomas checked through the thermal imager again and then looked back to Jericho and Catherine, making sure they were covering the right area and direction. Catherine had dropped to one knee, and he could see that the look of cold hard determination he'd seen on the range had returned. She shouldered the rifle and looked down the sights with an unblinking stare. Jericho had anchored himself into the ground with a rigid stance, ready to bring the thunder of the big nitro express. Thomas dropped the imager and slipped the Holland & Holland from his shoulder. Without the aid of the thermal imager, his vision was limited to about forty yards, and only then with the help of the fire.

Thomas knew that the lionesses would be edging closer. They would want to make the charge over as short a distance as possible, but were hampered by the light of the flames, and the open ground on the other side of the road and towards the camp. They expected the other lions to drive them in their direction, or at least distract them. A lioness on the hunt was the epitome of stealth, and they relied on getting close to their prey to make an ambush. They couldn't chase prey down over long distances.

A savage roar and the blast of a shotgun from the trail behind surprised them, and each jerked their head backwards at the sound. Thomas winced, knowing at once the lionesses were coming for them.

"Front," he yelled, not sure how many of their precious seconds had passed.

He caught the three wakes of the lionesses moving through the grass towards them, just before their tawny heads burst from the cover. They stayed low to the ground, their backs arched and hunched as they rippled closer. The guns seemed to fire in unison. Thomas watched the lioness barrelling towards him trip and plant into the dirt, and he instantly swung the barrel to the right to cover Catherine. Her lioness somersaulted backwards as her kneeling and close-range shot sent a shell spiralling through its top jaw and into the brain. Sheer momentum sent the lioness flying backwards, as if it had been struck by a prize fighter. Thomas saw Jericho's lioness had gone down too. But as Jericho lowered his gun, a streak of amber hued muscle sprung at him from the grass. Jericho dropped to his knee instantly and let the charge from the second barrel finish the job. The ensuing silence was only broken as Thomas drew back his bolt and Catherine worked her repeater to feed new rounds into the chambers of their rifles.

Instinctively, the three of them edged closer together. Back to back, they began to creep towards the centre of the kopje, where they would get the most light from the fire and be able to cover the angles better. They stopped about half way across the track that led to the staff camp. With a loud bark and thunderous growl, Rhodes the boerboel joined them, standing guard at Jericho's side. Thomas searched for Saka, and caught a glimpse of her eye shine as she looked out at them from the relative safety beneath Jericho's Jeep.

They could hear people shouting further down the track towards the staff camp. Thomas brought up the thermal imager to get a better view. There was a flash of hot white against the dull grey scrub as another lioness bolted from the trees and bounded across the path before disappearing into the brush again. As he scanned around, he caught glimpses of heat signatures as they streaked through the undergrowth. They seemed to be everywhere. He panned back round, only to meet the stony glare of a lioness, as it padded out of the grass by the entrance road.

Before he could drop the imager and raise his rifle, a blur of movement appeared from the right. Long slashing teeth raked the lioness's flank, making it spin round in surprise as it braced for the spring. But the attacker was too swift, disappearing into the darkness. The lioness seemed wild and maddened, roaring savagely and swiping at the empty air with her paw. What sounded like a ripple of excited bird calls floated up out of the grass, and Thomas immediately knew who the attacker was. African hunting dogs in packs were formidable aggressors, and he had heard many reports of them taking on lions. Saka was doing the same, but Thomas knew she wouldn't fare well on her own, even if aided by her natural agility.

Saka burst from the grass at full speed on the lioness's blind side, ducking quickly to land a second slashing bite to the underbelly. The lion spun again, a cuff of the paw just missing Saka's tail as she loped to a halt, this time standing her ground and facing the lion. Thomas was ready though, and had dropped the thermal imager. As the lioness turned her head towards Saka, a flicker of light from the fire brought her form out of the shadows. Thomas squeezed the trigger of the rifle. The crack echoed around the open area of the kopje. As the bullet smashed through her nervous system, the lioness leapt up in a violent spasm, hitting the ground as she rolled violently, biting at her own paws in shock and rage before slumping onto her side.

Thomas moved quickly, chambering another round with a

quick draw of the bolt as he dashed to cover the lioness, in case the first shot hadn't done the job. He let out a laboured sigh of relief as he saw the thick stream of blood seeping from her nostrils, and the pink stained saliva bubbling over her crooked and open lower jaw. The rippled skin of the lioness's snout and her lifeless amber eyes were frozen in a death snarl. Saka moved in and began to tear at the flank she had opened, but Thomas called her away. Both his head and hers swivelled as another roar, and more shouting, erupted from behind them.

The high pitched, blood curdling scream that lifted up into the darkness was full of pain and despair. It was the unmistakable sound of the acceptance of death. Thomas knew instantly that somebody had been taken. He and Catherine ran forward, as Jericho covered them from behind, Rhodes still by his side. They found Jelani, Keelson and the others half way along the track. Jelani was kneeling, as one of his men stood guard with the shotgun and another held a torch. Thomas followed its beam to the tracks crossing the path diagonally, perfectly intercepting the bare footprints of a man as he had sprinted towards the main camp. It was morbidly ironic that the instinct to run for his life had been what had ended it. Fleeing from the light and safety of the others in the staff compound had sealed his fate.

"It was Tambo," Jelani sighed. "He was most scared of lions. The roars were too much for him. He was probably trying to make it to the guns."

Some way off, a sickening crack echoed through the trees towards them. As they listened, they could hear muttered, rumbling growls and the soft squelching and tearing of flesh. Another crunch sounded. The lions had not hesitated to begin their meal. Jericho emptied both barrels in the direction the sounds were coming from as Thomas scoured the brush for any heat signature with the thermal imager. But the trees and scrub were too thick, and only a deepening line of shadows loomed back at him through the viewer.

A roar that sounded like it came from the kopje pierced the night, followed by another from the direction where they had gathered to watch Kanu Sultan. More roars from behind and in front of them rumbled at them. The lions were on the move again, closing in. They now knew for sure there was meat to be had here. Thomas spun as he heard the deep, heavy grunting of a lioness, as she passed close by through the trees behind them. The sound was almost warthog like, and one they made when excited or agitated. Each guttural exhale came as the feet thumped into the ground, as if the noise was being knocked from the body by the impact. He thought he saw a quick blink of amber-reflecting eyes for a moment, but they were soon lost to the darkness. He peered through the lens of the Thermoteknix binoculars again and took a sharp, involuntary intake of breath. Hot flashes and quivers of white broke the monotone grey and black forest surrounding them as the lions weaved through the brush.

Thomas took out the Anaconda from its holster and passed it to Jelani.

"Give it to one of the men, we're going to need as many guns as possible," he ordered.

Jelani nodded as Catherine also took her revolver out and gave it over. Jelani gave one to Mansa and the other to one of his trackers, a man named Chane. Most of the men were now sheltering in the tents, with only Jelani, Mansa and Chane staying with them. Mason, Karni and Keelson were close by, filming them from the open door of a tent. All was quiet, with even the insects having stopped their nocturne symphony.

A raged and penetrating roar thundered into the night. It sounded like the earth itself had opened up and cried out in savage anger. It was so loud that Catherine flinched, and Mansa nearly dropped the revolver he was holding. It was guttural, savage and authoritive. Thomas was in no doubt it was the animal Jelani referred to as the queen. As if to confirm his thinking, her loyal subjects began to call out in responsive moaning roars of their own. They could hear them all around, but they seemed to be moving off rather than edging closer. A quick peek through the thermal imager confirmed they were no longer surrounded. A few minutes later, the roars of the lions were much further away and distant.

"They're gone?" Jelani asked.

"It would seem so," Thomas replied. "It's still not safe to recover Tambo's body though. We'll do it at first light."

Jelani nodded silently as he handed back the Anaconda.

"Everyone stays in their tents, without exception," Jericho addressed everyone in a loud and booming voice. "There'll be two-man watches at both ends of camp. It's going to be a long night, but we'll get through it. Tomorrow we'll fortify things a little more. Get some sleep."

Jelani spoke with Chane and a few others as he organised the guarding duties for the rest of the night. Thomas, Catherine and Jericho began to walk back up towards their own tents.

"I'll take the first watch our end," Jericho shrugged. "Join me for the rest of our nightcap?"

"I think I need it," Thomas growled.

"I don't think I could manage it," Catherine said shakily.

Thomas looked over at her. She seemed a little pale and drained, her hardened exterior crumbling quickly. He nodded to Jericho as the Irishman headed towards the chairs and the fire pit. Thomas put his arm around Catherine and walked back to the tent with her. As they entered, she kicked off her sandals, stripped off her holster and outer layers, right down to her panties and a vest top, before flopping onto the bed. As Thomas put a hand on her back he could feel she was trembling, but not from fear, from sheer exhaustion.

"Go be a bwana with Jericho," she murmured, her eyes already closed.

Thomas smiled appreciatively as he leaned over and kissed her neck.

"I love you," he whispered.

"ngh-kay," she mumbled into her pillow.

Thomas picked up the holster and her gun, and placed it on the table beside the bed on her side. He made sure the door to the tent was secured before he slipped into the kitchen marquee. It didn't take him long to find the wooden box he was looking for, put away for safe keeping on his orders by Mansa. He opened it and took out the bottle of Lagavulin thirty-seven-year-old whisky. He grabbed a pair of glass tumblers and walked out to the kopje to join Jericho. He found the Irishman cleaning and reloading his formidable Merkel nitro express rifle. The DP-12 shotgun he'd used to dispatch the crocodiles leant against his chair too. Rhodes, the big boerboel, laid the other side of the fire, looking out into the dark.

"A dram for your thoughts," Thomas offered as he pulled out the cork stopper of the peat coloured glass bottle.

"A cigar for yours," Jericho replied, offering one of two

from a leather case he drew from his shooting vest pocket.

The cigars were Partagas Lusitania Gran Reserva Cosechas. They were made of only the very finest leaves cultivated from the Vuelta Abajo, Cuba's premier tobacco region. Even then, the leaves making up the fillers, wrappers and binders were all aged for at least five years. Thomas took one of the near eight-inch-long, torpedo shaped bundles. He used the silver cigar punch Jericho handed him to cut through the crisp outer skin at the end, and leaned forward to light it on a glowing ember in the bottom of the fire pit. They both supped at the whisky and let wisps of smoke from their cigars drift up into the African night sky.

"That last roar, that sound like a lion to you?" Jericho quizzed Thomas finally.

"There was something about it, wasn't there?" Thomas agreed. "It reminded me of a tiger. That angry, rant like snarl they have."

"Bloody loud too," Jericho lamented. "This female, this queen. She's a strange one. You ever heard a pride called off a hunt like that?"

"Is that what happened?" Thomas queried, raising an eyebrow.

"Seemed like it for sure," Jericho shrugged.

"No," sighed Thomas, "I haven't," agreeing begrudgingly.

They both sat in silence again as they smoked and drank into the night, deep in thought.

~

She lay hunched in the shadows, hidden below the thick and twisted branches of the thorn bushes a few feet from the soft sided dwellings the men used. Over an hour had passed and the bush was quiet. Some thirty feet away, she could smell the acrid burning of the tobacco in the strange glowing thing that dangled from the sleeping guard's lip. A fitful snore sent it tumbling to the ground where it fizzed out of ignition. His partner had not returned since she had started watching. It was time.

She flipped her paws over, dragging herself through the scrub on the velvet silence of her upturned fur, rather than risk the scrabble of leathery pads on the hard-baked ground. She paused at the edge of the scrub, now only a head length from the beige coloured canvas that separated her from the sleeping men inside. Her ears swivelled, as she centred in on the deep inhales and exhales that came from within. One set seemed closer than the others. The world around her was illuminated in an internal twilight of purple and sepia tones. She could easily see the loose flap of unsecured canvas, unlike the other panels of the dwelling. She inched out a little further, checking her surroundings constantly.

Finally assured, she pressed her nose under the loose flap. The strong sweet scent of the men inside was intoxicating now. She braced, raising herself up and making the opening larger. She surveyed the inside of the tent with casual curiosity. Her noiseless feet took her past the nearest man. He smelled of the earth and not unlike an old, abandoned termite mound. The second man she found smelt of fermented fruit, the taint thick on his breath. She ignored them both. She stared at the third. She held her head above his, his exposed body lying away from her towards the front opening, still secured as it was. She licked her muzzle, glancing once at the other men beyond him, before twisting her head to the side and casually sending her five and a half inch fangs through his temples. Her victim made no sound as she lifted his torso effortlessly from the ground. She dragged him back the way she had come, slipping through the hole she had made. Once clear of the tent, she adjusted her hold on the body, lifting it in her jaws as she carried it off into the scrub. The thorns of the whistling acacias stroked her fur like a grooming brush, but tore the clothing of the dead man and pierced and tore at the flesh beneath. She stood a moment as she watched several tawny bodies approach. They followed the trail she had laid down to the tent. They entered one by one as she did, each emerging straddling the man they had silently plucked, having made their slumber eternal. The lionesses slunk back to the shadows to consume their meals in peace. Only when she knew she was alone again did she settle in a clearing and begin to eat her own prize.

CHAPTER FOURTEEN

The night slipped away assassin-like, as the dawn arrived in its wake. The thin rays of light were not yet strong enough to bring warmth to the silent camp. Catherine reached across the bed, pulling herself closer to Thomas. She tugged at the still crisp French linen and began to tunnel deeper into the bedspread for warmth and comfort. Thomas did not stir, still deep in sleep thanks to the whisky.

It wasn't long after that, just as she began to doze again, that the shouts and wails began. Then she heard the noise of somebody hurriedly tapping against the glass door at the front of the tent. She sat up and threw her legs over the bed, trying to shake off her own grogginess as she shuffled across the floor. When she pulled back the curtain covering the door, she found Kelly Keelson on the other side, her eyes wide and her expression taut and fearful. Catherine reached for the handle and swung open the door.

"What's going on?"

"Jelani's men are leaving. The lions took out an entire tent of them last night, right under a guard's nose," Keelson replied.

"I'll be right there," the call came from behind.

Thomas pulled on his clothes quickly, stuffing his feet into his sandals and heading towards the door. He followed Kelly down the track towards the staff camp. Mason and Karni, who had taken the second watch, were already heading up to meet them. He looked to his left as Jericho stumbled grumpily from his own tent.

"What's going on?"

"Looks like we got hit last night after all," Thomas replied.

"Who did they take?"

"Six men. A whole tent," Keelson answered quietly.

"Christ," snapped Jericho, "how'd the guard miss that?"

"We're on our way to find out," Thomas shrugged.

Catherine caught them up, having stopped to pull on some clothes. By the time they reached the staff camp, it was a scene of chaos. Jelani stood in the centre of a group of his men. They were shouting at him, and Thomas noticed most of them already had their meagre belongings wrapped up and slung over their shoulders. As they approached, the men grew quiet and turned to look at them.

"What's happening?" Thomas asked, speaking to Jelani directly.

"They are scared," he replied, his brow slick with sweat. "They say the Petro-Loa came last night, and they do not want to face a bokor of Kanu's power and reputation."

"Well I wonder who put that idea into their head," Jericho muttered under his breath.

Thomas shot him a warning glance. But he let out a deep sigh and his shoulders dropped.

"Listen everyone," Thomas spoke up, lifting his voice to the gathered crowd. "I know you're scared. You have good reason to be. But I ask you this on behalf of those we've already lost, and those still here who need your help and protection. At least give me a little time to look into what happened. Don't give this bokor what he wants, or believe the lies he has asked you to stomach."

The men looked unconvinced, but a few placed their packs on the ground whilst others nodded in his direction. There was something fatalistic about their acceptance of superstition and the course of events. He had encountered it before many times. He remembered working with a village close to a camp he'd run several years back. The women there were regularly taken by crocodiles when they washed their pots in the river. Thomas had shown them how to erect a simple barrier of vertical poles that would have prevented the crocodiles approaching the riverbank unseen. The villagers ignored his advice. They simply saw it as the way of things. Those taken were fated. It was only when he waded out into the water himself and plunged the purposely cut sticks deep into the mud that the villagers accepted the barrier. But even then, they interpreted it as Thomas not being chosen to die, rather than mere luck or the practicality of the fence.

He could see the same dull acceptance of fate in the eyes of the men now. They expected him to investigate and then dismiss them and let them go, as no interpretation other than black magic would be acceptable to them. For now. He turned towards the empty tent they all seemed to be staring at and entered.

He stopped as abruptly as if he'd walked into a wall as he stepped inside. On the ground, arranged around the central supporting pole were six rumpled blankets, resting on the dry bare earth. He could smell the blood that had soaked into them. His senses were consumed by it momentarily. He saw the heavy droplets that stained the floor where they'd fallen, and the arterial spray coating the support pole and canvas walls. He closed his eyes, trying to block the visceral assault on his senses, only finding himself wrapped in the very silence that had allowed the lions to kill at leisure. The air felt stale and death drenched, clawing at his throat and skin. He opened his eyes and took a deep inhale of breath, steadying and hardening himself for the task he had set himself. He needed to be sharp, focused and alert.

He began to read the ground, dropping to one knee as he did so. He followed the drag marks of one unlucky man's heels, until they crisscrossed a set of paw prints. The lions had followed each other inside, using the already tried and tested trail of the one before. As he looked over the blankets, he noticed that most sported blood stains around a clean spot where the occupant's head would have been. The lions had bitten them through both sides of the skull, a favoured method for leopards and other big cats known to hunt primates. Only two showed the more violent, explosive blood loss that came from a suffocating throat bite. It was these two victims that had possibly flailed the most, not dying instantly, and almost certainly accounting for the excess blood on the walls and pole of the tent.

He followed the drag marks and prints all the way to the canvas back. He found the loose panel easily and lifted it up. He looked closely at the stretched and broken vertical seam of the panel. It had undoubtedly been forced open at its upper reaches, where the stitches were frayed and ragged. But further down, the tear was neater and less abrupt. As he looked closer, he was sure they had been cut with an upward slash of a knife. He remembered the flashing blade Kanu Sultan had used to decapitate the chicken, during the voodoo ritual he had carried out the night before. He felt a flash of anger as he also remembered the malevolent grin Kanu had worn.

He threw back the canvas panel and stepped out of the back of the tent. He immediately saw the set of deeper prints there, and he guessed by their size they were the queen's. He noted the impact cracks in the dry, clay-like mud where she had braced, pushing her weight down as she had lifted the panel and made the opening wider. Her pugmarks had cratered a little, and he examined the collapsed earth surrounding them. The harsh, ammonia laced scent hit his nostrils, and he realised that the ground had been liberally sprayed with the lion's urine, hence the mushy set of prints. But something bothered him about it.

"Cath, come round the back of the tent," he called out.

He hoped she wouldn't decide to walk through it. Moments later he heard her brushing past the scrub around the side of the awning. She appeared from the corner to his right.

"Take a look at this will you," he indicated, nodding to the stained area of ground he was kneeling over. "A lion has scent marked here and really gone to town. But it hasn't kicked up any of the brush or made a scrape. Something doesn't seem right."

Catherine joined him and took a closer look, jumping back immediately when the pungent smell hit her nostrils.

"I'm surprised at you Mr. Walker," she smiled, regaining her composure as she stood up. "I thought you'd be able to tell the difference. Don't you recognise it? The reason it's so strong is because it's chemical. It's probably a predator hunting lure or something like that. It's definitely not natural lion urine. This is something you would use to draw them in."

"You're right, of course you're right," Thomas exclaimed. "It makes sense too. I think the bottom of that panel was deliberately cut to give them an entry point."

"By Kanu Sultan, the man we saw last night?"

"Almost certainly," Thomas nodded.

"Why didn't they try to sabotage one of our tents? I'd have thought we were the more obvious targets?" Catherine asked.

"Our tents have wooden floors and reinforced structures. They're also harder to approach unobserved," Thomas replied. "It also depends entirely on what the objective was. If it was to empty the camp of most its staff, then we've already got a fight on our hands to stop that from happening. And if they do leave, then we'll be vulnerable."

"Not very comforting," Catherine replied, her face falling. "Maybe we're taking on more than we can cope with here?"

Her eyes fell to her feet as they turned together to make their way back around the tent.

"If you're not okay with this anymore, I wouldn't blame you," Thomas hinted as he pulled back a thorn encrusted branch of a whistling acacia. "I feel like you're taking things harder than the rest of us."

"I am tired," Catherine sighed admittedly. "I can't seem to shake it off. The same goes for my tummy, which has been squirmy since we got here. And I am very conflicted about what we're doing here. Last night for instance, I felt so exhilarated to take down that lioness. The excitement and adrenaline was incredible. Then I thought about what a beautiful animal she was, and the man who was killed."

"You felt guilty for how you had felt during the moment?" Thomas asked softly.

Catherine nodded. He could see the pangs of guilt and regret in her eyes as she looked down at the ground for a moment, avoiding his gaze.

"I feel exactly the same way. Why do you think I was in such a bad mood the other day after killing the two back at the cave? I think it's how every good hunter should feel," Thomas replied, hugging her with one arm across her shoulders. "No life should be taken lightly. She was a beautiful animal, she really was. But she was coming for you, to kill you. You did what you had to do. Other than a few francolins, everything we've had to take a shot at so far was pretty much bearing down on us. And that high you feel in the moment is just simple biochemistry. First, you get a hit of adrenalin to get you through the fight, then you get a dose of endorphins to help steady your overloaded nerves. It's a pretty powerful cocktail."

"I know." Catherine sighed.

"I need you, you know," Thomas said, giving her an affectionate hug. "I couldn't do any of this without you. I wouldn't be here without you. You always put others before yourself, especially me. You're so much stronger than I am. Why don't we put you first for a change?"

"Well, you know what they say, behind every great man, there's a woman rolling her eyes," Catherine replied, trying to smile.

"Look, so far Jericho and I have been running the show and making all the decisions," Thomas stated. "Why don't we start doing things your way? You're the most qualified wildlife biologist here, and to be blunt, I think it worked for us when we were hunting our scary toothed friend in Scotland. I'm probably better at taking orders than giving them to be honest. What do you think?"

"I think you're suggesting I'm a control freak," she replied, nudging him in the ribs softly. "But thank you. Yes, I'd like to try. I'd like to have a say."

"Done," Thomas replied with an encouraging smile. "Now we need to explain how Kanu pulled off his magic tricks to the others."

Thomas took some time to tell everyone gathered what they had found and explained Catherine's suggestion that the lions had somehow been lured to the camp. He slowly saw the men's expressions change from fearful to angry, as they began to realise they had been taken as fools. But he could also see some needed further convincing. Catherine suggested that they search the camp for other signs of baiting and lures, and then set about organising the men; instructing them to spend the day reinforcing the camp by building thorn bomas around the tents, and for large bonfires to be lit during the night. It was already becoming clear that with the discovery of the sabotage and the dozing guard, the men's perception of the situation was changing. He sighed with relief, seeing Catherine was already relishing being in charge. Thomas decided to walk out with Jericho to where they had seen Kanu Sultan.

"Looks like you were right," Jericho shrugged as they reached the welcome shade of the baobab tree, even though it was still early.

The ground was still marked by the blood of the sacrificed chicken, but it also bore the stain of the strong synthetic scent that had clearly been used to bring in the lions. As the wind changed and brought with it the rancid stink of the lure, they were in no doubt of its potency. The Motorola radio he was carrying bleeped, and Catherine informed them they had found another on the road that led to the camp. Kanu Sultan had been thorough, making sure the lures were placed at each accessible border of the camp.

"You don't happen to have any scent lures with you, do you?" Thomas asked Jericho, as they walked back in a wide sweep.

"No, don't get much use for them to be honest," Jericho replied. "Most of the animals I work with I'm trying to protect. That kind of thing is for the trophy hunters really."

"I don't have any either," Thomas said, shaking his head.

"Why, what's on your mind?"

"Oh, I was thinking about using Kanu's own tricks against him. And I also thought that if we could show some of our own that we too can bring the 'critters of the bush' in on demand, it would go a long way to showing Kanu up for what he really is."

"It's not easy stuff to come by in Kenya, what with trophy shooting being illegal," Jericho sighed. "But I know a trader in Usangi, across the border in Tanzania, who might have some, under the counter like."

"I think it would be worth getting if you didn't mind making the trip," Thomas implied.

"Aye, there's a couple of decent bars in Usangi, it's no bother at all," Jericho winked.

As they walked back, skirting through the brush behind the shooting range and up towards the main camp, Jericho stopped. He squatted down, hovering over a large print in the dry, crumbly earth.

"It's hers, the queen," Thomas stated. "I think it's from a few days ago when I was out here shooting francolin."

"She's certainly catholic in her tastes, I'll give her that," Jericho replied. "Quite the opportunist in fact. She must have lain here watching you the whole time."

"I think it's fairly clear she has no fear of humans whatsoever," Thomas stated flippantly. "I do hate it when animals haven't read the guide books, don't you?"

"Ain't that God's truth," Jericho grinned. "Big too from the size of that print."

"Big enough to throw her weight around, like with that adolescent male. I didn't want to say anything in front of Catherine, but this is easily the biggest lioness I've ever come across," Thomas agreed.

"Same here," Jericho nodded.

"And that roar is still bothering me too," Thomas admitted. "A lion's roar is deep and drawn. A leopard is more guttural and savage sounding. What did it sound like to you?"

"A fairly perfect blend between the two," Jericho replied flippantly. "Look, she's a big girl, with a decent set of lungs. There's nothing wrong with that," he replied with a grin.

Thomas gave him a despairing smile in reply. "I'm just thinking aloud," he shrugged. "But what if we're seeing some new change in behaviour here, perhaps brought on by climate change or the lack of food? What if it's more of an evolutionary change? Like Catherine said, lions are a vulnerable species and infanticide is one of the biggest localised threats they face. Maybe lionesses are getting bigger and stronger, just to increase the survivability of the cubs. I wouldn't be surprised if that male was killed because he was threatening them for instance. Jelani found prints of cubs not far from there."

"Maybe," Jericho smirked. "Sure, she's big and strong, and knows how to look after herself. But it was an adolescent she killed. She didn't mess with the big boys on the hill. I think as theories go, you're a little outside the box."

"It's served me well in the past," Thomas replied, looking out across the savannah as he felt a knot in his stomach. He had a horrible feeling they'd find out the truth soon enough.

CHAPTER FIFTEEN

They made the rest of the short walk back to the top of Anga ya Amani in silence. Jericho headed back to his tent, whereas Thomas made his way to one of the bath huts. He took his time to shower and then after, he filled the sink with piping hot water and took out his shaving kit. Although he didn't always use it, today he lathered his face with the traditional shaving brush before taking out the ebony handled Dovo straight razor. He began to shave, slowly and carefully sheering the grizzled stubble from his cheeks and chin. It gave him time to think and gather his thoughts.

Feeling refreshed and more awake, but still unsure about the nature of the lioness, he made his way back to the tent. He dressed quickly. He took the Colt Anaconda from the leather holster slung over the end bedpost, and slipped it into the inside pocket of his shooting vest. After the night's events, he wasn't prepared to relax so much as to walk around camp unarmed. He pulled on the boots he'd discarded underneath the bed the night before and walked out of the tent.

He found Catherine sitting at the dining table on the porch. She was writing quickly in a notebook, but stopped and looked up as he sat down on the rattan sofa opposite.

"All under control?" he asked.

"I think we've managed to avert the mutiny for now," she sighed. "They'll be busy most of the day reinforcing the camp."

"As will you be I imagine," Thomas added.

"You look ready for business," she exclaimed.

"I'm going to try and track them down properly. One lion on its own might not leave much of a trail, but a whole pride should give me something of an advantage."

"Is Jericho going with you?" Catherine asked, casually masking the concern in her voice as best she could.

"No, he's heading over the border to try and get his hands on some scent lures. I want to try and use Kanu Sultan's methods against him," Thomas replied with a shake of his head. "It will do us a lot of good to show Jelani's men that we have the same abilities. And it would be nice to have the upper hand for once."

Catherine studied him in silence for a moment, narrowing her eyes questioningly.

"Let's hear it, what's bothering you?" she asked.

"I was talking to Jericho about the strange behaviour this pride is showing. I suggested that maybe the females are getting bigger and stronger because of the changes in their environment and because of the risk to the cubs from the males. But there's something about their behaviour too."

"Well, we know sexual dimorphism is most exaggerated in species where there is intense, polygynous competition between males for access to females," Catherine stated, sitting back.

"Like lions," Thomas nodded.

"Yes, but as you say, these lions don't seem to exhibit those physiological differences," Catherine added. "In a way, they're more like wolves. Wolves show much less variation in their sexual dimorphism, and their social groups are made up of a monogamous pair and their offspring. This pride shows very close bonds. They even seem to have a clear alpha animal. Of course, this is all on your say so though," she smiled teasingly.

"Just remember what happened last time you doubted me," he laughed.

Catherine smiled then hesitated as a thought crossed her mind. "Come to think of it, I do remember reading about one species of cat that didn't show a huge range in sexual dimorphism, and had a pack structure more like wolves," she offered quietly.

"Oh really, which?" Thomas asked, confused.

"Smilodon, a sabre-toothed cat," she laughed. "All three sub-species were family pack hunters. Maybe we've found the Cannich cat's African cousin."

"Trust me, she's not that big," Thomas said, shaking his head.

"I'm only kidding," Catherine comforted him, getting up and slumping down next to him on the sofa. "I'm sure you're right and the changes we're observing are down to climate and behaviour factors. It's okay not to have all of the pieces of the puzzle you know?"

"I know," he admitted. "Best get out there and try to find some of the missing ones."

He stepped off the porch just as Jericho emerged from his own tent. The Irishman had also taken advantage of a fresh shower and a change of clothes. He carried a rather tattered rucksack over one shoulder, and slung it onto the passenger side of the customised, two-seat Jeep Wrangler. Thomas walked over to him.

"I'm going to take Rhodes with me," Jericho nodded as the big boerboel sauntered up to them. "Can you keep an eye on Saka?"

"I can go one better, I'll take her with me," Thomas replied.

"Good, that'll keep her out of the kitchen," Jericho grinned.

"Other than Rhodes, are you taking any protection?" Thomas asked. "Especially given the attention we've been attracting lately."

Jericho raised an eyebrow as he opened the glove compartment. Sitting inside was a bulky, odd looking revolver finished in hard chrome. Thomas could see it had an unusual design, with the barrel aligned with the bottom most chamber of the square shaped cylinder, rather than the top like most.

"This here's the rhino," Jericho explained quietly. "It's just about as ugly and as hard hitting as the real thing. I see it as Africa's version of the credit card. You don't leave home without it."

"Nice," Thomas replied with a sarcastic glance. "Seriously though, watch your six."

"Always do," nodded Jericho.

Thomas watched the Jeep roll out of camp. As the dust thrown up in its wake began to settle, he noticed Saka slink out from behind the kitchen. She was in the process of gulping something down when she spotted Thomas watching her. She froze, and her large, bat-like ears pricked up immediately as she dropped her head and prepared to spring away. Thomas guessed that as a professional thief, she was more than used to having retribution literally thrown at her when caught in the act, something she was now bracing for. Realising she wasn't about to be on the receiving end of such punishment, the mottle coloured canine relaxed and yawned casually, taking a few steps towards him.

"Feel like putting those skills to good use for once?" Thomas said softly and kindly.

Saka trotted over to him and as he knelt to greet her and butted him in the chest with the top of her head. She pushed her muzzle under the embrace of his arms, pushing against him and rubbing her cheek along his flank as Thomas made a fuss of her. As Thomas looked round, he saw Catherine leaning over the porch rail, her camera trained on him and Saka. She was smiling.

"It's not every day you get such a photo opportunity," she called out. "Do you think you might need a pack, out in the African sun?" she added sarcastically, lifting his canvas backpack from where he'd left it on the tent's porch. He walked over and took it from her, gently lifting her hand and kissing it in appreciation as he did so. He checked inside the pack to make sure it still contained everything from the day before; a radio, first aid kit, two canteens of water and his antler handled bowie knife. He gave her a quick nod and turned, but she pulled him back, handing him a black cattleman style hat. It had a tan coloured leather band, ordained with a single tooth of a mountain lion. The hat had belonged to Logan, Thomas's friend from Wyoming, who had been killed by the Cannich cat. He nodded again, putting it on as he walked back out into the sun.

"Just be careful," she cried out after him, still smiling.

"We're armed to the teeth," he replied, nodding towards Saka.

Mansa provided him with further supplies of biltong, trail mix and dried fruits. The thin African also passed him a sealed plastic bag of salted fish fillets for Saka.

"She seems to like them," Mansa said knowingly.

"Some hunter hey," Thomas shrugged. "Perhaps we should have called her mwizi instead," he added, using the Swahili word for thief.

"She is just true to her nature," Mansa replied courteously.

"After all, a hunter is a thief that steals life. She embraces this, as must we all. The only thing that separates us is the opportunity to show respect for our prey, not something all men share."

"That's rather profound Mansa," Thomas replied, "I'll do my best."

"Just remember, few plans or principles survive a first encounter with the enemy," Mansa replied. "When it comes down to it, there is still only one law of the jungle. Kill or be killed."

Thomas nodded, somewhat impressed by the elderly African's straightforward outlook. He packed the supplies into the bag and slung it over his shoulder. He grabbed his binoculars from the equipment tent too, before making a final stop at the gun rack. He slung his rifle over his shoulder and turned to head down the path, when he paused. He looked around almost sheepishly before reaching behind the rack and pulling out what looked like a sawn-off shotgun with a pistol grip. After chambering one round and slipping another two into the magazine, he collapsed the pump grip underneath the barrel, checked the safety, and stuffed the gun into a side pouch of the pack. He filled the cartridge loops of his shooting vest with '00' buckshot shells as he did so. He wasn't going to take any chances whilst out on his own, and he felt better having it at arm's reach. The gun was a Serbu Super Shorty, something he had carried for bear defence whilst working in Wyoming as a tracker.

As Thomas walked through the crew camp, he noticed Mason steadily tracking him with the camera. He smiled and walked over as Keelson joined them.

"That'll make a nice filler shot somewhere," Mason

laughed. "The great white hunter off to settle the score."

"I just want to see where our friends went," replied Thomas.

"We're going to document the fortification of the camp, then head out and get some stock footage," Kelly explained.

"Don't go too far," Thomas warned, "all the guns are elsewhere today, and after last night, I can't shake the feeling we might be being watched."

"You could always let us come with you and give us something real to film," Kelly pushed hopefully.

"I need to move quickly and quietly," Thomas explained, shaking his head. "Once I get a better idea of their territory, we can talk about group excursions okay?"

"You're making my job very hard Walker," Keelson scolded playfully.

"You practically got an entire series worth of action last night Kelly," Thomas laughed. "Get your stock footage and do some editing today. I will make it up to you."

"You'd better," she replied flippantly.

Thomas tipped the brim of his hat as he walked away, followed by Saka. He paused only for a moment as he reached the point from where they had watched Kanu Sultan the night before. He started to make his way to the baobab tree. As the parched grass became higher, up past his knees, Saka broke into a trot and came alongside. He knew she felt more confident when there were fewer people around. It didn't take long to reach the place where Kanu's convoy had stopped. He could still make out their tracks and the stained ground where the scent lure had been left. Saka sniffed at it, wrinkling her nose at the overtly powerful stink. Thomas slowed his pace and began to study the thick carpet of red dust that lay between the clumps of grassland and scattered trees. He soon found what he was looking for. Three good sets of prints showed where a small party of lions had homed in on the scent. This was the trail they had followed in. He guessed that the lions hadn't crossed the river, and had instead skirted around the camp to the east before heading south again. He decided as it was still early in the day, he might walk in the general direction the prints seemed to come from and see if they led to a crossing of paths further along, presuming the pride returned from whence they came as he suspected.

He made his way through the grassland slowly, stopping to examine any bent or crushed blades and patches that suggested the lions had passed that way. The savannah was dominated by pan dropseed and rye grasses, with mangled clumps of Bermuda grass, signifying where the soil had been disturbed, or where a bush fire had allowed it to spring up. He thought he could make out a path through it that had been flattened over, possibly by the passing of numerous bodies. Thirty yards in, his instincts were rewarded. A pile of lion scat signalled the trail of the pride. He crouched, carefully checking the wind direction as he waited for Saka to take interest. She flattened her ears as she approached the dung heap, dropping her head as if stalking prey. She nosed around the pile cautiously, making a hyena-like huffing as she did so. She skipped to and fro on her front paws, becoming more excited and agitated simultaneously. This was what Thomas had been hoping for.

Saka was hardly tame. She rarely followed commands of any sort. Just like a wolf, they had a different set of values to a domestic dog. Saka had never been playful or overtly affectionate as a pup. Suspicion, backed by cold, inquisitive intelligence had always been her predominant characteristic behaviour. She had never been gushingly eager to please like a puppy. She would grow bored very quickly, turning her powerful jaws on anything that had been chewable. In her case, that had turned out to be most things, including tents, saucepan handles, a revolver and any boots she could get hold of. She had loved leather boots as a pup, and Thomas remembered both he and Jericho had lost several pairs during training sessions that became learning experiences for them all.

Training any animal was easy to get wrong. The main misconceptions were that obedience could only be achieved as either a battle of wills or constant rewards. The trick with getting any animal, including humans, to comply unquestionably is to create the perception they have no other choice, and it is simply the requisite solution demanded by the situation. Presenting yourself as a dominant and arbitrary authority to a dog, especially a wild dog, whose pack instinct and hierarchy is based on strength and dominance, can lead to aggressive challenges. Thomas believed it was vital to show any dog that he had a place in the pack, and like most pack members, that he played an assigned role. For Thomas, that role was teacher and corrector, not always necessarily alpha. His job was simply to equip them with an understanding of what the world required of them. He did this by making them watch him, encouraging them to take their lead from him. Dogs did this naturally, but wild canines had to be convinced of its benefit.

Hunting dogs like Saka and her cousins, wolves, were natural problem solvers. Their comprehension was based on a more mechanical understanding of how things worked. They learn to do things that are in their interest, and to avoid those that aren't. Saka for instance, only had to watch Thomas undo the ties of the tent doors once to understand how they worked. Saka's competence was born from her desire to get outside and be free. A dog accepts their environment more readily, less questioningly. When a dog finds something it cannot do, its natural instinct is to turn for help towards the nearest human. A dog could be trained or shown how to open the tent doors, but it was far less likely to discover how to do so under its own, tireless investigation. In Saka's case, she would continue trying new methods, or adapt them until she found a solution. Even if the solution was simply give up, it lacked a reliance on Thomas or any other human for help.

This became the basis of his simple training with Saka. He had to exhaust every possible way of Saka not cooperating with him until it became her natural instinct to do so. Even then, he had restricted her to only the bare essentials of commands. 'Stay', the easiest, was so imbedded in her that she would be rooted to the spot for hours if he didn't release her. From rescuing her in the den, to fending off lions, her acceptance that 'stay' meant being out of danger was now natural instinct. 'Go on' was a release command, or one that gave her the freedom to explore further – something she needed little encouragement in and obeyed gladly. 'Here' was a simple recall, and again her understanding of Thomas's protective role played a vital role in her compliance. 'Out' was a warning command, telling her something was none of her business or dangerous. It had only taken a single encounter with a crested porcupine to convince Saka the benefit of this one. But it was the fifth and final command that Thomas had use for today.

Thomas always issued Saka's commands with the same guttural or softer tones that seemed universal amongst animals, but most closely echoed those made by wild dogs communicating in a pack. He also tried to emulate a behaviour that reinforced the command. As he watched Saka dancing round the lion scat, he slipped his rifle from his shoulder and brought it up, ready and poised as if beginning a hunt.

"Seek," he barked.

Instantly, Saka loped away, loose and alert. She travelled low to the ground, never bringing herself up to her full height. She craned her neck forward, her nose and muzzle only dipping slightly. She was following the scent, but her real gifts as a tracker were in her excellent eyesight and hearing. She moved like an English pointer dog, padding along the flattened path the lions had taken through the grass with an ambling gait that was surprisingly economic for her energy reserves, providing incredible stamina and the ability to hunt prey over long distances. Every fifty yards or so, she would stop, never taking her eyes off the path ahead as she waited for Thomas to catch up. They made their way in complete silence as the sun, and the temperature, rose higher.

~

The trail beaten Toyota bucked and shuddered as it forged a path through the lush elephant grass, the dulled chrome bull bars on its grill pushing the high reaching stalks down and aside like the bow of a ship. Kelly let out a deep sigh of contentment, throwing her head back as she did so and letting the sun warm her skin as it streamed in through the open window and roof. Mason was driving, and she felt content to take in the more aesthetic Africa stretching out in front of them, compared to the bloodier experience it had seemed so far. She closed her eyes, enjoying the warmth.

They were headed to the village where Thomas had killed the leopard. She was curious to see if their lives had changed for the better in the absence of the man-eater, or if the presence of the Daughters of the Darkness meant no respite for their way of life. She was also hoping to get an insight on how they saw Kanu Sultan, and if their perspective had changed since Thomas's arrival, especially after already reducing the pride's number. She knew the voodoo and supernatural angle would also play well to a western television audience, and couldn't help but hope the villagers would divulge their fears on camera.

She noticed a large white bird take to the air as the noise of the vehicle flushed it from the long grass. She watched it flap awkwardly, observing the terracotta coloured edges to its wings and crest. It reminded her of the herons that she sometimes saw at London's Richmond Park, a large open space in the capital, close to her flat in Putney Village.

"It's a cattle egret," Mason informed her, noticing the direction of her gaze in the rear-view mirror. "Recently they've started showing up in the UK, in places like Cornwall and Devon. Possibly the only good thing to come from climate change is the slightly more vibrant wildlife coming to our shores."

"Birds I don't mind," Kelly replied, still watching the bird's laborious progress in getting airborne. "You can keep the lions, tigers and bears though thanks."

"Oh my," Mason replied, smiling.

~

Thomas quickened his pace as Saka momentarily disappeared into a thicker patch of straw coloured rye grass. He slowed as a little flurry of banded martins gave away her position. The little, dark-chocolate backed birds with white bellies got their name from the thin black stripe across their faces, making them look like masked robbers. They cursed Saka with a high-pitched chirruping as she reappeared on the trail ahead. Thomas could tell she was losing interest; having been distracted by the birds, she was now looking for something else to do and skirted back round to him.

"Go on," Thomas called softly.

As she blended back into the surrounding grass, Thomas gave some thought to the other name given to her kind, the painted wolf. Out on the open savannah, her patchwork hide of black, brown and yellow mottles stood out. But here, in the deep brush and amongst the red and golden hues of the plain grasses, she was almost invisible. As he thought, he caught the sound of a high-pitched squeal rise up from a little further in. He realised that Saka's camouflage had been put to good use. She appeared again, closer to him, and as she threw back her head, he saw her swallowing the remains of a striped field mouse.

"That's not a bad idea," Thomas said, stopping for a moment to dig the supplies out of his rucksack.

He took a long swig of water from one of the canteens and tore off a chunk off biltong in his teeth. He offered Saka one of the salted fish fillets, which she gladly accepted. Unlike Meg would have done, she didn't pester him for more and instead lay down beside him. He idly wondered how Meg and Arturo were getting on at Catherine's mother's house. He imagined Meg being spoilt rotten, and nearly choked as he tried not to imagine Arturo the big black mastiff pulling Ally, Catherine's mother, along at full pelt through the quiet streets of Cannich.

As he took another gulp from the canteen, he picked up the slightest of movement from the corner of his eye, somewhere off to his left. He instantly jumped to his feet and brought the rifle up to his shoulder. It was then that he noticed the carefree chatter of the birds had ceased and the silence surrounding them. Saka too was up on her feet, her head bobbing up and down as she followed his gaze. The tiniest of growls lodged in her throat.

Thomas could see that the grassland gave way to a large thicket made up of various species of acacia, silver oaks and kapok trees. He looked through the scope of the rifle and scanned the woodland edge. He let out the breath he hadn't realised he was holding as he saw the hairy back of a bush pig slip into the shadows of the trees. As he wiped the sweat from his brow and looked up at the sun now directly overhead, he realised that most animals would be following suit and avoiding the heat of the day.

"It'll be cooler in there at least," Thomas said as he started walking towards the trees.

Saka padded by his side, panting slightly and seeming glad to be heading towards the offered shade. Seeing the bush pig had also reminded him of something Bah, the man from the ministry of defence back in Nairobi had said. Al Shabaab's forces to the north and east of Mombasa, and Kanu Sultan's operations as part of the supply chain, meant that Kenya was seeing a great number of forced conversions to Islam. He had noticed the bush pigs in the area seemed quite happy to forage near camp and human habitation, and he couldn't help wondering if it was perhaps due to no longer being a regular part of the menu. At the same time, with other prey items seemingly scarce, it would make sense that the predators would be likely to follow the pigs, in turn gradually habituating to human presence simply by association. It was the first theory that might make sense of the escalating attacks. Either way, he realised he should follow the pig into the thicket.

~

Kelly was pleased with the footage they had shot at the village. The people had spoken openly about living side by side with man-eaters. They had been a little more reluctant to discuss Kanu Sultan, but as she had distributed pictures of the six lions that had been killed so far, they had begun to take more of an interest. Proving that nearly a third of the pride had been killed was enough to plant a seed of doubt in their minds about Kanu Sultan's claims. There were at least three interviews that she knew she wanted to use.

The first, with the head man Whistle and his family, had brought a lump to her throat. The pain and anguish he seemed to be reliving as he told of the leopard attack, and the loss of his daughter, had almost been too much for her. He had expressed his humble thanks for Thomas's help with eyes shining with tears before becoming lost to his thoughts in silence. She had known straight away it would make for gripping television.

The second, with the hunter named Badru, had been much more volatile. He didn't seem fearful of Kanu Sultan, or the man-eaters, but he warned of their power and supernatural abilities. Kelly had taken pity on him as he had urged them to seek protection and leave, or suffer the consequences. She found it hard to believe that in the 21st century, such superstition was not only rife, but wholeheartedly accepted.

The third, with a gathered group of the village children,

had been much more upbeat. They had spoken of how they felt protected, and free to walk to school or play outside their homes. When pressed on the fact that only some of the man-eaters had been killed and the pride were still at large, one boy had shrugged and explained the lions had not returned to the surrounding villages as they were now being directed at those trying to kill them by Kanu Sultan. In short, they felt safe.

The villagers had seemed hopeful, even more energised as they had left. All except one. Standing at the side of the road, the tall, thin dark-skinned boy had watched them pass with an expression of dread. He had taken flight almost immediately, only his orange coloured jeans and the flash of his bare bronzed back showing up as he had dashed through the trees away from them. She had wondered where he could possibly be going and who he was. He had seemed vaguely familiar, but it had been Mason who had reminded her he was the boy who had run to the camp requesting they come deal with the leopard.

They were heading south-east, along a trail that bordered the Chyulu Hills National Park, making a wide loop back towards Anga ya Amani. They were looking for a flatter area of grassland to film a monologue and summary from Kelly. The igneous soil and well-watered slopes that led all the way to Mount Kilimanjaro in the south-west, seemed a little too lush and fertile compared to the amber and earthy tones of the scrub nearer camp. After about an hour, they found what they were looking for, and Mason brought the battered Land Cruiser truck to a halt on the crest of a hill overlooking vast, straw coloured grassland.

They spent some time raiding their supplies of water, fruit and biltong before setting up for the shoot. Kelly walked a little, drinking greedily from her canteen as she let her fingertips run through the waist high stalks. She paused and looked back, realising she had strayed some twenty yards from the car. She took off her sunglasses and shielded her eyes, partly to accustom them to the glare of the sun so she wouldn't be squinting whilst on camera, but also to take in the unfiltered view. The horizon was blurred by a heat haze, turning the few flat-topped trees in the distance into shimmering blobs of green and black. As she tried to focus on one, she thought she saw a glint of something reflecting in its canopy, but it was gone in an instant. She put it down to a trick of the light and turned back towards the truck.

"We're ready for you Kelly," Mason called out.

She waited as Karni fumbled with the black lapel microphone, as he fastened it to her loose fitting white blouse. She smiled, understanding his awkwardness.

"It's okay Karni, I trust you not to cop a feel," she whispered as he bent towards her.

"I'm sorry," he stammered. "Give me a boom mic any day."

"They're cumbersome and expensive my friend. Plus, it can't be that bad being this close to me," she purred.

"If you're flirting with me to make me feel better, it's having the opposite effect."

"Take much longer, and I'm going to stick your hand down there myself, so you have nothing to distract you and can attach the damn thing," Kelly warned flippantly.

"All done," Karni declared, walking backwards out of the camera's field of view.

He slipped on his earphones and began to monitor the feedback.

"How are the noise levels?" asked Mason.

"We're good. It's surprisingly quiet actually," Karni smiled.

"I just noticed. It is quiet, isn't it?" Mason remarked out loud. His face crumpled into a look of dread. "Oh shit...everyone back in the truck, now!"

Kelly only hesitated for a second. Facing Mason and the camera, she watched his expression distort into one of terror as the blood drained from his face. Spurred into action, she sprinted for the truck, flying towards the open front passenger door. Mason threw himself over the bonnet, whipping round and swinging off the frame into the driver's seat. Kelly was close behind him, throwing herself into the cabin and rising up to slam the door shut. That's when she noticed Karni was still outside. He still had his earphones on and was looking at them with a confused expression.

"There," Mason pointed behind Karni.

"Get in the truck," Kelly screamed.

The grass seemed to come alive. It rippled and flexed, converging on Karni from behind. As he sensed the movement, he bolted, grabbing his earphones and throwing them behind him in a hope to distract whatever was coming. It didn't work. There was an ear-splitting roar, then all the breath was knocked from his body. He found himself flying forward, and he saw Kelly's panic-stricken face pushed up against the window. His head struck the door below with such force that he slumped to the ground instantly, momentarily deaf and face down in the dust. An electrifying pain burst through his neck and shoulder, forcing his entire body to convulse and spasm. His trachea tried to open to pump more air into his suddenly oxygen starved body, but the clamping pressure on the back of his neck wouldn't allow it. His arms flailed, brushing against the sides of the truck, but growing weaker as the seconds passed. Face down in the dirt, he never saw his killer.

The lioness seemed huge to Kelly, inches away from her on the other side of the glass as she watched in horror. She pushed her feet against the closed door and squirmed backwards, her hands over her mouth. Mason dashed around the cabin checking the doors, windows and sunroof were closed. The two occupants of the Toyota watched as the lioness dragged Karni's body a little way into the grass. It turned to look at them, observing them with cold indifference. As it turned back to Karni's corpse, a second lioness appeared out of the grass. It placed a paw on the sound engineer's back, rolling him over by extending its claws into his flesh and using them for purchase. It lowered its head and sank its jaws into his right arm.

Kelly and Mason looked on in horror as a gruesome tug of war began, the two lionesses snarling and baiting each other whilst both refusing to let go of their prize. Suddenly, a third lioness appeared in front of the truck. With one easy bound, it jumped up onto the bonnet. It began to swat gently at the glass, just as a domestic cat would perhaps pester its owner for food. It looked in at the two people inside, its eyes wide and unblinking. It seemed to finally lose interest and jumped down, joining the other two in the squabble for Karni's remains.

"Well I for one am not going to just sit here and watch," Mason exclaimed.

He began beeping the horn repeatedly. The lions looked around, their curiosity aroused, but they showed no signs of fear or unease. They soon went back to their meal. Kelly noticed their blood-stained chins and cheeks with a shudder.

"Fine, let's see how you cope with two tonnes of truck coming your way," Mason growled, and turned the key to start the engine.

Just as he began to move the car, it was rocked by a sudden and vicious impact from the front, as a deafening explosion rendered them immobile. Mason watched in disbelief as smoke began to bellow from under the bonnet. There was the sound of popping and bubbling before another, much smaller bang made them all jump. A breath of flame quickly licked around the edges of the deformed bonnet before extinguishing into a second bellow of smoke.

"What just happened?" Kelly yelled at Mason.

"Something hit us," Mason stammered, "something big."

Kelly looked out of the window. The lions were still there. If anything, they seemed more interested in them now. All three had lifted their heads and edged a little closer, disregarding their meal for the time being.

"They weren't scared away by the noise," Kelly observed. "It's like they know we're in trouble. What do you think it was?"

"Well I'm not about to get out and take a look," Mason replied, "but I think somebody just took a shot at us. Better get on the radio don't you think?" he said, nodding to Kelly.

Kelly nodded back, her eyes wide and frantic. Mason was worried that she might be going into shock and reached over towards her bag.

"I've got it," Kelly said, quickly coming back to her senses. "Do you think we're still in danger from the shooter?"

"If they're packing heat with enough wallop to take out an engine, popping our heads off should have been no problem.

I'm guessing whoever they are wanted us stuck, possibly so the lions could finish the job."

Kelly remembered the glint she thought she had seen in the canopy of the tree towards the horizon. She tried to pinpoint it again as she peered through the windscreen. It seemed too far off.

"How far do you think that flat topped tree over there is?" she asked Mason, pointing through the glass.

"I'd say about a mile, maybe a little less," Mason replied. "Why do you ask?"

"I thought I saw something reflecting light in the canopy earlier, like a rifle scope maybe."

"That would be a hell of a shot," Mason exclaimed. "Not impossible though," he admitted, looking back again at the tree.

Kelly turned on the radio and checked the frequency.

"This is production crew to Anga ya Amani, come in, over," she broadcasted.

The radio crackled, but there was no reply.

"Maybe we're too far from the camp," Mason suggested.

"Anga ya Amani, come in please, this is a mayday."

Suddenly the radio crackled again, and Jelani's voice came through following the burst of static.

"We hear you production crew, what is your location, over."

Kelly looked at Mason as she had no idea where they were in relation to the camp. He grabbed the radio from her quickly.

"We're just a little way off the Chyulu Hills National Park road, heading east," Mason informed them. "We're about three miles out from Ulu village. We have one fatality and our car is going nowhere, over."

"We'll get out to you straight away, are you in any immediate danger?"

"Somebody shot our engine out. We're not alone out here, and I don't just mean the lions."

"We're on our way. Keep the channel open. I will also try to reach Thomas. If my thoughts are correct, he is walking straight towards you."

"Then warn him we have company, including three man-eaters, over."

"Wilco, over and out."

Mason looked round to find Kelly watching him expectantly.

"We just sit tight. Help is on the way. I suggest we keep our heads down just in case our shooter gets ambitious, but at least our friends out there can't get in."

"Let's hope they know that," Kelly shuddered.

~

Thomas knelt at a hole that had been forged through the intertwined branches of the candle bushes and whistling acacias. He could tell from Saka's relaxed body language that there were no lions within, but at over four feet high, it was obvious what had made it. He peeked inside, finding a smattering of pugmarks and even a strand of whitish fur stuck to an overhanging barb of the acacia. As he made his way in a little further on his hands and knees, he realised it was probably a day den, perhaps used by the mothers of the pride to hold up with cubs and escape the heat of the day. There would be several throughout the territory. The interior was warm and spacious, the branches reaching nearly eight feet overhead before doming naturally on either side. The thorny refuge also offered protection from the prying eyes of hyenas or other lions out in the open.

He sat in the centre of the den for a few moments. He closed his eyes, focusing on the lingering scent of the animals. It was pungent; not thick enough to suggest they had been there within the past few hours, but still no more than a day or two at most. The scent was raw and stale, full of earth and musk. It was unmistakable at such proximity. He opened his eyes and crawled back out again, just as his radio crackled from within his pack. He found it quickly and retrieved it. Jelani informed him of the situation. Thomas knew that if he kept heading south through the thicket, he would emerge on the other side of the plain where Kelly and the others were stuck. It was probably a walk of four miles or so he guessed, but he was determined to make it, even though he knew Jelani and the others were on the way. Before setting off through the thicket, he took a long swig of water from a canteen and streamed some into his hand, which Saka obligingly licked off.

The thicket was dark and cool. It was impossible to avoid the scratches of the acacias and wait-a-bit thorns, and he had given up trying. He felt clammy and claustrophobic. He knew why it made him feel uneasy. It had been a thicket just like this one where he had found Amanda's remains. He walked on, his rifle out in front of him. Saka slipped through the brush easier than he did, but stayed close and silent as they went. She could sense his tension, and was automatically scouting for danger, unable to identify the source of his anxiety. Thomas began to let out laboured and aggravated breathy sighs as he fought his way through the maze. As his arms grew tired and the humidity ate away at him, he realised that he was making a great deal of noise, and was following Saka's lead rather than his own sense of direction. He took a knee to gather his thoughts and take another swig of water, batting away the mosquitoes that rose to greet his sudden stop. Their buzzing reminded him of the rift valley fever that had stopped him from being there at the crucial moment Amanda had needed him.

"Get me out of here girl and there's a buffalo bone in it for you," he pleaded to Saka.

The thin, long legged canine padded over and gently butted his chest with her head, pushing her body against his as she passed. She made a high-pitched whistling noise and loped off through the branches. Thomas followed, knowing she was heading in the right direction. He let out a sigh of relief as he began to notice the branches and scrub thinning out. They were on the other side of the thicket. Within a few minutes he realised he could see sunlight and the golden hues of the savannah grass ahead. He stopped at the edge of the wood and took out his binoculars to scan the sweeping vista ahead of him.

Almost as soon as he did, he heard the distant sound of a car engine. He quickly sought the direction from which it came. In the far distance, he could see a flat-topped acacia tree and a cloud of dust disappearing into a heat haze. Before he could raise the binoculars to his eyes, it was gone. Saka stood at his side, watching expectantly.

Thomas stepped into the waist high grass and began to forge a path through, heading straight for the tree in the distance. Saka slipped from his left to his right and back again, always ahead. When she flushed a pair of yellow-throated sandgrouse, she paid them no attention but kept going, her keen eyesight drawn to something else. Thomas followed her upward gaze and frowned as he saw the black silhouettes hanging in the sky a little way off. The vultures were already gathering above where Karni's body probably lay he realised. As a dedicated opportunist, Saka knew that vultures meant a carcass, and the possibility of a far greater windfall than the two escaping birds offered. Her instincts would help guide him to Kelly and the others.

The straw like tufts of Bermuda grass gave way to an area that had been flattened and pushed down. He could see the tracks of a wide and heavy vehicle had gouged a trail heading east and he presumed it had been the one he'd heard racing off earlier. The trail was only a few yards from the flat-topped acacia tree, and Thomas quickly set about scaling the trunk, carefully avoiding the bite of the thorns as he did so. Close to the top, he found a convenient fork in a branch that offered a reasonable seat. He secured and steadied himself before slipping the rifle from his shoulder and bringing it up to look through the scope. He found the white backed vultures in the sky as they began to gradually drop lower, and shifted his gaze to the hillside below them. There he spotted the stranded Toyota with Kelly and the others inside. He pulled the radio from his pack.

"Come in production crew, this is Walker, have you in sight, over," he said, using the Motorola's hands-free feature.

"This is production crew, where are you Thomas?" Kelly's voice rang out from the speaker.

An electronic beep signalled the channel was clear and he spoke again, switching on the same feature on his handset.

"I'm in the same tree your friend was. I'm guessing he was monitoring local radio channels and heard your call for help, and decided his work was done for the day. I have a pretty perfect view of you from here."

"We still have some unwanted company. I don't recommend you turn up just yet."

Thomas looked back through the scope of the rifle. With both eyes open he studied the distant spec that was the truck and reached up with his right hand, adjusting the windage and elevation screws on the Leica scope. Once happy, he panned right and found an off-white blob sticking up out of the grass. It was the head of a lioness. He watched as it slowly stood up and moved towards the truck. It jumped up onto the bonnet and then made another bound onto the roof. It began to take deep, inquisitive sniffs around where Thomas guessed the sunroof was. The big lioness paused, as if its attention had been drawn by something. He presumed it now had an even clearer view of the truck's occupants. It began to swat at the glass panel, clawing at the edges. Then it started to place its weight on it, pounding on the roof with crashing force. Thomas guessed she carried about 280lbs, and wasn't sure how much of a beating the glass could take.

"Thomas, if you're in a position to let off a few shots, we won't complain. It looks like she wants in," Kelly's voice rang out from the radio.

"I'll see what I can do," Thomas replied. "You're not exactly fifty yards away though."

He watched the lioness through the scope, keeping both eyes open as he did so. He let out a long exhale as he began to work back from the truck and the lioness. At one third and two thirds back he stopped completely and watched the movement of the grass in order to gauge the strength and direction of the air currents. There was a slight crosswind, from his east to his west, and no more than about five miles per hour in strength. But over the distance, that was enough to throw his shot off by near enough four feet. He adjusted the windage screw again and settled the scope on the distant truck and its unwanted passenger.

Next, he slid back the bolt of the Holland & Holland rifle and ejected the magazine of ammunition. He placed it in the direct sunlight exposed on the branch beside him, and left it there. He knew he needed all the help he could get over the distance, and warming the bullets would have a small effect on the propellant within each of the 3.5-inch-long rounds, giving them a faster burn and a slight increase in reach. It would take nearly three seconds for the bullet to reach its target while travelling through the air at 2,375 feet per second. That gave the lioness plenty of time to move, or for the bullet to be thrown off course by a change in the wind.

"You may want to duck down below the windows to be on the safer side," Thomas instructed Kelly and others.

He began to slow his breathing down, all the time watching the lioness through the scope. She was hunkered down and determinedly clawing and swatting at the sunroof. She had her back to him and was slightly side on. He decided the best bet was to aim for an entry point just above the ribs and below the left shoulder. That would give him a solid body shot, reducing the chance of a miss, but at the same time offering a potential kill shot.

He checked the magazine and cartridges within were suitably warm to the touch before refitting it into the receiver underneath the rifle. He took three deep breaths, each time slowing the exhale in between. He remembered the old shooting saying of 'aim small, miss small' and focused with unblinking tenacity on a tawny coloured spot on the lioness's flank, a little below her muscle-clad left scapula. He squeezed the trigger, smoothly drawing it all the way back to the finishing position, even as the rifle kicked and released the projectile with a whip like crack of explosive force. He didn't blink, watching through the scope for any tell-tale indications of the miss he expected. Instead, the lion jumped straight up into the air and came crashing down, rolling off the windscreen and slumping into a heap by the side of the car. He'd hit on target, the bullet blasting its way through muscle, bone and sinew into the chest cavity, destroying the lungs and heart with the shrapnel and what was left of the expanded, misshapen bullet after impact.

The other two lions were up on their feet in an instant, and Thomas moved the gun slightly to focus on the nearest. It was then he heard the unmistakable sound of a V8 engine equipped with a supercharger. He sat up and looked round. The Big Cat was coming hard and fast along the trail from the opposite direction. By the time he looked back round, the remaining two lionesses had slipped off into the grass and were nowhere to be seen.

Thomas quickly scrambled down the tree, slinging his pack and the rifle over his shoulder. At a quick pace, it would take him about fifteen minutes to reach them, which was probably faster and easier than waiting for them to come to him. Saka surged ahead as before, as they headed into the savannah grass, which now came up to his chest. It was light and easily brushed aside, giving way to his touch almost immediately. The ground was only gently sloped and he had no trouble making way, but he was glad to hear the sound of a second car engine as Jelani and some of his men arrived behind the stricken Toyota, having come from the direction of the village instead. He was just wondering if they had possibly seen the lionesses leave, when he was struck by the same earthy, musky smell he had detected in the den. Saka appeared by his side, her ears flattened as she emitted a low warning growl. He had presumed the lions had fled into the nearby cover of the scrub and trees of the hillside. It was only now he realised they had instead entered the long grass, probably making their way to the thicket. They were coming his way.

Thomas had just enough time to drop the rifle and reach behind his head for the pistol grip of the shotgun from the pocket of his rucksack, dropping to one knee as he did so. The savage, guttural, brawling roar let him know they were coming for him. Saka was watching dead ahead and Thomas saw the grass shaking violently as something quick and heavy thundered towards them. He pumped the gun and pulled the trigger, a violent blast exploding from the end of the barrel just as the grass parted and the straw-coloured lioness sprang at him. She smacked into the ground in front of him, the bloodied right side of her face and missing part of her skull hidden from view below her crumpled corpse.

Saka instantly changed position, circling Thomas and coming up on his left side. He stayed knelt, listening to the moaning roar that echoed from thirty feet away. It was the long, drawn call that lions used to communicate with each other. She was searching for her partner, less sure and certain in the quiet following the gunshot.

"I'm still here. She's not," Thomas spat, his heart pounding in his chest as he searched the encompassing greenery for a trace of movement.

Seconds passed like minutes until he heard the lioness's call again, but now from further away and behind him. He didn't dare move until her third call sounded out over the grassland, even more distant and forlorn sounding. Thomas took a moment to put the gun away, but pulled his revolver from his shooting vest as he stood up and began to fight his way through what remained of the grass ahead of him. After several excruciating minutes, he emerged a little way down the hill from the Big Cat and where the others had gathered round Kelly and Mason. He saw Catherine comforting Kelly, who was clutching her and sobbing into her shoulder. As their eyes met, Thomas felt his heart break a little as he read the pain Catherine was gripped by. Saka yawned, a canine indication of unease and tension. She dropped her head as she jumped into the truck bed of the Big Cat, where Karni's body lay, wrapped in blankets Jelani and the others had brought. She let out a whimpering squeak before dropping her head onto her paws. Thomas wondered if she realised she had survived her brush with the lions while Karni had not, that life and death sat side by side on the bottom of the truck; the very embodiment of the struggle he was here to face, and the same one Patterson had faced before him. He felt a sickening feeling in his gut. As yet, in just over a century, nothing had really changed. Something would have to.

CHAPTER SIXTEEN

Jericho entered the town borders of Usangi with a dry throat and a sweat soaked back. He trundled through the dirt streets, slowed and stalled by the bustles and throngs of people flitting among the busy market stands. They carried goods ranging from garish coloured knock-off clothing to enormous bunches of lime green plantains. The town itself was the same mix of modernity and tradition. The northern border of the town was marked by a grand church, sitting cathedral-like in a position of self-importance. Its colonial columns and closed, white painted double doors were ignored by the locals, who favoured the smaller evangelical offering housed in a simple, elongated building made of wood on the other side of town. In amidst the two were shanty streets of smooth-walled clay huts with domed, thatched roofs, and simple timber cabins with sloping corrugated ones. The joint primary and secondary school was a much more modern looking structure, and rose up to the west over the single-storey buildings.

Having navigated the market, he turned onto Main Street. It reminded Jericho of something out of an old cowboy film. A number of plain terraced stores lined the road, some made of breeze blocks, caked together with sand coloured and muddied natural cement; others adding to the western feel with their dusty wooden verandas and low porch roofs. Jericho pulled in to the side of the road, next to the only two-storey building on the street, its powder blue facade stretching around the corner of Main Street and into a sleepy access road. It was a hotel, cafe and general store all in one. He was surprised that the Warthog was not the only car outside the establishment. Parked out front was a white Dodge Ram Rebel 4x4 truck, sporting blacked out wheel arches and bumpers. The chromed light rig and 18 inch wheels seemed a little out of place for a back-water town on the Tanzania border, where the vast majority of vehicles were older models of Land Rover Defender and Toyota Land Cruiser. Someone new was in town and they had cash to burn.

Jericho got out of the car and left the windows open. Rhodes got up from the passenger foot well and lumbered up onto the seat, panting happily as he looked out onto the town. Jericho rough housed with him a little in play, getting a good natured, bellowing bark from the big dog before he left him to guard the car as he headed into the store.

He passed through the saloon doors in the corner entrance, painted in the same blue as the outside, and paused for a moment to look around. To his right, were a number of plastic tables and chairs that served as the cafe. To his left was a long, oak decked bar, lined with empty stools with torn red vinyl seats. An elderly Tanzanian was behind the bar, wearing a dirty white T-shirt and an equally drab and dusty black cotton waistcoat. Jericho nodded in his direction. He was planning to stop at the bar, but thought it best to get what he'd come for first. He headed towards the rear half of the building, where he could see the backs of high aluminium shelf towers lining the cafe area. This passed as a supply store for the hunting outfits operating in the area, and he sauntered his way over.

He turned down the first aisle, ignoring the crude wire snares, poisons and traps that were illegally sold to the local farmers. He paused for a moment in the second isle, admiring some of the handmade machetes and knives, adorned with carved handles made from the horns of kudu, oryx and eland. One smaller blade was simply set in a polished piece of warthog ivory. Jericho often used the same material as natural night sights on his guns, as it did not yellow and fade like other types. As he passed into the third aisle, he found what he was looking for. The shelves were filled with various types of lures. Some were intended to call in predators and prey through mimicry of various calls. Most of these were electronic, and Jericho couldn't help smiling, knowing these were only bought by the westerners. Most of the local guides were well practiced in mimicking the local wildlife, and more than capable of calling them in without electronic help.

The scent lures were next, and he was surprised to find a large number of small 2oz bottles of lion attractant. Jericho knew a store like this would only lay down such a supply if there was a demand. He couldn't help but wonder if it was down to just one regular customer perhaps. He checked his wallet, wondering how much to get. Although the national currency was officially the Tanzanian shilling, trade was still best done in the good old U.S dollar, and the higher the bill value, the better the exchange rate. Jericho fingered a crisp $50 bill and scooped up three of the bottles.

As he turned the corner of the aisle and headed towards the counter at the back, he was startled by a stunning, young blonde woman ahead of him. She was dressed in a tight-fitting desert camouflage tee, with a deep plunging neckline that seemed sculpted round the teasing glimpse of her ample cleavage it allowed. As she bent down to pick up a hunting field guide on a lower shelf, he couldn't help but admire her skinny waist and what he imagined were long, silky legs wrapped in equally tight-fitting cargo pants. But she had a taut, muscular stance too. As she stood up and turned, she spotted him and flashed him a brilliant, perfect smile. Her blue eyes sparkled at him, and he could pick up a trace of jasmine wafting from her loose hair, that fell over her shoulders and reached towards her breasts on either side, Amazonian like. American thought Jericho, no longer left in doubt to whom the Dodge truck belonged. It was only then that he noticed the bald, heavily set man in a sand coloured safari shirt, watching him from behind. Jericho guessed the man was her guide and quickly went back to ignoring him.

Jericho guessed the blonde was in her early twenties at most, and watched as she moved to the counter and began talking to the Tanzanian clerk about an electronic predator call device on the shelf. He raised an eyebrow as he watched her hand over $500 without even attempting to haggle, but then realised there was something familiar about her. She turned back towards him, holding the device, which looked like a portable stereo system drabbed in camouflage. As she noticed the bottles of scent lure he was holding, she paused.

"You predator hunting too?" she asked in a deep, Southern drawl of an accent. Texan, Jericho guessed.

"Aye. How bout yourself?" Jericho nodded.

"I'm going for my first wild lion," she answered with a flirtatious smile.

"Forgive me for asking, but I know you, don't I?"

"I'm Tiffany Lee Amberson," she smiled again, flicking her hair back as she did so. "I'm a cheerleader for the Laredo Lions, but if you're a hunter, you may have seen my YouTube channel. I'm Game Girl."

"Of course you are," Jericho said, raising an eyebrow.

He had indeed seen her online videos. They depicted her

hunting alligators in Louisiana and taking on smaller predators like foxes and bobcats in her native Texas. Although he didn't doubt that she knew how to shoot, her preference for firing from close quarters on pre-baited animals made him think a lion was a little out of her league.

"The cats round here aren't the friendliest of sorts," Jericho warned her, glancing at the guide again. "Anyone shooting down range at them is okay as far as I'm concerned, but don't take it on lightly. These things make your mountain lions look like kittens and they mean business. They're bona fide man-eaters too."

"Good thing I'm not a man then," Tiffany exclaimed with a wry smile.

"That I can see," Jericho flirted.

"She's in safe hands," snapped the bald man from behind.

"Pity," Jericho replied under his breath.

He was pretty sure Tiffany had heard him. She went to slip past, brushing up against his chest ever so slightly, but hard enough so he felt the weight of hers against him.

"There's probably not another bar for miles, so if you're going to buy a girl a drink, there's no time like the present," she whispered.

"Well I'm going to buy me one, you're welcome to come too darlin," Jericho grinned.

After paying for the bottles of scent lure and checking on Rhodes, Jericho headed back into the bar. The afternoon sun was already swelteringly hot, and he was in no rush to get back into the Jeep to take on the long trail back to Anga ya Amani. He was glad to see that in the interim, Tiffany had lost her escort and was sitting at the bar alone waiting for him. He sauntered up beside her and ordered two King Oryx Dark lagers. The older Tanzanian in the waistcoat he had spied earlier, served them, pouring the black, tawny headed drinks into dusty glasses he took down from the shelf behind him. Jericho took a long drawl from his. It tasted like toast, coffee, liquorice and molasses all at the same time.

"It's not quite Guinness, but it's cold," he stated.

"I could get used to it," Tiffany smirked.

They ordered a second round, and then moved onto a pair of boiler makers before Jericho voiced his concerns a second time.

"Look, I know you're hardly a novice, but you should seriously think again about taking on the lions around here. I wasn't kidding about them being partial to people eating."

"I can't turn down the publicity of a Laredo Lion cheerleader taking down an actual lion," she shrugged. "The show is depending on it. The guns, my truck; everything is sponsored. I need to deliver."

"Hunted anything like that before?" Jericho asked after a pause.

"I'm the youngest person on record to have taken the big five. I was just fifteen when I claimed them. Lion, buffalo, rhino, leopard and elephant all under my belt."

"Forgive me," Jericho sighed, "but hunting in Tanzania isn't like a safari in South Africa. The bush is harsher, the animals meaner and the hunting harder, as well as being a two-way street."

"But it's okay for you to hunt them, is that it?"

She was smiling, but Jericho knew she was on the defensive now.

"Not lightly I don't," he said. "And, I'm not alone. I'm working with one of the best hunters in the world. We know each other well, and work together even better. We also have a top wildlife biologist in our camp too. You don't have that advantage. You're just a paying client to our friend Yul Brynner, wherever he's disappeared off to."

Jericho frowned, realising Tiffany had no idea who Yul Brynner was. Too young even for me he thought. As if on cue, the bald-headed guide walked back in through the saloon doors and eyed him menacingly.

"We'd better get moving. The lions will be lying up in the heat of the day," he said in a thick Afrikaans accent.

"You're going after them now?" Jericho exclaimed. "That's a terrible idea. You need to set a bait site up and leave it for a good few nights, so you know they're visiting before you put your client in harm's way."

"We know what we're doing," the guide replied.

Jericho guessed from his accent that he was from Namibia rather than South Africa. He was always slightly suspicious of outfits that crept north into territory like Tanzania. It wasn't easy hunting, but it was easier getting around the rules. Corruption was rife amidst the local authorities. That was why he was here too after all. He had no permit or jurisdiction to hunt in the country, but he did have cash, and that was all that mattered.

"Why not come and hunt with us, we could always use another gun. I have a very comfortable tent too I'd be willing to open to your good self," Jericho offered. "Not to you though," he added, nodding to the guide.

"That's a two-way street," Tiffany replied. "Why not come with us. We could use you too. My tent's not luxurious, but there's room for two. As long as we were lying very close together that is," she purred.

"I'm tempted darlin, I really am. But I don't like your set up. And I'm needed back across the border."

"Seems like it's not meant to be," Tiffany sighed.

She jumped off the bar stool and kissed him gently on the cheek. As she did so, she slipped a card into the back pocket of his trousers.

"I'll be around for a few more days if you change your mind."

"Not if the lions have anything to do with it you won't," Jericho quipped.

"That's enough of the scare mongering, Irish," snapped the guide.

Tiffany walked out through the saloon doors, but the bald man lingered. He walked over to Jericho and leant up against the bar to his side.

"I think it's time you left too Irish, on your way boyo," he said, prodding his finger into Jericho's deltoid, which was as hard as concrete.

Jericho smiled as he sank the rest of the boiler maker in one fluid movement. He didn't fail to notice the man's fingers tighten around the hilt of the belt knife he was wearing.

"You've heard God invented whiskey so the Irish wouldn't rule the world haven't yer?" Jericho asked.

Without waiting for the answer, Jericho kicked away the bald man's feet, slamming the side of his head into the bar with his left hand. The guide slumped to the floor, dazed, and with a trickle of blood oozing from his right temple. Jericho threw a $50 bill at the bar tender and tipped his hat as he got up.

"The thing is, I haven't had enough whiskey yet," Jericho whispered into the bald man's ear as he leant down.

As he left the bar, he saw Tiffany sitting in the driver's seat of the white Dodge truck. He smiled at her and shook his head at her stubbornness, which he couldn't help admiring. He climbed into the Warthog and reached into the glove box, his hand on the rhino revolver as he watched the bald man stagger out of the bar and past him. He relaxed as the guide climbed into the truck with Tiffany and they pulled off. Jericho started the engine and reversed out before heading in the opposite direction, still smiling.

~

Tiffany groaned as she checked her phone again. No signal and no connection. That meant no social media, picture messaging or other promotions she was planning. She would have to wait until they got back to the hotel they were staying at in Arusha. The Impala offered a little piece of luxury, civilisation and most importantly, Wi-Fi, amidst the dust, mosquitoes and spicy food; all three of which she blamed for her flighty stomach. At least for the moment they were travelling along the relatively smooth B1 highway, heading south towards Same, where they would turn off and make for the nearby Mkomazi National Park. That's when the road would get bumpy and she would have to fight to keep her breakfast down. She was hoping the alcohol would help, and so far, it seemed to be doing so.

They were heading for a private farm on the outskirts of the park, where they had permission to hunt and film. The land owner had been quite clever, planting a good number of shade offering trees in several clusters, all to the north of the property. He kept a few cows and goats, and had sunk a well too, but they and the shade were there to attract what brought in the real money. Wildlife from the National Park often strayed onto the land, with both predator and prey species enjoying the shelter, food and water it offered. Whereas most local farmers received less than the equivalent of $10 for the use of their land, Faraji, the land owner here, charged $150 for the use of his. It was still a small amount compared to the $50,000 billed for most safari hunts, but it easily covered the anticipated losses to his livestock and the expenses of keeping the land primed for the use of hunters. Her guide, Dali, had convinced Tiffany this was the place to go if she wanted a lion. As they turned off the highway and onto the dirt track that would eventually lead to the farm, she hoped he was right.

~

She lay hunkered in the long wisps of grass in the shade of a candelabra tree. The swathe of lush greenery that hid her had been bleached by relentless sun, and her pale mottled hide blended into the background almost perfectly. Twenty feet away, a caramel coloured zebu shorthorn cow grazed complacently, blissfully unaware of her presence. Her tail rose like a whip, swatting away some of the black and crystal blue bodied flies swarming her back. The cow raised its head and looked towards the thick clumps of grass for a moment, before going back to the greener shoots at its feet.

She lifted up onto her haunches and took a silent step forward, nosing through the thickly bladed grass, her ears flat, and whiskers reaching out ahead of her as they registered the waft of warm air breezing in her direction. She froze. Her ears pricked at the distant sounds coming from the stone dwellings where she knew the humans were. The cow heard them too and moved off, the bell around its neck clanging loudly as it lumbered away. She fought the urge to burst from cover and take it down, as was her instinct, and instead stood up fully and watched it go with casual flicks of her tail. She raised her head and issued five short grunts. As she turned towards the stone dwellings with a soft growl, eight tawny coloured heads appeared out of the grass behind her.

~

Tiffany took the Remington 770 rifle she'd been given as an endorsement for her YouTube channel out of its bag in the bed of the truck. She watched as Dali talked to Faraji. The bald man had his hands on his hips as the Tanzanian farmer pointed to the north. She presumed they were discussing where to set up. She checked the sights along the stainless-steel barrel of the gun and the scope. They'd gone to the trouble of finishing the rifle in her favoured camouflage pattern, neatly matching her clothes. She touched up her lip gloss using the side mirror of the truck. At least everything would look good on camera, including her. Out of the corner of her eye she glimpsed Dali leering at her. *Keep dreaming* she thought smugly.

She hauled the camera case and hydraulic tripod out of the truck bed.

"You can start helping any time you like," she yelled out to Dali.

The guide finished talking to the Tanzanian and handed him an envelope that Tiffany guessed contained the payment for use of the property.

"This is all certified and legal, right?"

"Of course, don't worry," Dali laughed. "I told you I'd look after you."

"I mean it. I want to see the permits, everything. I know why we're here, but hunting close to a National Park could bring down a lot of heat. It'll be great for publicity, but only if the hunt's legal."

Tiffany already had merchandise in the form of sweat and tee shirts, made up with the mantra 'hunting is my high and it's already legal' emblazoned on it. She knew the hunting of a treasured 'tourist' lion, near a National Park in Zimbabwe the year before, had led to a viral campaign against the rich dentist who had shot it. There would undoubtedly be another outburst amongst the greenies if she bagged a lion under similar circumstances. The only difference was that she anticipated the exposure and planned to put it to good use.

Dali walked over and picked up the camera case and tripod.

"Don't worry. All is in hand and perfectly legal. I have the paperwork right here," he said, tapping the chest pocket of his shirt. "We don't even have to go that far. The lions will come to us."

Tiffany nodded and began to follow him out towards a cluster of trees to the east.

~

She stopped about thirty yards from the nearest of the stone dwellings. Her nostrils were struck with a frenzy of different scents, and she moved her head slowly from side to side to take them all in. Somewhere to the north, brush was burning, and the particles of soot and carbon made her nose wrinkle. A similar, more chemical odour from the other side of the dwellings irritated her. She recognised it as the breath of the strange metal containers the humans used.

The first time she had seen a man on a horse, close to where she now lay, she had panicked, mistaking it for a single strange creature rather than two separate ones. She had dared not flee in case it would run her down. But her forced steadiness had allowed her to observe the man dismounting the horse, and the strange wrappings of leather and softer skins they used to ride. Later she had seen cattle harnessed together with dead trees and more leather and skins. She now understood the human ability to use animals in this way and dismissed their comings and goings without concern. Her continued observation had replaced fear with indifference. She had seen them use tools, just like the vervet monkeys and house crows that stayed close to their habitations, but was still cautious when they appeared with something new or unfamiliar.

The warm air brought to her a waft of jasmine, and she tensed as she caught the human scent clinging to it. The pride had staked out this land many times. They had occasionally taken cattle and goats here, but only at night, when the humans weren't around and had failed to bring their animals back to the stone dwellings with them. Today was different. The pride had split during the night, some staying north of the river, whilst the majority had crossed it and circled the lake to rest up and drink. Moving after a human kill was something she had learnt to do from her own parents. She remembered being chased and the exploding cracks of the sticks the men carried. She remembered the night her mother had not returned from the hunt. Men killed them and they killed men. She had fled the territory after watching her father die taking on two male lions. She had moved along the coast and gradually in land.

When she had killed a lioness stranded during a storm with her in marshland, she had discovered a den of cubs close by. It was the first time she had felt a maternal instinct, but it had remained strong since. Three of those cubs now made up some of the number with her today. The fourth had stayed the other side of the river during the night. Their own cubs bolstered the ranks of the pride further. With their numbers scattered though, she felt uneasy and defensive. She settled down again. They had watched the upright apes do this many times. There was still some waiting to be done.

~

Dali showed Tiffany the hunting blind that had been put in place for her. It was little more than a dried-up irrigation ditch that had been widened just enough for someone to lie down in. There was a soft mound of earth in front of it that would act as a rifle rest. Once she got comfortable in it, Dali would cover her further with grass and foliage from nearby. The blind was directly opposite a small copse of patchy trees. As they walked over the ground, he pointed out the numerous pug marks and the scratch marks on the trunks of the trees.

"We'll call blast from here. The wind is in our favour and Faraji has been keeping the livestock close by for the last few days," he explained. "You need to be careful though. The pugmarks are lion undoubtedly, but the tree scratches are leopard. You don't have a permit for a leopard."

"So what am I meant to do if one turns up and takes a liking to me?" Tiffany asked.

"Well you're a very pretty girl, it's only natural," Dali laughed. "But I'll be covering you from the blind back there."

Tiffany showed her contempt to the flippant remark in a scowl, as he pointed to a mound, where a screen of woven sticks and dried grass could just be seen sticking up out of the long grass about a hundred yards away.

"Best get ourselves into position hey," Dali suggested. "The afternoon is starting to get away from us and you need to be dug in well before twilight. Have a good long drink, as it'll be your last for a while. I'll set up that new toy of yours for the call blasting."

Tiffany took the rifle and placed it on the ground in front of her as she lay down in the blind. She rolled her shoulders to loosen her muscles and brought the butt of the gun up. She made herself as comfortable as possible. Dali returned and began to cover her carefully with the material around her in the long grass. She shot him a furious glance at his all too rigorous patting of her buttocks. He gave her a knowing grin in reply. *You won't be smiling when I get up again* she thought. She focused instead on making her own modifications to the brush around her head and in front of her; building the mound up until she was satisfied she was completely hidden from view. Dali finished covering the rest of her.

"Remember, if you need to pee, just do it. But whatever you do, don't move. The moment they know you are here, they're gone," he warned.

"I'm fine," she muttered. "Let's do this."

Dali walked back to the trees and turned on the call blaster. It had a remote control, which he pocketed before adjusting the volume to maximum. The screaming calls of a deer fawn in distress boomed from the speakers. The bleating, high pitched sound rolled out across the surrounding savannah as he walked back past Tiffany with a nod of his head, and made his way to the rear blind.

~

She moved slowly through the grass, looping widely to the south of the stone dwellings. She could sense the others, as they followed her movement in a wide spreading arc. After crossing the dirt track they moved more freely, gradually turning north as they swept forward. She came to a halt in the golden swathes of grass, about fifty yards from the mound where she knew a man was hunched, as there often was. She glanced to her left, noticing the amber eyes of one of her adoptive daughters fixed on her. She dropped her head, signalling her permission for the others to move. They crept forward together as an offensive line through the grass. She banked left, giving away her intention to skirt the first mound. The two sisters to her right converged on it silently. There was now just thirty yards between them and the man they sensed was there. He had positioned himself downwind, but so had they.

They moved one cautious step at a time. The big female's ears pricked each time the harsh bleat from up ahead sounded out, but she knew larger and better prey was much closer. She paused, hesitating to move past the mound until she knew the kill had been made. She hunkered down into the straw-like strands and waited.

~

Dali watched in growing boredom. He lifted the binoculars he'd brought with him and lingered as he savoured the view of the curve in Tiffany's buttocks they afforded him. He dropped the field glasses into his lap and glanced at the rifle leaning up against the blind in front of him. It had only been 45 minutes so far. He couldn't help letting his mind wander, imagining what the little cheerleader might let him get away with if he plied her with enough alcohol back at the hotel bar. Surely her own boredom would play a part. After all, what else is there to do he thought.

Suddenly, in his peripheral vision to his left, he thought he glimpsed something white creeping past the blind. As he turned his head, he was smashed to the ground and the breath was knocked from his body. He squirmed as he fought for a lungful of air, but he never took it. There was a clamping pressure at the back of his neck and then the world melted into blackness. As his consciousness slipped away, he thought he felt a pin prick in his legs, but then both it, and he, was gone.

Tiffany lay in her blind, her senses suddenly screaming and on alert. She couldn't believe that Dali had been so stupid to make a noise. It had sounded like he had dropped something, or worse had tripped. But all had gone quiet again in an instant. It was then she realised that she was trembling. Something wasn't right.

The pain in her left leg was so sudden and severe that her whole body convulsed with the agony. She screamed as she was dragged from the blind, scrabbling for the dropped rifle moments too late. She felt herself hauled upwards by whatever had her ankle, as she clawed at the ground to no avail. Her body was lifted into the air, as the loose covering of leaves and sticks were thrashed away. Suddenly the pain stopped, as the clamping pressure on her leg was released. She was shaking violently now, and she felt the panic in her chest rising as a low, guttural growl emanated from close behind her. She spun onto her back and froze in fright. A pale, long, fierce and feline face looked back at her with strange bluish eyes. She shuddered as it exhaled a wet hot breath, so close that she felt it on her skin.

As she tried to scrabble away on her hands, she saw the gaping wound in her right calf muscle through the torn trousers. She had already lost the boot somehow. The big cat swatted her onto her back with a casual blow of its paw. Tiffany screamed again as she watched it loom closer. The big female ignored the noise, opening her mouth and sinking her teeth into Tiffany's chest, the five and a half inch canines piercing the left breast and cutting off the girl's screams as a new wave of agony swept her body. Tiffany felt cold and numb as she began to drift away, her arms flailing as she weakened. Warm thick liquid began to pool in her throat, and her eyes bulged as she slowly began to drown in the blood collecting there and in her chest cavity. The clamping bite of the cat had already cut off the muscles that would have naturally allowed her to choke and vomit it up. A final violent spasm quivered through her limbs as life left her.

~

She began to feast on the warm human flesh immediately. The two sisters soon joined her. The five others had driven them off the man they had killed almost immediately. They could be heard scrapping over the remains, but the sisters knew the others would not be bold enough to approach them whilst she remained close. She ate steadily, watching them as she did, and warning them against coming closer with a low, purposeful growl. Satiated, she stepped off the carcass. This was the signal the sisters had been waiting for, and they pushed their noses past the bloodied and fleshy ribs as they savoured the remaining morsels.

She settled by the feet of the corpse, taking the bare and bootless one within her paws. Her rasping tongue began to remove the skin and released slow oozes of fresh blood onto her tongue. She enjoyed the sweet and coppery taste and began to gnaw, slicing off the toes with scissor like bites using her carnassial teeth. When she had finished, she tugged and clawed at the boot on the other foot until it came off, consuming it in the same manner.

She lay in the blood-soaked grass, panting casually as twilight began to paint the savannah in eerie sepia light. She stood and held her head high, and roared.

CHAPTER SEVENTEEN

Thomas sat on the rattan sofa outside on the tent's veranda and watched as the sun began to set. Catherine was curled up next to him, exhausted by the day's events and dozing fitfully. Every now and then, Thomas thought he could hear a muffled sob come from Kelly's tent next door. Saka lay in the warm dirt a few yards away and watched Thomas, seemingly succumbing to the apathy that gripped the camp. All was quiet.

Thomas turned his head as he picked up the noise of the Warthog's engine coming from down the track. Saka too, lifted her head and pricked her ears. As soon as the headlights came into view, she stood and stretched, yapping and squeaking excitedly as the car approached. Thomas waited as Jericho opened the door for Rhodes and grabbed his pack from the passenger side. As the Irishman walked up, Thomas could see he was tired from the journey. He tried to carefully dislodge himself from underneath Catherine's head, but she woke as soon as he stirred. He smiled at her kindly and nodded his head in Jericho's direction.

"Why do you two look worse than I feel?" Jericho asked, pausing by the deck.

"We had some lion trouble," Thomas sighed. "We lost Karni."

"Shit," Jericho spat.

"How did your shopping trip go?"

"Three bottles. There was more on the shelf too. I got the impression they had regular demand for it."

Jericho took the containers out of his bag and passed them

to Thomas. He examined them, guessing they were just repackaged commercially available scent lures for mountain lion. Although African lions were a sociable species, they still lacked a tolerance for other cats and would move in on any alien scent they picked up within their territory. It didn't really matter which feline species the lure was originally intended for; the lions would definitely be interested if they picked it up.

"When were you thinking of conducting your little experiment?" Jericho asked.

"I don't think we can afford to wait around and keep putting things off until tomorrow. There's no time like the present as far as I'm concerned," Thomas replied.

"Do you really think that's a good idea?" Catherine exclaimed.

"No, but I can't sit here doing nothing. Not tonight."

"What's the plan?" Jericho asked.

"For a start, you get the night off. You stay here and keep things in check in camp," Thomas smiled. "I'm going to set up in the tree where somebody took a pot shot at the crew truck and..."

"Somebody shot at them?" Jericho interrupted.

"Took out the engine, from about a mile away. Left them for sitting ducks," Thomas nodded.

He walked to the table opposite the sofa and picked up a piece of metal that was sitting on it, passing it to Jericho. The Irishman brought it up to his eye for a closer look, examining it carefully as he turned it over through his fingers.

"I think our problems just got worse," Jericho said with a sigh. "I've seen something like this before. That's a 50. calibre bullet, at least what's left of it. I dug a few of these out of a pair of black rhino in Tanzania last year. I only know one asshole using them, and capable of making the shot you're talking about. It looks like we've caught the attention of Viktor Kruger, a poacher. Nasty fellow. He's the one I think is after Sefu and my elephants."

"What's the connection to Kanu Sultan do you think?" Thomas asked.

"Oh, I imagine it helps to be friends with a local war lord and arms dealer. It's rumoured he favours a modified Christensen Arms rifle with a carbon fibre barrel. Not exactly an off the shelf item."

"With a year long waiting list from what I hear," Thomas nodded. "Can't imagine there's too many places in East Africa you can get 50. cal ammo either."

"I'm pretty sure he makes his own. No doubt Kanu Sultan probably refreshes his supply from time to time too."

"How dangerous is he? Do you think he may have been hired to kill us?" Catherine asked.

"I doubt it," Jericho shook his head. "At least not directly. You're not going to get shot, if that's what you're worried about. But left for the lions, or sold into modern day slavery, that's a possibility. We're not talking about Florence Nightingale here, put it that way."

"Very reassuring," Catherine muttered.

"Anyway," said Thomas, "I think at least two of the lions were lying up in a thicket not far from the tree he used. If the others return there, or even if the one that got away today is still around, I'm in the mood to dish out some payback."

"Speaking of which," said Jericho, "what's the tally?"

"I think they're down by eight now, not including that young male."

"That leaves fourteen by Jelani's count," Catherine added. "Still a substantial pride by any means."

"Exactly why we need to keep at them. They'll definitely be feeling the pressure," Thomas said. "They've never come up against resistance like us."

"That's a two-way street," Jericho said with a growl. "The score's even at the moment remember. I don't think we've got them running scared yet."

"Catherine is going to stay here with you on the radio," Thomas continued, ignoring Jericho's warning. "I'll take the Big Cat, lay the scent, and get comfortable in the tree. There's a good moon tonight, so I should be able to see fairly well, but I'll have a thermal scope anyway."

Thomas walked over to the gun rack and lifted his rifle from it. He carried it to the equipment tent and laid it on the table, quickly removing the day scope from its mount. He took out a small case and opened it, revealing a scope with a much larger aperture. It was an Armasight Drone Pro night vision lens. Its lithium batteries offered him approximately three hours of use, which would be more than enough to get him through the night. He took a moment to adjust the quick release mounts and then slid the scope onto the rifle. He checked the magazine and made sure the cartridge loops of his safari vest were filled with spare ammunition.

His rucksack hadn't been emptied since he'd returned to Anga ya Amani, and was still perched on the rear bench seat of the Big Cat. Like everyone else in camp, he didn't seem that hungry and wasn't planning on waiting around for dinner. The biltong would suffice. He took out the two canteens from the bag and refilled them with fresh water. Catherine appeared at his side, brandishing a new radio too.

"Just in case the batteries are getting low on the one you took out earlier," she explained. "Remember what happened last time you decided to go tree climbing."

"Well it wasn't so bad," Thomas laughed. "It worked out pretty well in the end as I recall."

"Yeah well, fool me once. Second time round, you'll be in serious trouble."

She kissed him, pressing hard against his lips. He pulled her closer. They both still sported bruises from the last few days, but they embraced the pain. It reminded them they were still alive, still fighting. And this was what they were fighting for.

"Best be off now, before I decide on stopping you altogether," Jericho warned, looking towards the setting sun.

Thomas walked out to the Big Cat and slung his bag onto the passenger seat. He put the rifle onto the rack in the light rig, and checked the Anaconda was still snug in the interior pocket of his safari vest. He slipped the black cattleman hat on, and tipped its rim in Catherine's direction as he started the engine and headed off down the track.

The savannah was painted in the deep rust red light of the setting sun. He guessed he had about forty minutes left before the light really started to disappear. As it was now, it was quite intense and he brought the rim of the hat down further to block out the glare. After a little while, the track turned naturally away from the direct path of the sun and he relaxed more. The supercharger whirred into life as he put his foot down a little and the tyres eagerly bit into the dirt as he belted along a straight bit of road. As he crested a slight rise, he saw the hillside where Keelson and the others had been attacked ahead. He looked to his right and spotted the flat toped acacia he'd sat in earlier. He tugged at the wheel and steered the Big Cat speeding into the long grass, the back end of the truck breaking loose for a moment as he did so. He corrected it with a grin, then turned sharply left as he discovered the track that Kruger had undoubtedly used and would lead to the tree.

Thomas brought the Big Cat to a halt a few yards from the acacia. He paused as he spotted a lone sable antelope bolt away then come to a halt a little further off, alert and watching. He knew there had always been a remnant population in the Shimba Hills reserve, to the east near Mombasa, but they were still a very rare animal, especially on the borders of Tsavo West National Park. He took it as a good sign, that possibly the Shimba population was expanding. They were without a doubt one of his most favourite animals. He could tell it was a male from the black glossy coat and the striking black and white markings on its face. Its impressive, scimitar shaped and heavily ridged horns were nearly five feet long, and clearly not just for decoration. The top foot or so of each was completely smooth, to allow for easier goring.

The bull sable let out a snort of indignation and Thomas decided now was not the time to get out of the car. He watched as the neck muscles of the sable bulged and the stiff hairs of its mane bristled. Sable antelope seemed to always emanate an aura of constant malcontent, as if they had a permanent chip on their shoulder. Thomas sighed, as he knew this was one of the reasons they were considered such a trophy amongst sport hunters. This bull was nearly 500lbs he guessed, a considerable prize, especially for an eastern sable as this undoubtedly was. As he watched the bull walk away, Thomas couldn't understand what trophy hunters gained from taking the life of such an animal. To see it bellow, snort and strut was a far more awe-inspiring experience. Watching a sable was never boring.

Thomas remembered taking drinks on the terrace of the private suite of the Belmond Khwai River Lodge in Botswana. He had been with Amanda, and they were enjoying their sundowners when the entire compound had erupted into turmoil. The luxurious camp boasted a swimming pool over twenty yards long. It was surrounded by a strong wire fence, with woven grass panels and an entrance via a baffle door, set up like the burladero of a bull ring. To any hippo or buffalo wandering close out of curiosity, the fence appeared solid, whilst guests slipped past the baffle into the tranquil and private pool area. But that evening it sounded like a riot in a zoo. Thomas had looked at Amanda completely bemused, as grunts and snorts were followed by the sound of hooves against flagstone. It was only when the snarl and roar of a lion had interrupted the symphony of noise that Thomas had dashed inside for his gun and headed for the pool area.

As he had edged round the entrance, he'd only had a matter of seconds to throw himself out of the way, as a colossal sable bull crashed through the fencing and into the baffle. It displayed incredible strength as it dislodged itself from the splintered wood and disappeared into the night with another rattle of hooves, trailing a section of the wire fencing behind it. As Thomas peered back round the baffle, he saw a dead lioness slowly sinking to the bottom of the pool. Her venting blood was slowly turning the water the colour of strawberry milkshake, and it was decided her hasty removal from the pool was perhaps the best next course of action to help return the evening to its former sense of calm. When he and several members of the lodge staff managed to remove it, they discovered the top section of one of the sable's horns sticking about an inch through the top of her skull. The root of the broken shard of horn was found just below her chin, and from there it had smashed through the rest of her skull and brain casing with little resistance. Only tossing the lioness into the pool had broken the horn, her bulky mass too much even for the sable's impressive weaponry.

Thomas gazed to the north, towards the lush forested hills of Chyulu Hills National Park. Somewhere out there, beyond his line of sight, was the pretty gorge that looked back over Tsavo West. Desert rose, peacock flower, elephant's foot and bauhinia had carpeted the rocky outcrops and crags, whilst lion's claw, St John's wort and sugar bush shrubs had lined the stone walls on either side. Stunning flame canopied Poinciana trees stood side by side with lavender boughs of cape chestnuts. It had been one of Amanda's favourite places, where she would often come to read or just contemplate their adventures. It had been a fitting place to scatter her ashes. He had never been back. He decided that it was something he should do, when all this was over.

Sure that the sable had finally moved on, Thomas climbed out of the car and took the bottle of scent lure out of the bag. He took the rifle down from the rack, and slung it over his shoulder as he began to backtrack down the trail. Every twenty to thirty yards, he would stop and lace an area of ground with the pungent chemical taint. Up close and in concentrated form it was unbearably musky and potent. Thomas made sure he stood upwind and let the breeze take the odour away from him. The one thing he didn't want to smell like, once up in the tree, was a lion. As he made his way back to the acacia and the car, he took handfuls of the dry earth and rubbed it onto his skin and clothing, dusting it off with clumps of parched grass to mask his own scent. He would try to stay upwind as best as possible, but he knew the breeze could change at any moment. His best bet was to stay quiet and still.

Thomas took a blanket from the truck bed of the Big Cat and tucked it under the strap of the rifle, so it was easy to carry as he scrambled up the tree. He took a final look back at the car and considered moving it back a little so it was even closer. But he was satisfied that if he had to leap to the ground and sprint, he would make the relative safety of the car before anything caught up with him. He pulled himself up into the branches, past the fork where he had previously sat. Not quite elevated enough for his liking, he clambered higher until he found a thick, flattish bough that he could swing his legs over whilst resting his back against the main trunk. He held himself in place as he folded the blanket in half, so the bottom part would cushion him against the bark and the top could be draped over his shoulders when he got cold. He squirmed and wriggled until he was comfortable and settled against the tree, watching the sun as it slowly began to set.

The landscape seemed Martian as it became painted in the intense red light, blending into the already amber and rust like colourations of the grassland and rocky outcrops. The thicket to the north was now silhouetted and sullen, just a group of dark and ominous shadows on the horizon. Thomas sat up as he heard the querying, rolling yowl of a spotted hyena. Moments later he watched it lope out of the grass and lift its nose to the air in the direction of the tree. Clearly it was picking up the chemical lure and didn't like what it signalled. Thomas guessed the animal was a good 170lbs and looked stocky and mean with it. Hyena females had to be bigger and more aggressive than the males in order to protect against infanticide. They also led the clans, some of which could be as large as eighty in number. The size and swagger of this animal almost certainly suggested it was both a female and an alpha. It wrinkled its nose in a growl, which then rose into a wailing yikker and the characteristic laughing call. It trotted away in a wide loop though the grass, occasionally looking back over its shoulder.

He couldn't help wondering that if one African species had developed the physical and behavioural morphology to cope with male dominance, perhaps it was now something they were observing in the pressured and vulnerable lion prides. Big cats were one of the most adaptive groups of mammals when it came to climate and behaviour. Perhaps it was only a matter of time before there started to be physical changes too. The big female that acted as alpha to the pride, or the Daughters of the Darkness as Jelani called them, could be the result of a simple and effective mutation. Or it could be something subtler. Lionesses already had close maternal instincts and bonds with the other females in their pride. It made them more effective hunters, as well as encouraged the sharing of responsibilities such as raising cubs. If there had been a dramatic increase in infanticide, it followed that only the biggest and most aggressive females and their progeny would be likely to survive. It was nature's version of selective breeding. If a lack of available prey led to heightened tensions amongst prides, then the resulting escalating territory squabbles and attempted takeovers could change the hormonal balances of the lions themselves. Both circumstances could result in dramatic changes to the lion's physiology over time.

Thomas brought his thoughts back to the present as the failing light began to give way to darkness. His eyes lifted skyward as he watched the uniquely African splendour of the unveiling of the night sky. Stars appeared in little flashes of light through the swirls of mauve, violet and indigo that became more and more intense as he stared. As he looked north, his gaze was drawn to one pinprick of light in particular, which he knew to be Regulus. It marked the great forepaw of the constellation Leo and was easily the brightest within it. To the ancient Greeks it had represented the Nemean lion, a beast whose golden fur was impervious to mortal weapons. Its claws were sharper than swords and capable of slicing through the armour of warriors. Only the hero Heracles was strong enough to vanquish it.

The lion had gone extinct in Greece and the southern reaches of Europe some 100 years B.C., and as he had discovered in Scotland, perhaps the cave lion and other more northerly suited species had lingered on even longer. What was clear from both mythology and history, including his own, was that lions and man had been pitted against each other for millennia. It was only in modern times, when the fight had slipped from one of supremacy and status to one of attrition, that the lions had found themselves on the back foot. Their range had slowly thinned, and populations retreated into east, central and southern Africa, and also to a tiny section of the Gir forest in India. In the combined seventeen nations of West Africa it was estimated only 400 lions remained, making them critically endangered there. Kenya had experienced a 60% drop in its lion population in a mere twenty years. And whereas countries like South Africa and Zambia reported an

11% increase in numbers, it was within fenced off reserves already filled to capacity and unable to accommodate further populations, or the natural spread of them. It was perhaps little wonder that a line had been clawed in the sand.

Thomas looked at his watch. The white gold casing of the Rolex Cosmograph Daytona glinted in the soft light of the newly risen moon. The lunar radiation illuminated the numerals in a cold, icy blue. In a few hours, it would be the first of October. As he looked up at the full and looming disc, he couldn't help smiling as he realised that if he had been in the Northern hemisphere, he would be under a hunter's moon. Towards the end of the month both he and Catherine would celebrate birthdays. He ran a finger across the slate coloured dial of the watch, tracing the echo of the engraving on its back. He cracked a sour smile as he looked once more towards the gorge where Amanda's ashes had been scattered.

Somewhere close by, a booming, hooting call sounded as a spotted eagle owl alighted from a nearby tree to begin its nightly hunt. As he concentrated on the sounds coming from all around, he thought he could pick up soft smacking noises and something large passing through the grass. Thomas decided he would risk moving slightly to take a closer look. He carefully and silently raised the rifle and switched on the scope. The grassland was suddenly illuminated in tones of hot white and cold grey. He swung the rifle left and easily picked out the bulky mass of a lone rhinoceros. He could see it was the rarer black rhino from the shape of its narrow mouth, and he watched as it used its prehensile upper lip to strip leaves from the branches of the tree it was under, a little way up the trail. Thomas felt the breeze pick up, and a few seconds later the rhino swivelled in his direction with an abrasive snort. Its oval shaped and hair tipped ears twisted and turned as its equally excellent senses of smell and hearing went on the alert, making up for its poor eyesight. With another snort the rhino turned tail, and a few seconds later was crashing noisily back into the timber of the thicket. Then he saw them.

Two flattish, white hot heads in the grass some three hundred feet away, still as statues and seemingly focused in his direction. They must have also come from the thicket he realised, perhaps following the rhino or more likely, the scent lure which was now wafting more strongly towards them. As Thomas slowed his breathing and tried to calm the thump of his heart in his chest, a third flash of body heat moved out from the thicket. He traced its path through the grass as he caught glimpses of the heat signature against the greyish black blades. It drew up between the other two and came to a halt. As he used his thumb to use the digital controls on the scope to sharpen the focus, he saw without doubt that they were three lionesses.

They moved forward together confidently, noses held high, ears pinned back and shoulders hunched. They cut through the grass in silent unison, slinking fifty feet closer as he watched through the scope. Thomas lined up on the central animal, which the other two seemed to be taking their lead from. He used the reticule to line up on the bridge of the animal's nose. Now less than a hundred yards, it was almost a sure target. He took a deep exhale and began squeezing back the trigger.

He hesitated. Something didn't feel right. He felt himself tensing, willing himself into stillness. Out of his peripheral vision he noticed how part of the branch next to him seemed to ripple and glisten in the moonlight. As his eyes darted from the scope to the branch, he realised he was looking at a long, serpentine body that ended in a blunt, coffin shaped head. Two unblinking beady eyes were trained on him and less than four feet away. It was a black mamba, and as he tried to gauge the length of its body back along the branch he realised four feet wasn't far enough for a snake that measured over twice that.

Thomas knew the venom of the black mamba consisted of a number of neurotoxins, chief among which was dendrotoxin. Before effective antivenin had been developed, being bitten meant certain death. The effect was almost instant, starting with coughing and dizziness, parasthesia and profuse salivation and sweating. Stroke-like symptoms would indicate the progress of the venom, with people usually experiencing muscle collapse around the face, neck and lower legs within 45 minutes of being bitten, and most usually succumbing within 20. That meant he didn't have enough time to make it back to camp if he was bitten, let alone administer antivenin. His heart rate would sky rocket before he finally went into neurogenic shock, and he would die either from cardiovascular collapse or respiratory failure. It usually took around eight hours, but he doubted the lions would wait for their meal that long.

There was nothing for it. Without hesitating, Thomas threw himself to the left, toppling from his seat on the branch and towards the ground. He saw the snake shoot forward, but then he was falling through the air and crashing into the ground with a thud that drove the breath from his body. As he took a great gasp and fought for air, he raised himself up onto his hands in a panic. The aggression of the black mamba was almost legendary, and stories of them chasing humans that had approached too close abounded. He cursed himself, knowing that was exactly what he had done. He hadn't checked the tree properly and had put himself directly in the snake's path. Whereas it would normally have fled, he had given the snake no quarter to do so by the time it happened upon him. Whereas some of the stories of the black mamba's truculence were no doubt exaggerated, he knew that once it was committed to a fight, it didn't back down.

It came silent and fast, slipping through the lower branches and then uncoiling down the trunk of the tree with deliberate and calculated purpose. The snake dropped to the floor a few feet from him, and he immediately scrabbled back on his hands and kicked away with his feet. With a loud hiss of warning, the mamba rose up and began to gape, mimicking a cobra as they were known to do. It was then he remembered something in a sudden moment of clarity. For a moment, he thought it might have fallen out, but he could feel it against his ribs. The Anaconda was too bulky to risk a shot, and in the time it took him to aim, the snake would have made its strike. But he did have another gun which he'd almost forgotten about. It was a small, two shot derringer that he'd put in the right-hand pocket of his safari vest on the first day they'd arrived in Kenya. Known as a snake slayer, this was exactly what it was meant for. Carefully and slowly, he held out his right hand and moved it away from his head. As intended, the snake followed the movement. Thomas drove his left hand inside the safari vest with all the speed he could muster, whipping out the gun and pulling the trigger instantly, only hesitating a moment before squeezing it a second time for good measure.

The snake was mid strike when its body was peppered by the first blast of shot. The second blast sent it flying backwards, as pellets half the size of a pea riddled its body and hammered it into the trunk before it dropped lifeless to the ground. Thomas looked up and groaned as he saw his rifle dangling by its strap from a branch still a good way up the tree. As he rolled onto his knees to get up, he started to feel the bruises and scrapes he'd accumulated in the fall, including a deep and painful gash on his right elbow.

He looked around carefully. The savannah was still and quiet. Without the night scope, he had no idea how much closer the lions had crept in the panic. He considered for a moment if he should call it quits and head for the safety of the Big Cat. That would leave him with only the Anaconda and considerably reduced his chances of taking out the lions successfully. He needed his rifle. He dusted himself off and took a few running steps towards the tree, making a scrabbling jump up into the lowest of its branches. He hoisted himself up and swung out to reach for the rifle a few feet away, when he heard a noise below him.

With his feet braced against the tree and both hands gripping separate branches, he glanced downwards, letting out a little gasp of shock at what greeted him. Golden eyes set in a pale tawny face looked up at him. The lioness's fur looked almost white in the moonlight, but he could still distinguish the colours. The lioness let out a burp-like grunt and looked behind her, no doubt at her approaching comrades Thomas considered. He didn't hesitate any longer, letting go of the branch he was holding with his right hand and leaning over to snatch at the rifle. He was distracted again by the sound of sharp claws as they shredded and splintered the bark.

Many assumed lions were not inclined towards climbing trees, and Thomas had often scoffed at them, wondering how many had sought refuge in the boughs of one only to hear the very sounds he was now. With each cautious and deliberate grapple of the trunk, the lioness's weight sent tremors up into the branches. Now only a few feet from being able to haul herself into the flat fork where he had previously sat, Thomas reached for the gun again. This time a violent shake of the branch as the lioness shifted upwards again, tipped the strap from the clutches of the tree, and it fell into his open hand. But Thomas knew he didn't have time to fire.

For the second time, Thomas jumped from the tree, managing to hit the ground with a roll, but still dropping the rifle and letting it clatter onto the stony earth below. As he tumbled upright, he pulled the Anaconda from inside his safari vest. Time seemed to stand still as two glowing coals of amber streaked out of the night towards him, and he noticed the white tufts of hair on the chin of the lioness as she rushed him. Thomas focused on them for a split second before pumping the trigger in an adrenaline fuelled panic. The three 44. magnum rounds found their mark and smashed through the lioness's skull, splintering her jaw from below, exploding into the brain case and taking out her left eye. The lioness slumped to the floor, dragged by her momentum through the dirt, like a macabre baseball slide that ended only a foot from the outstretched barrel of Thomas's revolver.

He jumped up and tried to sprint towards the car as he saw the second lion encroaching fast from the right. There was no sign of the third in the tree now behind him, but he knew it must be coming for him. He almost made it before a thumping swipe sent him tumbling sideways into the grass onto his back. He fought off the daze and panic that threatened to engulf him, and gripped the gun, swinging it over his chest as the stars above him were replaced with the rippling silhouette of the lioness. Thomas thrust his left arm upwards to meet the animal's throat as he sent the three remaining rounds in the cylinder through her chest. Next moment, he was smothered by the intoxicating musk and 300lb mass of the dead lioness.

He managed to struggle free and went to stand, only to find himself dropping to his knees in a sudden spell of dizziness. His head spun as he tried to focus on the black form that was surging closer. He could see his rifle on the ground a few yards away, but knew he would never make it. As he felt the wet, sticky patch growing on his back, he guessed the lioness that had swatted him to the ground had managed to claw him, even through the leather safari vest. He closed his eyes and lifted his head up to the sky, as his thoughts drifted towards Amanda's gorge again before they settled on Catherine. He wondered if Jelani would know to tell her to scatter his own ashes there. He hoped so. *I love you* he thought as he pictured Catherine's gleaming green eyes and soft curls of red hair. She was smiling, beaming at him and glowing in happiness.

It wasn't a roar, more like the sound of rolling thunder. Guttural, challenging, and angry, the sound seemed to penetrate every fibre of his being. But it didn't come from the lioness charging him. She had stopped short, frozen and gripped by fear just as he was. Both he and the lioness slowly turned their heads back up the trail, from where the sound had come from.

The moon was behind the hulking silhouette that stood statue like, poised and clearly looking in their direction. As it took a step closer, the lioness didn't hesitate any longer and bolted past Thomas in the direction of the thicket. Thomas looked at his rifle a few yards away, then behind him at the Land Rover. Something told him that discretion over valour was his best chance. Mustering the last of his strength, he staggered to his feet. His vision was blurring a little, but he could see the thing was coming for him. He stumbled backwards, groping in the darkness for the nearest door handle. As his fingers found the open side of the truck bed, he used it for support, pulling himself along to the rear door. He never made it. His foot caught on the bulky rear tire and he crumpled to the ground. He let out a deep sigh and pulled himself into a sitting position. His feet were out in front of him and his back rested against the car. All his fight was spent and he was out of time. It was coming.

It stepped along the trail with a casual gait that eschewed confidence. It was in no hurry, it knew its prey was cornered. As it strutted closer, Thomas could start to make out its features. Shoulder muscles that moved like pumpjacks, a chiselled flat head embraced by a flowing cloak of a mane. It was a male lion, undoubtedly one of the pair that had eyes on the pride's territory. It stepped into the moonlight and stopped, staring at him from a few yards away. It was without a doubt the most magnificent lion he had ever seen. The thick mane seemed jet black and covered the shoulders, and extended down towards the heavy set, rotund belly. Its flame coloured eyes flickered and glowed like torches in the darkness. It stood near enough five feet at the shoulder, and Thomas believed it would have easily measured over ten feet from nose to tail. It must have weighed all of 650lbs he guessed. The lion looked at him in disproving quiet. Looking at this animal he could see why they were called the king of beasts. Everything from its statuesque musculature to the domineering, imperious look it wore suggested regality. He felt almost surrendered to it. If he was going to be taken by a lion, this was the one.

It took a deliberate step towards him. The low rumbling growl came again, and it dropped its car engine sized head. Thomas felt no fear, just a sense of euphoric wonder as it came closer. Sometimes, when the body had been flooded by the full cocktail of flight or fight hormones and found itself still in a life-threatening situation, it would go into shock and shut down. Thomas considered this might be what he was experiencing. The effect had two possible outcomes. If the lion proceeded to eat him, the level of shock would deteriorate into numbness and unconsciousness, hopefully meaning he wouldn't feel much. Alternatively, as did occasionally happen, the lion might think he was dead and leave him alone.

The lion stood over his outstretched legs, its giant face a mere foot away from his own. It dropped its head again and took a long sniff of his scent. Thomas almost smiled as he saw the lion's snout wrinkle in obvious disgust. Then he heard a muffled grunt from somewhere behind the lion. He couldn't see its source as his entire field of vision was still filled with the animal before him. The lion turned away, stepping over his legs with deliberate care and walking off a few feet. That's when Thomas saw the second one. It was almost the twin of the first, except it had dark chocolate and rust coloured strands woven rope-like into its flowing black mane. As the first lion joined it, they both turned and looked at him. Thomas could see why the grunt he'd heard had been muffled. The second male was carrying the limp body of a bush pig in its mouth. It issued the grunt again and began to walk off into the darkness. The first lion looked back at Thomas for a moment before following it. He watched as its whip like tail lifted high up over its body and flicked back again with casual indifference as it disappeared into the gloom.

Thomas let the hammering beat of his heart slow before he tried to lift himself off the ground. He slowly made his way over to where his rifle lay and picked it up. He felt slightly less light headed as the adrenaline pumping through his system began to subdue. He dragged his feet a little as he made his way back over to the Big Cat and opened up the driver's door. He leant the rifle against the passenger seat and hauled himself into the cabin, closing the door firmly behind him. He rested for a moment before rummaging through his pack to find the radio. Catherine was on the other end almost immediately. He told her what had happened.

"What is it about you and trees," he heard her exclaim. "Can you drive?"

"I'm going to try to," he answered, "but I think it might be a good idea if you attempt to meet me somewhere in the middle. I still don't know how badly I'm hit. I certainly don't feel great."

"We're on our way. Stick to the track. If you feel dizzy or tired, pull over immediately and wait for us."

"Will do," Thomas replied, putting down the radio.

He started the engine and pulled the Big Cat around. His hands were still trembling, but he knew he had to try and get at least part of the way back to camp. He trundled the truck past the two limp bodies of the lionesses he had killed, before hitting the accelerator and tearing up the track as fast as he felt capable.

~

She edged through the grass with silent dedication. The scent of the males was thick and she moved cautiously, each step countered by a flick of her alert and pricked ears. Her whiskers stretched forwards in exploratory eagerness and she licked her muzzle, moistening her nasal passages and enriching the scents carried on the wind. She picked up her feet, bending her paws with precision to cushion their impact on the soft earth. She passed a large tree, and stopped short of breaking from the veil the long grass afforded her. She hunkered down onto the ground and waited, panting softly as she filled her lungs, ready for charge or escape as might be necessary. She lifted into a crouch and crept forward, slowly emerging from the blanket of greenery surrounding her.

Her eyes bulged as the intensity of the lingering scents bombarded her. She found the first of the dead lionesses lying face down by the side of the track. It was an older female, one that had belonged to the pride she had taken over when she had first settled in the territory. Her snout wrinkled into a silent snarl as her nostrils were stung by the waft of congealing blood that pooled beneath the lioness's head. She stepped away, finding the body of the second female a few yards from the first. This animal was smaller, younger. And familiar. It had been one of the cubs she had adopted during the storm on the marshland.

She nuzzled at the neck tenderly, patting at the limp shoulder of the lioness as she tried to roll it onto its feet. It stayed slumped and motionless on the ground. She opened her mouth as if she were about to sneeze, further enhancing her ability to taste and locate scent. She looked to the west, easily identifying the strong, prominent markings of the males from further off. There was an acrid, burning taste in the air too, like the scorch marks left on trees when fire fell from the sky, but much fainter. Then she caught it, the thin, coppery taint lacing a blood splatter on the ground. Man had been here too. She licked at the stained dust, enjoying the sweet and metallic taste that still lingered. She stood alert and restless, looking east in the direction the man had gone. As she padded along the trail after him, she rolled her head from side to side and began to bellow savage, snarling roars of intent that echoed across the savannah and dissipated into the darkness with her.

CHAPTER EIGHTEEN

Kanu Sultan stood in the impressive stone gateway of the former wildlife conservancy and listened to the sounds of the night as they echoed across the marshland. The faint angry roars faded slowly, only to be answered by silence. It was the voice of the queen, the strange one. She was smarter and larger than the others, that they knew. But nobody had ever seen her and lived to tell the details. It served his needs well as its part in the myths surrounding his powers and his domain over the animals, but clearly Thomas Walker was proving a thorn in her side as well as his. When the crickets and reed frogs began their chorus again and the sounds of the African night replaced the silence, he looked back towards the quiet waterway.

The Galana River led all the way to the east coast resort of Malindi, known as the 'little Italy of Africa'. But it was in the Gongoni township, on the opposite bank, that his kind of business was done. It was a hive for Al-Shabaab recruiters, who preyed on the unrest of the poverty-stricken locals, forced to give up their children to a vile sex trade and live in a hub for drug trafficking, all fuelled by the mafia-backed resort across the water. Adding to the powder keg was the Mombasa Republican Council, a political separatist group who also manipulated the strained tensions of the township to their advantage. Both groups needed arming and supplying. The government had no sway there and even less presence. It was the perfect destination for his business and a source of constant demand he was only too happy to supply. Adopting both Al-Shabaab and MRC tactics to intimidate and influence the impoverished farmers and villagers of Tsavo had in turn helped him secure his own seclusion from the authorities. But now Thomas Walker was bringing unwanted attention to the region. He lingered no longer and turned his back on the wilderness of the Galana marshes.

He strolled purposefully through the compound, back towards the lodge that now served as both his personal quarters and the base of his operations. His sharp eyes swept over the space until they came to rest on Musa, who was huddled up against the far wall. Kanu came to a halt a few feet from him, placing his hands on his hips as he surveyed the boy.

"Come with me Musa," he commanded simply, striding towards the lodge again. He didn't need to look back to know the boy would be following obediently.

Kanu passed the two guards at the entrance to the lodge and strolled through the lobby towards an open room to the left. Musa hesitated at the large double doors that marked the entrance, having never been inside before. Kanu beckoned him in with a look of impatience.

"Musa, a belief that your life has purpose and power is often the key to survival. Do you believe that?"

The boy neither nodded nor answered, his eyes wide in fear.

"There are always sacrifices you will be asked to make. Whether you are willing or not, that's what will decide your fate," Kanu continued. "When I was a boy, not much older than you are now, I was already on the streets of Mombasa. My father was a humble man who worked as a porter in a hotel. One day a drug lord came to our house, demanding money for protection. You know what happened then?"

Musa nodded. He knew the story well.

"He drove a machete through my father's chest, in front of my mother and older brother. But that was just the beginning of my nightmare. He then gave my brother and I a choice. Only one of us could live, and only then to prove our loyalty. Having spent years teaching me to fight, my brother hesitated. I did not. I took the machete and killed him. I knew I would become a soldier for the man who murdered my father, and that my mother would be forced to become either a prostitute or a drug mule. I chose life for us instead of death, it was that simple."

Musa nodded again, still fearful and unsure why Kanu was telling him a story they all knew.

"I was willing to kill my own brother to save myself and my mother. I am now giving you a similar choice. But it is not your family, but an outsider I ask you to kill. I am giving you the opportunity to finish the task I gave you seven years ago. So, Musa, what will you choose, life or death?"

Musa said nothing, but turned his gaze towards the wall of glass tanks that lined the far side of the room. His eyes fell to his feet.

"A good choice," Kanu huffed. "We will use the critters of the bush to purge the white hunter from our lands. Tomorrow night, you will kill Thomas Walker...with a little help from my friends."

CHAPTER NINETEEN

When Thomas woke, he could hear the soft chirrups of the speckled mousebirds as they foraged through the scrub behind the tent. He was lying face down in the bed, one arm dangling over the side and the other buried beneath the pillows he'd thrust aside during the night. He didn't want to open his eyes yet. The strong light he could detect beyond their closed lids threatened to sting his retinas before they were ready to embrace it.

He could feel the press of the pad bandaged to his elbow, and the dampness of the dressing on his back. Catherine had administered a strong dose of the hydrogen peroxide from the leopard kit, along with a shot of morphine. She had stitched him up too. He couldn't remember her doing so, but he felt the results of her handiwork just fine. He was stiff, sore and groggy. As a jolt of pain danced up his left arm and into his shoulder blades, he groaned and sunk back into the mattress. It was then that he felt a warm hand on the small of his back.

"Try not to move too much, from what I can see you'll feel every bit of it," Catherine exclaimed.

"How bad is it?" Thomas mumbled.

"Your back looks like a Picasso," she quipped. "It's a beautiful blend of swirls of blue, mauve and pink. There's even a little yellow bit, but I covered it with the dressing unfortunately."

"Try not to sound quite so smug."

"I've spent the night icing your back to bring down the inflammation, and practically showered you in sheep dip to stop you getting gangrene, and I cleaned and dressed your wounds, all of them. So I'll sound how I bloody well please thank you very much."

"Sorry. Thanks. My evening wasn't exactly a walk in the park you know though?" Thomas replied.

"Actually, you were in Tsavo West, so technically, it was."

Catherine smiled. He sounded miserable, and he clearly felt it. She peeled back the sheet and softly placed a cold press in the middle of his back, gently dabbing at the purplish bruises. She carefully pulled up the edges of the dressing and checked the four deep slashes. The stitches had held, but there was still a small amount of yellowish discharge staining the padding. She ripped it off with one quick yank.

"Ow," Thomas grumbled into the mattress. "I get it, you're pissed."

"I'm changing your dressing Eeyore, to prevent you from upping and dying on us later, is that okay with you?"

"Only if you can do it without sounding like you're enjoying yourself."

He could hear Catherine sorting through some kind of plastic box as she took out a pack of new gauze. She put it aside, and cleaned the scabbing ridges of the claw wounds with the cold press before patting the skin dry.

"I'll let you shower first before I put a new dressing on. You lost a fair bit of blood," she explained. "You were talking some fairly high-grade nonsense when we found you. Something about barbs or brothers I think."

Thomas lifted himself up and winced with the pain as he twisted round and sat up. His movement was deliberate and slow. He swung his legs over the bed and gathered his thoughts for a moment.

"Barbary brothers, that's what I said, I think," he grumbled, rubbing his temples.

"And what does that mean exactly?" Catherine asked.

"The two males we've seen traces of and know are hanging around. I saw them last night. I think they may actually be Barbary lions."

"Barbary lions," Catherine repeated quietly, studying him through narrowed and questioning eyes. "As in the Barbary lion that went extinct in the wild in the 1960s. The same Barbary lion that was only ever found in Algeria and Morocco? Would that be the one you're talking about?"

"The very ones," Thomas replied, smiling nervously. "That said, the Gaetulian lion of Libyan legend probably had a basis in fact, perhaps even being of the same species. If so, that would mean an extended range east. When we were discussing the Tsavo man-eaters, you mentioned the genetic studies of sub-Saharan lions that looked at mane length. Did you know those same studies detected markers that suggested the presence of Barbary lion DNA in their lineage? All those things point to the dispersal and spread of the species beyond what we have historically accepted as their geographical range."

"Jericho looked at the pug marks," Catherine sighed. "He agrees they were two large males. I don't doubt what you saw. You were however delirious, and may still be. Do you not think there's a tiny possibility that might be influencing you?"

"I know what I saw."

"Okay, so how did they get to Kenya then?"

Thomas could see she was only just holding onto her patience. She was hearing him out probably just because of the condition he was in.

"Let's say there was a possible remnant population in Libya, perhaps even Egypt. They have gradually been pushed further inland, into the mountain ranges and more remote arid regions to the south. The Barbary lion is uniquely suited to the environment, having already adapted to the Atlas Mountains and the bordering deserts. Ongoing conflicts and human incursion may have forced them to expand further. And most importantly, Barbary lions don't form prides. They usually hunt in pairs or small immediate family groups. It would help them be more inconspicuous. Give them fifty years or so and they could have easily got here, either from following the river deltas and mountain chains through Egypt and Sudan, or although less likely, via the more central ranges through Niger and Chad."

"Well, your fantasies are always relatively well thought through, I'll give you that," Catherine sighed.

"You would have had to see them to believe them. I've never seen lions that big. The first one, with the black mane was just magnificent. He was everything I have ever imagined a Barbary lion to be."

"Fancy that," Catherine cooed teasingly. "I remain to be convinced, let's leave it at that shall we."

Catherine helped Thomas up and tucked his arm over her shoulder as she walked with him to the door of the tent. She grabbed a towel and his wash bag with her free hand.

"Déjà vu, eh?" Catherine grinned.

"You really are enjoying yourself, aren't you?"

"You know how much I like being right and being able to say I told you so."

"Uh-huh."

She opened the door to the tent with her elbow and pushed

it open, helping Thomas as they shuffled slowly across the porch to the steps. He shielded his eyes against the morning light and was thankful as they turned away from it towards the bath huts. Thomas waited as Catherine got the water running and helped him take off the shorts he was wearing. He realised she must have dressed him again whilst tending him during the night.

"We had to bury your blood-stained shirt outside of camp," Catherine explained. "I imagine you'll be able to wash yourself, but I'll help get you dry and then fix your dressing."

"Thank you," Thomas said again as she helped him over to the shower.

After the initial stinging pulse of the water hit his bruised skin, he found his muscles quickly began to loosen and untwist. He was soon able to move his arms relatively easily and began to wash. He took his time, watching little trickles of blood and mud drain away with the water. When there seemed to be no more, he turned off the water and stepped out.

Back at the tent, Catherine pushed him down onto the bed and began to dab him dry. She fixed the gauze in place with medical tape, and sighed satisfactorily as she put the box down off the bed.

"All done," she smiled.

"I feel a lot better, albeit very stiff and sore," Thomas winced.

When he couldn't reach the fresh clothes on the rail, she grabbed them and put them on the bed for him. She couldn't help giggling as he rolled around the mattress, groaning and howling as he straightened out and slipped on some boxers and then the clothes.

"It's hammock, chair or bed for you today, that's it," she warned as he got up. "I'm sure there's some breakfast left if you can hobble quick enough."

She helped him through the door and down the steps. As he looked out over the kopje towards the breakfast table, he saw Jericho sitting there, his feet up and his Australian bush hat pulled down to shade his eyes, which were closed. Thomas realised it had been a very long night for all of them because of him. He decided they had all earned a day off. He slumped down beside Jericho, who opened one eye and acknowledged his presence with a grin. He sat up and stretched before passing him a cold, open bottle of lager.

"Finally, some real medicine," Thomas laughed, clinking Jericho's bottle in thanks.

"Tom was just telling me how those big males were probably Barbary lions," Catherine teased as she sat down.

"No doubt," Jericho shrugged tiredly. "I probably couldn't see them through all the leprechauns."

"Alright, I take your point," Thomas laughed, throwing his hands up in surrender. "Of those here though, who else has discovered a previously thought extinct species of big cat in their lifetime?"

"Yes, you were right once," laughed Catherine, rolling her eyes. "You're yet to make a habit of it. And technically, it was a hybrid."

"Fine, we'll see."

Thomas reconciled himself to breakfast, stabbing a pair of thick and juicy sausages from the serving plate at the table's centre and adding them to his own. He ladled scrambled eggs on top and plucked a still warm chapo from a woven basket containing many more of the sweet flatbreads. As he looked around the table he realised that somebody was missing.

"No sign of Kelly yet?" Thomas asked.

"She hasn't come out of her tent," Catherine replied. "Mason was here earlier but made himself scarce shortly afterwards. I think he's going over the footage they got. I'm pretty sure the camera was recording the whole time of the attack."

The mood in Anga ya Amani seemed apathetic and lethargic. Jericho was still tired from the long day before and the longer night that had followed. Catherine was near exhausted and Thomas realised that she probably hadn't slept at all. Mason and Kelly were quiet and skittish after their ordeal and were keeping their distance. Thomas lay slumped on the rattan sofa on the tent's porch and watched the staff come and go, moving around with a sullenness that belied their weariness. He knew how they felt. Beat but not yet beaten, and dreading what might come next. As he watched Jelani walk up the trail from the other end of camp, ashen faced and wide eyed, he realised that there was more bad news to come.

The news about the death of Tiffany Lee Amberson, a Texan cheerleader and something of a hunting celebrity, had come in over the radio and was quickly growing as a news story. Kanu Sultan had been swift to issue a statement declaring the incident as nature's revulsion of Western feminism. Jelani showed Thomas and Jericho the short video statement on Catherine's Toughbook laptop. As Kanu Sultan grinned and described Tiffany as a whore that had been paraded gregariously as an affront to Muslim beliefs, he added her death was deserved and inevitable. Such callous ignorance would not be tolerated, not even by the critters of the bush he had declared. Thomas noticed Jericho's rigid stance as he clenched his fist tightly, shaking with rage.

"I've had enough of this asshole. Let's just kill the fucker. And Kruger while we're about it," Jericho spat.

"It's certainly tempting. You don't happen to have either of their addresses, do you?" Thomas shrugged.

"Everyone needs to calm down. Picking a fight with a local war lord and his pet poacher are not part of the plan," Catherine interjected. "You know he's talking nonsense, don't buy into his propaganda. This girl was killed by the man-eaters, and those we can hunt down."

"Fine," growled Jericho. "But if I happen to find him crossing my path through my rifle sights, I'll be doing the world a favour, make no mistake."

The Irishman turned and stomped off towards the kitchen. Rhodes took a few steps in the same direction, but suddenly stopped as the sound of smashing glass reached their ears. The big fawn coloured mastiff looked at Catherine forlornly and only hesitated for a second before padding over and lying down at her feet beneath the porch table. Catherine reached underneath and scratched behind his ears comfortingly. Jelani drifted off too, back towards the staff camp. Catherine stood up with a sigh and reached down to rub Rhodes's head.

"You watch this one and make sure he doesn't go anywhere," she told the big dog.

Rhodes whined as she moved around the table and went down the steps. She crossed the short pathway that led to the kitchen tent and entered it. One of the orderlies was clearing up the smashed, empty whiskey bottle Jericho had left in his wake. Catherine helped pick up the last few pieces and mouthed a silent thank-you to the man, who nodded his understanding.

Catherine smiled as Mansa appeared, bowing politely in her direction.

"Hi Mansa, I was wondering if Kelly has had anything to eat today?" Catherine asked.

"Alas, I fear not," Mansa sighed. "I have not seen her."

"Can I steal a few things and take them to her?"

"We can do better than that. Let's make her something," the elderly African beamed in reply. "If you don't mind me saying so though, I think she needs to sleep and rest rather than eat."

"What would you maybe suggest then?"

"My hot malted chocolate, with a secret ingredient," Mansa laughed.

He took some milk and cream from a small refrigerator, powered by the network of generators that kept the camp lit and comfortably catered for. He heated the milk gently in a pan and began to prepare the cocoa and malted milk powder in another. He poured the cream into the powder mix, and sifted it gently over the heat until it had blended into a thick paste. As he reached across the counter to a tin, and took a pinch of dark red chilli powder, he winked at Catherine. Mansa then turned and plucked a bottle of Amarula cream from the shelf. He added a generous glug into the pan containing the makeshift paste before emptying the entire contents into the hot milk. He let it simmer for a moment or two, before taking it off the heat and pouring it into a thick ceramic mug one of the orderlies had brought over as he'd worked.

"Thank you, Mansa. If in doubt, go with hot chocolate," Catherine smiled.

"I've never known it not to work yet," Mansa nodded.

She took the mug from him and left the kitchen, heading towards Kelly's tent. She hesitated before knocking gently. On the other side, she distinctly heard the noise of someone startled into moving. A few moments later, the curtain behind the glass panelled door was brushed aside. Kelly paused and looked at Catherine with a confused expression. Catherine could see she hadn't slept. Her unkempt hair fell over her face in tangled strands, and her eyes were red and darting nervously. She opened the door and swung it open.

"Hey Kelly," Catherine said.

She felt torn and awkward all of a sudden. Up until now she had been somewhat distant with Kelly, perhaps even a little hostile. She was probably the last person she wanted to confide in or was expecting to appear in the guise of a friend.

"We were a bit worried that you hadn't eaten anything. Mansa has made you this and I wanted to check in on you," Catherine added.

Kelly nodded meekly, stepping aside so Catherine could enter. As she stepped in, she noticed that Kelly's tent was a little more femininely decorated than hers and Thomas's. Instead of a porch and veranda, it had an open lounge with a large wrap around sofa that hugged three sides of a dark mahogany coffee table. The bed, a four poster, was beyond and dressed with white linens. They were strewn aside, crumpled and heaped, flung back in the throes of a restless night. Kelly followed her gaze and gave her a timid, guilty smile of acknowledgment as they sat down on the sofa, across from each other at the junction of a corner. Catherine pushed the cup of hot chocolate over the table towards Kelly, who stared at it for a moment before picking it up with both hands.

She raised her feet up off the floor and tucked them onto the sofa, hugging her knees and resting the cup on top of them.

"It's not an entirely innocent concoction," Catherine warned, "Mansa thought you might need some encouragement to get some rest."

"I'm guessing none of us really slept last night," Kelly murmured. "My brain feels scrambled. What happened keeps running through my head. I was so scared...I just sprinted past Karni like he wasn't there. I didn't warn him. I didn't even look back. It's my fault."

"What you're talking about is called survivor guilt," Catherine said quietly. "It's something I've been dealing with ever since the attacks in Cannich. My friend Louise died. I didn't. First, I felt ashamed that I had survived and she hadn't. Later, I felt I'd failed her and others by not warning them, by not believing Thomas sooner. I felt responsible for their deaths. But it was more than that. Afterwards I felt almost as if I'd been spared by the cat, like I shared something with it. When Fairbanks and I were alone on the mountain, I wanted the cat to come. I wanted it to kill him, and it did. It was as if I willed it to happen."

"Did you feel guilty about that too?" Kelly asked, startled by Catherine's frankness.

"If I'm being honest, no. I felt nothing. It's what haunts me the most. I feel like stone whenever I think about it. Knowing that I have a coldness somewhere inside me that makes me capable of responding like that is something I have a hard time admitting."

"I've filmed in war zones. I'm in dangerous situations all of the time. I've always been so flippant about it. I can't help feeling that played a part in what happened. It was down to me to protect him and I dismissed the danger."

"I think you need to accept that everyone here knew what they were getting into. We have a good team here. The one thing I've learnt from everything I've been through is that facing it alone is the most painful route. What I've just told you I've never been able to tell Thomas, but I don't want you to have the same experience. You don't have to go through it alone."

Kelly looked at Catherine, still with a sense of fracture and fragility, but now with a glimmer of hope. Tears welled in her eyes and began to stream down her cheeks. She buried her face into her knees and sobbed violently. Catherine put her hand over Kelly's, waiting it out. After a while, Kelly seemed to stop, only occasionally jolting with a sharp intake of breath as she calmed again. When she did look up, she seemed more at peace than before.

"Have you felt like this all this time?" Kelly asked, seeming dazed and confused as she processed what Catherine had told her.

"Therapy helped," Catherine shrugged. "Most of the time, I'm okay. When I'm not though, I still go to a pretty dark place. I think Thomas has had a harder time of it than I. At least I know what's going on. It's just been that as he's tried to be protective with self-defence classes and training me to shoot, all it's done is remind me that I wanted someone to die and that they did. It makes me question what I would do if it happened again. He's equipped me to do the very thing I couldn't, but still wanted to happen. That makes me very afraid of what I might be capable of."

"That's horrible. Nobody will miss Fairbanks though," Kelly offered.

"But we'll miss Karni, and I will always miss Louise. In the here and now though, we need you. You didn't do this. The lions did, and we're here to stop them. You have a chance that I didn't, to do something about it. But maybe for now, drink your cocoa and try to get some rest. We're all doing the same today."

"Thank you," Kelly murmured, sitting up and taking a deep breath.

Catherine got up to leave and reached across to give Kelly a quick hug before turning away.

"Catherine?" Kelly called her back, as she headed towards the door. "There's one more thing. Mason wants me to go out with him tomorrow to do some more filming. I don't feel up to it. I know you have an interest in photography. Would you fancy going with him and helping him out? I just don't think I can face it at the moment."

"I think I'd actually love to," Catherine replied. "I look forward to it. Try to get some sleep."

"That's a two-way street," Kelly batted back to her. "Catherine...thanks. I really mean it. Thanks for being my friend."

"Well I wouldn't go that far," Catherine said with a mischievous smile as she opened the door. She paused, and smiled kindly at Kelly. "But you're welcome. Thank you too for listening."

"Any time," Kelly nodded.

~

The rest of the day seemed to pass slowly. Jericho kicked about the camp agitated and grumpily until he slumped onto the chair opposite Thomas. Mansa had supplied them with an almost constant stream of cold bottles of lager, and both had found their way to hammocks, where Jericho at least seemed to finally sleep off his discontent. Catherine had re-joined Mansa in the kitchen, putting a request in for a hot, sweet curry she had cravings for. He gladly accommodated and welcomed the help. As the sun began to set, their troubles too seemed to melt away into the shadows. They all came together around the fire at the centre of the kopje, as the rocky outcrop was bathed in magenta and crimson tones and the fiery disc began to slip below the horizon.

Kelly stood next to Mason, who put his arm round her in a fond hug. Catherine was in front of Thomas, and he wrapped his arms round her waist and held her to him. Jelani and Mansa joined them, carrying drinks and serving dishes.

"To Karni," Mason toasted, as he took a glass from the tray and raised it to the sky.

"To Karni," they all repeated, doing the same.

They all turned back towards the table and took their seats. The mood was still sullen, but a weight seemed to have been lifted. They had grieved and would still do so, but they were united again in purpose. They all seemed to sense it.

Catherine eagerly helped herself to the fat-jewelled chunks of buffalo meat, lightly coated in a sauce made from tangerines with crushed red and green chillies, as well as garlic, ginger and onion. She ladled heavy spoonfuls of fluffy brown rice onto her plate, flavoured with butter and pepper and burnished with shiny green peas. She ate greedily, as did the others. Food had been ignored for most of the day, but now their appetite had returned. As the flames of the fire grew tall, little ripples of laughter erupted around the table as Mason and Kelly shared stories and memories of Karni's adventures with them, blunders and all. Jericho boasted of his bar fight with the guide in Usangi, which then reminded him of several others, of which he regaled them further.

Slowly and amicably, as darkness descended, so did quiet. Kelly excused herself, followed by Mason. Jelani and Jericho moved to the chairs by the fire.

"An early night methinks," Catherine smiled warmly at Thomas.

"Up the wooden hill to Bedfordshire," he laughed. "Night all," he called, glancing back as he got up.

As he turned back round, movement caught his eye. Suddenly, out of the gloom appeared a thin, lithe figure sprinting towards him. Musa, the village boy was streaking across the kopje, eyes fixed on him. Thomas noticed the hemp sack he was carrying and gripping tightly with one hand. Thomas suddenly tensed and felt something was very wrong. He pushed Catherine behind him as Musa closed in and pinched the corner of the sack with his free hand. Then the dogs appeared.

Rhodes zoned in on Musa, emitting a menacing growl as the big dog flanked the boy. When he showed no signs of stopping, Rhodes broke into a full gallop. Saka slipped in behind, lowering her head and letting out an excited yikker as she joined the chase. Just as Musa seemed to realise his predicament, Rhodes leapt, knocking the boy to the ground. Musa scudded into the ground, landing on his back with a wallop that knocked the breath from his body. Rhodes towered over him, growling savagely, only to spring back several feet with a yelp, before standing his ground again and barking violently.

Thomas took a step back as a fat, squat head emerged from the bag Musa had dropped. The threatening audible hiss that accompanied the rippling, coiling body, left him in no doubt what it was. The puff adder crawled clear of the bag, inflating itself and tensing as it detected Musa's nearby scrabbling hand. It gave no further warning as it made a lightning strike, sinking its two-inch fangs deep into the boy's hand. It instantly recoiled, only to strike again as Musa failed to get clear in time. As Thomas dashed round behind, he grabbed Musa beneath his arms to drag him out of the way. Saka trotted in, head bobbing and teeth bared as she closed in on the snake.

The puff adder lived up to its name, enlarging its body and coiling back on itself as it detected the encroaching dog. Its head followed Saka's every move and mirrored it. At well over two feet long with a thick, stout body, Thomas guessed it was a male by the size. Its sandy coloured scales were decorated with what looked like dark brown and orange chevrons. It struck, finding only empty air where the tip of Saka's nose had been. Instead, the hunting dog had dashed to the side, uprooting the snake and flipping it onto its back, landing a quick and slashing bite of her own to the puff adder. The snake writhed and coiled as it tried to escape, but each time, Saka expertly cut it off and attacked its exposed tail or back. Slowly but surely, the puff adder began to lose its strength and veracity. Its body was covered in gashes and tears from Saka's teeth. It lay still, barely hissing as she closed in confidently. She pounced, taking the snake's head in her jaws and crushing the skull with a series of fast, crunching bites. Satisfied, she dropped the dead puff adder on the floor and trotted over to Catherine, rubbing up against her legs in a cat like manner.

"Jelani, get the antivenin kit, would you?" Catherine asked, running over to Musa who was already going into shock.

Jelani nodded his head and dashed off towards the staff camp.

Thomas knelt by the boy and placed his hand on his back, helping him sit up,

"Okay Musa, I'm going to need you to stay calm," he explained. "The quicker your heart beats, the faster the venom is going to move through your bloodstream, so we're going to take everything nice and slow. I'm also going to need you to keep your arms below your chest, so the venom has to make its way up hill to get to your heart. Don't panic, we have antivenin on site and it'll be here any second."

Musa nodded slowly, but his eyes were still wide with panic. He was breathing rapidly and as Thomas took his pulse, he could feel it was racing.

"Musa, it's really important that you calm down. I want you to breathe in for a count of four seconds and then breathe out for the same amount of time. Do it with me, okay?"

Musa met Thomas's eyes and began to control his breathing, taking air in through his nose and exhaling the same way as Thomas counted out for him. Thomas quickly felt the pulse begin to slow, and he could see the boy was less frantic. Jelani arrived back with a large, white, plastic carry case. Thomas carefully raised Musa's hand to inspect it. He sighed, already noticing the swollen and discoloured flesh around the fang marks of each bite. The venom was working quickly.

Catherine opened the container and took out a drip bag of 0.9% saline solution. She then glanced over the vials and quickly selected five marked SAVP Polyvalent Snake Antivenin. Taking a sterile syringe and injector from its wrappings, she quickly administered all five vials into the solution.

"Let's move him," she said. "Get him into a tent and onto a bed where I can set this up easier."

Thomas, Jericho and Jelani picked up Musa together and then stared blankly at Catherine.

"My tent's nearest," Kelly spoke up. "Put him in there."

Without hesitating, they shuffled quickly towards its glass doors, Catherine carrying the drip and Kelly picking up the case behind her. She then sprinted ahead to open the door.

"The sofa's fine, put him down there," Catherine ordered as they entered.

They put Musa down onto the wide, firm cushions and made him sit up again, stooping him forward to lower his arms towards the floor.

"Hold this high," Catherine instructed Thomas as she passed him the IV bag.

She unravelled the full length of the tubing, punctured the IV bag with the attached spike and pinched the drip chamber. As she opened the roller valve and release line, she checked the feed, satisfied there were no bubbles as the fluid began to make its way down the tubing. She then took out a 25-gauge catheter from the white box.

"Now unfortunately Musa, this is going to hurt a little bit. It's quite a big needle, because you're young and we need to administer a lot of medicine quickly. Brace yourself."

She turned over the arm Musa hadn't been bitten on. She turned to Jelani, who passed her a belt tourniquet he had anticipated she'd need with a smile. She nodded her thanks as she fitted it. She then ran her fingers along the vein and palpated it until she was happy. She swabbed it with an alcohol soaked cotton ball and then opened the catheter. She inserted the needle with a quick push, feeling Musa flinch as she did so. She checked the flashback of blood in the catheter's hub and smiled with relief before pushing it in a little further. She took a few moments to carefully edge out the needle and nestle the catheter in place. When she looked up again, Jelani was waiting with sterile strips of bandaging and some tape.

"You've done this before," she smiled, taking them and using them to fix the catheter in place.

She took off the tourniquet and checked Musa's vitals. The boy seemed to be doing well, but he was still looking around the tent at all who had gathered, wide eyed in fear.

"Are you going to kill me Bwana?" Musa stammered.

"Just the opposite," Thomas nodded.

"If we were going to kill you, we wouldn't have just wasted nearly a $1,000 worth of antivenin on you," Jericho growled. "Out of interest, why did we do that? You do realise he was trying to kill you. That snake was intended for you."

"I figured," Thomas nodded. "That's a strange way to thank someone for coming to your village Musa."

As Thomas looked at the scraggly teen, he couldn't help but feel a great swell of pity. The boy was clearly gripped by panic. There was something about his demeanour that suggested he was expecting a severe punishment for his actions, and a physical one at that. Even as Catherine fussed over him, the boy flinched at her every touch.

"Musa, we're not going to hurt you," Thomas assured him quietly. "But why were you trying to hurt us. Did Kanu Sultan make you do it?"

The boy fixed Thomas with a fearful gaze but nodded silently.

"Where did you get the snake from?"

"It's his. He collects them," Musa stammered.

"How long have you been with Kanu, Musa?" Catherine asked.

Musa looked at her. A thick stream of tears began to pour down his cheeks. Catherine sat down by the boy and took his hand in hers.

"I know you're scared. Would you feel better if I asked the men to step outside for a moment, so we can talk?"

Musa nodded, wiping away the tears with his free arm.

"Gents, why don't you give us some space? He's not going anywhere for a while and I don't think he really wants to hurt his doctor, do you Musa?" Catherine asked, turning back to him.

Musa shook his head violently.

"We'll be just outside," Thomas nodded, touching Catherine's elbow with a caress of his fingertips.

"I still say we should have let the dogs finish him off," Jericho huffed under his breath as they exited the tent.

Thomas thumped him in the back good naturedly before turning back and closing the door behind him.

"Okay Musa, it's just us now," Catherine quipped, checking the drip again.

"Well, just us and a camera," Kelly added. "Musa, I think you have an important story to tell. I think you've been abused and hurt viciously by Kanu. We want to make sure he can never hurt you or anyone else again. But that means telling your story. What d'ya say?"

Musa nodded. Catherine noticed a little colour was coming back to his cheeks. He seemed calmer and more alert. Clearly what Kelly had just offered appealed to him very much. She waited as Kelly quickly set up the camera on a tripod and started recording.

"How long have you been with Kanu Sultan?" Kelly asked. "How did you come to join him?"

"It has just always been. I don't know how old I was, but my earliest memories are of Kanu taking me from the arms of my mother. She was dead. I remember the hyenas and Kanu driving them away. But when he took me, as we went away they came back and started to eat her. I have been to that place many times since. I know it is where Kanu takes his prisoners to die. He lets the critters of the bush clean up after him."

"Why did you feel you couldn't come to us for help?"

"Because...the Bwana. I brought a great evil into his life."

Musa stopped, fresh tears welling in his eyes and rolling down his cheeks.

"When you say the Bwana, do you mean Thomas?" Catherine asked, surprised.

Musa nodded. "I was so scared, I never knew..." he began to sob almost uncontrollably.

"Nobody here is judging you Musa. Just tell us what happened," Kelly reassured him.

"It was seven years ago. Kanu walked me into a camp and just left me. He told me that if the Bwana awoke and found me there, he would kill me. I was very afraid, and I cried. Then I saw her, the Bwana's wife. The one with hair like yours," Musa pointed at Kelly. "I was so scared, I ran. As fast as I could. When I heard her coming after me, I ran even faster. I didn't know Kanu was waiting for me. He grabbed me and we left, but he waited until he was sure the lions were coming. It was so quiet. I never heard them take her, but Kanu wouldn't leave until he was sure. I... I led her to them. It was me."

Catherine was staring at Musa in shock. She glanced at Kelly, who seemed just as disturbed as she was. They were both processing what they had just been told. If Musa was telling the truth, then it meant only one thing. Kanu Sultan was responsible for Amanda Walker's death.

CHAPTER TWENTY

Catherine stretched and pushed back against the wooden frame of the chair as she looked out over the kopje, watching a burst of light the colour of a blood-orange begin to creep towards her from the horizon. The night had been cold and she had been restless, but now warmth was returning to both her and the ground with the sun's arrival. As its reach found the cracks and crevices of the outcrop, agama lizards began to peek out from within. A stunning male scurried out into the open, snatching up a dormant cricket whose senses had been dulled by the cool of the night. Catherine admired his striking cobalt blue body and his pumpkin coloured head. A duller, brown headed and mottled cream bodied female strutted past him awkwardly, flicking her tail hard in his direction as she passed to express her annoyance at his proximity. Both settled a few feet from each other as they took up basking positions. Catherine decided to join them, closing her eyes and letting the warm touch of the sun rest on her skin.

"Did you sleep at all?" Thomas asked as he walked up behind.

"A little I think, how about you?" she replied, reaching out for his fingertips with her own.

"Actually, I slept pretty well," he said, sounding a little surprised. "I think finally knowing what happened to Amanda and why she left the tent helped bring me a little peace."

"You don't blame Musa, do you?" Catherine asked, concerned.

"No," Thomas assured her, smiling softly. "If anything, I'm

even angrier on his behalf. Poor kid must have been terrified. He can't have been any older than five or six at the time. How is the patient anyway?"

"He's stable and resting. Jelani moved him down to the staff camp, he didn't seem comfortable in Kelly's boudoir as it were."

"What are your plans today?" Thomas quizzed.

"I offered to help Mason with some scouting he wanted to get done. I thought I might get the jump on him and head out early. It would be a shame not to use this light."

"I'll let him know, where are you going to be?"

"I thought I'd head back across the river towards the scrub out that way, where we encountered the elephants. It would be nice to see them again."

"Take the Big Cat and obviously go armed. And take a radio," he smirked.

"Unlike you, I have no intention to head out anything less than fully prepared," she grinned back mischievously.

Catherine busied herself putting her pack together, grabbing her camera, binoculars, radio and supplies. She checked in with Mason to make sure she knew where she would be before heading to the car. She started the Big Cat and let it idle for a while as the climate control kicked in, then trundled off slowly towards the river crossing below the camp. She checked in both directions for hippo and crocs before plunging the car into the water, surging through with ease to the other side.

About a mile and a half from camp, as she worked her way along a declining ridge line, she stopped to get her bearings. She climbed out of the cabin and onto the truck bed, where she laid out a map on the cabin roof. She pulled on her sunglasses.

Jericho had told her that he thought the elephants had moved west. As she studied the map, she could see that the scrub gave way to forest in that direction, and a little way in there lay what looked like a pristine lake. If the elephants were moving away from the river, this would almost certainly be their next stop, as she knew they would rarely choose to be more than a day's journey from water.

As she looked down onto the plain she was above, she could see she was likely to be right. The landscape of towering termite hills and patchy scrub was scarred and etched with the ancient trails of elephants that had used the same direct routes, possibly for centuries. She remembered Thomas had told her that what was considered the best road in Uganda had in fact been a well-worn elephant track, just like the ones she was looking at now. She clambered back into the cabin and headed down the ridge in their direction. It didn't take her long to find further confirmation that she was going the right way. Large dry clumps of dung peppered the wake of the elephants, as did their tracks and imprints in their dust.

She stopped by a slightly older pile of faeces that was now sprouting green shoots of some hidden seeds within. She let out a contented sigh at the sign of a healthy ecosystem in action. For years it had been suggested that elephants could have a devastating impact on a landscape if left unchecked, something that had resulted in their control and cropping throughout much of their range. It was only relatively recently that their true contribution had been realised. Although at first their intrusion into new areas could be seen as destructive, the long-term effect was the opposite. Their first and foremost role was in seed dispersal and fertilisation, as she could see in the fertile droppings she was looking at. Fruit trees in areas where elephants had disappeared had been found to be in decline, as their seed pods fell straight to the ground where they would be damaged or destroyed by beetles and other insects. Those that did survive would eventually be killed off by the shade of their parent tree. Although some smaller animals such as antelope did help disperse the seeds, their digestive tract didn't provide the perfect levels of nitrogen and enrichment that those of elephants did. Even dung beetles played their part, preferring elephant faecal matter to others, and rolling it away into snug burrows that further helped dispersal and germination.

Further to that, the felled, uprooted and damaged trees left in the wake of a herd on the move provided new homes for rodents, geckos and insects that roamed their cracks and crevices. As they naturally cleared paths through forest areas, they would create savannah and scrub, which in turn was more open to another great changer of landscape and new growth, fire. After years of misunderstood management of wildlife and landscapes in the hands of man, a new principal was emerging that she was full heartedly behind. Let nature be nature and get the hell out of the way. Man's biggest mistake so far with conservation was short-sightedness. Little could be achieved or observed in five years. But given fifty, nature could really do something.

She continued to follow the track-way across the scrub towards the trees up ahead. The path was still wide enough to accommodate the car, and the elephants had opened up the woodland for a fair way in. Concerned that she didn't want to block the path completely if it became too narrow and she encountered a nervous elephant, she pulled off the track a little way and decided to leave the car in the shade of an impressive baobab tree. Before heading off, she checked her pack and took out the tube of la prairie sun protection emulsion. The expensive sunscreen was something Thomas had found for her. As a redhead, she somewhat envied Thomas's dark hair and sun resistant skin, but even he looked pale compared to the blonde and bronzed Jericho. With the help of the lotion she would brown a little, and her freckles would come out a little more, which she rather liked. She applied it liberally to her face and arms before putting her sunglasses back on and shouldering the rifle. She slipped on her hat and set her sights on the interior of the forest.

She walked along the dusty trail, stopping every ten yards or so, as Thomas had taught her. She quickly identified the large, almost square footprints of a mature female. She assumed it was a female by the accompanying smaller, more jumbled prints of the calf accompanying it. She could see the mother's steps were side by side, indicating she was moving slowly to accommodate the pace of her infant. Further along, she found the tracks of two larger juveniles, whose hurried steps betrayed their playfulness as they criss-crossed those of the others.

In the shade of the trees it was much cooler, although a film of sweat still clung to her skin in the humidity. As the scrub and vegetation became thicker, she slowed her approach and became more alert, listening to the haunting sounds of the forest. She froze as the piercing cry of some kind of bird of prey rang out through the branches, instantly bringing silence to the patch of trees she was working her way through. Moments later, the angry replies of what she knew to be yellow-billed hornbills reassured the woodland residents that the danger had passed and the sounds of chirrups, chirps and rustlings returned.

A little further in, she began to pick up the rumblings of her quarry. She threaded her way through the vegetation towards the sounds until she came to a break in the trees. She stopped a good ten yards back. The grass was long enough to hide her if she crouched, and she did so instinctively, edging closer to the opening. At its perimeter, she came to a halt and hid herself by resting against the trunk of a small neem tree with a low, umbrella-like canopy that helped conceal her further. Her heart was beating fast and she could feel the thud of its thunder in her chest. She knew she was smiling and couldn't help it. It had hardly been a difficult or long walk, but still she found herself breathless and her eyes gleamed and sparkled at the sight before her. This is what she had imagined Africa to be like.

Stretching out in front of her was the natural crater of an eroded and long dead volcano. Its gentle and organic slopes were adorned with lush grasses, punctuated by the many trails of the animals that journeyed there from the forest. The reason they did so, lay at the heart of the crater in the form of a flat, crystal blue lake. She guessed that it wasn't only the water that drew them, as the volcanic soil would also be an important source of mineral rich clays and salts. She gazed in awe at the accumulated herds.

Nearest was a group of approximately ten Grévy's zebra mares, who were being watched over by a lone stallion. A little way from them was a Beisa oryx with a young calf. Ordinarily a true desert species, this female had split from the herd and sought the refuge of the crater to give birth and nurture her infant for a few weeks before returning to the more arid environment from which she came. They in turn were kept company by four greater kudus, which she identified from their distinctive white stripes on their backs. Her gaze paused on the bull's impressive corkscrew spiralled horns that measured nearly six feet in length. The leisurely grazing of the antelopes was interrupted by the barging, snorting arrival of a pack of giant forest hogs. The huge, heavily built pigs were covered in vast swathes of thickly matted black hair that turned silver along their spines and across their muzzles. Several of the boars sported foot-long tusks on either side of their mouths and would have easily weighed in at 400lbs. The other animals instinctively gave them a wide birth, and the oryx and kudu moved closer to the zebra. They all joined a group of about thirty wildebeest a little further beyond, clearing the view for her.

The elephants were nineteen in number. She counted eleven cows, including the matriarch. With them were four older juveniles and four calves. Her breathing was slow and relaxed as she watched them play and forage together. She felt the knots in her neck loosen and dissipate, and she rolled her shoulders as she let out a long, contented sigh. She reached for her bag and the camera within. That's when she heard it, or more felt it to be precise. It started with a giddy sensation and queasiness that made her reach out for the support of the tree. As she moved, a deep, penetrating rumble sounded from close by. Her head spun to the right. The thunder came instantly, with a blood curdling trumpet and the cracks of the trees as they parted and splintered in the bull's wake. Catherine froze as Sefu charged, his ears spread and trunk raised high in a posture of unmitigated rage and threat. At thirty feet, he stopped mid-charge and let out a screeching, ear-piercing bugle. Catherine gasped in fright, but instinct urged her to hold her nerve. Sefu seemed more surprised than enraged now he had drawn closer.

The guttural, reverberating clacking noise the big bull was making sounded gentle, almost inquisitive now. His mighty ears folded back and he shook his wrecking-ball sized head in a gesture she knew indicated delight. Sefu stomped to within ten feet, Catherine unable to move or take her eyes away from his towering form, even though her mind was screaming at her not to make eye contact in case he felt challenged. She could easily have stood beneath his chin with ample room to spare. Sefu stretched out his trunk towards her, taking a big whiff of her scent. Using the prehensile tip of the snout and the softest of touches, the elephant knocked off her hat and brushed a stubborn sticking-up sprout of her hair. He paused, almost resting his nostrils on the out of place strands as he took in a second whiff. Seemingly satisfied, he swung right and moved slowly out from the trees and into the expanse of the crater. Catherine's lungs seemed to burst as she let out the breath she had been holding. She struggled to suck down air as she watched the colossus that was Sefu move closer to the herd, his trunk and head swinging back and forth in seeming contentment.

She became entranced by the elephants, taking pictures when she remembered and enjoying the spectacle when she didn't. She watched as one of the cows lumbered up to a silver oak tree. As the cow approached it, she lifted her trunk high into the air, placing it flat and vertical against the bark, as her tusks slipped either side of the tree's circumference with ease. The cow then shook the tree violently with a few casual rams of her head against the trunk. The result was a sudden downpour of loose limbs, branches and debris from the canopy. Content, the female began to pick through the bounty with the tip of her trunk.

The first crack didn't quite register with her, as its echo brought every animal in the crater to a standstill. The animals seemed to look round in bewilderment, as did Catherine as she tried to place the sound. Her eyes darted to one of the lone cows in the elephant herd. It was swaying its head to and fro as if trying to ascertain the source of the sound. As it turned, it seemed to become overbalanced and crumpled to its knees before keeling over completely. Only then did Catherine notice the smear of blood behind its head on the left side of its skull. She froze, still trying to process what had happened. Another shot rang out, this time sending one of the giant forest hogs spinning into the dust. The remaining animals didn't hesitate any longer, scattering in a thunder of hooves, squeals and grunts. Only the elephants remained, although most had moved back to the trees at least. They seemed unwilling to leave their fallen herd member lying out in the open.

The screaming roar was so loud it made Catherine jump and cower closer to the tree. She heard the splintering and smashing of wood as Sefu thundered through the trees like a juggernaut. He exploded into the clearing with a screeching trumpet that declared murderous rage. Her eyes darted to the other side of the crater, where she noticed movement. The source of the gunshots and Sefu's focus was now obvious, as men began to emerge from the trees. She counted eight in all, all dark skinned and dressed in what looked like tan coloured military fatigues. One carried an AK47 over his shoulder whilst the others brandished grizzly looking machetes and long -bladed knives. Two headed over towards the forest hog as the other six approached the dead elephant. They seemed unworried by Sefu's display and the violent, rumbling drone that emanated from him constantly.

With a second roar of unbridled wrath, Sefu charged. He careened forward, lifting his head to bring his curved and near nine-foot-long tusks up. They gleamed in magnificent readiness as he covered the ground with tumultuous screams. Before the man with the AK47 could react, Sefu was on him. The trunk hit the armed man like a wound spring, sending him tumbling backwards in a cartwheel of flailing limbs. Sefu didn't stop, his giant feet smashing into the man and rolling him along the ground like a football. As he tried to scramble away, Sefu reached out with his trunk and coiled its tip around the man's ankle, pulling him back beneath his great mass violently. The elephant stamped on the man's chest with one triumphant blow of a single foot, then sank onto his knees. As he did so, the tip of his tusk sliced through the man's right shoulder, separating his arm from his body as Sefu crushed the remaining life out of him with methodical thrusts of his knees and chin. Catherine watched transfixed as the man was turned to bloody pulp before her eyes.

Another of the soldier poachers ran forward to grab the AK47 that had been dropped some yards away. Sefu spun with a surprising turn of speed, a savage, growl-like sound caught deep in his throat. The trunk snapped out like a whip and caught the man on the side of his head, sending him spinning into the dirt, but not before a lucky squeeze of the trigger peppered Sefu's side. The frantic elephant roared with renewed rage and charged instantly, dropping his head and tusks as he scooped the man from the ground and tossed him high into the air. He landed in a crumpled heap in a cloud of dust, and Sefu thundered over to finish the job. As the dust cloud whirled and encompassed the great beast and his victim, they momentarily became invisible. Only the reddening of the cloud and the sounds of squelch and cracking bones gave hint to the man's fate.

Sefu emerged from the cloud in a full charge at the remaining men, who began to scatter in hurried shouts and high-pitched cries. All froze as the crack of another shot rang out and echoed along the edges of the crater. Sefu too stopped. As Catherine watched, he seemed to be rocking back and forth on his feet unsteadily. He raised his trunk high, forming the shape of an 'S' as he wrapped it around his head and began to feel the edges of his face with its tip. Catherine knew this was a protective behaviour elephants adopted when they were frightened. She stepped out from the trees, her body trembling. All sound seemed lost except the thrashing of her heart in her ears as she noticed the trickle of blood seeping from the wound in the side of Sefu's head. She turned rigid, and her eyes fixed on those of the defiant bull as another shot sounded. Sefu's legs gave out from underneath him completely and he rolled over onto his right side. He struggled violently to keep his head and shoulders elevated as he tried to roll back up. But his strength was leaving him.

Catherine was running now. She saw the angry soldiers reaching for her in seeming slow motion as she passed them. Her gasping breaths came short and struggled, in time with the fall of her feet as she raced over the ground towards the dying elephant. As she reached Sefu, she spun on her heels, raising her arms above her head and spreading them wide in a protective stance. The soldiers stood back and did not approach, unsure of the feral woman now in their midst. As a third shot near deafened her, Catherine felt the soft touch of

Sefu's trunk on her shoulder. She turned slowly, shaking uncontrollably. As her eyes met his bloodshot, questioning gaze, time seemed to stop. She hardly noticed as his trunk tenderly swept around her waist and pulled her out of the way and to the side, placing her behind his left shoulder. She never dropped her gaze, confused at first by his actions. There was something regal in his eyes, an acceptance of death, but also an unrelenting intelligence and nobility that shook her. She realised these were his last moments and he was trying to protect her. Pressed against his skin, she felt the impact of the final shot but did not hear it. The only sound she focused on was the fading thump of Sefu's heart. It was long after it stopped that she felt herself being roughly grabbed by the wrist and dragged away towards the trees.

CHAPTER TWENTY-ONE

"She's not picking up on the radio," Mason said, shaking his head. "I think it's time we headed out after her."

"Agreed," said Jericho. "We know where she was headed. The three of us jump in the Warthog and get her back to camp before dinner I say."

"You'll get no argument from me," Thomas growled. "Jelani, can you provide Mason with a shotgun from the rack and bring mine and Jericho's rifles too. We'll head out as soon as we're all ready."

Jelani nodded and scurried away towards the equipment racks. Thomas had seen the worried look in his eyes and wanted to give him something to do. He would ask him and the men to sweep west just in case she had tried to double back that way and run into trouble. Given that would put her at the heart of the pride's territory, he hoped that wasn't the case.

"She probably just took a radio with a dead battery." Jericho tried to reassure him, thumping Thomas on the shoulder.

"Then why didn't she show up to meet Mason?" Thomas shrugged.

"It's her first time in Africa, and for a photographer, distractions don't come much bigger than an obliging herd of elephants," Jericho suggested.

"Not Catherine," Thomas replied softly. "She's maniacal when it comes to doing things by the book. She almost would have certainly checked the batteries of the radio, and she wouldn't be gone this long without heading back, no matter how enthralled she was."

"I know. I was just trying to make you feel better."

"Stick to what you're good at," Thomas warned.

Jelani returned to them carrying the guns. He handed the rifles to Jericho and Thomas, then passed a pump action shotgun to Mason. Thomas glanced at it, noticing it was a Mossberg tactical model, easy to use and a good choice for someone not used to guns like Mason. He leaned over and showed him where the safety was. The gun had an ammo clip attached to the stock, which Jelani had filled with six shells. Thomas checked he had cartridges in his shooting vest still, and made sure the five-shot magazine was full before clipping it into the rifle. Jericho tapped the gleaming brass bullets edging around his own belt to indicate he was ready too. By the time Thomas had taken Jelani aside and asked him to conduct a westerly search, Jericho and Mason were waiting in the Warthog. Thomas climbed into the truck bed and banged on the roof. The V8 roared as the big Jeep tore off down the track towards the river. Thomas searched the scrub and landscape ahead for any sign of Catherine or the car. As he looked up at the sun, he realised that there were probably only a few hours of daylight left at most.

With Thomas's keen eyes studying the trail ahead and Jericho backing him up from the driver's seat, following the path of the Big Cat from the other side of the river was easy. The wet tyres had bit deep into the mud and left a deeply rutted and discoloured path in their wake. It also didn't hurt that Catherine had told them roughly where she was heading. Jericho slowed and stopped as Thomas caught the tell-tale signs of where the Big Cat had come to a halt, and signalled him to slow down by thumping the cabin roof.

"He wouldn't be letting me do that to his pride and joy," Jericho grumbled to Mason as they pulled off again, still following the tracks.

They worked their way down a ridgeline and onto a scrub and termite mound strewn plain. It was easy for them to see what had drawn Catherine there. The elephant trails were as easy to follow for them as they had been for her. As Thomas's eyes darted over the trail ahead, he spotted the creased ripples in the dirt that signalled where the tyres of the Big Cat had clawed at the ground as Catherine had brought the car to a stop. He slapped the roof of the cab again and Jericho obligingly drew to a halt. It didn't take long to see why she had stopped. The relatively fresh droppings would have confirmed that she was on the right track, which meant so were they. As he crouched down, he spotted the shiny, almost ultraviolet backed dung beetle that had frozen at his approach. A few inches from where it sat was a neat heal print from Catherine's boot. Thomas followed the direction it seemed to be heading and saw what had undoubtedly caught her attention. Less than a mile ahead, through the haze, he could see the tree line of a forest. As he climbed back into the truck bed, he could see Jericho had seen it too from the impatient glance he threw him. The Irishman knew this was where both the elephants and Catherine would have been headed. He knew of the lake at its centre and instinctively put his foot down. The engine complied happily, tearing ahead with renewed purpose.

Just as they entered the trees, a concealed drop sent them momentarily flying before the bumpy landing put them into a careless drift that ended abruptly, as they sideswiped a small

African pencil cedar sapling. With nothing holding him back, Thomas was thrown from the truck bed and tumbled heavily into the hard, red ground.

"Sorry boys," chirped Jericho. "That Ray Charles Driving School has a lot to answer for."

Thomas picked himself up unsteadily, grabbing his hat from the ground and dusting it off. He was facing away from the other two still in the cab of the Warthog, and his eyes were drawn to a glint of metal a little way ahead. As he put the hat back on, shielding his eyes further from the sun, he realised it was the Big Cat. He walked towards it, following the bent and folded stems of Bermuda grass the car had left in its wake, as Catherine had turned off the trail and parked up. He heard the doors of the Warthog open as Jericho and Mason followed him. The car was untouched, and he could still see the discarded contents of Catherine's pack that she had left on the passenger seat before heading off. He took the spare keys from his own pack and opened the car, quickly searching through the interior and checking the gun rack. She'd taken her rifle and pistol from what he could see. If he hadn't been so worried, he would have smiled as he caught the scent of the expensive sun lotion he'd given her still lingering in the cabin. He had noticed over the last few days that being back in the bush had heightened his senses again, something he would be pleased about if not so distracted.

He twisted round sharply as a distant cry caught his attention. It sounded like a squabbling, hissing series of cackles. He looked up and to the north, knowing what he would see. Dotting the sky were the black silhouettes of vultures as they descended, eventually falling from sight beyond the trees. The sheer number of them meant only one thing. Somewhere up ahead there was a body, and the birds were already feasting.

The three of them tracked their way through the scrubby forest, guns raised in readiness and not knowing what they might find. As they approached a break in the trees up ahead, Thomas found himself biting his lip and taking short raspy breaths. His mouth was as dry as the dust on the ground and his heart thumped in his chest like a jackhammer. He hesitated, sensing the hole that seemed to be forming in the pit of his stomach. He didn't dare imagine what might be out there in the clearing. He sensed Jericho move in close behind him.

"Easy does it fella. It's not your sweetheart they got. It's mine," the Irishman growled softly.

Thomas's head snapped round in momentary confusion, but he followed Jericho as they stepped out into the clearing. His eyes were drawn to the large crimson headed birds that seemed to line the crater they were standing in. They were lappet-faced vultures, the biggest of their kind in Africa. The flaps and folds of skin that hung from the sides of their heads and gave them their name made them look like some kind of vulgar, mutant, predatory turkey. Their vicious black curved beaks were the only instruments that could break through the tough dried hides of the carcasses they fed on. Even other vultures, like the griffon and white-backed ones now gathering in droves, had to wait for the arrival of the lappets before they could eat. They were therefore head of the table, cursing angrily at any that dared approach whilst they were still enjoying the choicest morsels. They kept the competitors back with angry wing slaps and slicing snaps of their beaks. The only birds that they tolerated were the equally grotesque looking marabou storks, whose intimidating size and long, wide straight beaks gave them equal standing. The storks would use their weaponry to enlarge and deepen the entry points into a carcass, which then opened up the table to the lesser vultures scrapping for their place. Even in this wretched and macabre dance, nature adhered to a hierarchy that would benefit all.

As he scanned the trees he spotted the solitary form of a male bateleur eagle. Compared to the others, it was an incredibly handsome bird, with a black head, neck, belly and breast. The back, tail and mantle were coloured chestnut, and the upper parts of the wing appeared silvery white. But the flash of red, featherless skin at the base of the beak gave away the bird's role here. It too was not against scavenging, and Thomas knew that it had probably been first on the scene, having a predilection for the eyes and tongue. It only donned the regal pretence associated with its kind as it waited for the larger and more aggressive birds to clear the area once more. The vultures had even quite possibly followed the bateleur to the scene.

There was no difficulty in finding what had drawn the birds to the crater. The scene of slaughter and butchery was laid out before them like a morbid diorama. Nearest to them was the straggled carcass of an elephant cow. Her legs were pushed out to her sides, her knees only slightly bent in an ungainly sprawl. Thomas knew that if he looked closer, he would find rope burns on the legs where she would have been pulled into position. The vultures had already bored into her side, and were now busy widening the opening. The internal organs would be the first to go, followed by as much of the meat as they could tear from the insides before larger predators arrived. Thomas knew it wouldn't be long, especially with the stench of blood scorched by the dry heat of the day wafting over the savannah.

As his gaze wandered over the carcass, he couldn't help the gasp that escaped his lips as his eyes came to rest on what was left of the cow's head. The golf ball sized eyes had already been gouged from their sockets, leaving only fleshy, bloody pits in their absence. But it was beyond them that the true butchery had taken place. There was simply nothing. The head had been cleaved, hacked through by hatchets, machetes, or perhaps even a chainsaw. The only thing that remained of the face was the lower jaw and lip. Everything else was gone. It was as if some giant thing had come along and bitten off the face. Globules of fat, tattered flesh, and a gaping hole in the centre of the cross-sectioned skull where the brain had been, was all that remained. The vultures had already dined there with glee. The ground where he stood had soaked up the waterfall of blood, that must have flowed as if it had been rain. He knew the hyenas would lick away any remnants they found once on scene, even swallowing the blood splashed stones to aid their digestion.

The poachers that had done this of course wanted the ivory, and this brutal method not only allowed them to remove the tusks intact, but also provided them with a meal in the form of the fatty and muscular trunk. They hadn't bothered taking anything else from the carcass, which was strange given the demand for bush meat. As Thomas looked up, he saw Jericho standing in front of a much larger elephant a little further away. As he started to walk over, he was distracted for a moment, as a white-backed vulture flapped down and landed clumsily on a pile of fleshy mush to his right. As he looked, he spotted the torn strands of the tan military fatigues sticking to the broken, twisted stumps of bone, in a glue of blood, skin and pulp that was all that remained of one of the poachers. Thomas had to stop himself from gagging as it slowly dawned on him what he was looking at. He hesitated no longer, lifting his rifle high and letting off a shot that sent the vultures cart wheeling into the air with disgruntled screeches. Most lazily drifted into the nearby trees to wait for the men to leave, as they knew they would.

The body of Sefu had been left in a similar way to that of the cow, but their attack on him seemed more brutal. They had cut deeper into his skull, and the wounds seemed more jagged and vicious. It was as if they had wanted to hurt him even after death. His tough hide was yet to be pierced by the vultures, and the bullet holes in his side that had sent streams of blood down his flank and belly now swarmed with flies, their bodies glistening black, blue and green in the sun. With the quietening of the vultures, their droning buzz quickly filled the silence. Thomas, Jericho and Mason walked around the bull's remains and were shocked to find a further, final insult to the great bull's dignity. An ugly gash and open wound was all that was left of the elephant's sexual organs. They had been hacked off and removed.

"God-damned limp-dicked sons of bitches," Jericho spat. Thomas and Mason looked at him questioningly.

"Trading ivory with certain Asian markets has led to the discovery they also believe consumption of certain parts will improve their sexual prowess," Jericho explained, shaking his head. "There are now several syndicates operating out of Mombasa. Ivory has become known as the white gold of jihad.

The worldwide trade is estimated to be worth around £12billion. About £5billion of that finds its way into the hands of assholes like Al-Shabaab."

"How is the Kenyan Wildlife Service meant to be able to compete with that?" Mason asked in disbelief.

"Honestly? They can't." Jericho shrugged.

"Catherine was here," Thomas stated quietly, crouching on the ground beside the elephant.

The others immediately saw what he was looking at. A number of small, bloodied boot tracks led away from Sefu's carcass. Thomas followed them, never taking his eyes away from the ground. Jericho and Mason followed.

"How do you know it's Catherine?" Mason asked.

"I recognise the tread pattern of her boot," Thomas replied. "She's also putting up some resistance. I can see where she's dug her heels into the ground."

"I hate to say it, but that's a good sign. The more she fights them, the more likely they'll leave her alone. They're lazy, that's why they do this. But they aren't exactly feminists and she's unlikely to come out of this untouched," Jericho said.

"I'm going after her. She won't have to fight them for long," Thomas stated.

"The thing is, it's more likely she was taken on Kanu's orders. If this is the work of Kruger, and I think it is, then he wouldn't have taken Catherine without being asked to. Kruger isn't out to get you, but we know Sultan is. Kruger's probably already delivered his prize," Jericho offered.

Thomas considered his options for a moment. He didn't like any of them.

"Okay, we split up. I'll take the Big Cat back to camp and try to convince Musa to tell me where Kanu's camp is. You try to track Kruger from here, but keep in touch."

"Same goes for you old boy," Jericho nodded.

"Mind if I tag along with you back to camp?" Mason asked Thomas.

Thomas nodded, just as a savage roar lifted up from beyond the trees. They all spun at once in the direction it had come from.

"Doesn't look like we're going anywhere yet," Jericho sighed as he broke the barrels of the double rifle, placing a long brass-cased bullet in each.

CHAPTER TWENTY-TWO

Catherine sat coiled on the bench seat that ran along the sides of the lorry bed she had been dragged to and thrown in. There was a small space around her in the otherwise crowded interior, and the dark-skinned men watched her wearily. Several of them had already made the mistake of underestimating her, only to find her kicks a little too well placed and powerful for their liking. She hadn't come through it unscathed though, and she could feel the heat of the bruise on her cheek, put there by a back-handed slap from the largest of the men. She was fairly sure that the slam of her retaliating elbow had broken his nose though. They had backed off then, but mainly because the white man with the thick South African accent had told them to. He was up ahead of them now, and occasionally she caught glimpses through the lorry's front window of the flashy six wheeled Mercedes jeep he was driving. She glanced behind to the flat-bedded Toyota that followed them, carrying the spoils of their hunt. The rear of the lorry she was in was covered in canvas, held in place with a flimsy looking frame that lined the rear compartment. She had considered throwing herself from the sides, as the gaps between the metal loops were easily large enough, but the canvas was tied down too tightly. For the last fifteen minutes, she had been tugging at the knot that held the panel behind her in place, made easier by having her hands bound behind her back.

Just as she felt the knot begin to give, the three-vehicle convoy turned sharply, slamming her against the side momentarily before the lorry trundled to a halt. As the men around her began to pour out of the back of the truck, she could see they had pulled into some kind of compound. Shanty style, single storey buildings made of wood with corrugated iron roofing, surrounded them on three sides. Beyond the buildings there was a maze of desert camouflage walled tents.

"Out," the big man commanded.

The dried blood around his nostrils almost made her smile. He glowered at her as he watched her rise and stagger forward, balancing made difficult from her trussed arms. As she neared the opening, his hands shot out and grabbed her by the shirt, throwing her to the ground. She had been expecting it, and twisted to fall on her side and back rather than her front. She was quick to turn again to make sure the kick that followed hit her in the base of the spine. She couldn't help the cry of pain it summoned, and she knew it gave her assailant some pleasure to hear it.

"Back off Hondo, you'll damage the goods," said the smug South African voice from behind.

The man, dressed in a white safari suit with matching hat and a tan suede shooting vest, leant down and dragged her back to her feet by the elbow. She winced and struggled to catch her breath still. She felt a little giddy as she found herself on her feet again.

"Take her to my tent," the South African nodded, handing her back roughly to the burly Hondo.

She was marched through the compound, shoved ahead of her escort towards the tents. As she looked around she noticed the elongated open shed that stretched along the back wall. It was lined with cages containing all manner of live animals. She spotted something that looked like a cross between a cat and a racoon curled up inside the nearest, and realised it was an African civet. A caracal, a small species of cat was in the cage next to it, and bobbed its head up and down as she went by. It's larger cousin, a cheetah, snarled and swatted at the mesh of its own tiny prison behind. She thought she could just make out the black pointed ears of a pair of servals beyond that too.

As her eyes wandered, she saw smaller animals like lesser galagos, also known as bushbabies, as well as vervet monkeys and a lone, morose looking chimpanzee. Passing a tower of wicker boxes stacked in the corner, she realised each contained a single Jackson's chameleon. None of the cages had been constructed to allow the creatures inside them much comfort or space. They were purely intended for transport. All victims of the illegal wildlife trade, they were destined to be sold as pets or farmed for their parts and fur. But as she had witnessed back at the crater, they were the lucky ones.

The point was driven home to her as she was thrust through the entrance to a large white marquee style tent sporting a dramatic, pyramid shaped roof. The interior was dressed in bright and vibrant Arabian patterned fabrics, coloured rose-pink, cherry and gold, and lined with matching tasselled plush cushions. At its centre was an ornate, gold-painted four poster bed, covered in crimson silk sheets. A garish pink and gold chaise-lounge sat to its side. But it was none of these that drew her eye. It was the pair of gold tipped elephant tusks that ordained the foot of the bed, the skins of lion and leopard that covered the floor; the lone gorilla skull displayed on top of a Roman-esque stone column. Everywhere she looked there were sickening personal trophies. Another single elephant tusk sat mounted in a solid slab of black marble, shaped to hold it in place perfectly. The ivory itself was intricately carved, depicting a herd of elephants winding through a forest towards a lone hunter, crouched and waiting for them with rifle raised. She found herself bristling, wanting to smash it into a thousand pieces. She turned away, only to find herself looking at a similarly mounted rhino horn, capped with an iron sheath that ended in a razor-sharp tip.

"It's Persian," the South African voice came again, from behind. "War dress for their beasts. Worth several hundred thousand pounds I'm told and over 1500 years old. Also proof that man will always look to conquer those mightier than himself, wouldn't you say?"

She turned and saw the man grinning at her. He seemed almost victorious. He skirted round her and she snapped round to follow him, never taking her eyes off him for a second. This seemed to amuse him further and he raised his eyebrows in mockery as he nodded towards Hondo. The big man nodded and ducked out through the doors of the tent.

"My name is Viktor Kruger, what do you think of my little collection?" he asked, slumping down onto the chaise-lounge.

"I think you must need a microscope to find your own penis with this much compensation around you," Catherine seethed.

The smile vanished instantly. He studied her intently.

"I commend spirit, but not rudeness my dear. It's Catherine, isn't it? I prefer Cathy. Do say my dear girl; I'd have hated to grab the wrong prize. Can't be too many redheads running round here, but you never know hey?"

"Only my fiancé calls me Cathy. My mother calls me Catherine when I'm in trouble. You're neither shitbrain. You can address me as Ms. Tyler, or preferably not at all."

"So defiant," Kruger laughed cruelly. "But you are in

trouble my dear. A year from now you might not even remember your name. It and your fiancé will be like some distant dream, somehow familiar but still nothing more than a fantasy."

Kruger tilted his head to look past her and beckoned with his hand. Catherine turned to see a haggard looking old native woman shuffling past her. She wore an orange shawl that nearly covered her from head to toe. She bowed her head towards Kruger then swiftly turned to Catherine. The woman had deep pits and lines across her face, and her eyes were steely grey and cold. She walked around Catherine once, prodding her in the buttocks and ribs.

"Cut that out you old witch," Catherine warned through clenched teeth.

The woman ignored her, continuing her appraisal until she faced Catherine again. Without warning, and startling quickly for someone who seemed decrepit and fragile, the woman grabbed Catherine's trousers at the waist and unbuttoned them, dragging them down to her ankles along with her panties in one deft movement. Unable to lift her feet, Catherine slammed her right knee into the old woman's left eye socket, sending her stumbling backwards. Kruger tutted loudly as if he was scolding a child, and casually lifted a revolver from behind the back of the chair. Catherine recognised it as her own. He only had to move it slightly in her direction for her to turn rigid. The memory of the mountain and the sound of bullets ricocheting off the surrounding rocks rooted her to the spot, as the old woman regained her feet and continued her examination, muttering incomprehensible curses under her breath as she did so.

"I don't usually trade whites Ms. Tyler," Kruger explained.

"It makes the authorities nervous and likely to do something rash like actually investigate, so I'm afraid I need to get rid of you rather quickly. I'd kill you myself, but that really would attract their attention."

She couldn't help the involuntary tremble as the woman's fingers roughly parted her pubic hair and pressed meanly on the edges of her vagina. Her legs felt weak and she thought that her body might collapse in on itself in any given moment. A cold sweat formed on her brow as her head sank towards the floor. She hardly noticed as the woman stood up straight again and began to squeeze her breasts. The sharp pain brought her back from the cold confusion of her thoughts, and she glared at the hag in shock.

The old woman turned and bowed her head again towards Kruger. She held up her right hand and showed two raised fingers.

"Two hundred?" Kruger queried sitting up, feigning disappointment. "That's the trouble with fundamentalists. Only a few years ago I'd have gotten a good couple of grand for you at least."

The woman nodded again.

"Why so high? Our friends won't normally even pay $75 for a woman of her age, even one as good looking as her?"

"It is not just her they pay for," the old woman laughed, turning before she left the tent. "But also her child."

CHAPTER TWENTY-THREE

Jericho had barely closed the action of his rifle when a tawny coloured blur erupted from the scrub in front of him. He swivelled, swinging the gun from his hip and squeezing the trigger. The blast from the right-hand barrel sent its glowing projectile faithfully into the chest of its target. The lioness crashed into the dirt, sliding to a halt about twenty yards from them.

"Back to back boys," Jericho yelled, reversing his steps towards Thomas and Mason.

Thomas raised his rifle as he spotted a glimpse of honey coloured fur skirting the bushes ahead of him, but the lion was using the natural dips and contours of the crater to stay hidden. As it dropped out of sight, he caught another movement from the corner of his eye and instinctively dropped to his knee. He brought the scope up, trying not to blink so as not to narrow his field of vision. But again, the flash of fur was all he saw before it vanished just as quickly. They were being surrounded.

A low, continuous growl came from the bushes about thirty yards ahead of Mason. Thomas and Jericho instinctively turned their heads in the same direction, but didn't let their guard down. Thomas was almost impressed when he saw a lioness to his right break cover and bound to a new, nearer hiding place amongst some sickle bushes.

"Look, straight ahead," Mason pointed.

As Thomas looked round, he saw a golden coloured lioness standing out in the open. It seemed to be watching them nonchalantly, standing still, but behaving non-threateningly. If anything, the lion seemed curious. Thomas couldn't help admiring the animal. Her bronze colouring practically glistened in the sunlight, a sure sign of being well fed. Though not tensed, her muscular shoulders and neck gave hint at the power and strength she was capable of. Thomas found the stare of the lioness unsettling. It was too self-assured, almost cocky. He realised why just in time.

He spun round, reaching out with his right hand to turn Jericho's shoulder back towards the danger they were facing. Thomas didn't have time to bring the rifle up, instead dropping to his knee and angling the barrel upwards before eagerly yanking on the trigger. Half way through its spring, the lioness that had been stalking him whilst its partner distracted them, somersaulted backwards, as the big calibre cartridge smashed through its lower jaw and back out into the sunlight through the top of its skull. The lioness crashed back down into the dust, her body gripped in the violent spasms of death as her muscles tried to send messages to a part of the brain that was simply no longer there. Thomas watched in horror as another two lionesses burst from either side of the bushes, passing their fallen comrade without a glance. Their amber eyes were set on only one thing; the three men in front of them.

Jericho too found himself in the path of a charging lioness. As he raised his rifle, lining up the sights along the barrels neatly to a point just ahead of the sprinting cat, he smugly discharged the second chamber, only to realise in horror that he had been a little over confident. The lioness had just enough time to anticipate the discharge of the gun, and dug her heels into the dust, turning to her left as a spot on the ground ahead of her erupted in a spray of loose stones and a volcanic spray of crumbling earth. Her snaking tail shot upwards and countered her sliding, scrambling acceleration. Jericho stumbled backwards as he tried to reload in vain, knowing he would never make it. But the lioness merely grazed him as she steamed past, and he realised too late that Mason was the intended target.

The lioness reared up with a roar, her outstretched claws mooring themselves in Mason's side. With his back turned on Jericho's position he had been completely exposed, and the lioness buried her teeth into his shoulder and neck, as her weight knocked him forward onto the ground. Mason managed only one short cry of surprise before he began to be dragged away. The waiting lioness who had served as the distraction, now eagerly bolted forward, opening her jaws to greet him. A shot rang out and the oncoming feline stopped stock still, her facial features frozen in a mixture of surprise and pain. A crimson stain appeared in the centre of her chest, and the lioness crumpled to the ground as her legs gave way.

Mason felt the lion still carrying him bite down savagely as she turned direction, now steeling away towards the safety of the nearest trees. He yelled in pain but kept his head, lashing and kicking out at his attacker. Face down and unable to turn, there was little damage he could do to the lion, but he hoped to cause enough interference to make her think that dropping her meal would make for a faster getaway. Unfortunately, the lioness was already stooping to duck under the branches of a meanly barbed acacia bush, the famous wait-a-bit thorn. Mason knew he was only a few feet from death, and that once shielded by the undergrowth, the lioness would kill him. He closed his eyes, praying for another shot to ring out, but it never came. All he heard was a strange grating sound, like something metallic being dragged over hard ground. He opened his eyes in confusion and glanced downwards. He nearly cried out loud when he saw the carry strap of the Mossberg shotgun caught on his belt buckle, and he quickly scrabbled for it, pulling the weapon into his hands. He awkwardly gripped the gun over the fore end with his right hand, and used his left to shove the end of the barrel into the lioness's ribs. The gun was tight against his chest and at a slight angle as he pulled the trigger.

The cat was knocked to the ground as if it had been hit by a speeding truck, dropping Mason from its jaws instantly. As he rolled onto his knees with the last of his strength, he was horrified to hear the lion emit a ferocious hiss as it too found its feet. It slumped to the ground, its legs giving way instantly. But then it began to crawl through the dirt towards him, writhing and clawing its way closer. Mason pumped the gun in a panic, the concentrated glance down it took to do so momentarily distracting him. When he looked up again, he was shocked to find the lioness only a few feet away, teeth bared and still advancing. He was beginning to feel light headed and dazed. He didn't have the strength to lift the gun and instead balanced it on his thighs. Just as he felt the world begin to spin away, he managed a panicked pull of the trigger that sent a spray of lead straight into the face of the lioness. He slumped over, falling face down into the dirt as he drifted into unconsciousness. The last thing he heard was the huffed last breath of the lioness lying next to him.

As he furiously reloaded, Jericho watched the lion casually dragging Mason towards the bushes. He quickly lined up a spine shot, only to see another lioness trot out from the undergrowth in front of them. He swung the barrels towards the new target and this time made sure of his mark before firing. He saw the bullet hit home before movement to his right made him spin round, gun still raised. Two lionesses were sprinting towards him and Thomas, only seconds away from the spring. The men both fired simultaneously, the deafening shots ringing in their ears and muting the chaos. A cloud of dust sprang up in place of the lions, blinding them too. As the dust swirled in thick cyclonic drifts, Jericho was disorientated by the muffled sound of a shotgun blast. The screeching, monotone chime reverberating in his ears made it sound like it had been fired underwater. Both he and Thomas were frozen to the spot, guns raised, and eyes feverishly searching their limited field of vision.

Thomas felt the thud of his heart begin to slow as the dust began to settle. He could make out the two crumpled forms of the dead cats, sprawled out on the rocky ground where they had fallen, snarls frozen into their faces by the sudden arrival of death. He turned and sprinted towards Mason, Jericho instinctively covering him. As Thomas turned the cameraman over, he could see it was bad. The lioness had raked Mason's right arm and side viciously with her claws, ripping into the flesh as effectively as oversized fish hooks. The shreds of his shirt were soaked in warm, wet blood that streamed from the wounds. Worse still was his shoulder, torn apart by four-inch-wide punctures from the clamp of the lioness's upper and lower canines.

"There's a med kit in the car," Thomas motioned to Jericho, shouldering the rifle and hoisting Mason up from under his arms.

Thomas squatted, allowing Mason to fall over his

shoulders as he sprang up, carrying him in a fireman's lift and snatching up the shotgun as he did so. Balancing Mason by locking his arm over his ankles, he used his other hand to firmly grip the pump of the gun, violently jerking it with a downward thrust of his arm to load. With a flick of his wrist he tossed the Mossberg upwards, catching it by the pistol grip. The weight of the weapon nearly made him overbalance, but he corrected his footing quickly, bringing the barrel up and pointing it ahead of him.

"Show off," Jericho grumbled. "What exactly was the issue with asking me to do that for yer?"

"It seemed quicker. Get going," Thomas growled.

Jericho covered from the rear, only ever a few steps behind Thomas, as he scanned the now empty crater. As they entered the trees, Jericho noticed the gathered vultures begin to descend again from the canopy, a sure sign that the predators were not in the immediate vicinity. He didn't let his guard down, knowing they could just as easily be heading in their direction still. Thomas's progress was slow as he balanced both gun and Mason. His back and legs were screaming by the time the Big Cat came into view, and he staggered towards it with renewed purpose.

A few yards from the car, Jericho sprinted forward and opened the rear passenger door. Thomas bent down and rolled Mason from his shoulders onto the seats of the rear compartment. Jericho was already rooting in the truck bed for the first aid kit. Finding it, he dashed round to the other side of the car and opened the door, close to where Mason's head now lay.

They both worked quickly, cleaning the wounds with hydrogen peroxide solution in a quantity that would have had most men screaming with pain. Mason's limp and silent body only worried Thomas further. They both did what they could with the lacerations and puncture wounds, plugging them with sterile gauze swabs and wrapping them in military field dressings.

"He needs a hospital," Jericho said, shaking his head.

"Do you know where the nearest one is from here?" Thomas asked.

"No clue," Jericho shook his head. "Look, I say stick to the plan. You get back to camp as fast as you can. Jelani will know where to take him, and there are better supplies there anyway for you to at least stabilise him. I'll head out after the poachers. If I find anything, I'll radio you."

"And vice versa," nodded Thomas. "Don't do anything rash. These guys clearly play rough."

"So do I. And I'm inclined to, after what these bastards have done," Jericho spat.

Thomas stretched out his hand. Jericho took it and shook it firmly. There was a playful glint in the Irishman's eye that made Thomas smile despite the gravity of their circumstances. With a tip of his hat, Jericho turned and strode towards the Warthog. Thomas too kicked into action, jumping into the driver's seat and starting the Big Cat. With a roar of the V8, he turned the truck around and pressed hard on the accelerator, as he guided it back up the trail with a determined turn of speed. Jericho watched him go in the rear-view mirror before he too moved off, in the opposite direction.

~

She moved through the scrub effortlessly. She usually avoided travelling during the day, but the pride had split during the night and now a number of them were missing. The lionesses had called for them in nervous, ranting roars from the kopje where they had rested, but no answer had come. Only she had slipped from the rocks into the maze of thorn bushes, termite mounds and outcrops that lay between there and the waterhole where she knew the others preferred to hunt. She felt more at ease once under the cover of the pale foliage of the acacias. The world around her was painted in mottled shades of blue, brown and mauve, but she instinctively knew she was safer behind the thorns than the slabs of rock and the other trees. They somehow felt different, as if her whole body was more attuned to them. She froze as a startled bush pig jumped up from in front of her and dashed into the scrub. The movement registered in her vision as a flash of iridescence, and she watched the animal disappear, letting it go without further thought. Her instinct and focus were singular.

As the light began to fade she felt less exposed and vulnerable. She began to lope through the scrub. The scent trail the others had laid down was still strong and becoming easier to follow. The waterhole was close now and the warm smell of the trail invigorated her. She felt the anticipation of their presence and began to speed up. Then she froze. Her ears pricked up and she opened her mouth, sharpening her hearing even more acutely. There was a kill ahead. The clamour and bickering of the vultures made her uneasy for some reason in the absence of other sounds. Turning her head allowed her to taste the taint of blood in the air.

An angry growl escaped her throat before she hunkered down into the long grass. She listened intently before moving forward, crawling on her belly to the edge of the trees. Her muscles hardened and tightened in readiness as she rose a few inches for a better view. The vultures were everywhere, fighting angrily for their place at the banquet table. The elephant carcasses were being ignored in favour of the fresher, more easily accessed meat suddenly on offer. She now knew the warm scent of the others and that of the blood came from the same source.

She burst from cover in a spring of pent up savagery she could no longer contain. She barrelled into the first group of vultures, who had been too slow to react to the roar that had erupted from her as she charged. Her front paws swatted at the two nearest birds in hammer blows that drove their crushed heads into the dirt. Her jaws snapped around the torso of a lappet-faced vulture, beating its wings in panic as it tried to take to the air in vain. As she bit down, its struggles instantly ceased and she spat out its lifeless body in a blood-lust fuelled snarl. Slashing swipes of her claws brought down another two vultures before the others were out of reach and back in the safety of the trees again.

She patrolled the crater with wrathful shakes of her head, issuing grunt-like snarls of warning to the gathered scavengers. She paced from one body to another, revisiting the fallen lionesses several times. Two she licked at the faces of, and rubbed with her chin and cheek. Her attentions became more frantic and violent as they remained cold and still to her touch. She lay nose to nose with one of her adopted daughters, her hot wet breath lashing the snout and whiskers of the dead cat. She lay statue-like, unable to judge the amount of time that had passed. She only moved again when a white-backed vulture decided to investigate her own still body. She extinguished its life as if swatting a fly.

That was when the other scent came to her on a wisp of breeze from the east. She paused at the pool of blood a few feet from one of the lionesses. She licked at the congealed liquid, instantly recognising the salty, coppery taste. She lifted her head, staring across to the other side of the crater. Her shoulders pumped hard as she skirted the waterhole, eagerly following the scent. She slipped through the trees until she came to a larger opening on the edge of the forest. The air was now tainted with sulphur and carbon, the meaning of which she recognised. She looked out across the plain to the south, towards the place where the men and their soft-sided dwellings were. As the sun began to set, painting the landscape in hues of pink and crimson, she broke into a run towards the camp.

CHAPTER TWENTY-FOUR

Thomas slammed on the brakes as he passed the main entrance to Anga ya Amani, sliding to a violent halt just outside his own tent and throwing up a cloud of red dust. He sounded the horn in three long blasts before kicking open the door and jumping out. Jelani had been sitting out on the kopje and was at his side in an instant. He froze when he saw Mason's wounds.

"My friend, what happened?" Jelani stammered.

"He took a hit from a lioness. We followed Catherine's trail to a small patch of woodland where we found two elephant carcasses. I don't know if that's what brought the lions in or if they were already there," Thomas explained.

"Elephant carcasses?"

"Poachers. Jericho is on their trail now. They may have also taken Catherine, but we can't be sure. We need to get Mason stabilised and to a hospital."

"The nearest one is in Voi, about thirty miles away."

"Would you be able to take him?" Thomas asked.

"The trucks and the men are still out searching for Miss Catherine. I don't think we can wait around until they get back," Jelani answered, shaking his head.

Thomas passed him the keys to the Big Cat, grabbing his bag and rifle from the passenger seat.

"I'm going after Catherine, and I need to speak to Musa if I've got any hope of finding her. Take the Cat. It's the fastest option anyway."

"I understand my friend," Jelani nodded. "I will see if there is anything I can do to make Mr. Mason more comfortable before I leave."

"Thank you," Thomas nodded, turning to head towards the staff camp.

"Don't underestimate Kanu," Jelani called after him. "He's bad business, bokor or otherwise."

"I know. Watch your own back too."

Thomas hurried down the path towards the staff tents. It was eerily quiet, the normal clamour and bustle of camp life noticeably absent. The silence was broken by the sound of the Big Cat's engine roaring into life as Jelani headed out. Thomas stopped outside the tent Musa had been given. He couldn't help but notice it was the one the lions had cleared out only a few days before. He could still smell the disinfectant that laced the canvas walls, and the bleach that had been used to remove the blood stains. He parted the doors slightly with a little pressure from his middle and index finger to peek inside. Musa was sitting on the bed, clearly aware of his presence and watching him. Thomas smiled, pushing the flap of the door aside and stepping into the tent.

"Hello Musa, how are you doing?" Thomas asked.

"Good Bwana, I'm okay. I feel much better," Musa answered.

Musa sat on his camp bed, his feet tucked beneath him and his arms wrapped around his knees, pulling them tightly into his chest. He watched Thomas with wide unblinking eyes in the way a gazelle watches a leopard out in the open. The boy was fearful and didn't trust him. Thomas wondered if he thought he was there to kill him. Surely the failure of his attempt would earn him a considerable punishment in Kanu's camp, perhaps even death Thomas thought. He clearly expected to still be punished for his forced part in Amanda's death. Thomas slid the rifle from his shoulder carefully, and deliberately rested it up against the wall of the tent. He did the same with his bag. Thomas took a seat on the neatly made empty camp bed opposite Musa.

"Musa, I know you feel that you were somehow involved in my wife's death," Thomas said, resting his elbows on his knees as he leant forward gently. "It wasn't you who killed her, it was the lioness, this so-called queen. I don't blame you at all."

Tears immediately welled in Musa's eyes. They began to stream down his cheeks uncontrollably as he nodded his head in silence. Thomas went to pick up a bottle of water from the small bedside cabinet beside them, but paused. He smiled and instead opened the drawer of the cabinet. Inside, as he suspected, was a hidden stash of cans of Coke and sweets. Jelani had a real weakness for them, especially the fizzy drinks. Thomas had correctly guessed that Jelani had moved into the tent, offering his own to the remaining men, who would have been hesitant to stay in accommodations marked by the man-eaters. He took one of the cans of Coke and handed it to Musa, who took it readily. Thomas knew only too well that such things were often used as rewards for child soldiers. Jelani's own past was reflected in his freedom to consume them as an adult, and the pleasure he took from it. Thomas had seen the white scars on Musa's skin whilst he had been treated the night before, little rice-like flecks against the dark flesh. The mark of a belt or whip.

"Musa, you telling me what happened to Amanda is something I have wanted to know for a very long time," Thomas assured him. "I feel very proud of her and what she did. And you were very brave to tell me. I feel that I can finally be at peace about what happened. Thank you for giving me that. But I need to ask you to give me something else too."

"Yes Bwana," Musa nodded eagerly.

"Catherine, the woman who is to be my new wife – I think Kanu has taken her. I need to go after her. I need you to tell me where his camp his. Do you think you'd be able to show me on a map?"

Musa nodded again, much more slowly this time. Thomas quickly went to his bag and took out a map. He unfolded it and spread it out on the bed in front of Musa.

"This is where we are now," Thomas showed him, pointing to where the camp was marked on the map towards its south-east corner. "This is the village where I killed the leopard," Thomas said, moving his finger directly south. "Where will I find Kanu?"

Musa studied the map. He used his finger to trace the path of the road that led east out of the village. He paused at a junction, where one path looped back around the hills towards Anga ya Amani. Instead, his eyes darted further across the map. He dragged his finger along the road further east. At a point marked as the Mavia Maiu rocks, Musa's finger shot away from the road at a sharp angle, now following a series of craggy outcrops. It finally came to rest in the centre of a marshland fed by the Galana River. Thomas could see it was surrounded by arid scrubland with no direct access by road. The wildcat king would be able to see anyone trying to approach from any direction, although he noticed the river offered a little more cover and protection. He could follow it in to the camp possibly.

"This is where I'll find Kanu?" Thomas asked.

Musa nodded.

"Thank you, Musa," Thomas nodded. He began to put the map away.

"You go alone?" Musa asked.

"For now, but Jericho and the others hopefully won't be far behind," Thomas replied. "I'm not looking for a confrontation, just hoping to sneak in and get her back."

"That's good. They not see you coming on your own. If you follow..."

"The river," Thomas said, nodding in agreement.

Musa smiled. "The rocks are high, and the marsh grass is too."

"Good to know. Will you be alright with the others away?"

"Yes. I am pleased. Pleased I could help."

"I'm pleased too Musa. Try to get some rest."

Thomas picked up his rifle and bag and headed out of the tent, walking back up the trail towards the kopje. He slipped behind the kitchen tent to a small clearing where the ATVs were parked. He walked past them to the Triumph scrambler, brushing away the layer of red dust that had accumulated on its coffee coloured petrol tank. He made sure the gun was pulled tight across his back before putting on the rucksack, further securing the rifle. He straddled the bike, starting it with a deft kick and a flick of the ignition. With a quick glance upwards, he noticed the darkening sky and switched on the big headlight at the front of the bike. He twisted the throttle and raced through the camp, heading down the track back towards the staff area. He passed Musa's tent with a quick glance, catching the gleeful eyes of the boy as he did. Then he was out into the grassland, cutting a path through the long swathes of greenery towards his destination.

~

Saka raised her head, watching Thomas go and bounding forwards a few steps with her ears pricked up on alert. She babbled her jabber of squeaks and squeals in protest for a few seconds before falling silent. Her head dropped as she swung around, back towards the main road that led into camp. She glanced at the big tan boerboel and then back at the trail into camp. She quickly scampered across the kopje to the big dog, who was tied to a stake outside Jericho's tent. She began to gnaw through the leather leash that kept him there. Rhodes jumped to his feet before she was through. He too could sense what was approaching along the trail. He pulled against the damaged leather, snapping it easily with a powerful and defiant shirk of his shoulders. He growled once in the direction of the camp entrance before turning and following Saka at a fast trot in Thomas's wake.

~

She walked along the centre of the trail, her head rolling from side to side. All caution was gone now, replaced with an unbridled fury. A continuous growl sat in her throat as she passed through the stone pillars at the top of the trail, padding into the camp that she could already sense was empty. She paused, confused by the lingering chemical taint that had changed direction. She was just about to follow it, when she caught the fresh scent of the dogs. Underneath was the sweet, salty musk of a human's sweat. He had walked along the trail in both directions and now the dogs were following. This was a hunt she had made before. She had learnt that dogs and humans were often found together. Her cobalt eyes flashed with deathly intent as they caught the glow of twilight. The tip of her thick tail thrashed the ground purposefully as she crossed the kopje and headed downhill along the path ahead of her. She stopped outside a familiar smelling tent. She knew there was someone inside it. She lifted her nose high, her whiskers reaching forward as she picked up the slight ripple of static charge in the air around the human, only separated from her by a thin layer of material. She licked her muzzle, her nostrils flaring as they caught the waft of ammonia and fresh perspiration coming from the hairless ape. It wasn't the one she sought. She turned back to the trail, dropping her head to again pick up the scent of the dogs. She began to trot as she too headed out into the grassland.

~

Musa stared at the thin gap between the canvas doors with unblinking, bulging eyes. His entire body shook and trembled despite his muscles being taut and rigid. He clutched his knees against his chest even tighter than before, as the small puddle of urine collected beneath the bed. All thoughts of the threat Kanu presented had vanished from his mind.

"The strange one," he whimpered. "The strange one."

CHAPTER TWENTY-FIVE

Jericho patrolled the perimeter of the forest, looking for any sign of the poachers. If they had butchered two elephants on the spot, and had enough men to haul off the take and Catherine at the same time, he knew there would be a trail to follow. Sure enough, on the western edge of the woodland and heading north, he found what he was looking for. The path of a heavy truck snaked into the distance, the deep welts it had left in the soft trail bed obvious and easy to follow. Jericho left the Warthog running as he got out to examine the tracks. A closer inspection revealed the tread patterns of at least two other vehicles following in the wake of the truck, letting it do the hard work of flattening out the route ahead. He looked out in the direction the tracks led, as he crouched down and took a handful of dry dirt from the ground. He rubbed it over his hands. The action steadied his nerves and helped him think. Resolute, he stood up and dusted off his palms, heading back to the Warthog.

At first his progress was slow. He wanted to be sure that he didn't lose the trail of the truck. But as the light began to fade, he put his foot down. As he crested a slight ridge, he saw the trail joined a curved, mud road that led into a thick patch of woodland. He put the Warthog in neutral and coasted down the slope onto the trail. His caution was rewarded when he picked up the sound of men shouting up ahead. He rolled the Warthog off the road and a little way into the trees, turning off the ignition completely. Interested to know what he was up against, Jericho took off at an angle into the dense forest on the right-hand side of the road. He moved quickly but still cautiously, stooping to hide his silhouette and outline as much as he could.

About 500 yards in, his clothing quickly becoming dampened by the humidity, he stopped to get his bearings. The sounds of a busy camp were much closer now, but the vegetation was still too thick to make anything out. He decided to risk climbing a nearby neem tree with a conveniently angled trunk. He was only a few feet up, his feet scrabbling for purchase, when a low and threatening growl from nearby made him freeze. It was immediately answered by a flurry of squawks, screams and further growls from multiple animals. He drew himself a little higher and froze again as he found himself looking into a pair of deep-set brown eyes, about thirty feet away. He had been seen. As his urge to duck and run was about to kick in, his senses caught up with his instincts and he made himself look again. He let out a deep sigh of relief to steady himself. The morose dark face staring back at him belonged to a chimpanzee, sat in a dirty and cramped wire cage. As Jericho's gaze shifted, he saw the cheetah, caracal and other cats. His eyes came to rest on the crude and large padlocks that kept the otherwise flimsy cages secure. A grin crept across his face as an idea formed.

After climbing a little higher into the tree and watching and listening for some time, he was fairly sure of the layout. He guessed there were no more than about fifteen men in the camp, based on the two large green barracks tents on the far side of the compound. There was a guard at the partially covered entrance from the road, and Jericho could hear his snores from the tree. Over-confidence and laziness was a typical militia trait, and all the men in the compound had the swagger of former militia men. Two more patrolled the back of the open part of the compound. Their minds and hands were more interested in the self-rolled cigarettes they were both smoking. Weapons seemed scarce. He had seen one of the guards carrying what had looked like a World War II M1 carbine, but a few others had the ubiquitous AK47s. The men seemed scattered through the camp, something he could use to his advantage if he remained undetected.

He carefully made his way down the tree and threaded his way back through the forest to the car. He slipped around to the open back, and dragged a heavy tool box out from underneath the raised spotlight rig. He rummaged through it until he found what he was looking for, a pair of compact bolt cutters. He slipped them into his back pocket. At the same time, he retrieved the Rhino revolver and placed it in its holster, and slung the DP-12 shotgun over his shoulder. He paused at the side of the road, making sure he was still alone before ducking across and back into the trees. The shroud of darkness that was beginning to descend helped cover him further. He decided to wait it out again at the tree, for his eyes to adjust to the fading light. After several minutes, the newly risen moon broke from a low cloud bank and he made his move.

The wall of cages made it easy to approach the compound from that side. He made careful movements and stayed low, knowing that if he disturbed the animals too much, they might also draw attention to him. He wanted to remain in the background as far as they were concerned. Their attention was best served centred on the handful of guards he had seen. He crept into a small corridor formed by two rows of cages and made his way as close to the ones nearest the compound as he dared. The bolt cutters made quick work of the padlocks on the bottom row of enclosures. The first released was a crested porcupine that blinked at him with sleepy eyes before beginning to snuffle at the now open door to its former prison. Next along was a pair of common jackals. A honey badger snarled at his sudden appearance, attacking the door with its formidable teeth. He decided to let the intelligent mustelid figure out how to open its now unlocked cage by itself. A rare striped hyena was next, then the cheetah and caracals. A savage growl drew his attention to a large cage underneath that of the cheetah. A handsome male leopard glowered at him.

Hell, better out than in Jericho thought, clipping through the padlock. He didn't open the door, hoping to retreat before the leopard figured out that freedom beckoned. A pair of servals were liberated before he came to the chimpanzee. It watched him with curiosity as he cut away the padlock. It sat bobbing its head as he threw the padlock onto the floor, then looked up at him with its lower jaw dropped. Although it looked as if it were surprised, Jericho knew the expression signalled one of happiness or acceptance. But suddenly the chimp's demeanour completely changed. The pupils of its eyes became pinpricks and it flipped its lips to expose the upper and lower canines. Jericho knew that many people mistook this for a smile, but it was a formidable posture of threat. The chimp was showing the weaponry it had available and was willing to use. Without warning, the chimp flew at the door, bursting through it with such force that it swung into Jericho's crouched form and sent him spinning backwards into the dirt. That's when he saw the silhouette of the guard that had turned into the corridor of cages. The chimp was on the guard before he realised something was amiss, the primate's heavy fists bludgeoning him to the ground before he could even cry out. The chimp hammered a series of blows to the guard's head and chest, before stopping and looking at Jericho with wide eyes of elation, its lips forming a cone shape as it issued soft whoops.

"Good for you, big fella," Jericho whispered with a smile.

The chimp swung into action, opening the doors to all the cages that Jericho had visited. The animals needed little persuasion after the tottering chimpanzee had encouraged them out of the cages, with bangs to the mesh with its powerful hands and the same soft whoops. Jericho took out the revolver and stepped forward, his presence as well as that of the chimp further encouraging the other animals to follow their instincts out into the open compound.

A second guard, the one carrying the old-fashioned carbine, walked back along the compound and paused as he passed the dark corridor of cages. He squinted into the shadows. The animals seemed unusually restless and he thought he had seen something. Two green glowing spots of light stared back at him. He stepped closer, only to recoil in horror as a rippling, roaring mass of teeth and claws clothed in amber and swirls of black spots launched out of the darkness towards him.

Jericho began to edge backwards as the leopard went to work, dragging the squirming guard back into the secluded cover of the now empty cages, jaws clamped over the man's throat. The big cat's hind claws had already gutted the guard. One front paw was wrapped around the militia man's head, its claws embedded in his scalp to prevent movement and struggling. The other paw sat hooked into the chest, where its pressure kept the prey still, and monitored its shortening, failing gasps for oxygen as it died. Leopards really were natural born primate killers. Jericho decided to backtrack, and to try edging along the close-knit group of tents beyond the cages. As a shout went out and a spray of gunfire followed it, he knew his planned distraction was doing its job.

~

Catherine kept looking down at her tummy, confused and questioningly. Somehow, she knew the old woman had been right. She had suspected for a few days now. Her stomach had never seemed to settle since she'd arrived in Africa. Her favourite foods and even drink tasted strange and overpowering. Her hormones had been off the chart too. It all made sense. Kruger had left her alone in the tent, called away for something. The big guard, Hondo, stood at the entrance watching her. A few moments later, Kruger returned, carrying a curved, single ivory tusk.

"This Ms. Tyler, and the small menagerie you passed on your way in, is the cause for all your discomfort, both present and that to come," Kruger stated, putting the tusk down on a wooden cabinet to the side of the tent. "The men and the trucks cost me say, $30 a day. This though, to the right buyer will bring me $300,000. The matching pair perhaps as much as three quarters of a million. We also grind the root and a few feet of each tusk into powder worth $1,500 a lb. Not bad for a day's work eh? Tomorrow, we do it all again. I'm sure you know the black market in animals and their parts is the third biggest illegal trade after drugs and weapons? And we just happen to do a little work for a gun runner too," Kruger said, grinning. "Makes getting ammo convenient."

"Makes you sound like somebody's errand boy," Catherine replied.

"Seeing as I'm adding slave trader to the résumé, you may want to watch your temper," Kruger jeered.

"Not likely," Catherine scowled.

Kruger looked towards the door as the sound of gunfire caught their attention. Shouts, and a flurry of barks, roars and animal chatter followed. Hondo took a step forward then paused, looking at Kruger for permission.

"Go check it out," he nodded.

Catherine's gaze had settled on the tusk, its tip lying away from her and towards the man who had killed its barer. It gleamed, and now as she looked at it just an arm's length away, she saw why Sefu had been given his name. Kruger was still distracted by whatever was going on in the main camp, and didn't notice as she slowly rose from her chair.

"Sword," she murmured out loud.

"What?" Kruger snapped, turning back. "Hey, put that down."

Even shortened and cleaned of some of its bulk, the tusk was still unbelievably heavy. Catherine didn't have time to hesitate. She charged forward, plunging the tip into Kruger's belly, hurtling at him with all the might she could muster and pushing him backwards towards the ornate gold bed. As she rammed him against the corner post, there was a moment of resistance before she felt something give, followed by a shudder and a cry from Kruger that made her spring back in surprise.

Kruger was already slipping to the ground, his hands clutching at the tusk that had torn its way through his abdomen with the brute force of Catherine's charge, helped by the sudden stop brought by the collision with the bedpost.

"Sword," Catherine repeated slowly, her eyes meeting

Kruger's wild stare rather than watching the pool of blood that was beginning to collect at his side. "The elephant you killed was named Sefu. It means sword in Swahili."

Kruger was pale and sucked down deep, raspy breaths. His eyes bulged as he looked at her and then down at the tusk. Catherine followed his gaze. She could see the natural curve of the ivory had followed the path of least resistance upwards, perhaps slicing through the gut. Guessing by the dark colour of the blood, it had ruptured something, most likely the liver. He was bleeding out fast. Kruger stuffed his hand inside his vest, pulling out the revolver he had taken from her things earlier. His strength was leaving him now though, and he dragged the barrel over the floor towards Catherine, unable to lift it. She reached out casually and took it from him. She checked it was loaded and stood up, tucking it into her trousers. She made her way to the door of the tent and looked out, but not back.

~

Jericho slipped between the canvas walls of two supply tents, only to freeze as he saw a blur of movement coming towards him. He let out a sigh of relief as a bat eared fox dashed past without even a glance. As he heard another short burst of gunfire followed by a scream, he brought up the revolver and edged a little further along the narrow corridor between the tents.

He stole a glance back towards the compound and saw it was in turmoil. A tent on the far side was partly collapsed. Another was on fire. The smashed gas lamp that had ignited it lay in pieces on the ground not too far away. Jericho watched as a man stumbled into the open, kicking at something clinging to his ankle. As the panicked soldier angled the barrel of his AK47 wildly towards the offending blur, he pulled the trigger, killing the honey badger that was clamped to his flesh but also riddling his own leg with bullets. He collapsed onto the floor and was immediately swarmed by the two jackals, their snapping jaws ripping into his clothing and body with a panic fuelled clamour.

Just as Jericho turned back towards the tents, a heavy fist smashed into his jaw and sent him spinning into the dirt. A little dazed, he tried to flip onto his back, only to find himself pinned by a boot that came down onto the base of his spine. He craned his neck upwards and froze as he saw the cheetah a matter of yards away, its body taut and poised for the spring. It had possibly been stalking him all along. As he heard the bolt of a gun being pulled back, he threw his hands over his head to protect the neck and buried his face into the dirt, the rim of his hat cutting off his view of the cheetah as he did so. He knew what was about to happen, the cat already half launched into its attack. He just had to hope it happened before whoever had the gun on him could pull the trigger.

There was a muffled cry, then the sudden lifting of the pressure on his back. Without hesitating, he jumped to his feet and spun to face the potentially combined threat of his attacker and the cheetah. He realised that as he had been thrown to the ground he had dropped the revolver, but that wasn't what drew his attention. It was the gnarled growl of the cheetah. The man that had attacked him was laid out on the ground, the cheetah straddling him lengthways. Jericho felt a slight pang of pity as he saw the big man's foot twitch. The lithe cats did not boast the strong, sharp teeth of their larger cousins. Their fangs were relatively compact and unable to penetrate tough hide, but were perfectly adapted for clamping around the smaller throats of the Thompson's gazelles and springboks they favoured as prey. To be killed by a cheetah meant a slow, fear filled death via asphyxiation. The burly soldier was being suffocated by the patient cat. It occasionally shifted its weight or position to avoid his flailing limbs, but the fight was over. It had won. Jericho retrieved his gun and slipped past the cat, which lifted its hind quarters, following his movements as he went. Once the threat was gone, the cat settled down again, as the man whose throat it held in its jaws finally stopped moving.

Jericho almost chuckled when he saw Catherine burst from a large white tent ahead of him. She staggered towards him and flung her arms around his neck. He didn't mind she struck the back of his head with the butt of the revolver she carried as she did so. He could feel her chest heaving, and her body trembled against his for a moment.

"Fancy seeing your good self here," Jericho laughed, returning the hug.

"You really are a sight for sore eyes," Catherine said, wiping away the tears that threatened to stream down her cheeks.

"Not that it isn't nice to see you, but I think we'd best be off," Jericho suggested, looking around.

Jericho grabbed Catherine's hand and led her straight into the trees, not looking back at the shouts and screams that still came from the camp. Catherine did though. She saw the old woman who had examined her emerge from a tent, a look of wild panic on her face. She also saw the crouched form in front of the woman, its tail thrashing the ground either side of its coiled hind legs. For a brief moment, Catherine's gaze met the frantic searching eyes of the woman. Then she was gone, engulfed by the dark, shadowy silhouette of the leopard. Catherine turned away in silence, her eyes fixed to the ground as Jericho led her back to the car.

Jericho threw the guns and his pack into the back of the truck before checking on Catherine. She was shivering from the cold, still only dressed in the shirt and trousers she had put on that morning. Jericho pulled his jacket from behind the seats and placed it over her shoulders.

"I'd normally get you back to camp and safety as soon as possible," Jericho sighed. "But I think your man might be in a spot of bother. Truth is, I wasn't expecting to find you here. We thought Sultan had taken you. We had to split up, and Thomas is heading for his camp. I think he might need a bit of backup, what d'ya say?"

"Sultan means to kill us, or at least disappear us, that much I know," Catherine nodded.

"Thought as much. Are you okay?"

Catherine's face suddenly hardened. Jericho thought he saw a flash of anger, or maybe it was resolve, ignite in her eyes for a moment. It was replaced almost instantly by a steely coldness that took him a little aback.

"Let's finish these bastards," Catherine stated.

"Catherine," Jericho said with a smile, "Thomas is my greatest friend, but I think I'm beginning to downright adore you."

As Jericho started the engine, he heard a crackle from the radio that was mounted to the dashboard. He grabbed the receiver.

"This is Anga ya Amani calling Warthog, come in, over," came Kelly's hurried voice.

"Warthog receiving, was just about to give you folks a

call," Jericho replied, "I've found Catherine. Is Thomas there?"

"No, he left. Only I and a few others have just made it back to camp. Musa is in hysterics though. He's been screaming about some monster in camp. There are big lion tracks leading straight through and I can't find the dogs."

"See, I go away for one afternoon and the whole place goes to hell," Jericho said with a feigned sigh. "Don't worry about the dogs, they can look after themselves. Do you know where Thomas was headed?"

"Musa told us Kanu's camp is somewhere in the Galana marshlands, possibly an abandoned wildlife conservancy near Kilalinda."

"I know it," Jericho replied. "Any word on Mason?"

"No, again we only just heard. We're trying to assemble some help, then we're going after Thomas," Kelly told them.

"We are too. I can cut across country from here. We'll probably get there before you do, so just make sure you bring the cavalry."

"Will do my best. Out."

Catherine looked at Jericho questioningly.

"A monster? And what happened to Mason?" Catherine asked.

"Probably just that big female Thomas was talking about," Jericho replied as he reversed the truck back out onto the road. "You know all this voodoo crap they've been throwing around, it's all buffalo shit. Pay it no attention, although it does probably mean the lions are on Thomas's trail too," Jericho sighed. "Mason was mauled quite badly by a lioness back at the crater, but I'm sure Jelani already has him at a hospital."

Jericho stamped on the accelerator and tore off down the

road, passing the now quiet and deserted poachers camp at speed.

"Do you think it will be the lions or Kanu Sultan that will get to Thomas first?" Catherine asked.

"Knowing his luck, it'll probably be a photo finish," Jericho sighed, changing down gear and straining the engine as much as he dared as they left the cover of the trees altogether, and made it back out onto the savannah.

He saw something up ahead and hit the brakes, careering to a violent stop in a cloud of red dust. He reached for the glove box, opening it and pulling out a pair of binoculars. As he brought them up to his eyes, he quickly spun the focus ring, bringing the large moving objects into sudden clarity. The remnants of the elephant herd shifted to and fro nervously having already heard the car's engine, and no doubt spotting the bright headlights that shone in their direction.

He panned to the left, spotting a small group of lights in the far distance, which he knew to be the reportedly abandoned wildlife conservancy on the Galana River. He rested the binoculars in his lap, smiling at Catherine.

"You know, some ideas are so good you can have them twice in the same day. You've heard of the charge of the light brigade? Now it's the heavies turn," Jericho grinned.

CHAPTER TWENTY-SIX

Thomas twisted the throttle as he cut through the swathes of scrub. As he neared the river, the vegetation began to thicken. Acacia bushes and fever trees became more frequent, slowing him down and tearing at his clothing as he passed. He brought the bike to a stop as he surveyed the way ahead. The last rays of tangerine sunlight touched the sharp volcanic pillars on either side of him. As the sun disappeared, the terracotta landscape changed to one seemingly bathed in ultraviolet light, with deep blues and mauves now replacing the vibrant reds, pinks and orange. The moon was still finding its place in the sky as the stars began to appear.

That wasn't the only change he felt. With the light went the warmth. A cold breeze touched his cheek and the back of his neck, sending an involuntary shiver down his spine. He narrowed his eyes as he looked for a clearer path. Straight ahead seemed to only promise more of the same rocky outcrops and unwelcoming thorns. His gaze shifted to the right. As his eyes grew accustomed to the growing darkness, he spotted a narrow gully that led into a sharp descent. He blipped the throttle again and rolled the bike into it, following the path over precarious rocks and small drops. The scrambler coped with the punishment, and as he turned a sharp bend, he realised he had chosen well. The trail descended into the wide, flowing Kilalinda marshlands. He could see the reed grass swaying in the gentle caress of the wind like waves on an ocean.

Beyond to the north and east, he could pick out the

pinprick glow of lights in the centre of the adjoining Galana marshes. It could only be Kanu's camp. He turned off the scrambler's headlamp and descended into the long grass.

~

The distance she had travelled was beginning to wear her down. She loped along, her breath releasing in grunting gasps with each heavy impact of her paws. The big dog was easy to follow and wasn't far ahead now. It left a visible trail where its cumbersome girth ploughed through the brush, and its stink and slobber tainted the air. She could afford to rest for a moment. She stopped, padding into the long grass and lying down. She lifted her nose high into the air, comforted by the familiar smells of the marshland that came to her on the breeze. She filled her lungs with deep draws of air through her nostrils, closing her eyes as she allowed her taut muscles to relax and refuel. She lay there in the gathering darkness still and alert, aware of her surroundings but confident in them too. As a hyena greeted the fall of night with a ripple of laughter, she stood and made her way further into the marsh. She slipped down a bank to a stream that was lined with tall reeds, offering her seclusion as she drank. Satiated, she crossed the water with an effortless bound, and headed for a tower of rock, in the centre of the meadow on the other side of the stream. She rippled over the crumbling sandstone slabs, the cracks and crevices of which housed the searching roots of acacia bushes clinging to the outcrop. They offered her cover until she edged out onto the ledge, which allowed her to overlook the marsh more fully. She stood tall, carefully changing her footing until the wind was behind her. She allowed her lungs to fill again and then lifted her head, roaring with a savagery that punctured the night. Deep within the kopje, amongst dry and dusty root systems and the dark walls of rock, a hyrax family trembled in the echo. Out on the marsh, a group of whistling ducks took to panicked flight and a pair of waterbuck raced and jumped for the darkness of the trees. The roar carried far, igniting a primal fear in every animal that heard it. It told them to run and hide. Death was afoot.

~

Nearly two miles to the east, Thomas heard the roar and stopped the bike. He turned his head, quickly gauging the direction and distance. It was undoubtedly the queen of the pride. She was behind him and closing. He knew that the marshland was at the centre of the pride's territory. Perhaps that was why Kanu had chosen it as a base, as well as its logistical and tactical advantages. He guided the scrambler into a narrow ditch, and kept the revs low as he splashed his way upstream. He banked left when the ditch widened and he started to catch glimpses of the Galana River through the reeds to his right.

The abandoned wildlife conservancy was directly ahead now and he decided he couldn't risk going further on the bike without giving away his approach. He still didn't know what he was letting himself in for, or what to expect other than a bristling camp of armed mercenaries. Stealth and surprise were the only allies he had for the moment. As he turned off the bike's engine, he froze as he caught the unmistakable sound of the brush parting behind him. Still straddling the bike, he was completely vulnerable. He carefully and slowly reached inside his shooting vest for the Anaconda revolver, hesitating for a split second before snapping around and shoving the gun underneath his left arm to bear down on his would-be attacker.

Rhodes met his gaze with the forlorn and disapproving look of a true mastiff. The big dog lowered his head and trotted past Thomas, whose heart was still racing as Saka too slipped from the shadows and joined the fawn coloured boerboel.

"You two nearly gave me a heart attack," Thomas whispered, holstering the gun, and panting for breath as he recovered from the fright.

He got off the bike and crouched beside the dogs. Rhodes let out a soft growl of contentment as Thomas rubbed his back comfortingly. He was glad to have their company and knew he could rely on their training to keep quiet. He could see by their alertness, and the way they observed the lights of the camp up ahead, that they already saw this as a hunt. He began to creep forward, staying low and keeping the dogs behind him.

~

The others began to converge on her immediately. They had been made skittish by her absence during the day, but her roar had signified her return to the territory and the start of a hunt. Now fewer in number, they were more cautious as a collective and less inclined to separate. But she gave them confidence, and they came to her willingly. They stuck to tunnels, long forged through the reeds, that hid their approach. Occasionally, a pale flash of fur or a careless brush of the foliage in passing would hint at their passage, but otherwise they paced their yet unseen quarry from the refuge of the reed bed.

~

Thomas viewed the buildings that made up what had been the Kilalinda Wildlife Conservancy and now served as Kanu

Sultan's base. It reminded him a little of how Wild West forts were depicted in movies. A large courtyard was surrounded on all four sides by high stone walls with towers at each corner. They had probably originally been intended to allow guests to view the wildlife of the surrounding marshlands. The network of wetlands and savannah would have attracted many animals from miles around. Now they afforded Kanu Sultan a prime view of the surrounding territory. Thomas hoped the wildlife had learnt quickly that their new neighbour had less than friendly intentions towards them. He knew a remote outpost like this would have to be as self-sufficient as possible, and that meant a reliance on bush meat. The eerie quiet and absence of life made him feel on edge and confirmed his fears.

As they had told Thomas themselves, the government's limited resources couldn't deal with more than one threat at a time as it was, and the terrorists in the North were a much higher priority than a pillaged ecosystem. But just like the ecosystem, the terrorists and Kanu Sultan were all linked and reliant on the status-quo. If you removed a keystone predator from a thriving system, it would soon crumble and fail. Thomas could only hope it would be the same with Kanu.

From what he knew of the wildlife conservancy, a large headquarters building, an open garage and a game lodge were all housed inside the courtyard. He was approaching the back wall of the camp, still hidden by the high reeds and sloping banks of the waterway. Ahead of him, he could see a jetty roughly hacked out of the river clay and reinforced with rock-lined sloping walls. It extended out to a quiet stretch of water, fed by the river itself and lined with the same tall reeds that were helping him stay hidden. They served the same purpose here. Although he couldn't see it, he guessed there would be a boat, or even a few, moored on the other side. They, and even possibly the camp itself, would be well hidden from the main waterway.

Both the jetty and rear of the camp seemed quiet. He had remained motionless for some time, waiting for a movement or sound to give away the presence of any unseen patrol, but none came. He decided there was nothing for it but to move out of the reeds and take a closer look at the camp. He moved quickly, darting from the bank of reeds and into the shadow of the nearby boundary wall that loomed above him. As he did so, he came face to face with a thin young guard as he turned the corner. Both were startled, but it was Thomas who acted first, swinging his rifle from his shoulder and up in a fast sweeping movement. The heavy wooden stock connected powerfully with the young patrol man's chin, and Thomas followed up with another blow to the side of the dazed guard's head, knocking him to the ground unconscious. Thomas glanced around him before rolling the guard down the bank and into the cover of the reeds. He then peered around the corner the young man had come from.

There was a large arched entrance into the courtyard about twenty yards away. It looked like it had possibly once contained a set of gates, but now it was empty and opened out onto a low walkway that led to the jetty. Thomas edged towards it, his back against the wall. His mouth was dry, and his heart was still pounding in his chest as he checked the handle of the Anaconda with his fingertips. He steadied himself before risking a peek through the archway.

The first thing he noticed were the two huge spotted hyenas that lay in the centre of the courtyard, both secured by steel chains attached to spiked collars. They snarled with lazy malcontent at the men wearing tan coloured military fatigues who passed them by. Thomas was surprised by the seemingly small number. There were about six altogether in the courtyard itself, standing in pairs as they talked and smoked together. They appeared relaxed. His gaze wandered to the wooden staircase in the far corner, that led to a walkway around the perimeter wall, and linked the towers at each corner. He scanned them, only finding one occupied; the tower to the north that looked in the direction of the savannah, the nearest roads, and civilisation.

Two of the guards stood either side of the mahogany double doors that marked the main entrance to what had been the game lodge. Their AK47s rested against the wooden slats of the building. Thomas wondered if Kanu was perhaps using it as his personal quarters. His eyes shifted to a stairway to his left that led down, perhaps to cellars or a storage area. His gaze then flitted to the barn like structure that served as a garage. He could see the same Range Rovers that had formed Kanu's convoy on the day he had laced Anga ya Amani with lion pheromones, and a few battered Toyota trucks. A simple plan formed in his head. He realised that the most likely places to find Catherine, if she was here at all, was either down the stairs or in Kanu's adopted residence. He'd find her, make for the vehicles, and get out of there as quickly as possible. If she wasn't there, he'd slip back out and escape on the bike.

The stairs were nearest. He watched the patrols as they crossed back and forth over the courtyard, waiting for an opportunity to slip past unnoticed. He nearly yelled in fright when something wet and soft touched his elbow, but he spun quickly on his heels to find an inquisitive Saka at his side. He held up the flat palm of his hand to indicate she needed to stop. She turned and trotted back to where Rhodes stood. The mastiff glanced out over the reeds then back to Thomas. The dogs were uneasy about something.

As he turned back to the courtyard, he noticed the two hyenas were lying with their backs to each other. He didn't see any food or water bowls nearby, and their position meant they had probably been in the sun for the best part of the day. It was perhaps one of the ways Kanu kept them irritable and bad tempered, but he hoped he might be able to use it to his advantage. He looked to the ground and soon found what he was looking for; a smooth flat stone. He waited until he was sure the backs of the guards were turned and then threw the stone in a wide looping arc. His aim was good and it hit the nearest hyena in the ribs, making an audible impact as it did so. Just as he'd hoped, the hyena immediately jumped up and turned on its unsuspecting partner.

The hyenas tumbled back and forth, snarling and yikkering as they scrabbled for purchase. The one Thomas had hit with the stone managed to clamp its jaws onto the ruff of raised fur along the other's neck, forcing it to the ground. Already the guards in the courtyard were all running towards the squabbling animals, just as he'd hoped. As the men formed two gangs of three and picked up the chains to pull the hyenas apart, Thomas dashed through the open archway and made it to the stairs, hurrying down the steps quickly. They turned to the right at the bottom.

He found himself in a long narrow corridor. There was a light switch on the wall to his left and he flicked it on. An old yellowed lantern spluttered into life at the end of the passageway, producing just enough light to illuminate the three cells along the right-hand side. As Thomas took a step forward he was immediately hit by the stink that came from their interiors. He peered in through the rust spotted grills that covered the entrance to each one, noticing the dark stains on the straw-coloured floor. Blood and excrement in the most part he guessed. He was at once relieved and frightened to find all the cells empty. Catherine wasn't there. He presumed a prison block was something Kanu had installed on moving in. It was hard to imagine a wildlife conservancy had need of them.

He made his way back up the stairs and peered out across the courtyard. His view was blocked by a pair of shiny black military boots that faced him. He slowly lifted his head.

"Kind of you to join us Mr. Walker," Kanu Sultan said, smiling down at him.

~

She froze, half emerged from the reeds, a paw extended and reaching for the ground. The others behind her came to a halt too, their senses on edge as they crouched in the cover. A soft murmur came from a patch of scrubby reeds and buffelgrass nearby. She pushed her nose through the soft stalks and blades. They parted at her touch. There she found the man, prostrate and still. She paused as she caught the slight movement of his arm. The sounds he made were strained. He was in pain, possibly injured. She took another silent step closer. And then she sensed it. The lingering taint of her prey. She surged forwards without hesitating, opening her jaws and sinking her fangs into the man's temples. Disorientated and only just coming around, his world went black again, permanently and painlessly. She squatted over the body, urinating onto the man's chest and heaping dirt over the corpse with scrapes of her hind feet.

The pride moved off. When a few of the others paused at the man's body and sniffed at the fresh scent of blood, she growled a low and menacing warning. They instantly turned away and followed her out of the grass and reeds.

~

Thomas was led into the game lodge. As he had suspected, Kanu had made himself at home there. The towering pot plants, palms of some kind, appeared to have gone uncared for during his occupancy, but the rest of the decor was clearly to his liking. They stopped in the lobby as a guard stripped him of his weapons and threw them onto one of the chairs.

"I see you treat yourself well," Thomas said quietly, eyeing Kanu with disdain.

"What can I say Mr. Walker. My customers have deep pockets and bad intentions. In Africa that is what we call a business opportunity."

Kanu smiled. He crossed the lobby towards an open room to the left.

"Perhaps you would be interested in some of my pets Mr. Walker," he suggested, as a guard pushed Thomas forward with the butt of a rifle.

As Thomas entered the room he noticed it was lined almost wall to wall with glass tanks of multiple shapes and sizes. Inside each were long serpentine forms that slithered to and fro, searching the perimeters and tasting the air with their forked tongues. Even inside, the snakes could sense the coming of night and were becoming more active. Thomas remembered the puff adder that Musa had brought to the camp. Now he realised it had been given to him, not just caught. Kanu clearly revelled in perpetrating the myth as a shaman who controlled his 'critters of the bush'. Having them handily caged and captive was no doubt useful.

The glass tanks housed several venomous species that he recognised. Green and black mambas, gaboon vipers, puff adders and several species of cobra called the room home. In the largest tank, positioned at the bottom and closest to the floor, was an enormous, coiled rock python. Thomas peered through the glass at the reptiles. He noticed they all seemed in excellent condition and were well fed. Each of the enclosures were fitted with arrays of sun lamps and moisture pads, and provided plenty of space for the animals.

"You take very good care of them," Thomas acknowledged.

"They demand a higher level of attention than some of my other charges," Kanu replied, smiling.

"Like those hyenas out there, left without food or water?"

"Oh, they'll be fed soon enough Mr. Walker. A concerned conservationist like yourself is the perfect man to see to that I'd say," Kanu replied, laughing.

Thomas didn't need to ponder too long on his meaning. He ignored the threat.

"Or a pride of lions that have found their territory stripped of natural prey?" Thomas probed further.

"One of the reasons I've brought the hyenas inside the walls of the compound Mr. Walker," Kanu exclaimed. "But on the contrary, human beings are perfectly natural prey. We have simply forgotten," Kanu explained. "The oldest caves of this continent are testament to that. The bones of man and beast locked in eternal conflict. Whilst the wolf lay down beside us around ancient fires, something unable to shirk its primal intentions stayed in the darkness. And there they have remained."

Thomas didn't answer. He knew Kanu was right. A six-million-year-old Kenyan fossil skull from a human ancestor had been found heavily damaged, not by erosion or disturbance, but from blunt force trauma. Something had pierced the bone several times. It was only when an inquisitive geologist happened to match the wounds to another fossil, the teeth of a leopard discovered in the same cave, that the identity of the killer was revealed. Other fossils in Tanzania, a mere 1.8 million years old, depicted a similar tale of human predation. In Uganda, it was estimated from leopard faeces that up to five percent of the chimp and gorilla population were taken by leopards. Cats and primates had been a part of natural predator and prey relationships for millions of years. It was they more than anything else that humans feared were creeping silently towards them in the darkness.

It made him think of the Zhoukoudian cave in China. A macabre collection of skulls nearly two million years old had been discovered there, and at first had been thought to be evidence of early humans practicing cannibalism. Further scrutiny suggested a predator such as a leopard was in fact the culprit. In the end, however, it was discovered that death had come in the form of the giant hyena, Pachycrocuta brevirostris. It was then he had something of an epiphany. Although they resembled dogs, hyenas were feliforms. They were in the same family as mongooses, civets, and most importantly, cats. Some twenty million years ago, hyenas and cats had separated on the evolutionary tree. Both had appeared in eastern Asia, but it was hyenas that had reached Africa first. Most species of hyena, just like cats, were solitary. Only the spotted hyena exhibited complex social behaviour. They hunted in groups and the females were in charge. What if lions were following the same evolutionary path as their distant cousins, but were just a million years or so behind? It might explain abnormalities like the lionesses of the Okavango exhibiting manes, or the matriarchal led pride they were dealing with here in Tsavo.

"I can see I am no longer amusing you Mr. Walker," Kanu stated dryly. "I can assure you the feeling is mutual. I hear you have killed eight of my pets..."

"Sixteen actually," Thomas stated.

Kanu seemed taken back for a moment.

"That's over two thirds of the pride," one of the guards behind Kanu said, seemingly to himself.

Kanu whipped around instantly, drawing a large, gold coloured pistol from his belt. It sported garish tiger stripes over the metalwork and Thomas recognised it as a Desert Eagle. Kanu seemed to shrug apologetically at Thomas as he pointed it behind him without looking and pulled the trigger. The resulting boom sounded like the blast of a canon and the guard was thrown backwards against the wall. The hole in his chest, the size of a dinner plate, showed the blast had hit him square on.

"I can't abide interruption Mr. Walker," Kanu said.

"Is it only your conversation you're concerned about, or have I cut in on your plans too?" Thomas challenged.

"They're intact enough to still be of major concern to you Mr. Walker, I can assure you," Kanu replied with a sneer.

He nodded at the guard behind Thomas, who prodded Thomas in the back with his rifle and began to usher him back outside. Thomas reluctantly followed Kanu and his entourage, left to his thoughts again. It was just a shame he had nobody to share them with in what might be his last few moments.

~

She lay crouched, coiled tight against the ground. The earthen bank hid her well enough as she viewed the wooden and stone structure. Her tail lashed the ground with pent frustration. The others were spread behind her in a narrow fan, all focused on an opening ahead of them. She raised her head slightly as she sensed movement. The two dogs had slipped through. The breeze came from behind and had taken the pride's scent to them. With a singular guttural grunt, she rose to her feet and padded past the opening, heading to the other side of the structure and downwind.

~

Thomas couldn't help feeling nauseous as he was led across the courtyard towards the hyenas. After hearing the accounts from Musa and others, he had a good idea of what was about to happen. Although related to cats, hyenas didn't share their table manners. A cat would kill you swiftly and efficiently, but not a hyena. Just like a bear, they were happy to consume you whilst you were still warm and alive. They stopped a few yards from the nearest of the two spotted fleabags. It inquisitively got up and approached, straining at the taut end of its chain, head slightly cocked as it surveyed them with hungry interest. It was not the way he would choose to go. He reacted instinctively as he caught a movement out of the corner of his eye.

He moved like lightning and slammed his elbow into the nose of the guard behind him on his left, sending the man wheeling backwards, a heavy stream of blood gushing from his burst nose. Before the guard toppled over completely, Thomas grabbed him by the lapels on his fatigues, wheeling round in a move that saved him from a spray of bullets from the other guard's AK47. Thomas let go of his human shield, depositing the body within reach of the salivating hyena. He braced himself for the impact that would follow the next squeeze of the trigger, almost thankful for the comparatively painless alternative it offered him to the bone crushing jaws, but it never came.

Rhodes moved with a speed and agility that seemed unfitting for his size and bulk. He let out a deep and booming howl that bounced off the stone walls. As the big tan boerboel leapt at the second guard with more of a roar than a bark, Saka dashed in to torment and distract the other hyena. Rhodes floored the guard, grabbing him by the throat and dragging his squirming body through the dust. Thomas leapt forward and grabbed the AK47. He dropped to one knee and looked around. Saka was doing a good job, keeping the hyena at the end of its chain but staying safely out of reach of its jaws. He spotted the guard in the north tower taking aim in their general direction and sent a volley of bullets in his direction. He saw the guard spin backwards, clutching at his shoulder and tumbling out of sight.

Kanu seemed to have disappeared, but just as Thomas stood, he sensed the sudden presence of someone behind him. Something broad and heavy hit him in the back of the neck and he slumped to his knees again, dazed and only just on the brink of consciousness. Kanu slipped back into his field of vision. Thomas's head was spinning, but he saw Saka sprinting back towards the archway through which they had entered the camp. Thomas winced as a deep bark from Rhodes was met with a casual blast from Kanu's pistol. He heard what sounded like a heavy wet sack hit the ground behind him, and knew the big dog was down.

"You have quite the knack for causing me trouble Mr. Walker," Kanu grumbled, his charm and humour now gone.

"You think I'm bad, wait till the guy whose dog you just shot catches up with you," Thomas replied, still a little dazed.

"I have friends in low places too Mr Walker," Kanu replied, grinning. "At the moment, they are entertaining your fiancée, but I'm sure the Irishman can be added to their to-do list."

Thomas didn't reply. He wondered if Jericho had found Kruger. If so, had he found Catherine? He knew Jericho would have raised hell if so, of that he was certain. Everything else less so, including their fate and his.

"It's a pity I can't extend your visit any longer, it's been quite entertaining," Kanu said with a sigh.

"I've been bored half way to hell myself," Thomas jibed, not even looking at Kanu.

"Then allow me to speed you on the rest of the way," Kanu quipped, raising the big pistol and aiming it at Thomas's head.

Kanu paused, distracted by something. Thomas heard it too, a deep and heavy rumble like the approach of thunder. He didn't know what it was, but it brought him back to his senses. He sprang forward from the ground. His days of playing rugby and Australian football were long over, but he could still put some heft into a tackle. He shoulder-barged Kanu in the chest, sending the African flying backwards. The pistol flew out of Kanu's hand, landing in the dust beside the nearest hyena. It eagerly took it within its jaws and began to gnaw on the barrel. It held the gun between its paws, enjoying its new toy.

Kanu pushed Thomas off with a powerful shove. Thomas rolled, quickly jumping to his feet. Kanu did the same, reaching behind his head. A hint of blood coated his fingertips from where his skull had met the ground. He stared menacingly at Thomas as they began to circle each other. Thomas could see from his stare that the games were over. The African spun on a heel, delivering a devastating spin kick that landed just below Thomas's right ear. He was knocked to the ground instantly. Instinct told him to get up, but it was like gravity had tripled in the last few seconds. It felt like his brain was being sucked into his body.

A second kick to his ribs sent him rolling through the dirt but at least seemed to restore gravity. He managed to scrabble to his feet just in time before Kanu's boot crashed down where his head had lain just moments before. Thomas was quick enough to block an elbow slam by raising his arms, but was then too slow to meet the straight counter punch to his exposed stomach that followed. He doubled over and staggered backwards, Kanu rushing in too quick for him. Another spin kick sent Thomas face down into the ground again. He stayed there, only vaguely aware of the wet sensation on his face. He was bleeding. Thomas pushed his hands underneath his chest and pushed up, spluttering for breath. Kanu's boot met the small of his back and applied enough resistance to make his struggling pointless. Thomas slumped, knowing he was beaten.

"Don't beat yourself up Mr Walker, let me do it for you," Kanu taunted him. "I'm afraid you didn't stand much of a chance. I survived the streets of Mombasa only because my brother had taught me to fight. Vita Saana is an ancient martial art I adopted in later life. It has an especially aggressive technique known as the lion system. It fitted into my propaganda rather well, and it has practical applications as you just found out."

"Didn't do your brother much good though if the stories are true," Thomas sneered, remembering some of the background information Jelani had given him prior to his arrival.

"They are true. I killed him," Kanu replied quietly. "I did it to prove my loyalty to the drug lord who had killed our father. I had to show him that I wasn't going to carry out my revenge. That came years later. Best served cold as they say, just as your corpse will be to the lions."

"Is that them now?" Thomas asked casually, looking past Kanu.

Kanu spun around as he heard one of the guards open fire. Others were running towards the entrance. As Kanu peered into the darkness, he realised what Thomas meant. The night air was filled with noise. Savage roars and bellows penetrated and echoed along the stone walls of the compound. Three lionesses suddenly appeared, sprinting into the courtyard. They were on edge, moving with purpose and with no attempt to conceal their presence. One took a swipe at a guard who was too close, cutting him down without stopping. With a thunderous scream, their pursuer crashed through the entrance after them. The elephant came after them like a freight train, splintering the wooden panelling of the nearby garage wall and flipping a flat-bed Toyota truck neatly onto one of the Range Rovers. Thomas couldn't help but smile.

Over the uproar and chaos, Thomas heard a shot ring out. The tower guard he had previously wounded toppled over backwards and crashed to the floor. Another scream sounded in the darkness as the lions found themselves cornered, and turned on Kanu's men as they too found themselves trapped.

A thud and a crack sounded from the front wall before it exploded in an avalanche of rock and earth. Five more elephants stampeded into the compound, acting faster and more efficiently than any wrecking ball. Through the rubble and dust, Thomas caught a glimpse of a car with blazing headlights and a spotlight rig coming straight towards the compound. As the vehicle approached, he heard the engine and recognised it. It was the Warthog.

Thomas rolled and jumped to his feet. There was only one place that might offer him cover, and that was the stairway at the edge of the compound that led to Kanu's makeshift prison block. He was half way there when Kanu caught up with him, knocking him to the ground again with a slam from the side. Thomas flipped onto his back and rose up on his elbows as Kanu towered over him. The African was smiling. They both knew it was over. Thomas was no match for Kanu.

The Warthog roared over the debris of the demolished wall and landed with a thump, skidding to a halt in the centre of the half-destroyed camp. Jericho jumped from the jeep, firing his shotgun into the air with one hand and turning the elephants away from the car and back towards the open entrance. His other hand held the rhino pistol as he covered the swarming compound. Thomas glanced over as Catherine swung out from the passenger seat, her pistol drawn and pointed at Kanu. Nothing mattered anymore. She was safe, and she was here. He felt euphoric and lay on his back, smiling contentedly at her as she approached. His elation seemed matched in intensity by Kanu's disappointment. The African lowered his raised, tensed forearms and knotted fists.

He moved so fast that Thomas hardly had time to call out. A roundhouse kick knocked the pistol flying from Catherine's hand and he whirled past her, spinning on his heels to come at her from behind and slipping one arm underneath her chin, tucking the other behind her head in a choke hold. He grinned at Thomas again, but it was short lived. Catherine reacted instinctively. She arched her back and pulled downwards, dragging Kanu forwards with her. As he tried to move backwards, she placed her clenched left fist into her open right hand and then powered her elbow straight into his groin. As Kanu doubled over, she pivoted on her hips and stabbed at his eye sockets with two rigid fingers. They found their mark and Kanu released her, stumbling backwards. But Catherine wasn't finished. Her left hand dropped to the ground, acting as a pendulum to the right leg that delivered a smashing kick that landed just below Kanu's left ear. It was his turn to be sent tumbling through the dirt.

"I love you," Thomas exclaimed, smiling.

"Who wouldn't?" Catherine shrugged.

She crouched and offered Thomas a hand. She needed both in the end to haul him up. She turned back. The gun had been flung several yards behind her, well out of Kanu's reach. He was still groaning and writhing on the ground. Catherine kept her arm around Thomas's side as they walked over towards the gun. She left him for a moment to pick it up, then came back to him. As she glanced back towards Kanu she dropped to her knees and let off a shot, as he disappeared through the archway that led to the marshes.

"Quick little bugger, isn't he?" Jericho exclaimed, joining them. He threw the shotgun to Thomas, who caught it by the strap. "Let's end this, that bastard can't get away. I'm sure it would be bad for all our health."

"What about Kanu's men?" Thomas asked. "Surely there

must be more of them?"

"You mean those guys?" Jericho replied, nodding behind.

Thomas glanced, noting about a dozen men on their knees.

"There's a new bokor in town, didn't you see the elephants obeying my commands?" Jericho said with a wink.

"How did you get them to charge the lions?" Thomas asked.

"What lions?"

As if to answer, a blood curdling roar pierced the night. It brought the chaos and noise of the compound to standstill and silence.

"Jericho...Rhodes, I think he took a hit. He's..."

"I saw him," Jericho nodded sombrely, "He's breathing. Take more than a bullet to knock the life out of that one I tell you. Be on your way now," he nodded.

"I'm coming with you," Catherine stated, checking her gun.

They both headed towards the archway and slipped through it. The lights from the camp faded quickly, leaving them in inky blackness. But the moon was full and lit their way a little. Thomas was able to follow Kanu's muddy footprints from the compound. As he'd feared and suspected, they were headed for the jetty. But then he saw something that made him stop. Something that had made Kanu stop and change direction too. The huge round pugmark was unmistakable. The queen was here. It had been her roar that had floated up from the marsh.

~

Just as she had tensed for the charge into the open, she had registered the rumbles of the elephants and the vibrations of the metallic beast following in their wake. She had slunk back into the marsh, unable to call back the others who had already slipped between the stone pillars. As she lay in the underbrush listening to the shouts, gunshots and screams of the elephants, she vented her frustration, as a ripple of energy swept along her spine from the tail and burst forth in a roar. A continuous growl emanated from her throat as her tail thrashed from side to side. Then she saw him. The man passed through the crumbling opening in the stone and was headed for the river. The warm night air brought his scent to her and she sat up, recognising it instantly. She had detected it many times before, often when hunting. Many times, his taint had been on the other men she had killed and eaten not far from here. It had laced the pungent territory markings that she often travelled miles to investigate too. This man had encroached on both her food sources and home. She slipped into the water and surged towards the jetty, snarling her intentions.

~

Kanu Sultan stopped in his tracks as soon as he heard the snarl. For the first time in as long as he could remember, he felt fear. He peered out across the water, towards the lagoon and the river beyond that offered escape. He saw the bow wave as something large moved out of the reeds and headed for him. As they reflected in the moonlight, he watched two blue glowing orbs snake their way closer. Instinct told him to run, but the unfamiliar terror he felt rooted him to the spot. At a distance of about ten feet, he began to see the whitish head that belonged to the eyes fixed on him, the body already rising from the water. Suddenly released from his fright, he turned to run as the river exploded in a tidal wave of water, fangs and fury.

~

Thomas lowered into a crouch, bringing the shotgun up. Jericho had fired two shots into the air. Thomas remembered to pump the gun, loading the next two rounds into the DP-12's twin barrels. If Jericho had loaded the gun fully, that meant he had fourteen left. Catherine stayed behind him, her pistol raised too. They dropped down the bank and into the marsh grass and reeds. The trail of both Kanu and the cat were obvious, a flattened path that led east. They had barely gotten ten yards when a scream lifted up from ahead of them. It was a chilling sound, a cry of pure terror. They began to edge forward again.

"I don't like this," Thomas whispered.

"What's to like?" Catherine shrugged.

Thomas turned to look at her. His face was full of warmth and affection.

"Don't get soppy," she nudged him. "We have a job to do."

~

Kanu sprinted through the reeds, his eyes wide and his lungs on the verge of bursting. He felt the presence of the cat, its thunderous paw strikes sounding out closer and louder with each step. He stumbled, but his momentum kept him going for a few seconds more, before all breath was purged from his body with a tremendous blow from behind. He smashed hard into the mud and the few inches of water at the base of the reeds, dazed by the strike. Clarity painfully burst back into his consciousness as what felt like molten iron pins ripped into his leg. His body was lifted into the air and thrown several feet as the queen whirled around, an angry roar escaping as she released the clamp of her jaws. Kanu crumpled to the ground, but he struggled to his feet. His damaged leg gave out instantly, just as the blow came from the side. He wailed in agony as the queen buried her teeth into his chest, lifting him from the ground, and tearing her way deeper into the reeds. Her blue eyes locked on his, emblazoned with tenacious rage.

She dropped the man as soon as she reached solid ground. She brushed past him, a casual flick of her tail opening his forehead, as its barbed tip lashed him. She stood before her prey, which whimpered and cowered on the ground. The stench of the coppery, salty blood filled her nostrils and a sound that was half purr and half growl signalled her delight at this. She stepped forward, taking one of the man's feet in her mouth. She bit down, enjoying the sensation of the crunch of the bone and ooze of blood it released. The man's screams became a catalyst to her probing claws and stabbing teeth. She licked the blood from the mangled feet, removing what was left of the skin. She sucked on the exposed flesh then ripped away the fat muscles from the calves.

Kanu took short gasping breaths as he went into shock. His eyes bulged and glazed as they looked up into the night sky. His brain still distantly registered the jolts and tugs that rippled along his nervous system as strips of flesh were ripped from him by teeth and claws. He heard the popping sound as his lungs collapsed, followed by something not unlike the noise made by a deflating balloon. Vomit filled his throat as his sternum cracked and his stomach emptied, simultaneously venting his bowels as his body shut down. No screams were left now, only pain as more cracks signalled the splintering of his ribs. The last tremors he felt were of her muzzle pushing its way through the opening in his abdomen, instinctively nosing up into his disintegrated chest. Her tongue lapped at the blood drenched innards before she sucked the fleshy, beating mass into her mouth. She ripped his heart from its mooring veins, arteries and tendons as if they were string. Life left Kanu's eyes just as he registered the great white head above him, its chin and jaws stained with the dark residue of his own blood. She swallowed her prize as new sounds came to her from across the marsh. Her ears pricked and she let loose a low rumbling growl as she melted back into the cover of the reeds.

~

Thomas and Catherine followed the bloody trail another forty yards further before they found Kanu's body. It looked like his chest had exploded. His left side had been eviscerated and his clothing shredded into blood drenched clumps. The tattered remains of his legs ended in the blunt pulp of what was left of his feet. The right one had been removed and lay in the grass half-consumed. It was like a hole had opened in the grassland, the walls of which were soaked with blood. The small indent in the greenery was a crucible of slaughter. Globules of matted tissue and fat dripped down from the swaying blades and bent over reeds. This had been an act of savagery, something beyond feeding or hunting.

"So much for the wild cat king," Catherine stuttered with horror.

"She's out for revenge," Thomas whispered in shock.

"I hate it when you talk like that," Catherine said, reeling back and shaking her head. "You know animals don't operate on those kinds of levels..."

Thomas grabbed her by the hand and led her away from the scene, unable to stomach the visual and olfactory assault on his senses any longer.

"Seriously, now is when you want to have a conversation on the semantics of emotional intelligence in higher mammals?" he said with disbelief, as he turned them back towards the compound.

"Well yeah. Going on today's events so far, we might be dead later."

Thomas turned his head in her direction with a look of surprise and a hint of prideful fondness.

"You're very cool under pressure," he said. "Looks like those Muay Thai lessons have more than paid off."

"Let's just say that a question I've been asking myself for some time has been answered," she replied, returning his gaze with equal warmth. There was no hint of the coldness and holding back he'd sensed before.

Thomas kept moving. With Kanu dead, he could afford to deal with the queen later. Then he heard it, a low, gruff, rasping growl. It built in volume and intensity. It filled his ears and set him on edge. She was out there, somewhere close by and watching them. She hadn't finished yet. Thomas and Catherine instinctively went back to back. The growl ceased instantly, replaced by silence. They began to scan the surrounding reeds and buffelgrass.

"Keep moving back towards the camp," Thomas whispered. "We're where she wants us at the moment, let's change that around."

Catherine nodded and began to edge forwards only to come to an abrupt halt.

"What's the matter?" Thomas asked.

"Something just passed through the grass ahead of me," she stammered. "It was pretty damn big, and it looked greyish. Whatever it was, it was moving fast."

"Sounds like our girl," Thomas rasped.

He caught the sound of the grass rustling before he saw the shimmer of movement to his left. She had skirted past them, slipping through a maze of corridors only she knew. She could approach virtually unseen, but it was clear she wanted to be behind them.

Catherine continued forward, more urgently now. They both froze as the sound of a gunshot echoed from within the compound.

"Fuck'n lions," yelled Jericho's angry Irish voice, full of rage. The marsh went quiet again.

As Catherine went to move off, Thomas touched her elbow with a gentleness that told her to stay put. She slowly turned her head.

Thomas was breathing rapidly, his mind racing as he studied the form that had just stepped out onto the path. In the pale glow of the moon, the wide and brilliant eyes seemed to shine blue. There was something other worldly, almost ethereal about the stare that met his. The face was feline, but not lion shaped. It had the blunt, taut features of a leopard, but on a much more massive scale. It was also the wrong colour. As Catherine had said, it did indeed appear to be grey. Revealed by the moonlight, it looked almost white. But the strangeness didn't end there. It had a bear like hump that marked its massive and powerful shoulders, covered in a dark coloured ruff of bristled fur. Thomas thought it could easily be mistaken for a mane at a distance. From there, the coat became brindled along its back, contrasting with the faint spotted markings that lined its belly and flanks.

It was as if the animal had called them out. She was tired of lurking in the shadows. She stood as still as a statue, only emitting a purr like growl. She would occasionally tense, or drop her head cautiously, as she regarded him with a stare that belied a cold and calculating intelligence. And that's when

Thomas realised what was happening. They were being ambushed. It was just like Musa had told them when Amanda had run into the long grass. This queen wasn't challenging them. Nor was this some noble acceptance of fate. It was simple distraction.

Thomas swivelled the shotgun on his hip and squeezed the trigger, blasting an area to his left. He heard a yowl of pain as the unseen lioness hidden there died where she laid in wait. He swung back, ready to pull the trigger again, but she had already vanished back into the maze. As he stepped backwards, he nearly tripped over Catherine who had become rooted to the spot. A lioness was barrelling towards her, teeth bared, and the white of her chin shining like a beacon as it streaked through the long grass towards her. A second shot echoed into the night from the direction of the compound, this time slightly closer. The lioness tripped and somersaulted off the path into the grass. There was a soft splash as the body crashed into a hidden pool of standing water.

"I got one up here too," came Jericho's distant voice over the reeds. "Was there more than three?"

"The queen's out here too," Thomas yelled back. "Only, I don't think she's a lion at all."

"Good to know, I'll just shoot the next thing that comes out of there that isn't you."

"Or me," Catherine shouted back.

Jericho muttered something that neither of them heard.

The ear-splitting roar was terrible and thunderous. It was the most horrible thing Catherine had ever heard. She winced and trembled at its sound. Thomas tensed his grip on the shotgun and pumped it to reload. Catherine screamed as something exploded at them from the reeds, a hurricane of teeth and fury. Thomas's finger snapped at the trigger twice in quick succession before it hit him.

The world went black and silent for a moment, but he was still conscious. It was the roar that had deafened him and he realised with horror that it was the animal itself that cut off his vision. He gasped for breath as it suddenly vanished and he found himself looking up at stars. With his ears still ringing he tried to sit up. He still had the gun in his hands, but when he tried to move, he yelled out involuntarily with pain. He guessed that the thumb and index finger on his right hand were broken, as was his ring, middle and little finger of his left. He could feel the breeze cooling his forehead, which was slick and wet with blood. His shoulder too felt wrong. He looked down. It was torn open, perhaps grazed by the queen's teeth.

"Catherine?" He called out shakily.

"I'm here, coming right for you."

"Don't, I don't know where she is."

Thomas looked around. The pain, and a blow to the head in the tumble he was only just registering, were taking their toll. He was close to drifting into unconsciousness. Something stirred in the darkness low down in the reeds. It crawled and clawed its way towards him. Blue glazed eye shine appeared out of the black, as the silhouette of her grey head loomed closer. He'd hit her with both blasts from the shotgun in the chest, but her heart was still pumping. She had one last kill still to make. Thomas shuddered with a shockwave of pain as he flipped the shotgun up awkwardly onto its stock. He used his elbow to slam down on the pump handle as hard as he could. He let out a gasp as he heard it load and lock in place. He looked back up and recoiled in horror as he found she had inched her way to within a foot from his outstretched boot, jaws open and eyes set in unblinking determination. He let the shotgun fall onto its back and shoved the ring finger of his right hand into the upturned trigger slot. He pulled backwards. The world went black.

CHAPTER TWENTY-SEVEN

When Thomas awoke again, he found himself lying prostrate in a hospital bed. He was dressed in a simple undershirt and was in a private cubicle. His vision was slightly blurred, but as he came to, he found his surroundings strangely familiar. He strained to see further. Sheet plastic curtains were pulled around his white metal bed. He relaxed a little when he saw Catherine, curled up asleep in a chair a few feet away. He saw a label on a pill pot next to his bed. He was in the Nairobi hospital; the same place he had found himself after Amanda had died. It was possibly even the same ward.

When he looked back at Catherine, she was awake, grinning at him with glinting eyes of relief and mischief.

"It's nice to have you back sleepy head," she cooed, leaning in close.

"I was just thinking the same thing," he replied.

He felt very stiff and sore, and decided not to move too much. Catherine lifted his eyelids and moved his head from side to side as she examined him.

"Ow," he protested.

"Is that our brave Bwana I hear," came an Irish accent from behind the curtain.

"What's left of him," Catherine replied.

The curtains parted and Jericho stepped in.

"You had us worried there for a little while," Jericho laughed.

Thomas reached up with his hand to stroke his chin. It was covered in a few days' growth of stubble.

"How long?" he asked.

"Three days," Catherine replied. "I think your head took one too many knocks. You've also got some pretty nasty lacerations and bruising, but I guess your body has been making good use of the rest. You look an awful lot better than you did."

"Will I be able to play piano again?" Thomas joked, holding up his bandaged fingers.

"You should be able to," Catherine laughed.

"Amazing, considering he couldn't before," Jericho added.

"I'll get the doctor," Catherine said softly, kissing him on the forehead.

She slipped past the curtain, and returned a few moments later with a tall, African doctor. He had hints of grey in his tightly curled hair and crow's feet around the eyes, but he offered Thomas a kindly smile. Thomas replied with a grimace as his vitals were checked.

"You're in pretty good shape considering what you've been through. A few days of rest and some more fluids, and you should be just fine," the doctor declared.

After a few more checks and detaching a drip Thomas hadn't noticed, the doctor left them.

"Mason is recovering in the next ward. Jelani is sorry he couldn't be here too, but he's rather busy. Looks like you stirred up something of a hornet's nest," Jericho explained. "First, Kanu's operation has been completely shut down, and his men surrendered as soon as the authorities arrived. Secondly, those two males that you had a brush with. It appears you might be right; they bear all the look and swagger of Barbary lions. The plan is to take some samples of hair and saliva at a bait trap and look at their genetics. But more than that, they've moved in to the pride's territory. There's only three younger females left, and they seem happy to have the protection of the brothers as you called them. Anga ya Amani is about to become Kenya's most desirable safari camp for scientists and tourists alike. With Kanu gone, we're hoping the game will come back, and that under the leadership of the brothers, the pride will return to more natural prey. The government is already drawing up plans to expand the Tsavo park borders to protect them."

"But that's not all," Catherine interrupted. "It looks like you may have inadvertently discovered another new species of cat."

"The Mngwa," Thomas answered with a nod. "It translates as something like the strange one."

Catherine nodded.

"It was originally described in field journals from the late 1930s by William Hichens, a British clerk stationed in Tanzania. It was also tracked by a hunter named Patrick Bowen in the fifties. But it's never been proven to exist."

"Until now," Jericho laughed. "Kelly was practically doing somersaults. The Field Museum want both it and some of the others for their research and exhibits. There's a pretty heated bidding war for the documentary. I also found some items in both Kanu and Kruger's camp to make things worth my while," he grinned. "Catherine made sure they wouldn't need them again."

Thomas glanced at her and smiled. He knew there were lots of gaps in the story to cover, but it looked like they had a few days to do so. He settled back into the pillow and closed his eyes as he listened to Jericho recount their adventures.

CHAPTER TWENTY-EIGHT

Three weeks later, he found himself looking up at the distant peak of Mount Kilimanjaro. It was a bright African spring afternoon in early November. The gorge was as beautiful as he remembered. Most of the flowers were already in bloom, and splashed the terracotta rocks with further colour. There were bright pink desert roses, gold and red peacock flowers, and delicate blue elephant's foot mixed with vivid purple bauhinia. The flat-topped acacia tree was still there, marking the entrance to the gorge. It offered him shade today, just as it had when he had scattered Amanda's ashes. It was here that he had returned to say goodbye.

He looked down at his watch and released the clasp on the bracelet. He held it in his hand as he turned it over and read the inscription.

"Live free. Live wild. Love forever."

He knelt, looking out at the gorge. What he had said to Musa had been true. Knowing what had happened to Amanda had freed him of the burden of his guilt. He didn't know if it was because Kanu had met the same fate by the same animal, or if it was just from knowing he himself hadn't been to blame. Deep down though, he knew the peace came from knowing Amanda had died simply being true to herself. Kindness, compassion and bravery had made her leave the tent that night. He knew she would have been happy to be laid to rest in Africa. He decided there and then that this was where she and his memories belonged. Here, surrounded by peace and beauty, and protected from guilt and the past. It was time to go.

"You're going to be late for your own wedding," Jericho called from the Warthog, parked a little way behind.

"I'll blame the best man," Thomas said with a grin, turning around and walking towards him as he refastened the watch.

They drove in silence, only exchanging boyish smiles and playful shakes of the head. Jericho punched him on the arm and then crushed his shoulders with a powerful, one-armed hug.

"I'm happy for you man," he said.

"And that's what I am, happy," Thomas replied. "I've also don't think I've ever seen your car this clean," he joked, looking over the cabin.

"Well it's not every day she gets to be a wedding car."

They roared through the gates of the world-famous Finch Hattons private game camp. Thomas spotted two Range Rovers that seemed somehow familiar. He shot a questioning glance at Jericho.

"It's not like Kanu was using them...and you insisted on flying in your guests and families. How else was I supposed to get them here? Finch Hattons were very happy to accept your contribution," the Irishman explained, grinning like a Cheshire cat. "You're honeymooning here too, aren't you?"

"Presidential suite," Thomas replied, raising an eyebrow. "I wanted to show Catherine the real Africa."

"Some would argue you already have," Jericho laughed as they walked through a gazebo gate into a wild flower meadow.

Thomas stopped in his tracks. It was stunning. The early evening beckoned with a light warm breeze, and the sun was just beginning to set. Candle lanterns marked walkways lined with flower baskets that led to the front. There, a kindly looking Kenyan registrar in a black shirt and round glasses waited for him. He and Jericho passed along the gathered guests. Thomas saw his sister and parents sitting next to Catherine's mother, and he gave them a knowing nod and a grin. Kelly Keelson and Mason sat just behind them. The reporter turned producer beamed at them both. Jericho made a little bow in her direction.

The registrar smiled kindly at them as they took their place to his left. Thirty seconds later, the small group of musicians behind the registrar began to play. A piano began the main theme from Christina Perry's A Thousand Years, and Thomas had to stop himself from letting a tear roll down his cheek as the cello joined in. Two violins added their voice, interweaving the melody with Wagner's bridal march perfectly. Thomas could barely breathe. His back was turned to the congregation, and he saw Jericho stiffen as his jaw dropped. The Irishman turned to meet his gaze, his face lit up in wonder. Thomas turned.

There she was. There were no words. Her beauty and grace defied his attempts to categorise them. Her short hair was tied back in two natural curls that complemented her neckline. A braid of delicate pink and white flowers nestled against the dark copper strands. Her eyes were a deep turquoise as they caught the setting sun and became fixed on him. The pink lips and the corners of her mouth crumpled into a cute and honest smile that brought his thumping heart back to something of a normal pace. The dress she wore was striking yet quietly beautiful. It was embellished with ivory Venice lace and the material itself was subtly naked. It hugged her form, showing her breath-taking figure. The V-neckline and short sleeves made it seem less formal, and suited her perfectly. It ended in a sweep train that gave the impression she was floating through the meadow towards him. As she took her place beside him and inhaled a deep breath, it was only then that Thomas noticed it had been her brother walking her up the aisle. Thomas couldn't take his eyes off her.

Time seemed to stand still. He could hear the registrar speaking. He consciously had to force himself to respond to the questions he was asked, even when he finally said "I do." They both had tears in their eyes by then.

When Kelly caught the bouquet, she couldn't help blush as she glanced in a ruffled fashion at Jericho. Thomas and Catherine both cried during their speeches. Jericho had everyone laughing and crying again with his. Before they knew it, night had fallen, and they took to the floor of a beautifully adorned barn to take their first dance. Fittingly 'A Thousand Years' played again, this time in its original version.

"I won't let anything take away what's standing in front of me," Thomas whispered as he pushed his fingers through her hair, repeating the lyrics. "The two of us, together from now on."

"I have something to tell you," she purred in his ear. "It won't just be the two of us I'm afraid." She gazed into his eyes, aglow with affection and tenderness. "I'm pregnant," she whispered. "Eight weeks."

Thomas couldn't help but cry. He picked her up off the floor with one hand and whirled with her, and she clung to him and threw her head back in a girlish laugh. They didn't stop dancing for hours.

It was much later when Thomas joined Jericho at the railings of the game lodge, looking out over the savannah. The

Irishman slapped him on the back with a hearty embrace. As they surveyed the silhouetted trees and darkness, lifting their eyes to the stars and nearly full moon, a savage and searching roar echoed out of the landscape. Jericho turned to Thomas and smiled.

"If that isn't the roar of a Barbary lion, I don't know what is," he laughed.

Thomas returned the smile, and picked up his beer as he walked back to the dance floor with his best man. He glanced back just once before Catherine's hand found his, and whisked him away.

~

The big grey and white mottled male lingered for a while. He had travelled up the coast, occasionally catching the scent of the female before he had begun to track her inland. But now the rich aroma had vanished without trace. He knew he couldn't stay here, having already picked up the markings of the two male lions. He had learnt a long time ago to remain hidden and avoid confrontation. He growled at the lights in the distance once, then padded away back into the night.

EPILOGUE

There was no trace of the warmth of an African spring as Jericho passed through the gates of a remote Welsh facility, just outside of Snowdonia National Park, a few weeks later. Thomas and Catherine were still on honeymoon, and safely out of the country as had always been the plan. The security here wasn't Army, but they had a military swagger for sure. Private contractors that could be kept off the books no doubt. He was directed towards an open hangar, where a dark coloured Jaguar saloon sat. He drove the hired Hyundai SUV over and parked.

He climbed out of the car and made his way to the group of men waiting for him. They stood around an enormous crate that was waiting to be loaded onto an AVIC Y-20 cargo plane. As with the hunters and trappers he had already procured, he had vetted the crew himself. They could be trusted to keep their mouths shut and had been paid handsomely to do so.

Jericho couldn't help smiling as he approached the jumpy looking man from DEFRA, his contact. Pettigrew was a gerbil of a man and he knew it.

"Mr. O'Connell, late as usual," Pettigrew complained, puffing his chest up.

Jericho ignored him.

"I trust all is in hand?" Pettigrew enquired nervously.

"Everything is arranged to take her off your hands and out of your country, if that's what you mean Mr. Pettigrew," Jericho replied.

"And your friends?"

"Still in blissful ignorance that a number of sabre-toothed kittens made it into the Scottish wilds thanks to an idiot who thought they'd make great pets. And that you are still hunting and killing any big cat you find, in direct violation to UK law, and the directive you gave them. How's puss?"

Jericho looked past Pettigrew to Ryan Glass, his head trapper.

"Sedated and ready for her trip," the rough looking man replied.

Jericho walked over to the crate. It had been designed to his specifications, reinforced with carbon steel throughout. He peeked through one of the ventilation holes. The hulking mass of the animal inside was all that he could make out, but he saw enough to be happy. Her fangs were more than visible as she rested on the floor of the crate. A heavy snort and snore reverberated around its interior, shaking the walls.

"According to the notes we found in the owner's journal, she's not even two years old yet or even fully grown. He named her Tama, after a Native American spirit." Pettigrew explained.

"Strangely fitting," Jericho said with a grin. "I presume we have that journal?"

Pettigrew handed it over, begrudgingly.

"It's for the best, can't have you hanging onto any evidence or being associated with any of this," Jericho explained with mocking sincerity.

He nodded at the assembled crew to start loading the crate. Pettigrew handed him a black holdall.

"Feels about right," he mused as he judged the weight of the payoff. He turned away and began to walk back towards the car.

"Why not kill it Mr. O'Connell?" Pettigrew called out.

"Because she is a miracle of nature Mr. Pettigrew, and one of a kind," Jericho yelled as the aircraft's jet fans began to turn over. "She's not one of your leopards or pumas. She's a superstar and deserves to shine. Also, my hypocrisy only goes so far. Thomas wouldn't want her killed without reason, and neither do I."

"What about the other one?"

"She must be dead. We found no trace of her," Jericho replied.

He opened the door of the SUV and climbed in. He put the holdall down on the passenger seat and patted it with a sigh of satisfaction.

"At least...not in this country," he shrugged, watching Pettigrew climb into the back of the Jaguar saloon.

As Jericho stopped at a mountain crossroad a few minutes later, he watched the cargo plane climbing overhead, turning west and headed towards the Atlantic. He paused to watch it go before pulling away, back towards the airport and his own long flight home.

THE END

A Note from the Author

Thank you very much for reading The Daughters of the Darkness. By doing so, you've supported an independent author and the independent publishing industry. This is my second novel, and a direct follow-on from the first, Shadow Beast. If it wasn't for thousands of readers like you, taking a chance on an unknown writer, it would never have been possible. So once again, thank you.

For us little guys, spreading the word is really important. So, I make one request. Whatever your thoughts about the book you've just read, good, bad, or otherwise, please consider leaving a review on Amazon, Goodreads, or both! It really can help make the difference.

About the Author

Luke Phillips has always been a keen student of the natural world. When studying zoology at Liverpool John Moores University, he was surprised to find the Loch Ness Monster referenced in the first lecture he attended, as an anecdote about what could be out there. But even before then, having spent time on the shores of Nessie's home as a young boy, and with a keen imagination fuelled by creature features glimpsed through childhood fingers covering his eyes, his interest in myths and monsters was evident from an early age.

He lives in the county of Kent in the UK, and was always encouraged to write by teachers and readers alike. The Daughters of the Darkness is his second novel.

THOMAS WALKER WILL RETURN IN PHANTOM BEAST

Made in the USA
San Bernardino, CA
09 July 2019